By Her Command

ALSO BY DANIELLE GRAINGER

THE DENTON HEIGHTS SERIES
Under Her Wing (Book 1):
The Shasti and Madison Story

In Her Cage (Book 2):
The Jaleesa and Tina Story

Within Her Grasp (Book 3):
The Marta and Shanice Story

By Her Command (Book 4)
The Rowena and Minjung Story

THE BERNADETTE SERIES
Wrecking Bernadette (Book One)

(S)mothering Bernadette (Book Two)

Becoming Bernadette (Book Three)

Desiring Bernadette (Book Four)

Loving Bernadette (Book Five)

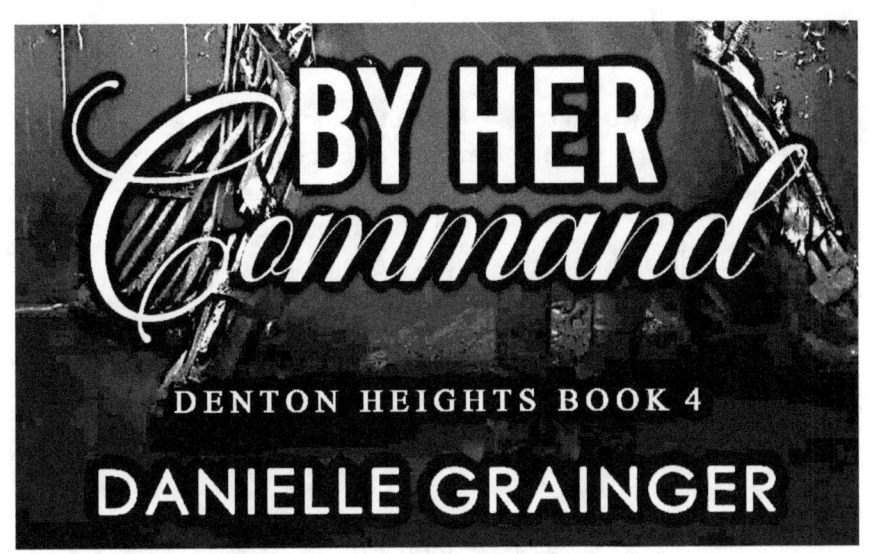

BY HER Command

DENTON HEIGHTS BOOK 4

DANIELLE GRAINGER

eBook ISBN   978-1-953734-32-7

First Edition 2024

9 8 7 6 5 4 3 2 1

Cover design by Sarah (Forcoverservice)

Published by:
Bibi Books Publishing Company, LLC

Dedication

By Her Command is dedicated to our diverse community of folks
who have searched for a place in this world.
Know that you have a right to not only find it but thrive in it as well.

Acknowledgments

Nothing is done in a vacuum, and that includes writing. I want to thank my friends and family for understanding my need to isolate and craft stories that keep knocking on my brain. What a relief it is to finally get them out "on paper."

Thanks also go out to my splendid and supportive Beta readers. Jiske, you're always ready for me to send a manuscript for your perusal, and you even encourage me to finish it so you have something to read. (Notice I didn't say "nag."). Olivia, you always have time to check my grammar, spelling, punctation, and a myriad of other technical things. I promise that I truly do my best to make it perfect for you, but apparently, I'm only human, after all.

And lastly (but not least), hugs and thanks go out to you readers. Your polite and generous communications fill my soul and keep me going. If you keep reading, then I'll keep writing. Deal?

Author's Note

Many readers contact me wanting to know the backstories behind Domme Rowena and her submissive Minjung. To do it justice, I had to go back in time. This book, "By Her Command: Denton Heights Book 4," begins on the timeline before Book 1 in the series ("Under Her Wing") but progresses through Books 2 and 3 in the series ("In Her Cage" and "Within Her Grasp") and then ends *after* those first three.

So, even though "By Her Command: Book 4" chronologically begins before Book 1, it's best to read it as the fourth book in the series. In other words, read books 1, 2, and 3 before tackling this one.

Thank you to all my wonderful readers and to those who have taken the time to write to me. I love hearing from you and treasure your feedback.

— Danielle Grainger, September 2024

Table of Contents

Chapter 1

Rowena

The curtains were closed, but the door was unlocked, and there would be a knock on it soon. Rowena Tate looked around the hotel room that wasn't. This room, like all the others on this floor of the former hotel, had been converted into an office of sorts. There was no bed, just cheap but clean living room furniture and a kitchenette. She hated events like these, having been to more than her fair share, but she'd been without a submissive for a while and needed to find one that could not only run the household but could also satisfy her more personal needs. Needs that had been untended for far too long.

Rowena laughed as she ran her finger over the first candidate's picture. The woman in the photo was an attractive East Asian woman about Rowena's age. Something in the way the woman held her head and looked right into the camera caught Rowena's attention. But the reason she laughed wasn't because of the picture; it was because her sister had no clue that it had been her nagging that led Rowena to this event in downtown Chicago.

Over the last several months, Rowena's older sister, Mallory, had been gently trying to motivate her to get the Cincinnati plant in shape. The mere thought of trying to fix it so Daddy would be proud of her was overwhelming. He had trusted her with it, and that's how, almost ten years prior, she'd left St. Louis and moved to Denton Heights, a bedroom community of Cincinnati, to be a family presence at the plant. At first, the plant ran itself smoothly. It made good profits, and both her parents praised her for her business acumen. And she let them think that. But she knew the truth. She was an imposter. She hadn't done much of anything for the plant except make occasional visits. She'd speak with management and then to the workers on the floor. But now, nine years in, something was going on at the plant that she couldn't figure out. Profits were down, and employees were leaving in droves. Recent visits yielded no insights or clues as to what was wrong or how to fix it.

Her best friend Hayley had been the one to encourage her to stop brooding and at least get her own house in order before tackling the plant. Like Rowena's sister, Hayley knew how to gently plant seeds in Rowena's brain, so ultimately, Rowena thought it was her own idea to seek out a new submissive who could run the household. Hayley was one of two trusted friends who knew a few of Rowena's secrets. Not all, of course. A woman must keep certain proclivities to herself, naturally. Still, it was Hayley who recommended Miss Kat's Domestic Servants Agency, so here Rowena sat behind a cheap desk in a private room for their exclusive spring event.

And it certainly was exclusive. One did not simply show up to an event like this. Dommes and Doms had to be recommended and subsequently invited. She had Hayley to thank for the introduction. The room she waited in was tidy and organized except for the purposely stale coffee overheating in the pot and the wadded paper scattered on the floor around the trash can. Earlier, she had tossed them from behind the desk, purposely missing. She'd laughed when she accidentally got one in. Laughing helped calm her nerves. She expected the prospective submissives to be nervous, but she was uncharacteristically nervous, too. She'd rethought her outfit repeatedly that morning but stuck with her low-cut business suit showing a generous, but not too generous, amount of cleavage. The suit was all business, and that's how she intended to conduct this first day's round of interviews. She'd picked five submissives to interview that day. Three before lunch and then two after. Unfortunately, protocol at these things meant absolutely no play or touching on day one. It had been a long time, too long, since she'd had a submissive bound and gagged, anticipating her favorite flogger.

Rowena laughed and said out loud, "That's what day two is for."

A soft knock on the door pulled her back to the task at hand. "Come," she said with an authoritative tone. She purposely kept her head down, reading the bio on the first candidate, even though she'd already read it several times. The door opened, someone entered, and then the door closed softly. Rowena did not look up—not yet.

After a long but not uncomfortable minute for Rowena, she glanced up and was pleased on many fronts. The submissive woman stood quietly near the door, head down, hands behind her back. She was obviously waiting for instructions.

"Come in. Sit." Rowena did not point to a chair and was again pleased when the submissive pointed to one and asked, "Would this one be all right, Madam?"

Rowena nodded. Good. The woman hadn't made assumptions and asked before sitting. But how much of this was an act, and how much was true submission? She had forty-five minutes to root it out.

"Your name, please?" Rowena asked, trying not to lose her cool at the striking woman sitting in front of her.

"Minjung Lee, Madam."

Good use of honorifics. So far, so good. And her manner of dress suited her well. She wore black, and the color complemented her long black hair. Rowena had always loved the naturally dark hair of East Asian women like the one sitting in front of her. She achieved a similar color from her stylist. The ultra-short form-fitting skirt the woman wore was certainly enticing and hugged her form sensually. The matching low-cut short-sleeve blazer was clearly designed for a camisole or blouse underneath. Minjung wore neither and simply had a scarf around her neck tucked beneath the blazer, effectively blocking the cleavage. It was a clever yet subtle choice since any Domme could simply ask for the scarf to be removed. Scarves could be used to bind hands or become a blindfold. And that belt cinching her waist snugly could become a makeshift collar and leash. Rowena wouldn't do any of these things. Not today, anyway.

"What brings you here today, Meanjean?" Rowena purposely mispronounced the woman's name to see what her reaction would be.

There was none.

"Thank you for seeing me this morning, Madam. I have experience running households, and my most recent contract just ended. I'm looking to serve a Madam in a full-time and full-capacity position."

"And tell me, what does a house manager do?"

Minjung paused for a moment before speaking. It wasn't a panicked pause—more of a taking a moment to think pause—and for whatever reason, that pleased Rowena.

"A house manager can mean many things, of course, Madam. In my prior assignments, I've looked after every aspect of running the household. For example, on a larger scale, I supervised the cleaning staff, maintenance and landscaping people, kitchen staff, and the like. On the more personal scale, I saw to my Dominants' needs making sure they were comfortable and happy."

"'Comfortable and happy,'" Rowena echoed. "Give me examples of your household management."

"Yes, Madam," Minjung said with a slight nod of her head. Her posture was exemplary as she sat erect, her head held steady, and her hands clasped in her lap. "I made weekly meal plans that they approved or adjusted. I made appointments. I also helped as an office assistant for some by handling phone calls, filing, and light bookkeeping. Things like that." Minjung's cheeks tinged slightly. "I was also available for their enjoyment, satisfying any and all physical needs." She paused for a moment and added, "Within my hard limits, Madam."

"Always," Rowena said. Respecting limits was essential for a safe, sane, and consensual arrangement. "I need coffee." She pointed to the coffee setup on the sideboard. "Would you get me a cup?"

"Oh, yes, of course, Madam." Minjung stood up, took three or four steps backward, and then turned to tend to the coffee. She was most certainly earning points for etiquette. That was tipping the scale in her favor, for sure. So many submissives these days simply weren't. Their Dominants pampered them so much that they were soft and sloppy. The community in Denton Heights was no exception. She could count on the fingers of one hand, not including her thumb, the old-school Dominants she was friendly with. The others could keep their new-age, everyone-has-feelings bullshit.

But this sub, the one getting her coffee, was not of the new age. She had been well trained.

"Madam?" Minjung asked, holding up the coffee pot.

"Yes?"

"This coffee seems to be stale and overcooked. Would you like me to make a fresh pot? Or I can pour this for you if you like." Minjung's expression was neutral, which amazed Rowena. Clearly, a new pot was in order, but Minjung wasn't making assumptions.

"A new pot for sure," Rowena said. Normally, she would say thank you, but she needed to establish and maintain her authoritative demeanor. There was a hierarchy to be established here.

Minjung dumped the old coffee into the kitchenette sink, cleaned the pot thoroughly, and asked how strong or weak Rowena liked it. "Madam?"

Minjung asked again.

"Yes?"

"May I continue to answer your questions while I do my task?"

"Perfect idea," Rowena said and watched as Minjung inspected the bag of coffee Rowena had brought from home. A slight nod of Minjung's head gave approval to the freshness. "Would you ask for help when you're unsure about something? Can you work independently, or would you wait for me to tell you what you have to do?"

"I would ask for clarification for anything that was unclear, Madam. I like to work independently, though, because it shows my Dominant that I am competent and capable. She need not worry that I can handle things. I would hope, though, that a Dominant would understand my need to ask a lot of questions at the beginning. Once I feel autonomous, then I can relax into my tasks, and my Dominant can relax into hers."

"Like the coffee-making," Rowena mused out loud. "You asked for clarification, got it, and proceeded to work independently."

"I suppose so, Madam," Minjung said as a slight smile graced her face.

Rowena hid her own smile under a hand as Minjung reached down to pick up every single one of the paper balls and toss them in the trash can. *Independent, indeed,* she thought.

As the coffee brewed, Minjung prepared a tray with sugar, half-n-half, and whatever else she found on the sideboard.

"Tell me about your last position," Rowena said. "Why are you not collared?"

Minjung lowered her eyes, and her very demeanor deflated.

Warning bells went off in Rowena's head. Did Minjung do something to get released? Was she going to speak ill of her last Domme? That would not be acceptable.

"I had a six-month contract in Master Kevin's house here in Chicago," Minjung said.

Rowena was surprised. Minjung's stat sheet said she was a lesbian and preferred being submissive to dominant women. Something about her prior arrangement wasn't sitting right. "Go on," Rowena encouraged.

"Basil was the house manager, and I was his assistant, so I basically worked for him. During parties, I served Master Kevin's guests. Sometimes, I was furniture. I was always clothed at Master Kevin's."

Rowena detected a change in Minjung's tone. "Being clothed, was that an issue for you?"

"Yes and no," Minjung said as she poured the coffee into the only mug in the room. "He is a gay man. His household and subsequent parties were all men, so I preferred to wear clothing in front of them."

"Parties full of men? Did you at least give consent?" Rowena was incensed on Minjung's behalf.

"Madam?" Minjung asked, clearly unsure what Rowena was asking. She brought the tray of coffee and accompanying condiments to the desk.

"Did they use you at those parties?" Rowena asked as evenly as she could.

"Used me? Oh," Minjung said with sudden understanding. "No, Madam. I was never to be touched at the parties or ever." Minjung hovered over the coffee service and asked, "Would Madam like me to serve?"

"Yes," Rowena said succinctly. "Two teaspoons of sugar and make it light."

Minjung stirred sugar in, poured some cream, and awaited Rowena's inspection of the color.

"A little more creamer."

Minjung splashed the barest amount in and stirred.

"More."

Another bare amount.

"Yes, that's it," Rowena said. She reached for the mug and took a sip. "Mmm," she moaned, pleased to finally have someone make coffee the way she liked it. "I might hire you just for this skill."

A small, amused smile crept up Minjung's face, but she lowered her gaze as she sat down.

"So, your physical needs haven't been properly seen to in at least six months?"

"No, Madam, they have not."

"You must be terribly frustrated. I couldn't go that long," Rowena said, knowing it had been longer than that for herself, and she was ready to burst with need.

Minjung cleared her throat. It was a delicate thing but endearing. "I have indeed been frustrated, Madam. And, although Master Kevin and Basil have been very kind and generous to me, the placement didn't allow me to…"

Rowena encouraged her to finish.

"I didn't feel I was reaching my full potential there. I did what I was told, but it was automatic. I was basically an unthinking robot. Please understand that it is ingrained in me to serve, but I also crave a connection with my Dominant, a connection of mutual respect. And by this, I mean that she benefits from *my* submission and not just anybody's submission. That *I* am a big part of the reason she's happy and thriving in her own life."

"Hmm," Rowena said. This was not an answer she had expected. Minjung seemed to be quite adept at communicating her needs. Rowena set her coffee down on the tray but clumsily spilled a large portion. She bolted out of her seat and reached for the napkins just as Minjung did.

Minjung flinched and covered her face with her hands as if to ward off a blow.

"You're okay," Rowena said gently. "I just spilled some coffee. I wasn't going to hit you. I don't hit my subs in anger."

Minjung sat upright, put her hands in her lap, and nodded. "Yes, Madam. Thank you, Madam."

The responses were automatic.

"Did someone in Master Kevin's household abuse you? Tell me the truth."

Minjung looked up, surprised. "Oh, no, Madam. No, no. They treated me well there."

"Mm hmm," Rowena said, not quite believing the submissive woman sitting in front of her. "When were you released?"

"Two months ago."

"Two months on your own," Rowena said. There was a history of abuse somewhere in her past, maybe in the recent past. She didn't want to take Minjung down that road right then, but perhaps at tomorrow's play session. If Minjung agreed to one, that is. She switched topics.

"Tell me more about being furniture. It sounds interesting. Not my kink, mind you, but if it's yours, it can be accommodated."

Minjung's eyes lit up as if she'd just been promised ice cream. "At Master Kevin's, sometimes I was a side table. I was on my hands and knees and had to be perfectly still. Guests would put their drinks or plates on my back. One time, I was the dinner table. Plates of food were placed all over my body for guests to grab."

"I couldn't be still that long."

"Oh, but Madam, it allowed me to retreat into myself. As furniture, I was not capable of speech, thought, or even action. I was just…there and nowhere all at once."

"Hmm," Rowena said again. "You like being objectified then?"

"Oh, yes, Madam."

"This stat sheet says you prefer working for women?"

"Yes, Madam."

"Why?"

Minjung paused thoughtfully and said, "I connect more with women. Women see me. Master Kevin was a fair and authoritative Dominant, though. I liked his dominance, but I needed more than he could give me. I'm not bisexual, so there was no physical satisfaction there, except for an occasional flogging from Basil when I requested it."

"Ahh, flogging is my personal favorite thing to do. Tell me why you requested floggings from Basil."

"Floggings, any kind of impact play, send me to another place. Some call it sub-space. Maybe that's what it is, but I occasionally need them for relief. Basil never gave me aftercare, so it wasn't quite as satisfying as I had hoped." Minjung looked up and said, "Madam, I want you to know that I am a capable house manager. I am good at anticipating needs, following instructions, and acting independently. I want you to know that I am more than a simple bean flicker." Minjung said the last sentence in a rush.

Rowena burst out laughing. "How do you feel about bean flicking?" She made no move to hide her grin.

Minjung's blush returned, but she spoke well about the types of sexual services she could provide another woman. She also spoke about some of her own needs, including the need for bondage and impact play. "My hard limits are listed in the application, Madam. We can discuss those, but I'm fairly firm on them."

"For the most part, they match up with mine," Rowena said with a chuckle. "One last question for you. I am obviously a plus-size woman. Tell me what obstacles that might cause for you."

"You are a woman, Madam. There are no obstacles."

Rowena's momentary insecurity about her weight dissipated with Minjung's answer. Minjung's bashful smile also helped dispel Rowena's concern. It might be temporary, but she'd take it.

She outlined the required tasks and responsibilities for the house management position she was offering. Minjung asked a few thoughtful questions, which told Rowena she was serious about the job. When Rowena segued back to the more personal physical expectations, Minjung didn't falter and seemed eager to be of service. Rowena had to be sure because her own libido had been piqued during their discussion.

"Minjung, I see here that your medical tests came back clean and clear. I'm sure you've seen that mine did as well, so I'm going to request a play session with you for tomorrow."

Minjung's eyes lit up.

"Obviously, you have the choice to accept my request or reject it. You have free will."

"Free will, Madam?"

"Of course," Rowena said. "I'm looking to hire an exclusive house manager who can service all of my needs. But I am not looking for a slave. I hate that people use that expression in the lifestyle. It's so disrespectful to the real insidious meaning of the word. So, please know that you will always have free will within the bounds of our contract, and you will always have safewords."

"I understand, Madam." Minjung's expression seemed to soften as she absorbed Rowena's words. "I appreciate how clearly you convey your needs and expectations."

Rowena's own body relaxed as well. She stood up and said, "Thank you for your time, Minjung."

Minjung's hands had been resting on her lap, but then she did a curious thing that modern-day subs knew nothing about. Minjung moved her arms so they rested on her thighs, and then she turned her palms up.

Rowena almost sighed at the gesture of respect. Minjung had been trained well.

"Thank you," Rowena said.

"Thank you for seeing me today, Madam." Minjung rose, took three steps backward, and headed toward the door. She turned before opening it and said,

"Thank you" again.

Once the door closed behind Minjung, Rowena blew out a sigh and then jotted a few notes on Minjung's application. She logged into the placement service's website and requested a play session with Minjung for the next day's more intimate interviews. If Minjung did not accept the play session, then Rowena would move on. It was that simple. She was hiring a house manager who could also service her physical needs. She wasn't interviewing for a wife. She did hope that the thirty-six-year-old candidate would accept, though. She seemed to be a seasoned submissive servant who would be well suited for the house manager position, at least.

Rowena stood to fix the coffee pot scenario. "Who abused you, Minjung?" she murmured to the coffee pot. "What's in your past that still haunts you?" She set the coffee to overcook in the machine and placed her clearly unclean coffee mug nearby.

Back at her desk, she read up on the next candidate she had selected. Without looking, she wadded up several pages torn from a legal pad and tossed them near the trash can. This time, she didn't make a single one.

There were five quick knocks on the door, and then it opened, "Can I come in?"

Rowena looked up. A mid-twenty-something blonde woman bounced into the room.

"Hi, I'm Bunny," the woman said as she grabbed a chair and pulled it up to Rowena's desk. Bunny wore her hair in long pigtails down her back. The ends of her long-sleeve button-down plaid shirt were unbuttoned but tied by the hem flaps, so her breasts were accentuated. It was a flattering look. Rowena appreciated the white bra highlighted underneath. Yes, this candidate was as cute as the photo in her bio, and Rowena had to admit, that's why she had picked her to interview.

"Your full name, please?" Rowena asked without smiling.

"Bunny Haas."

No honorifics so far, Rowena thought. Not a good start. But, then again, protocol could be taught, but Rowena wasn't sure if she was up to the level of training this one might require.

"What brings you here today, Bonnie?" Again, she purposely mispronounced the candidate's name.

Bunny burst out laughing. "It's Bunny. B u n n y," she spelled out. "So many people get that wrong."

Rowena didn't nod, smile, or even acknowledge the correction. She was waiting for the candidate to answer the question. After a clearly uncomfortable silence for Bunny, she finally answered.

"Oh, uh, my last girlfriend wanted to see other people, and since I'm not really poly, I'm moving on." Bunny threw her hands to the side as if to say, "Tada."

"I'm interviewing for a house manager position," Rowena said. "What do you think a house manager does?"

"Manages the house. Duh," Bunny quipped and burst out laughing.

That laugh alone was enough for Rowena to mentally cross this one off her list, but she decided to give the young woman another chance. The woman's nerves could be taking over.

"Well, uh," Bunny continued, "I guess I would do the housecleaning and any cooking you would need. Of course, I know a lot of good Uber Eats drivers, so that would be cool. Uh…" She looked off to one side, thinking. "I don't know. I guess you would tell me what I have to do, right?"

Rowena managed a chuckle. "Right now, I need coffee. Would you get me a cup?" She pointed toward the coffee setup on the sideboard.

"Oh, sure." Bunny bounded out of her seat, pulled the pot of clearly overcooked coffee, and poured it into the dirty mug. The balled-up paper wads remained unnoticed and untouched at the woman's feet. She hustled back and placed the mug on Rowena's desk.

"You didn't even spill a drop," Rowena praised. It was meant as sarcasm but had kind of come out sincerely. Rowena wondered if she was losing her touch after living alone for so long.

"Thank you," Bunny said, drinking in the praise that wasn't.

Rowena should have ended the interview there. One of her biggest pet peeves was when anyone or anything wasted her time. But for some reason, she didn't. Maybe she needed a baseline for the subsequent candidates. She wasn't sure why, but she continued the interview.

"So, tell me about your last position," Rowena said.

"Oh, yeah, well, like I said, my girlfriend went to work, and I stayed home. I cleaned and cooked sometimes and put together workout programs for her.

She really liked them. Oh, and I can do those for you, too. We could start off easy because clearly, you need to build up to more strenuous workouts."

It took all of Rowena's strength to keep her expression neutral. As the woman talked on about her ability to help "obese" people lose weight and become more fit, Rowena threw her hands up at the next generation. She did some mental math and realized the woman was fourteen years younger than she was. That was too much of a gap. She made a note for herself to stay within a certain age range.

New submissives, if Bunny could even be considered one, were clearly cut from a different cloth. Rowena was only thirty-eight, but she considered herself an old-school Domme, and this child sitting in front of her was not anything close to what she needed or wanted.

"I must say that you have a wonderful fashion sense, Bunny," Rowena said, starting her dismissal of the potential submissive sitting in front of her.

"Thank you," Bunny said and tightened the knot in her shirt ends. "I wanted something that said, 'sexy' but also wasn't too 'do me now.'" She laughed, which made Rowena smile.

"Unfortunately, I don't think you're right for this position. I'm seeking someone with more experience than you have. Thank you for coming in today." Rowena stood up.

"Oh, is the interview over?" Bunny asked, remaining seated. "I thought we had another thirty minutes to go."

"I have all I need," Rowena said and gestured toward the door. "But I wish you good luck in your next interview. You'll be a good fit for someone here; I'm sure of it."

The young woman stood and said, "You think so?" She bit her lower lip.

"Absolutely," Rowena said sincerely. "And your dance card will be quite full tomorrow, I imagine."

"Dance card?"

Rowena did her best not to shake her head. She should not have selected someone so young to interview.

"Your day-two interviews should be full," Rowena amended.

"I hope so," Bunny said. She stuck out her hand, and Rowena shook it. "Thank you for your time." She turned and headed for the door.

"Oh, and one word of advice, Bunny," Rowena said.

"Yeah?"

"Be sure to use Ma'am or Mistress in your next interview."

Bunny inhaled through clenched teeth. "Oh, my God. I forgot that part. I'm so sorry, Ma'am."

Rowena nodded once and added, "You might even begin your next interview by asking how she'd like to be addressed. That will score you some points."

Bunny pointed at Rowena and said, "Good idea. Thanks, Ma'am. Have a good day."

And with that, Bunny bounded out the door and out of Rowena's thoughts.

Chapter 2

Minjung

Minjung stood outside the same door she'd gone through the day before. Today, however, she needed to take an extra breath to calm her nerves. This was a performance interview, and she had to do well, or this old-school Domme wouldn't choose her. Minjung had responded favorably to Madam Rowena's demeanor and style, but today, both would show more of the cards they were holding.

The dungeon master, or whatever the equivalent was for a hotel floor, stood sentry near the elevators. The woman looked like she could handle herself, so Minjung felt safe going to a hotel room to engage in physical play with a stranger she'd met once for less than an hour. If this Domme didn't pan out, then maybe the retired woman in her early sixties would. Mistress Barstow had some health issues, and Minjung would certainly be able to help her out with them. Unfortunately, Minjung hadn't felt the dominance from her that her soul so desperately needed.

Minjung smoothed down the sleeveless black mini dress that landed mid-thigh. It was almost a micro dress, but not quite. The front zipper was zipped all the way to the top but could be pulled down to her naval. Hopefully, that would happen quickly because the form-fitting faux leather was a bit unbreathable. For shoes, she'd chosen simple black flats. She wore no jewelry, and the only makeup was the cover-up around her left eye.

She checked her burner phone for the time and watched as it changed to precisely nine o'clock in the morning. She waited for two more beats and then knocked twice softly.

"Come," said the voice from inside the room. It was only one word, but it conveyed confidence and control and calmed Minjung's nerves somewhat.

Minjung took another deep breath as she pushed down the lever. She repeated her entrance from the day before and stood quietly waiting for instructions. Madam Rowena was silent, but Minjung knew she was watching from the couch. Minjung took the time to consciously relax her neck, shoulders, core, and every other muscle group that wanted to remain tense.

"Come here," Madam Rowena said.

Minjung nodded and moved. Madam Rowena pointed to a low armless chair, and Minjung sat. She had planned to somehow graciously fall to her knees and wait for instructions, but a chair was a nice surprise. Minjung turned her palms upward.

"Thank you, Minjung," Madam Rowena said. "And thank you for accepting my day-two interview request."

"Thank you for requesting me, Madam," Minjung said without raising her eyes.

"Look up."

Minjung looked up and sighed softly but audibly. Madam Rowena was a striking-looking white woman who wore a burgundy and black lace-up corset top that tastefully accentuated her buxom form. A small amount of cleavage peeked out the top, teasing the woman gazing at it. The long floor-length black skirt somehow made her look every bit the Dominant that she was. Her hair was pulled back into a tight bun. All of it, including the focused gaze, affected Minjung's breathing.

"I had originally thought I would give you an impact session that you seem to crave," Madam Rowena said, "but late last night, I changed my mind. I'm sure you have a few more sessions today, and those Dommes will probably flog, spank, and cane you to their hearts' content. Some will even try to find your limits. So, I'll let them do that. Instead, I'd like to delve into something else."

Minjung assumed Madam Rowena was going to test her bean-flicking skills or something. She hoped this one wasn't a foot enthusiast. Minjung would do it; it wasn't a hard or even a soft limit, but it wasn't really her kink.

"You mentioned clothing yesterday," Madam Rowena said. "Please correct me if I'm wrong, but it seems to me that being naked helps deepen your submissive state. Is this correct?"

"Oh, yes, Madam." Minjung tried not to sound too eager, but this was perfect.

"Excellent." Madam Rowena motioned for her to stand, and Minjung was pleased that at five foot five, she was shorter than the Dominant standing in front of her by a couple of inches. Being taller than a Domme never felt right.

Madam Rowena moved closer. "I'm going to touch you now. Would that be okay?"

"Yes, Madam. That would be okay." Minjung's voice cracked in anticipation. And since when did a Domme ask permission? Madam Rowena was different, that was for sure. Hopefully, it was a good type of different.

"Your safewords are red and yellow? Correct?"

"Yes, Madam."

"I'll honor them." Madam Rowena took a step closer. "But please understand that I will stop any and all activity if you tell me to. We don't know each other. Trust has yet to be established, correct?"

"Yes, Madam."

"Good. For this session, you are permitted to speak, cry out, whatever you wish." Madam Rowena reached for the top of the zipper and pulled it down so slowly that Minjung almost whimpered. "But should you become my servant, there may be times I'll ask you to remain silent." The front zipper reached its lowest point, and Madam Rowena pulled the dress off Minjung's shoulders. She walked behind, unzipped the lower zipper, and shimmied the dress down Minjung's body, leaving her completely nude.

At Madam Rowena's nonverbal command, Minjung stepped out of the dress pooled at her feet.

"Your body is beautiful, Minjung," Madam Rowena said with clear admiration. "You obviously take care of yourself."

Minjung shuddered at the praise. She wasn't used to it. It was no surprise that her nipples rose to the occasion.

"Very nice," Madam Rowena said.

Touch me, please, Minjung urged with her non-existent telepathic powers.

Madam Rowena's hand came close to one of Minjung's erect nipples but didn't touch. The hand then touched skin as it traced the outline of Minjung's breasts. She walked behind Minjung, and the heat from the hand settled over Minjung's buttocks and then her lower back. It was an inspection, not a formal one, but she had expected it. The woman and the hand continued to circumnavigate Minjung's body until coming full circle and facing her once more.

"Sit," Madam Rowena commanded.

Minjung shuddered in arousal. It was the tone in the command that did it. It was the dominance. That was what she craved more than anything.

"If you were to become my servant, know that I occasionally invite other Dommes to my home. You would be kneeling at my side. No, actually," Madam Rowena amended, "you would be sitting on a low stool or chair like this one. I read about your knee issues in your bio and that most certainly can be accommodated within reason."

Minjung sighed in relief.

Madam Rowena chuckled. "See? I read your info sheet." She chuckled again and then grabbed Minjung's chin. "You will not embarrass me in front of the other Dommes." It wasn't a question, so Minjung did not respond. "They will have free reign to touch you, of course. You are an object, after all. Not exactly a side table, but a prized possession to be touched and handled."

Madam Rowena released Minjung's chin, ran a hand down one shoulder, and stroked her biceps. "So toned and in shape." She then ran a hand across Minjung's chest. She circled one breast and then the other as if testing the feel of each. "One Domme may want to fondle your breasts like this as she greets me in my home. We may talk about the weather or even the Dow Jones Industrial Average, but all the while, she will be touching you like this." Madam Rowena was standing so close that Minjung could smell her subtle scent. Was it rose? Maybe a body spray? Whatever it was, it was pleasant and suited the woman wearing it. The hands began a slow kneading of the flesh, making Minjung moan.

"Another Domme may come over and snap a nipple between two fingers and twist, gently at first, of course."

Yes, yes, yes. Squeeze hard, Madam, Minjung willed. She did, and Minjung cried out at both the suddenness and the pain. Her head lolled back slightly.

"She would continue to squeeze this nipple and realize the other needed equal treatment."

Minjung gasped when her other nipple was pinched, rolled, and squeezed like the first. Her legs parted slightly. Her hips arched minutely, but she couldn't presume Madam would take her all the way. Edging might be her thing.

The fingers left the nipples only to flick each one in turn. Pain shot to her center. Yes, this was what had been missing. Pain. Pleasure. Both. Her mouth opened as she tried to stifle her moans with breathy exhales.

"Another Domme might simply put a hand on your cheek and stroke your face gently."

Minjung sighed softly at the touch. The sigh turned to an unexpected moan when a hand touched her thigh and traveled to the inner portion of her leg.

"Now, the Dommes would know and understand that you are mine, of course, and they would know that you are not to be touched in this general area." Madam Rowena cupped Minjung's sex. "This area, which seems to be incredibly wet at the moment, is mine. They would know that. And your Mistress does not like to share her toys."

Minjung arched her pelvis. She was taking liberties, she knew, but she was reaching a heightened state of arousal she hadn't reached in over a year, maybe longer.

The hand that had been stroking her face went away, making Minjung whimper at the loss, but then both hands grabbed her inner thighs and yanked them apart. Minjung whimpered again, but this time, at the gain. The hands pulled her forward in the chair.

"Oh, yes," Madam Rowena continued as if giving a lecture, "they would understand that they would never be allowed to do this." Two fingers slowly encircled Minjung's very wet inner lips, first one and then the other in a figure eight. "So aroused," Madam Rowena murmured, clearly pleased. The circling continued, but the location changed as the fingers slowly entered Minjung's body. Minjung arched her pelvis, wanting and needing more.

The two fingers slowly circled inside until they tilted up and oh-so-fucking-slowly massaged the upper wall. Madam Rowena knew her way around a woman's body, too.

"They would understand," Madam Rowena continued, her voice quite husky, "that this G-spot and all of this belongs to me and no one else. I own this pussy and the rest of the body that goes with it. Another finger dipped below, and Minjung jumped when Madam Rowena lightly circled the base of her clit.

"A clit can be sensitive, and those other Dommes might not take care of my property as well as I do. Of course, when I increase the pressure and the speed as I rub the clit and G-spot, the more likely my property might burst into flames. And that is encouraged. It rewards the owner of the property."

Owner. Property. Yes, yes, yes. Minjung bucked to Madam Rowena's rhythm.

"None of those other Dommes will ever get the pleasure of seeing my property have her first proper orgasm in a long time."

Minjung arched her pelvis and froze. The orgasm slammed into her body, and she screeched her release. She continued to buck her hips to Madam Rowena's rhythm. She moaned in time to the pulsing aftershocks once she returned from the stratosphere. Her body became flaccid, and she melted back into the chair.

Madam Rowena hadn't stopped her ministrations, though. Was she trying to give Minjung another orgasm?

"Red, Madam. Please, red, red," Minjung gasped out. "I'm sorry. I'm not used to—"

"You're okay, Minjung. It's okay." An arm went around her torso and held on.

They sat like that for several minutes until Minjung had caught her breath. "Madam?" she said once she could speak.

"Yes, Minjung?" Madam Rowena stroked Minjung's face again.

"Thank you, Madam. That was unexpected. I haven't had attention like that in so long."

"I know."

Minjung sat up. "I need to please you, Madam. Let me—"

"Nope, nope," Madam Rowena said. "I appreciate your offer, but I want you to come up here with me." She stood and reached for Minjung's hand pulling her toward the couch. Before reaching it, though, Madam picked up a light blanket and threw it around Minjung's body. "Come sit with me."

Minjung sat next to Madam Rowena as instructed and allowed the Dominant to put an arm around her and pull her close. Minjung wasn't sure what to do until Madam Rowena suggested that she close her eyes and relax.

"You're safe here," Madam said softly. "Just be still for a little while."

Minjung found herself powerless over Madam Rowena's soft tones and steady arm around her. At Madam's insistence, Minjung settled her head on Madam's soft, pillowed breasts, letting herself unwind.

"You need this more than impact play, I think," Madam Rowena said softly.

"Thank you, Madam." Minjung closed her eyes, took in the rose-scented cologne of her benefactor, and relaxed her body one muscle group at a time.

Minjung moaned as she woke. She stretched her body and reached up to wipe drool from her mouth. It was then she realized where she was and woke up fully. "Madam," she said with alarm. "I am so sorry. I must have fallen asleep." Minjung sat upright, and the arm that had been holding her disappeared. Minjung bent over low and turned her palms up in respect.

"You're fine, Minjung," Madam Rowena said with a chuckle. "My arm was going to sleep, but you needed this."

Minjung willed her speeding heart to slow down. Had she ruined her chances with this Domme? How weak was she? "I'm sorry, Madam," Minjung said again, not knowing how to make it right.

"No need. On the contrary. I'm extremely flattered that you were able to relax enough to have such an epic orgasm and then fall asleep in my arms." Madam Rowena paused for a moment and then added, "That was special. And even if you don't accept my offer of employment, I will cherish the memory of our session today."

Minjung could not control the tears that began. She would not allow them to escalate into sobs. She thought that was finished. But Madam Rowena had shown her so much kindness that it was almost too much. It was different. *She* was different.

Madam Rowena clicked her tongue and stroked the blanket over Minjung's back. "You're okay, Minjung. Let me get you some water."

"I should serve you, Madam," Minjung protested and started to rise.

"Not today," Madam Rowena said and stood up. She came back with a bottle of water and handed it to Minjung, who drank heartily.

"Thank you, Madam. You're very kind."

Madam Rowena chuckled. "Don't let that get around now. I have a reputation to uphold."

"Madam?" Minjung said and took another drink of water.

"Yes?"

"Were you serious just now when you said you were going to offer me the position?"

"Yes."

Minjung's throat closed with emotion.

"But I don't want you to respond now," Madam Rowena cautioned. "You have other appointments today, and I'm a realist knowing there might be something better out there for your particular needs. And, besides, you may not want to move to the suburbs of Cincinnati."

"Cincinnati?" Minjung had never been there. And it would be a long way from…here.

"Mm hmm," Madam Rowena said. "It's a nice city. But I won't try to sway you either way. It will be your decision." She headed back toward her desk. "You probably have another appointment after this one, so if you need to freshen up in the bathroom, feel free. Shower if you wish. I have toiletries in there for general use."

"Yes, thank you, Madam. I will." Minjung felt like she was betraying Madam Rowena by admitting to having more appointments, but Madam Rowena most likely did as well, so maybe it was expected at these things.

"I also have a care bag for you to take with you." Madam Rowena held up a tote bag and showed her the contents. Minjung was confused. It was a Michael Kors designer bag filled with snacks and drinks.

"Madam." Minjung was at a loss for words. The only thing she could think to say was, "Thank you."

"It's the least I can do," Madam Rowena said. She gestured toward the shower. "Go on. Freshen up. I'm sure your ass is about to get swatted by your next Domme, and you want to look your best." She laughed a hearty belly laugh and sat down at her desk to read over some papers.

The butterflies filling Minjung's stomach accompanied her into the bathroom, but caution accompanied her as well. This all seemed too good to be true. And things that seemed too good usually weren't. What was the flip side of this kind and benevolent Madam Rowena? Did she have an evil, sadistic side? Why was the house manager position open? These and a dozen other questions peppered Minjung's brain as she let the warm water rinse her clean.

~~~

Later that evening, Minjung sat at the desk in her assigned hotel room, three floors up from the Dommes' offices/playrooms. Her journal was opened to a new page.

Saturday, April 14, 9:07 pm
My ass is sore. My thighs, back of my legs, and breasts are sore, too. My body has been beaten and bruised by enthusiastic Dommes having their ways with me. Of the four, three gave me impact, two had me give them an orgasm, and the other two let me have my own orgasm. The first was epic. Madam Rowena offered me a contract as her number one pick. Mistress Barstow also offered a contract, but it says I'm her third choice. Third choice. Young me would have been insulted by that, but at this point, I'll take anything. Even third place.

Mistress Barstow took a while to orgasm this afternoon. Her auto-immune condition was acting up, she'd said. But the way she held my head in place between her thighs and encouraged me was cute. I would gladly take the chance on her as my Domme since I know I can help make her life better. But, yeah. I didn't feel much dominance from her. She was leading, yes. But in charge? Not really.

Madam Rowena, though? She currently has no full-time staff at present. She must have a small home. When she outlined what my responsibilities would be, they all seemed reasonable. She's closer to my age (I think) and definitely has that dominant demeanor. Thinking about it makes me squirm in this hotel chair, much like I did in her office this morning. I was mortified when I fell asleep in her arms, and I'm kind of shocked that she actually offered me a contract after that.

It's settled. I will mark Madam Rowena's offer as my first choice and Mistress Barstow's as my second. I need a position, so Daddy Sheila will be third. Funny how my final picks are all white women. White Dommes are in the majority at this event, so that makes sense, I guess.

Time to check the boxes now.

It was a good day. Day Rating: 8/10.

Minjung hesitated before clicking the boxes on Miss Kat's Domestic Servants website. She didn't want to be impulsive. Each offered a six-month contract. What if Madam Rowena turned out to be a nightmare? She'd be stuck for half a year.

She leaned back in the chair. She needed a distraction so she could marinate on her decision. She minimized Miss Kat's screen and opened the email app.

"Oh, shit," Minjung said out loud. She had an email from Jenna. "Only took you two weeks to reach out," Minjung growled. "I should have blocked you after it happened."

Curious, Minjung didn't open the email but read the first few lines that showed.

> JENNA: Minjung! Where you at? Your shit's gone. Did you take it? Last I seen, you was in that ambulance. You almost broke his nose, you know. You gotta come back. He's ...

Minjung blocked Jenna, clicked the trash icon, and closed the email app. She went back to Miss Kat's website. As planned, she clicked Madam Rowena as her first choice, Mistress Barstow as her second, and Daddy Sheila as her third. Once certain that her responses registered, she powered down her tablet and set the alarm on the bedside table. If she were lucky, she'd be signing a six-month contract with someone the very next morning.

Chapter 3

Rowena

Pen in hand, Minjung signed her name underneath Rowena's signature. Bennie, the dungeon master, took the pen from Minjung and signed her own name underneath as the witness. The contract spelled out duties for a house manager for six months with an opt-out for either party after two full weeks. Rowena didn't want either of them to feel stuck if it became obvious that the relationship wasn't going to work. The more intimate nature of the agreement had been spelled out in vague language, but Rowena made sure Minjung verbally expressed in front of Bennie what those terms could mean.

"Congratulations, Ma'am," Bennie said to Rowena and handed each of them a box. "Mistress Kat is pleased that you were able to make this connection today and wanted you both to have a small token of gratitude for choosing her placement service."

Rowena arched her eyebrow in surprise. She urged Minjung to open her box first. She did and pulled out a small silver charm. It was a lock. Rowena was not surprised when hers was the accompanying silver key.

"Please thank your Mistress for us," Rowena said to the dungeon master.

"I will, Ma'am." Bennie took a step back. "If that will be all?"

"Yes, yes," Rowena said. "You serve your Mistress well."

"Thank you, Ma'am." The burly woman backed all the way to the door. "Now that an official contract has been signed, you are permitted to lock this door, Ma'am. But rest assured, I will be down the hall should anyone need me for any reason."

"Thank you, Bennie."

"Ma'am." Bennie tipped an imaginary hat and backed her way out of the room.

"Go lock that," Rowena ordered Minjung.

Minjung nodded and did as commanded.

"Why are you still dressed?"

Minjung's eyes grew wide at the surprise question, but then a small smile settled on her face. Rowena sat back in the desk chair and watched intently as Minjung removed her white vintage blouse with lace sleeves. The blouse tapered in at the waist and fit her trim figure well. Rowena, however, was more interested in what was underneath the blouse. And, although Minjung had worn black capris, which were now shimmying down her legs, jeans would have also gone well with the blouse. Minjung had an excellent sense of fashion, and Rowena couldn't wait to add to her wardrobe. Not that Minjung would be wearing clothes that often back at the house, however.

"Attention," Rowena said brusquely as soon as Minjung laid her clothes down on the chair she had just vacated.

Minjung stood tall, legs together and arms at her sides.

"Excellent." Rowena stood. She pulled the crop out of the top drawer and tapped the business end in her free hand. "I won't use this on you today." She flicked the crop, producing a satisfying whooshing whistle. "You have too many bruises and wounds from those over-zealous Dommes with something to prove. I will simply let this crop be a prop for us this morning."

Rowena moved closer and touched the tip of the crop against the dark bruises on one of Minjung's breasts. "Any pain here?" She moved the crop to the other breast. "Or here?"

"My nipples are very sore, Madam. Everything else feels okay, except when pressed."

"Which I won't do." Rowena chuckled evilly and added, "I'm a sadist, but not a mean one. If that's even possible." She threw her head back and laughed deep from her belly. To her own ears, she sounded like Ursula from *The Little Mermaid.*

Rowena used the tip of the crop to lift Minjung's chin slightly. She took in the yellowish bruise around Minjung's left eye. It was almost healed and hadn't been caused by the Dommes. She didn't comment on it but could tell that Minjung understood that she'd seen and registered what it was. Rowena moved to Minjung's back and groaned at the bruises and bright red blotches all over Minjung's back, including her kidney area. She growled under her breath. "I'm going to touch you gently. Be honest and tell me if it hurts." She placed her hand over one kidney and then the other.

"It doesn't hurt, Madam," Minjung said. "I called red. Mistress Barstow apologized for her poor aim and admitted her mistake."

"Looks like a lot of mistakes." Rowena traced the blotches. "Inspection," she said, calling for another submissive pose.

Minjung laced her fingers behind her head and spread her feet apart.

Rowena growled again at what she saw. Her hand barely covered the deep dark purple bruise on Minjung's upper thigh. "How does this feel?"

"It doesn't hurt too much, Madam." Minjung paused for a moment and asked, "May I add something?"

"Go on."

"It's a badge of honor to please a Mistress with my body. It excites me to see it in such a clear and tangible way."

"You like to see the bruises and welts."

It wasn't a question, but Minjung answered anyway. "Yes, Madam."

"I was right not to flog you yesterday. Those wannabes did enough damage."

Minjung remained silent like all classically trained submissives knew they should.

"You will be servicing me today," Rowena said. "Pleasuring me on the couch. Stand in wait position while I freshen up."

Minjung kept her feet spread but clasped her hands behind her back.

"Good," Rowena said and headed to the bathroom. She washed her hands and took a moment to slide off her panties and tuck them in a bag. A quick washup there gave her confidence for her first session with Minjung. She also wanted to keep Minjung waiting a little while. It was all part of the Domme/sub game, wasn't it? It helped Rowena get more into Domme space. Truth be told, she hadn't had a full-use submissive in almost a year, and she needed to get her nerves out.

When Rowena came out of the bathroom, she didn't look at or address Minjung. She headed to the couch but didn't sit or lie on it. "Come," she commanded. Minjung was standing in front of her in seconds. "Take off my skirt."

Rowena had purposely chosen a wrap-around skirt with a side tie. Minjung easily undid the knot and pulled the skirt off. She folded it neatly and placed it on an empty chair.

"I want you to take things slowly. Get to know my body. You'll be spending a lot of time there." A surge of arousal hit Rowena. Just the thought of having a full-time submissive was heady stuff. Rowena sat on the couch and then lay down, a pillow under her head. She placed the heel of one foot on the armrest while the other foot remained flat on the floor. This left an opening for Minjung to maneuver and explore Rowena's body.

"Use one of those chair cushions for your knees."

"Yes, Madam." Minjung reached for the cushion. "May I touch you, Madam?"

"Mmm." Rowena moaned at the question. Arousal was such an unpredictable thing sometimes. The littlest thing could get one going. "Yes, you may touch me."

Minjung placed the cushion on the floor and eased her way between Rowena's spread legs. Minjung didn't lunge in right away and took a moment to take in the scene before her. Another rush of arousal hit Rowena.

"Beautiful, Madam," Minjung said.

Another rush. "Mmm," was all Rowena could manage.

Minjung picked up the bare foot resting on the couch and kneaded the flesh expertly. Was this a small taste of her foot massaging skills? That would be explored soon. Maybe the first evening at the house.

Minjung moved on to lightly massage Rowena's calf and worked her way up past the knee to her thigh. Rowena fought hard to squelch the urge to cover her ample thighs. She really needed to get toned. Hopefully, Minjung wasn't disgusted by how out of shape she was.

Stop, she chided herself. *Enjoy this. Minjung knew what she was signing up for.* Rowena forced herself to relax into the unfolding scene.

"You have beautiful skin, Madam."

"Mmm." Rowena arched her pelvis. She needed Minjung to move along but didn't want to rush this first time.

Minjung must have sensed Rowena's urgency because she quickened her pace. She leaned forward on her elbows and inhaled deeply through her nose. It almost looked like she was sampling the bouquet of a glass of red wine. Minjung moaned, but it was barely audible. A small smile lit up her face as if she were pleased with something.

Soft kisses graced one of Rowena's inner thighs, making her exhale the breath she hadn't realized she'd been holding. Soft lips traced a path up one thigh and then down the other, skipping the most important spot in between.

The kisses made another trek back up and stopped just short of the goal. Minjung's tongue reached out and stroked the fleshy skin. Devouring kisses accompanied the tongue. As expected, Minjung moved to lick and suck on the flesh on the other side but didn't linger. She seemed completely in tune with Rowena's needs.

Rowena's head lolled back, and her eyes closed when Minjung's lips finally pulled in Rowena's lower lips. *Yes, this was it.* Minjung sucked the labia into her mouth and dove in. Her nose traced a path up Rowena's center. Rowena jumped when the nose made accidental contact with her swollen clit. Or maybe it wasn't accidental. Minjung's tongue took over with sweeping licks, devouring everything it encountered.

"Look at me when you do that," Rowena said, her voice breathy. Minjung looked up, and they made deep eye contact. She continued to lick and suck and kiss Rowena but hadn't yet paid any attention to her clit.

This is my submissive servant. She's mine. Rowena's core tightened at the thought. *Mine.*

Rowena couldn't take it any longer and grabbed Minjung's head, refocusing her attention on the swollen bundle of nerves that so desperately needed devotion. Minjung knew what to do and consumed Rowena as if it was her last meal. Rowena felt a distant spark. It was like flint hitting steel, but she didn't ignite. Not yet. She held Minjung's head still and bucked rhythmically over her lips and hardened tongue. Rowena even rubbed herself over Minjung's nose.

She let Minjung's head go, arched her pelvis high, and said, "Make me cum. Make me—" Another spark. This one was bigger. Minjung took Rowena's pearl into her mouth.

"Fuck," Rowena grunted. And then it happened. The spark ignited. She rode the momentary stillness as long as she dared, and then her nerves shattered. She bucked her hips while Minjung held on. Wave after wave of pure pleasure coursed through her body through every limb, muscle, and sinew.

Rowena moaned as the waves continued. She stilled the head between her legs with one hand. "Mmm." More aftershocks. They were velvet waves unlike any she'd experienced before. Another. These weren't multiple orgasms, just generous aftershocks caused by a submissive skilled in the sexual arts.

When her eyes focused again, Rowena looked at her new submissive and quipped, "You pass."

Minjung smiled and turned the most wonderful shade of crimson. "It was a pleasure, Madam. You have a wonderful taste."

Was Minjung full of shit, or was she sincere? Who knows? Whichever it was, it felt good to hear. Rowena pointed to the armless chair and said, "Nadu from the chair."

As Minjung moved to do the submissive pose, Rowena closed her legs and sat up. She stood without saying another word to Minjung and went into the bathroom, taking her skirt with her. She took that moment to look in the mirror and blow out a sigh. Minjung was a dream submissive. Hopefully, it wasn't too good to be true.

After freshening up and getting dressed, Rowena came out and took in the most gorgeous sight. Minjung sat in a perfect Nadu pose with her palms facing up. This pose indicated that she was available and ready for any instruction or action her Dominant commanded. Palms up indicated respect for Rowena, even though Rowena had commanded her into the pose.

"At ease, Minjung. You may relax. I am, however, extremely pleased that you know these poses. This means you're well-trained in the classical manner of submission."

Minjung nodded.

Rowena grabbed a bag from behind her desk. "We have a few details to discuss." She sat on the couch. "You may look up when I speak to you. In fact, I prefer it. I'll tell you 'Eyes down' when I want that. So, the default will be to look at me when I speak to you. Understood?"

"Yes, Madam."

"You have been addressing me as 'Madam,' and that is fine. But you may also use 'Ma'am' or 'Mistress.' Understood?"

"Yes, Madam."

"I have to get back home this evening to be ready for the opening bell tomorrow morning. You live here in Chicago. Yes?"

"Yes, Madam."

"Okay. You need to recuperate from those bruises, so I want you to stay here to get your things in order before coming to me. How much time will you need?"

Minjung furrowed her brow in thought. "I'd say three or four days, Madam."

"That's all?"

Minjung nodded.

"All right then." Rowena reached into the bag by her side. She pulled out an iPhone. "This is yours. I've programmed my number into it, and yours is already in mine. Do not, under any circumstances, give my number out to anyone. Is that understood?" She asked the question with more force than she'd meant.

"Yes, yes, Madam," Minjung stammered, clearly hearing the seriousness of the command.

"I have worked hard for what I have, and I will not have anyone or anything ruin that for me."

Minjung nodded her understanding.

Rowena paused for a moment. "I'll send my usual driver back up here to fetch you when you text me the day, time, and location. I'd like at least a one-day heads-up for that. I have good people working for me, but I also respect their time."

"Yes, Madam."

"Excellent." Rowena deliberately relaxed her shoulders. She'd learned this small trick for dispelling tension from her voice coach back in boarding school. She still used the technique to this day.

Rowena smiled at Minjung. "You did well," she said softly.

Minjung looked down. "Thank you, Madam."

"What questions do you have for me?"

"I..."

"Go on."

Minjung cleared her throat and said, "I think there may have been a mistake in the amount of my allowance."

"Go on."

"I didn't want to bring it up with Miss Bennie in the room, but it seems too much, Madam. Or maybe it was a monthly allowance?"

"Weekly. As the contract states."

The look of shocked disbelief that fell over Minjung's face almost made Rowena laugh.

"Like I said, I have good people working for me, and I pay them well. Remember that you are a hired servant. You are earning a salary. I don't know what your other arrangements were like, but you are one of my employees now."

Minjung closed her eyes and took a breath as if to calm herself. She reached up to wipe tears that had welled up. "Thank you, Madam. You're— This—" She exhaled loudly and finally said, "You are very generous. I hope to live up to your expectations."

This time, Rowena did laugh out loud. "Me, too, Minjung." *I hope to live up to yours.*

~~~

It was early Friday afternoon, one whole week since Rowena had met the submissive servant that her hired driver had gone to fetch from Chicago. The latest text from Minjung said they were less than an hour away. Rowena sat in her office at her overlarge desk. It had been made from the finest mahogany that money could buy. The stock sheet on her screen remained unexamined. She was too antsy to work and closed the screen. She took a sip of her usual afternoon coffee and smiled at the thought of Minjung taking over this task for her. Minjung would take over a lot of tasks, and if last Sunday's post-contract liaison was any indication of what was to come, Rowena was going to be one happy Dominant. They hadn't even explored impact play yet. Judging by Minjung's bruises, she could tolerate a lot.

Devious scenarios flashed through Rowena's head. Wrists fastened to an overhead bar at just the right height so Minjung was forced to stand on her tippy toes. Or would that aggravate her knees? She had to find out more about the knee issue. Anyway, the flogger would have to be first. Light strokes then harder and harder until Minjung's entire back was red and pulsing. Wait! There would be nipple clips, of course. Maybe they would also be attached to her labia so that every time she flinched, her sensitive bits were stimulated. How about a clothespin zipper?

Rowena squirmed as a shot of arousal hit her. Her phone dinged an incoming text. Was it Minjung? Were they here?

> VICTORIA: Is your new slave there yet? I'm coming over.

Rowena groaned. She loved her friend dearly, but now was not the time to educate her on the misuse of the word slave. Minjung was *not* a slave. Using that term was so disrespectful to the true horrors of slavery. The Underground Railroad had run straight through Cincinnati during America's abhorrent history, and that fact was never to be disrespected or taken lightly. Rowena groaned again. A scolding would have to wait. She punched Victoria's contact info and called.

"Is she there?" Victoria asked instead of greeting Rowena. "I can't wait to get a look at her. It's about friggin' time you got somebody permanent."

"Shut up," Rowena said. "You're not coming over."

"C'mon, woman," Victoria pleaded.

"No. She needs to acclimate, and I need to acclimate to her in the house."

"Are you going to share her?"

"Stop. No."

"You never did play nice with others." Victoria laughed and then added. "Okay, okay, I get it. You want to keep her for yourself for a while, but if she needs extra training or workouts, I can help you out."

"You aren't going anywhere near her, Victoria." Rowena smiled and took a sip of coffee. Her friend was mostly giving her grief, but there was a small part of Victoria that liked to sample other people's treasures. "You need to get a serious girlfriend and stop messing around with flings."

"Hey, what can I say," Victoria said, sounding like a Don Juan. "Women love me. I'm just giving them what they want."

Rowena laughed and looked up at the analog clock on her office wall. She still had time to look over Minjung's room one last time. "I may have an afternoon tea next week," she said. "It'll be small. You and Hayley."

"Hayley I like," Victoria said. "And her cute sub, Ashley, is a dream, but please tell me Hayley's going to leave her husband home."

"Nope. It's a safe space for them to be themselves. And if you're still playing with Sarah, you can bring her, too. Nobody new. I don't like strangers in my home."

"I'll bring Sarah," Victoria said. "So, I know I don't need to remind you, but you have a little over a month to get your new girl trained for her unveiling at the masquerade ball in May."

"I'm not going to that," Rowena spit out. "Just to see them all playing at D/s? No thanks. This is a lifestyle, not a weekend joyride."

"Seamus is hosting with Miss Matilda."

"Are you kidding? He sold out? I'll have to give him shit for that."

"You know how much he loves attention."

"Yes, he does," Rowena said. "You'd think one sub would be enough, but he has three."

"And he's talking about getting another. A *little*."

Rowena groaned. It was the only response she could muster. Seamus was really selling out.

Victoria laughed, but then her tone turned serious when she said, "Rowena, c'mon. When are you going to let your hair down and let people in? You're stagnating in that big house of yours."

"I *am* letting people in." Rowena knew she didn't sound convincing. "I have a new full-time submissive on the way as we speak."

"Who you're paying to live with you."

Rowena tried not to deflate. She loved Victoria, but sometimes, her words hit a little too close to home.

A loud bell sounded in the background of Victoria's phone. "Shit. School's out. I have to patrol." Victoria was ex-military and was head of security at an elementary school in Denton Heights. She took her job very seriously. "Let me know how it goes when you get a chance."

"Don't—"

"I won't. I'll only come by when you give me permission." Victoria laughed out loud. "Gotta go. Bye." She disconnected the call.

Rowena slid her phone app closed. Rather than think about Victoria's razzing, she stood up from her office chair and headed to Minjung's room, which was tucked in the corner on the east side of the second floor. Rowena's suite of rooms was on the west side of the third floor, but Minjung wouldn't be privy to that floor for a while. They'd play in the playroom down in the finished basement. The room masqueraded as a fitness room, which Rowena used on occasion. Okay, fine. She rarely used it to work out. She didn't have a garish St. Andrew's cross but instead had bolts embedded in the walls and ceiling for chaining submissives. The spanking bench could be construed as a workout bench. Her implements of impact, gags, blindfolds, rope, cuffs, and other bondage equipment were kept in a locked closet next to a stand of free weights. It all looked so innocent. Disguising the queening chair had been easy. A cushion placed on top of the opening in the queen's throne hid it nicely. The jail cell was harder to disguise, but she kept some barbells with weights inside and a few of those big exercise balls as if it were a storage closet.

Rowena could not take a chance that some worker or repair person would wander into the playroom and spread the word about kinky Rowena Tate over on Western Ridge Road.

Daddy would definitely not be pleased if he found out, but she was too careful for that to happen. Living in the suburbs of Cincinnati, over five hours away from St. Louis, was her way of living the life she wanted without upsetting the family's apple cart.

She usually took one of the elevators to get upstairs, but Dr. Moreau suggested she exercise more, so she climbed the stairs to the second floor. Slightly out of breath, she took in the plain room. There was a queen-sized bed, a couple of dressers, two bedside stands with lamps, and basically nothing else. Rowena would find out what Minjung's needs were and would buy more furniture to suit her new submissive. The ensuite bathroom was fully stocked with toiletries, and the linen closet was packed with soft goods.

The beep from the security camera in the front of the property sounded. A spike of adrenaline hit Rowena. "She's here," she gushed in a high, tight voice as she hustled out of the room and down the stairs into the kitchen to check the camera. Her hired driver was at the gate.

Rowena pressed the intercom button. "You made good time, Ash."

"Yes, Ma'am," Ashley said as she spoke into the camera from the driver's seat. "Your person is in good spirits and is excited to see you."

"Good." Rowena hit the gate-open button and watched as the town car drove into the fenced-in property. She smoothed down her untucked silk blouse and headed to the foyer to wait for the sound of tires on the circular drive. She flicked the switch for the outside fountain and was rewarded with the soothing sound of rushing water.

Why was she so nervous? This was absolutely ridiculous. She relaxed her shoulders and then her jaw. A small smile crept up her face as she thought of the burdens Minjung would be able to take off her shoulders. Managing an over seven-thousand-square-foot home and seven-acre property had become too much for her. Housekeepers, landscapers, and repair people helped, but she had to manage them. Minjung would do all the managing now.

The black town car stopped in front of the steps leading up to the front porch, and Ash stepped out of the driver's seat. Victoria was right. Ashley was a beautiful young woman. She had her blonde ponytail tucked underneath her chauffeur's cap. Rowena loved that Ash's Mistress required her to wear the whole chauffeur's regalia, complete with a black suit and shoes and a thin black tie. The white shirt underneath was form-fitting and showed off the young woman's assets quite nicely. Secretly, Rowena was glad that Hayley had taken a shine to Ashley and made her a fulltime sub. Although Rowena was more of a one full-time sub at a time Dominant, she'd known that Hayley hadn't been fulfilled with her submissive husband as her only sub. As Rowena stood watching from the front foyer, she firmly decided to have that small tea party once Minjung was fairly well acclimated.

Ash must have known that Rowena would be watching because she helped Minjung out of the car as if Minjung was a princess. Minjung stepped out looking like a fashion model in her black straight-legged slacks and cream-colored sweater over a white blouse. A barrage of feelings battled for dominance within Rowena. Possessive pride was winning out over the nerves.

Should she say it? Would it be corny? Yes, it would, but she would say it anyway.

Rowena opened the front doors and stepped out on the landing. Minjung saw her and stopped moving. She bowed her head and turned her palms toward her new Mistress.

"Welcome home, Minjung."

Chapter 4

Minjung

'*Welcome home'? Could it be home?* Minjung hid her face in her hands, trying to get her tears under control. After a too-long moment, she wiped them away and looked up. "Thank you, Madam. Thank you." Her voice broke on the last word.

Madam Rowena nodded and then directed her next words to Ash, the hired driver.

"Ashley," Madam Rowena said, "will you please help Minjung bring her things into the foyer and then up to her room?"

"Yes, of course, Ma'am," Ash said and opened the trunk.

Madam Rowena nodded and, without another word, went back into the house.

Minjung swallowed hard, trying to get her emotions under control. She turned to open the back door of the car and pulled out her backpack. She put it on and clicked the strap across her chest. She reached back in and pulled out one of the boxes. With her upper body in the car, she took a moment to breathe. She was overwhelmed. What had she gotten herself into? The house was so big. No, it wasn't even a house. It was a mansion. The lighted fountain in the driveway was sort of calming but amplified her benefactor's obvious wealth. The concrete walls surrounding the property made it seem like a fortress. She should be ecstatic, but she'd had more than a decade of experience with privileged people and knew it could go one of two ways.

"That went well," Ash whispered out of the side of her mouth, breaking Minjung out of her thoughts. "You're one lucky woman."

"Am I?" Minjung asked meekly and then kicked herself mentally. She hadn't meant to let her nerves show like that.

"It's okay to be nervous," Ash said as she pulled one of Minjung's suitcases from the large trunk. "Listen, my Mistress has been saying for months now that Miss Rowena needed a full-time sub." She pulled another suitcase out and set it on the drive. "I don't know if you know this, but Miss

Rowena takes in wayward subs from time to time. About a year ago, I think it was right when she'd let her own full-time sub go, my contract wasn't renewed with my former Domme, and Miss Rowena took me in for a couple of months."

"She did?" A pang of jealousy spiked in Minjung's core.

"Oh, no worries," Ash said. "She said I was attractive but too young for her. No sex. That was kind of refreshing since Dommes can sometimes be…Ahh, you know."

"Sure," Minjung said noncommittally. But she did know. Although she craved the dominance of another woman and longed to belong to someone, sex always came with that. Not that she was complaining, but she struggled against calling herself a sex worker. She had tried to come to terms with the label since it was a valid profession, but she still struggled. She also didn't know Ash that well and wasn't about to share her intimate thoughts with this virtual stranger. She'd done that with Jenna and look what it got her. She reached up and touched her almost-healed cheekbone and eye socket.

"I mean," Ash continued, "if a foster sub wants impact or wants to wear a plug or whatever, Miss Rowena will help them out, but that's about all. She makes sure they get back on their feet and move on. Like she did with me." There was reverence in Ash's tone, making Minjung wonder if Ash had a crush on Madam Rowena. Minjung did not like that thought, not one bit.

Minjung cleared her throat and changed the subject. "Thank you for your help today. That was a long trip for you. There and back."

"I'm a service sub like you," Ash said as she gestured for Minjung to check the trunk. "I will be rewarded well by my Mistress when I get back home."

"That's good," Minjung said. She gestured to the trunk. "That looks like all of it."

Everything Minjung owned in the world got moved to the foyer just inside the front doors. Her world consisted of the backpack strapped tightly to her body, three moving-sized boxes, the Michael Kors bag, and a matching set of three suitcases. The suitcases were kind of bittersweet. They had been a parting gift from Mistress Kelly, her former Domme, who had ended the contract when she decided to get out of the lifestyle for a while. Mistress Kelly was the one who had recommended her to Master Kevin. What Minjung hadn't told Madam Rowena during the interviews was that Master Kevin only took her in because he was doing his friend a favor. Minjung knew it wouldn't last, and it didn't.

Minjung tried to keep her expression calm and even. It was quite the opposite of how she really felt. The overlarge foyer didn't help matters. It was almost as big as Jenna's entire apartment. The circular space had a palm tree growing out of a planter box in the middle of it. Two staircases flanked the foyer and led to a second and then a third floor. A chandelier hung from the third floor over the palm tree, making Minjung wonder how she was going to clean it. Hopefully, Madam Rowena hired out for specialty jobs like that. The only sane thing in the room was a side table with a vase of cut flowers. There was a wooden box that looked like it might be where Madam's mail would be placed.

A door opened, startling Minjung. Madam Rowena came out and asked, "Is this everything?"

"Yes, Ma'am," Ash answered.

"Excellent. I know you're anxious to get back to your Mistress," Madam Rowena said to Ash, "but I'd like you to help Minjung move her things up to her room before you go."

"Yes, of course, Ma'am," Ash said. "My old room?"

Madam Rowena chuckled and then gave directions to a room on the second floor.

"Ahh," Ash said knowingly. "The east-wing suite?"

Madam Rowena nodded.

"Ma'am, may we take the elevator off the kitchen, or would you prefer we use the stairs?" Ash pointed to the staircase nearest them.

"The elevator, of course," Madam Rowena said. "Buzz me when you're finished and meet me down here." She turned toward Minjung and said, "You may take a few minutes to freshen up from your long trip, but don't take too long. We have a lot to discuss this evening."

"Yes, Madam," Minjung said.

"We'll be down in a bit," Ash said.

As was protocol, neither of them moved as Madam Rowena turned and headed back through the door she'd come through. Once the door closed, Minjung blew out a sigh.

"This way," Ash said as she picked up two suitcases.

Minjung plunked the Michael Kors bag on the box that held her journals and some books, picked it up, and followed Ash into the heart of the house. Different emotions battled for dominance. Anxiety was winning. Her adrenaline had kicked in and wasn't helping at all. It had been a long trip from Chicago, but at least she hadn't had to take a six-hour bus ride. When she'd left home over twelve years ago at age twenty-four, she took a bus to Portland in the middle of the night. Portland still seemed too close to San Francisco, so after a couple of nights on the streets and not finding what she wanted, she took another bus to Seattle. And it was there that she found the lifestyle community she'd been looking for. Too bad, like most things in her life, it hadn't lasted. But that was the past, and this was the present.

Ash narrated as they walked toward the elevator. "That room right in front of us is called the great room. It's the room for company."

With its cheery couches, wingback chairs, and side and coffee tables, the great room looked like a showroom. Even the lamps were perfectly matched to the light brown furniture. Light brown wasn't doing the color justice; it was probably called *biscotti* or something fancy like that.

"Your Mistress holds afternoon teas there sometimes," Ash continued. "I served at a few and even attended as a guest a couple of times with my own Mistress."

Minjung drank in the information. She'd make notes later in her new calendar journal she'd specifically purchased for this new assignment. She had a ton of questions already written out in the notes section. What else was there to do on a six-hour car ride?

"This way." Ash pointed to the right. "This leads toward the kitchen and formal dining room." Ash gestured to the right again. "Dining room there."

It was another showstopping furniture showroom.

Ash paused in front of the elevator and pushed the button. "Kitchen here, obvi. You'll be spending a lot of time here, for sure. There's a butler's pantry behind." She pointed to a doorway off to the right. "It leads to the dining room as you would expect, although Mistress Rowena often eats at her desk. Occasionally, she eats at the kitchen dinette there overlooking the koi pond."

"Pond?" The word escaped Minjung's mouth before she could help herself.

Ash just laughed. "Yeah, but it's empty now. She hasn't had any fish since

Kaylynn forgot to feed them, and they, uh, became un-alived."

Minjung had many questions about that last statement but stashed them in the far reaches of her mind. She had other more pressing matters at the moment.

The elevator door opened, and they stepped in with their cargo. Ash hit the button for the second floor. Just before the doors closed, she said, "The TV room is just beyond the kitchen, although she sometimes calls it the family room. She works puzzles in there while watching her shows and baseball games. She watches a lot of baseball."

Minjung wanted to ask what Madam Rowena's favorite shows were but decided she needed to play things cool. She was not going to become besties with Ashley or anyone. Having friendships or making ties was too risky—look what happened with Jenna. So, instead of asking, Minjung simply nodded.

The elevator opened up into a small alcove with a bathroom off to one side. Would this be her bathroom, Minjung wondered.

As if reading her thoughts, Ash said, "That will be for guests, not that your Mistress has many overnight guests. Miss Victoria sometimes. Lydia was here one time in between Doms. And, duh, how can I forget? Her occasional fosters, too." Ash led the way to a loft area overlooking the kitchen. "This space was designed to be a study room for kids or an office or something. Your room is beyond here. She led the way through the loft area into a short, wide hallway. Fanfold doors sat at the end. "Your washer and dryer are behind there."

Whoa, she'd have her own washer and dryer? Right next to her room?

"Your laundry and hers will never mix," Ash said. "Ever."

Minjung took note of Ash's cautionary tone and then followed her through the open door into a large bedroom.

"This is you."

It was another showroom, and Minjung couldn't take it all in at once. There had to be a mistake. The room was bigger than any she'd ever stayed in, including the one she'd grown up in. The bedspread on the queen-sized bed looked high-end and expensive. There were two dressers and two side tables. It was more furniture than she'd ever had. Minjung's eyes widened. Was that a balcony?

Ash put the suitcases down near one of the dressers. She took in Minjung's gaze and said, "Nice, right?" She opened the French doors to the balcony. "Come look."

The view was spectacular. The balcony faced east, but the light from the setting sun behind the other side of the house lit up the trees with deep oranges and yellows.

"Beautiful," Minjung said.

The mid-April lawn hadn't yet begun to grow, but Minjung knew the lawns and the rest of the grounds would be stunning. Just beyond the three-car garage stood acres of oak trees. She wasn't sure how much property Madam Rowena had, but it seemed adequate for a private lifestyle. The concrete walls disappeared behind the trees, keeping the view pristine.

"C'mon," Ash said. "Two more things to show you up here, and then we'd better get the rest of your stuff."

Ash opened the full-sized walk-in closet, which was as big, maybe bigger, than the supply closet she'd slept in at Master Kevin's. Next was a full-sized bathroom. It had a shower that was separate from the jacuzzi tub.

"Are you sure this is the room Madam meant?"

Ash laughed. "Yes." She laughed again. "See? I told you you were one lucky woman."

Minjung nodded but knew not to get excited about these perks or get used to this lifestyle. These were not her things. If she could relax and recover in this suite, then she would be better able to serve her Madam. That was all that mattered.

"Let's take the stairs back down," Ash said and led the way. "This way, you'll know how to get around."

Minjung followed Ash out of the suite, through the loft, and into the elevator alcove. Instead of heading for the elevator, Ash continued past the restroom and into an open area. Minjung stopped in her tracks. A walkway bridge with railings on both sides connected the east wing, where Minjung's suite was, to the west wing, on the second floor. Minjung took a few tentative steps on the bridge and then looked down.

"I know," Ash said. "It's an amazing design, isn't it?"

"Breathtaking."

"C'mon," Ash said. "We don't want to keep her waiting."

They double-timed it down the stairs flanking the foyer, grabbed the rest of Minjung's possessions, and deposited them in her suite.

"She told you to freshen up," Ash said as she was about to head back out Minjung's bedroom door. "You do know what that means, right?"

"Yes," Minjung said, unable to stifle her grin.

"A change of clothes, too," Ash advised. "But make it snappy. She's probably just as anxious as you are."

"Thank you for your help, Ashley," Minjung said. The wheels were already turning as to what outfit she could throw together quickly.

"I'm glad to help, and I'm sure I'll see you soon. My Mistress is chomping at the bit for me to tell her all about you."

"No pictures," Minjung blurted but regretted the impulse immediately. Ash hadn't even been holding her phone. Paranoid might just be Minjung's middle name.

"Yep, yep," Ash said. "Your Mistress made that clear to mine. And mine made that clear to me." She headed out the door and said, "Tootles," as she left.

Minjung wanted to take a moment and breathe but couldn't take the time. She tossed the largest suitcase on the bed and dug out her deep V-neck Henley top, casual black track pants, and a black thong. She threw the smallest suitcase on the dresser and pulled out some toiletries. She didn't have time for a shower but instead took a quick washcloth bath, brushed her teeth, and then her hair. She pulled her hair back into a loose ponytail. She didn't have time for anything more elaborate.

Once freshened up and dressed, she put on her faux leather flexible black flats. She pulled the new planner and her latest STD test results out of her backpack and then tucked the pack into the cabinet of the side table closest to the door. The backpack might look ordinary, but it was her lifeline. It held her personal papers, her current journal, some cash that she needed to add to, and a few versatile pieces of clothing and shoes. It was basically her go-bag. After leaving home, she'd learned to expect the unexpected and be ready to flee quickly. She would have done that in Chicago, but he'd knocked her unconscious. She wasn't sure, but he must have dragged her out of the apartment, down the stairs, and into the communal laundry room for someone to find her. That's where she was when she regained consciousness as the paramedics were loading her onto a stretcher.

"I hear you like it rough," he had said.

No, no, no, Minjung pleaded with the memory. *Not now.* She exhaled deeply, patted her go-bag one more time, and headed out of her new room. Taking the stairs seemed quicker, so she hustled through the elevator alcove, past the bridge, and down the stairs into the foyer. She took a moment to breathe as she stood outside the door Madam Rowena had gone through earlier. She had to get her nerves under control. One more breath, and she knocked twice.

"Come," Madam Rowena called.

Minjung opened the door but kept her gaze down. She wanted to look around, but protocol wouldn't allow that. She'd see it soon enough. Without turning her back to her new Domme, she closed the door. She held onto her planner but clasped her hands as best she could in front. She waited.

"You have an impeccable style, Minjung," Mistress Rowena said after an overlong moment.

"Thank you, Madam."

"Eyes on me."

Minjung looked up. Ahh, this was an office. Her Mistress sat at a large desk with four stacked computer screens off to one side. Papers and folders were piled neatly on the other side.

"Come. Sit here." Madam Rowena gestured to a low stool near her desk chair.

Minjung sat, placed the planner and test results in her lap, and raised her palms up to her new Mistress.

"Thank you for the respect. We have a few things to discuss." Madam Rowena's chair groaned under her weight as she shifted. She wore a black and white smocked-waist top, which was flattering for her body type. The blouse went well with the white flared pants she wore. Madam Rowena also had flawless style, and not only in clothing.

At first, the conversation was light. Madam Rowena asked how the trip from Chicago was, and Minjung gave glowing praise of Ash's driving skills. Her new Domme also asked if Minjung's new room was suitable. Minjung had to swallow down emotion before answering, "Yes," but then added that she'd never experienced such hospitality before.

"I take care of my people," Madam Rowena said. Clearly, this was a point of pride. "I want you to be comfortable."

Madam Rowena's demeanor was calming and Minjung found herself relaxing into the conversation. What also helped was that Madam Rowena's soft brown eyes were alert and focused on Minjung. There was a lot of intelligence behind those eyes, for sure. And, frankly, the whole combination was arousing Minjung in a good way.

"Thank you, Madam," Minjung said. "I have new test results, Madam. Since the auction." She held the printout with her clean STD tests.

"Excellent," Madam Rowena said. "That was very forward-thinking. I like that." She glanced at the results and added, "I'm still clean as well, as you saw at the auction."

Minjung bowed her head in a nod, indicating that she understood.

Madam Rowena then launched into an overview of the typical daily routine. Minjung was to manage an app on their phones for appointments and schedules. Both could enter appointments, but Minjung would most certainly remind her Mistress of anything coming up.

"I know you have questions, but before we get to those, tell me what will happen tomorrow." A hint of mischief danced in Madam Rowena's eyes.

Minjung understood why her Mistress's eyes sparkled that way. It was a test. Madam had given out a lot of information in a short time, and her request seemed daunting. But Minjung was ready. She inhaled, matched her Mistress's mischievous glint as if to playfully say, 'challenge accepted,' and said out loud, "Saturday means the market is closed, and Madam Rowena can sleep in, but probably won't. For now," Minjung said without looking down at her notes, "coffee will be served at the dinette but there will come a time when coffee will be brewed and served in Madam's suite on the third floor." Minjung then rattled off Saturday's breakfast, lunch, and dinner menus and was pleased when Madam nodded at each thing, adding a couple of things she hadn't conveyed before.

"You may eat before or after I do, but there is never to be a mess left in my kitchen." Madam Rowena raised an eyebrow. "Understood?"

"Yes, Madam." Minjung's core tightened at the slight push of dominance. More. She wanted more of that.

"You'll need breaks. Your Chicago application said you want daily exercise breaks."

Minjung nodded.

"That can be accommodated. I typically work on my puzzles or read after lunch, so that might be a good time for you to exercise. I'll show you the exercise facility tomorrow after breakfast."

"Thank you, Madam." This was the perfect opportunity to ask, and she had to ask it now, or the opportunity might never come up again. "Madam?"

"Yes?"

"May I also walk the property on occasion?"

"Walk? Outside?" It sounded like this was a foreign concept for her. "Sure. I suppose so. Just stay inside the property boundaries. It's seven acres, and that's a lot, but you'll bring your phone with you so I can contact you if necessary or vice versa."

"Yes, Madam." Minjung also knew it was so Madam Rowena could track her. And that was okay for now. Minjung knew how to take off the tracking feature. She also knew how to ditch a phone that was traceable by people she didn't want to be traced by. Take Chicago, for example. She wasn't sure if he and Jenna were able to trace her, but she couldn't take the chance and ditched the burner phone a couple of hours after signing the contract with the woman sitting in front of her.

Madam Rowena told her that no one would be coming to the house for the first week she was there. No cleaning or landscaping crews and no friends would show up. This was to give the two of them a brief period of getting to know one another without outside distractions or obligations. A red flag went up in Minjung's head. No contact with anyone for an entire week? That sounded like isolation, which was a definite no-no in any new relationship.

This bit of news validated Minjung's paranoid escape plan and need for a go-bag. It was already too late tonight, but tomorrow, she would walk the fence to find any places she could climb or squeeze through in case she needed to get lost again. She reminded herself, though, that she had a two-week opt-out clause she could invoke if she needed to. She could use the cash, that was for sure. Knowing she had a plan in place, she firmly decided to let herself relax into the situation and do the best job that she could. Besides, she had a cell phone and could call Ashley for help or 911 if it went that far. Paranoia and intuition had kept her alive in the past, and she hoped her vigilance would keep it that way.

Madam Rowena looked over her notes one last time and threw her pen down on the legal pad. "Disrobe and then sit back down."

"Yes, Madam." Minjung stood, moved off to the side so she wouldn't trip over the stool, and began a methodical removal of her clothing. Madam Rowena's gaze watched every movement, but Minjung made no attempt to create a sultry and sexy striptease. She was not going to make any assumptions in that regard.

Once her clothes were folded and placed on a coffee table in a lounge area that Minjung hadn't noticed before, she came back and sat on the stool.

Madam Rowena leaned forward. "How are these?" She gestured to Minjung's knees.

Minjung usually wasn't self-conscious about the scars, but Madam Rowena seemed overly attentive to them, which made her nervous.

"Fine, Madam," Minjung said but then thought better of her response. "Actually, they are a bit stiff from sitting in the car for so long."

"I see." Madam Rowena wheeled her office chair closer and traced the scars along one knee and then the other. "Sports-related?"

Minjung clenched her jaw. She hadn't been expecting that question. She willed her mind to go anywhere other than the reason she had to have that first surgery. The second surgery had been needed because of physical activity and stupidity on her part, but Madam didn't need to know any of that. The pause before answering Madam's simple question had been overlong, so Minjung simply said, "Partly, Madam." It was kind of the truth because the first surgery had not been sports-related at all, had it?

Minjung flinched when Madam Rowena reached for Minjung's cheek. She raised her arm in defense. She was so frustrated with herself. Why was she still flinching? Chicago was already in her rearview mirror, and it had been over a decade since she'd left home. Madam was not either of them.

"I wasn't going to strike you," Madam Rowena said softly. "But it's obvious you have something in your background that makes you guard like that. You don't have to discuss this with me now, but I need to know if you would like me to bring in a trauma counselor or some other kind of professional."

Minjung relaxed the muscles she realized were tensed up and took a moment to respond. "That's very kind, Madam. I think I am okay. Being here and not there is already helping."

Madam Rowena nodded. "May I touch your cheek?"

Minjung nodded.

Madam Rowena pressed lightly on Minjung's cheekbone and then felt around the bones surrounding the eye. "Any pain?"

"Not anymore, Madam."

"I would like to take you for a physical exam. Maybe this weekend. This needs to be checked out. Would that be okay?

"Yes, that would be fine, Madam," Minjung said, surprised that her new benefactor was this concerned about some healing bruises.

"Good. I'll set that up." Madam Rowena stood and said, "Inspection."

Minjung leaped to her feet and assumed the inspection stance with hands behind her head and legs spread. This pose was familiar and calming.

Madam Rowena opened the bottom desk drawer and withdrew a crop. "Again, this is simply a prop for this evening. After your inspection, the only activity I have in mind is making full use of this." She ran the tip of the crop over Minjung's mouth.

Minjung smiled, her lips beneath the crop tip.

Madam Rowena chuckled. "You like pleasuring your Mistress, don't you?"

"I do, Madam."

"Go on," Madam Rowena said as the tip of the crop trailed over Minjung's body. "Expand on that."

"The taste of a woman is unique," Minjung said. "I feel privileged that the woman allows me to touch her so intimately. It boosts me to please her this way."

"Does your tongue ever get tired?"

"Of course, but I switch it up by using fingers or nose or chin so my tongue can rest and regroup."

"'Regroup,'" Madam repeated with a chuckle. She continued her crop inspection and a soft moan escaped. Was she getting aroused? Maybe. Probably. Minjung would hopefully be able to learn the telltale signs soon enough.

The crop gently tapped Minjung's inner thighs, and she separated her legs further apart. "Is this okay on the knees?" Madam Rowena asked.

"Yes, Madam. My knees are fine." That was a lie. Minjung knew she'd be on her knees soon enough and didn't want to disappoint her new Mistress, especially since they were on their first official evening together.

Madam Rowena tossed the crop on her desk and stepped so close that Minjung thought she was going to kiss her. But she didn't. Instead, Madam Rowena's hand found Minjung's very aroused center.

Minjung couldn't help moaning her excitement as she tried not to move. Her hands were voluntarily clasped behind her head, not bound or chained. Her legs spread by their own volition. This dominant woman was touching her intimately. She moaned again.

"Someone's wet," Madam Rowena announced. She swirled a finger around Minjung's budding clit and then pulled away, causing Minjung to groan her disappointment. Madam Rowena simply chuckled and popped her wet finger into Minjung's mouth. "Clean this."

Minjung took great delight sucking and licking her Domme's digit clean. When Madam Rowena began thrusting that one finger in and out of Minjung's mouth slowly, another involuntary moan escaped.

The finger retreated and a pillow got tossed on the floor by Madam's feet. "Take these slacks off me and get to work."

Minjung grinned at her benefactor and eagerly complied.

Chapter 5

Rowena

The border had been completed the day before Minjung arrived, but now it was time to separate colors. Rowena sat at the table in the family room and pulled out orange and yellow pieces, putting them into separate piles. Funny how her initial intentions for a jigsaw might start out one way, but sometimes the pieces pushed her in other directions. Like now. For whatever reason, the blues and greens were calling out to her. With a sigh, she abandoned her initial plan and worked on what the puzzle seemed to want.

She stole a glance at the tracking app and watched Minjung's progress around the perimeter of the property. Why anyone would want to risk tripping or hurting themselves out there in the woods was beyond her. There was a perfectly good treadmill in the playroom downstairs. She'd even shown Minjung the space that morning, but Minjung had chosen to go outdoors anyway. Minjung had definitely seemed impressed with the space and even stroked the vinyl spanking bench lovingly. They'd use that soon enough. Once Minjung was deemed healthy and injury-free, Rowena would have the green light.

She sucked air through her teeth as she thought about the ways she would break in her new sub. She had to break her in before the initial two-week trial period was up, though. So far Minjung was a dream, but it had been less than twenty-four hours. She hadn't pre-cooked the omelet that morning and then reheated it to a dry mess as Kaylynn would do. No, Minjung waited for her to come down to the kitchen and cooked it right away. She'd had all the ingredients ready, and it was quite good. The coffee was wonderfully hot, too. The side dish of grapes was weird, and Rowena ignored them. And when the hell did grapes enter her house, anyway? Victoria. It must have been. She'd been rooting around in the kitchen the other day. The lunch Minjung made had been pretty good, too. Minjung made her a grilled cheese sandwich just the way she liked it and tomato soup from one of Chef Blake's Easy Meals from Tyttle Foods.

Was Minjung too good to be true? Some submissives were good actors, though. She'd had posers, many of them, in fact, who ultimately hadn't been able to satisfy Rowena's needs in the long run. She had to find out if Minjung was one of these posers and quickly. A six-month contract was a long time to put up with a sub whose every other word was a safeword.

But, no, she wasn't going to let her thoughts go back to Kaylynn, her last full-time poser submissive. Nope, nope, nope. Rowena dug into the box and pulled out a handful of puzzle pieces. Blues went into one pile, greens into another. The rest went into the top of the box to be sorted later. But Kaylynn had seemed so perfect in the beginning, hadn't she? The mid-twenties woman kept up the charade for quite a while until she got uppity and decided that she didn't care for impact play or bondage anymore. Oh, but she liked the paycheck and the accommodations, didn't she? Sure.

Rowena grunted, tossed the puzzle pieces in her hand back into the box, and sat back. Jigsawing was supposed to be calming and meditative, so why was Kaylynn ruining it for her this afternoon? With a sigh, she stood up, walked four steps to her recliner, and plopped in it. She hit the controller and was soon reclining with her feet up. Maybe she'd take a quick nap. She hadn't gotten much sleep the night before because so many different emotions were running through her. Apprehension over whether she'd made a good choice battled with excitement about having a new submissive in the house. Minjung's oral skills seemed to be quite good, making Rowena squirm at the memory of the service Minjung provided her in the office last evening. Unfortunately, impact sessions were going to have to wait until tomorrow's green light from Dr. Moreau. It had taken a while, but she'd finally found a female doctor well-versed in BDSM. Rikki Carmichael's Aunt Matilda had made the recommendation.

Thinking about Matilda also brought mixed emotions. She loved the older woman dearly as a mentor and friend, but Matilda could be judgmental and scathing with her advice. At some point, Matilda would want to look over Rowena's new submissive and give advice, wanted or not.

"Usually not," Rowena said out loud and then sighed. She had to get Minjung used to the scrutiny newcomers always received in this tight-knit community. Rowena had a small tea planned so her close friends could meet Minjung. "Hayley, Victoria, and their respective subs," she mumbled. "Mm hmm." Rowena had to see how Minjung handled herself serving and attending to the needs of a small group. No sense in subjecting Matilda to a disaster if it could be avoided. And then Rowena would be able to save face.

Rowena closed her eyes and started to relax when she remembered that she was tracking her new sub. She'd also tracked Minjung throughout the night, too. The woman was a virtual stranger in her house, after all. Minjung's phone hadn't left her room at all during the night. Not that Rowena had restricted Minjung to her room, but many things were revealed when subs thought their Mistress wasn't looking or aware. When sleep wouldn't come, Rowena gave in and went to her lounge space off her bedroom. This room was a bonus living room where she kept a second home security setup so she could monitor all the cameras, both outside the house and inside. She didn't go as far as to put cameras in bedrooms, bathrooms, her office, or the playroom/fitness room, but all the common spaces had cameras. There had been no movement, with the one exception of the black and white cat outside that seemed to cut across the circular drive going who knows where.

She woke up her phone and saw that Minjung was heading for another lap around the property. Hopefully, her sub's outing was to keep in shape, not to get away from Rowena.

She jumped when the phone dinged in her hand. It was a text from Victoria.

VICTORIA: Still have a sub? How are things going?

"Eager much?" Rowena said to the phone.

ROWENA: All is well so far. And, no, you cannot come over.

VICTORIA: Spoilsport. I have a date tonight anyway. I've got a new clit vibrator to try on Sarah.

ROWENA: Fun. She's lasted longer than most. Is this a record for you?

VICTORIA: Shut up.

ROWENA: Bring her to the tea next Saturday. Or is Sunday better for you?

VICTORIA: Either. Let Hayley decide.

ROWENA: I'll let you know, but plan on tea next weekend. Did you put fruit in my fridge?

VICTORIA: LOL. Of course. I thought you'd want your new sub to feed you grapes.

Rowena scoffed. She'd met Victoria through Matilda, and they'd hit it off right away. Apparently, they were both on the more sadistic side of things when it came to BDSM. It was nice having someone who understood her need for ultimate power.

ROWENA: Not buying that excuse. And, btw, most people take food OUT of my fridge, not put food IN.

VICTORIA: Fine. I put some actual fruit and vegetables in there, so your poor submissive wouldn't have to eat that crap you buy.

Rowena laughed out loud. "Oh, my God." She scoffed at Victoria's insolence. She was the only one, besides Matilda, that she let get away with that kind of thing. Of course, Rowena could dish it right back.

ROWENA: She put some grapes in a cup for me this morning.

VICTORIA: And yet here you are, still alive. LOL

ROWENA: Didn't eat them.

VICTORIA: You're too much.

Rowena chuckled as she typed in her next text, knowing her friend wouldn't be offended.

ROWENA: Fuck you.

Her phone rang, and she knew who it was before she looked at the caller ID.

"No thanks. You're not my type."

Rowena chuckled into the phone. "You're an ass."

"Probably true," Victoria said. Her tone changed as she asked, "Has your new sub been to Moreau yet? Has she passed inspection? Is she in perfect health?"

"The appointment's tomorrow."

Victoria made an excited noise. "So that means if she's healed up from that matchmaking conference you went to, you can strap her down in your playroom tomorrow and have your way with her."

"Mm hmm," Rowena said. Victoria's words were music to her ears. She hadn't had a proper sub in a long time. Too long.

"Why don't you just go to Shasti? Why go all the way to Cincy? Shasti's a doctor right here in Denton Heights, and since she's part of our community, she obviously knows the score."

Rowena took a deep breath, knowing that Victoria would hear it. "That's exactly the reason. I don't want someone local knowing all my business."

"'Nuff said. Forget I asked," Victoria said. "And I think maybe it's also because Shasti is the newcomer, and Matilda's attention shifted to her. We were the chosen ones, but now we've been cast to the side for someone shinier and newer."

"Sounds like your love life."

Victoria burst out laughing.

"To be blunt," Rowena added, "I'm not sure about Shasti yet. She says she wants a *little*."

"What's wrong with that?"

"Creeps me out," Rowena said. "Age play?"

"Nah, that's not what it is. It's not pedophilia or whatever warped concept you've got going on in that head of yours. *Littles* are grownups that somehow missed out on nurturing or something. They just want to be cuddled and have lots of stuffies."

"Why aren't you a *little*, then, Vic?" This she said half seriously.

"Shut up, asshole," Victoria also said half seriously.

Rowena was getting sleepy and needed to end the call, but Victoria beat her to it.

"Hey, I have to get ready for my date. Gotta charge up the new vibrator."

"Have a good date. And I don't want details."

"But you'll get them anyway," Victoria said with a devilish tone. "Text me tomorrow. After the appointment."

"Maybe." Rowena disconnected the call. She never committed to texting or calling anyone. Not even her family. Mallory was due for another call to nag Rowena about inspecting the plant. She wasn't in the mood to be harassed, so she pushed thoughts of her family aside, closed her eyes, and did her best to relax.

Rowena sighed as she stretched her arms overhead. She must have fallen asleep. She opened her eyes and fumbled for the controller to put the footrest down. It was then she saw Minjung. The sight of her new submissive startled her; Rowena had been without a permanent sub for a long time, and she wasn't used to a submissive sitting on a low stool, eyes closed, waiting. Was Minjung sleeping? Her posture was fully erect, and her hands were face down on her thighs.

Rowena accidentally coughed, and Minjung's eyes flew open. The submissive's palms turned upward.

"How long have you been there?"

"Maybe twenty minutes, Madam."

Rowena checked her phone for the time. She'd only had a half-hour nap. "Get me coffee," she said and stood up. Her puzzle awaited.

"Yes, Madam." Minjung stood, backed away, and headed to the kitchen just on the other side of the family room.

"And cookies," Rowena called after her. "The iced cinnamon ones, not the shortbread."

"Yes, Madam," Minjung called back from the kitchen.

Rowena sorted a few puzzle pieces and then texted Hayley.

> ROWENA: I'm giving a tea next weekend. Which day is better for you? Saturday or Sunday?

She put her phone face up on the table and went back to sorting. Jigsaw puzzles were solvable problems, and that's why she liked them. There were infinite strategies but only one final result, so you definitely knew you'd gotten it right. Rowena found it soothing. There were no deadlines and no one telling you how to do it or that you were doing it wrong. She picked up a particularly deep blue piece and remembered another of the same color in her pile. She rooted it out, and voila, they fit together. Every piece that connected sent a tiny little dopamine hit. And this was a one-thousand-piece puzzle. *Let the good times roll*, she thought with a laugh.

Her phone lit up as Hayley's text came in.

> HAYLEY: Sunday would be lovely. How are things going? I know better than to call, but do call me soon, dear. I have so many questions about your new sub.

Rowena laughed at her over-polite friend. She and Victoria were polar opposites in that regard.

> ROWENA: Things are fine here. Sunday at 3:00. We'll have finger sandwiches, little cakes, and the usual. It will be my submissive's first event.

> HAYLEY: Shall I do the 'checks-and-balances' speech? Or will Victoria do it?

ROWENA: How did you know Victoria was invited?

HAYLEY: Oh, please, dear. You two are as thick as thieves.

Rowena chuckled at her friend's observation.

ROWENA: You'd better do the speech. Victoria won't be as thorough as you will be.

HAYLEY: Perfect. Anyone else coming?

ROWENA: Just you and Victoria. But please bring your subs. I want mine to see how well-behaved yours are.

HAYLEY: You make me blush, my friend. Minjung has already met Ashley, so that might be good.

Minjung entered the room carrying a tray.

ROWENA: I have to go.

HAYLEY: Looking forward to next Sunday.

Rowena turned her phone over and patted a side table near her puzzle table. She was not going to take a chance that her new submissive might spill something on her brand new puzzle that was right out of the box.

"Madam?"

"Yes?"

"Would you like me to stir in the sugar and creamer?"

"Yes, yes," Rowena said impatiently and went back to sorting.

After several long seconds, Minjung told her the coffee was ready. She stood as if unsure whether to hand the cup to her Domme or not.

Rowena reached over and grabbed the cup on her own. "Sit here." She gestured to an empty chair at her puzzle table. She reached for a cookie and took a small bite. The sip of coffee afterward was divine. The combination was perfect, but she wouldn't tell Minjung that. It was best not to get subs used to praise because, many times, Rowena just wasn't in the mood to do so. And, besides, small things like making coffee were expected. Praise would be reserved for bigger things, like lasting longer than Rowena during an impact session. Now, that would be an accomplishment.

Minjung sat as instructed, her hands in her lap.

"Help me sort." Rowena explained the blues and greens piles and Minjung nodded her understanding.

They sorted in silence for a while until Rowena asked, "What questions do you have?" She never asked subs *if* they had questions because they would often default to "No," and then communication was compromised.

"Thank you, Madam." Minjung stopped sorting to look directly at Rowena.

"No, no." Rowena gestured to the enormous pile of untouched pieces. "Keep sorting. You don't have to look at me this time."

"Yes, Madam." Minjung went back to sorting and then said, "It will take me a while to become autonomous with ordering groceries, so I want to ask for your leniency in that regard."

"Of course." Rowena flicked away Minjung's concern with a hand flip. "I'll put my list in the app, and you can add to it. But before you send the order to the delivery service, I'll look it over and approve it."

Minjung's shoulders visibly relaxed. "Thank you. And Madam?"

"Yes?"

"May I also add a few personal things to the list? They can be deducted from my earnings, of course."

"What kinds of things?"

Minjung blushed and made an odd noise before saying, "Feminine products, for example. And perhaps leafy greens and vegetables. I also enjoy sparkling water, but I can drink tap water if you wish it."

"Sparkling water? Like for mixed drinks?"

"Oh, no, Madam," Minjung said as she sorted. "They're flavored carbonated waters. I like the coconut flavor the best."

"Sounds awful," Rowena said with a laugh and then added, "All those things are fine." She didn't look up from her puzzle. "You'll be showing me the list anyway, so I can nix whatever seems excessive."

Rowena then informed Minjung about the doctor's appointment the next day. If all was healed from the overzealous Dommes and the blackened eye, then Minjung could anticipate her first impact session in the playroom afterward.

A relieved smile crept up Minjung's face as she continued to sort puzzle pieces.

"Does the thought of an impact session downstairs please you?" Rowena asked, knowing that it obviously did.

"Oh, yes, Madam," Minjung said with much relief. "It's been a long time, Madam."

"Indeed."

Was Minjung a pain junkie? Was Minjung hoping that Rowena would be a fetish dispenser so she could get her fix? Matilda's grand-niece Rikki Carmichael currently had a submissive just like that. Anyone with eyes could see it. Everyone knew it except the one person who should. Rikki was oblivious to how badly her submissive Eileen was using her. Was Minjung going to be like that? Tomorrow's session downstairs might tip that hand. Or it could go the other way. Minjung could be a softy like Kaylynn.

"Ask another question," Rowena said. The questions Minjung asked would reveal the things that were important to her. Would the next one be about playtime or sex?

"Do you have recipes you would like me to try to make for you, Madam? Family recipes or favorites? I have experience with many different dishes and don't mind learning more."

Interesting question. Perhaps Minjung was holding her cards closer to the vest than most submissives would in her situation. Yes, this one was intelligent. But so was Eileen, who knew just the right smoke screens to keep Rikki ignorant.

Rowena told Minjung that making recipes might come in time since she preferred frozen Chef Blake meals. She then sprang the afternoon tea party on Minjung and looked for a frightened reaction. She got none, and Minjung asked about the menu for the afternoon and if there would be a variety of teas or just one. Would Minjung serve each guest, or was there some other protocol in the Tate household?

Minjung's questions amused Rowena. She answered them one by one and realized that it was going to take a lot to fluster this one. Perhaps Minjung was a three-thousand-piece puzzle and not the three-hundred Kaylynn had turned out to be.

Rowena always did like a challenge.

"Madam?"

"Yes?"

"Thank you for taking me in," Minjung said. "You have an amazing house, home, and property." The handful of puzzle pieces went unsorted as she looked over at Rowena.

"Thank you," Rowena said. "I've worked hard to get what I have."

Okay, sure, Daddy's money had paid for the house and property, but if the trust fund money ever stopped rolling in, she'd be financially set from her own investments. It's basically what she did Monday through Friday. She'd been interested in the stock market since her Economics teacher at Miss Primrose's School in St. Louis had them participate in a mock stock market challenge. She'd easily won the competition because she was one of the few students to actually research the trends in the market to buy and sell accordingly. And to this day, she dedicated her week to continuing that success. Mostly success, that is. There were no guarantees in that line of business, of course, and she planned accordingly.

"Madam, I noticed some cardinals building a nest on the north end of the woods," Minjung said. "I am happy to be out of the city."

"Oh? And what if I had lived in Cincinnati proper? Would you be miserable?"

Minjung chuckled and looked down. "As always, Madam, I find ways to be unmiserable."

"'Unmiserable,'" Rowena repeated. "Humph." She had not been amused by the chosen word that probably wasn't a real word. Had Minjung just tipped her hand? Was Minjung no different than Kaylynn or Eileen? Would she 'find ways' to get what she wanted? Like the rest, would Minjung get her kicks until it wasn't satisfying anymore and then leave? Leave like they all did?

Disappointment and anger intertwined in Rowena's core. She scooped up a handful of puzzle pieces. *So, what will it be then, Minjung? Will I be asking you to leave after two weeks, or will you last the full six months without breaking character?*

"Leave me," Rowena said without preamble.

"Yes, Madam," Minjung stood up, took three steps back, turned and walked out.

Chapter 6

Minjung

Minjung didn't go far after being dismissed by Madam Rowena. She went to the kitchen to continue her food inventory in the pantry, cupboards, refrigerators, and freezers. As she made notes, she wondered why Madam had suddenly sent her away. *Because I asked to put things on the list*. It was the sparkling water. She shouldn't have asked. Who did she think she was anyway? Tap water would be fine. Minjung chided herself. She shouldn't have made demands. But, then again, she'd need feminine supplies soon and couldn't just walk to the neighborhood market to pick them up. There was no market or anything in this isolated area.

And isolated it was. On her three laps around the property that afternoon, she not only moved her muscles and exercised her lungs, but she also did reconnaissance. The tall concrete walls surrounding the entire seven acres seemed impenetrable. There were no holes or gates with any imperfections she could find. The only way to the other side might be to climb, and that would not be fun if she had luggage and her backpack. She had spotted a place where the wall didn't seem as high, but she also hadn't ruled out digging underneath, either. But for that, she would need a shovel or something.

As she'd walked that afternoon, she enjoyed the lovely spring day and thanked the universe for getting her out of that Chicago situation. Hindsight made it pretty clear that she shouldn't have accepted that position at Master Kevin's. Instead, she should have moved to a new city when Mistress Kelly released her. Especially because six months later, Master Kevin let her go at the beginning of February. It had been the heart of the winter, and since she didn't want to live on the streets, she was forced to take Jenna up on her offer to sleep on the couch. Her gut told her not to. It turned out her gut was right.

And right now, even though her gut wasn't screaming for her to flee, it could at a moment's notice, and she had to be ready. During her next walk around the property, she would stash a backup go-bag near a semi-climbable section of wall, just in case she had to leave quickly without being able to go to her room to get any of her things. Madam Rowena had cameras everywhere, so she'd have to take things outside a little at a time and stash them.

She heard Madam Rowena mumble something in the other room, but it hadn't been a call for Minjung. She checked her phone, just in case. No text from Madam.

Master Kevin had mercurial moods and was rough with his submissives sometimes. Minjung had gotten lucky that Mistress Kelly implored him not to touch her. She'd felt guilty that the others bore the brunt of his anger, but there was nothing she could do about it except tend to their bruises and cuts. Would Madam Rowena turn feral like Master Kevin? In less than a day, Minjung had already seen a vast mood shift. Something had definitely changed at that puzzle table, but Minjung had no clue what had happened.

The food inventory was done, and Minjung took another look around the kitchen, making note of the appliances, both large and small, as well as anything else she came across in the drawers and cupboards. She did this as quietly as she could, of course. She didn't want to disturb her Domme in the next room. Since Madam Rowena sprung that Sunday tea event on her, she only had a short time to get acquainted with the kitchen. She made a note to pin down the menu for the event so she could get those things on the grocery delivery list.

Minjung decided that it was simply going to take time to get a feel for and be able to read Madam Rowena's moods. Apparently, her Domme was eager for an impact session since she had somehow convinced a doctor to give Minjung an examination on a Sunday. She would pass the physical exam, of that Minjung was certain. The bruises from the Dommes had already turned yellow and were fading. The marks around her eye were barely noticeable at that point, and her ribs didn't hurt anymore.

Not knowing what to do with herself, she started on a deep clean of the kitchen. Madam Rowena had a cleaning service that came in once a week, but it seemed they had gotten a bit complacent in their work. Everything looked clean on the surface but when she wiped underneath the upper cabinets, her rag came back filthy. This would take some time. She made a note in her journal to ask where the kitchen and downstairs bathroom towels were to be laundered.

"Stop doing that," Madam Rowena said as she walked into the kitchen. "I have maids for that."

"Yes, Madam," Minjung said. She was not going to protest or even show her the dirty cleaning towels. Instead, she looked down and clasped her hands behind her back.

"Get my dishes from the family room, wash them, and meet me in my office." Madam Rowena headed toward the front of the house.

"Yes, Madam." Minjung moved quickly to retrieve the coffee tray. She brought a clean rag with her and wiped down the side table. After washing and drying the dishes, she put them away and hurried to Madam's office.

She knocked twice and waited.

"Come."

Minjung entered and was instructed to sit on a low stool near the couch where Madam Rowena was sitting. She sat facing her Domme and folded her hands in her lap.

"I will not be used," Madam Rowena blurted.

Minjung had no idea what Madam was referring to, so she remained silent.

"You will not use me to get my money or to get your kicks or, or..." she huffed, clearly upset. "Or whatever." She threw her arms up in exasperation.

Minjung remained silent. Protesting might have sent her Domme into a higher tirade, but at least now Minjung understood why she had been dismissed so suddenly.

"Say something," Madam Rowena barked, clearly irritated.

Minjung looked up. "I apologize if I've done something to offend you, Madam. It wasn't my intention. I have no desire to take advantage of you in any way. I hope I didn't give that impression."

Madam Rowena didn't speak for a moment and then said, "You didn't do anything wrong. I just want to warn you that I won't be taken advantage of. I have to be careful. Very careful. So that's why I'm watching you, and at the first sign of anything amiss, you'll be gone so fast, you won't know what hit you."

An exhausted disappointment bubbled in Minjung's core and settled there. Tears she hadn't known were so close to the surface spilled out, and she used one hand to cover her eyes. Desperate not to appear weak in front of Madam Rowena, she pinched her thigh until she cried out.

"What are you doing?" Madam Rowena asked coldly. "Why are you crying?"

This only escalated Minjung's despair. She slid to the floor onto her wrecked knees and lowered her head in supplication. Her forehead came to rest on one of Madam Rowena's slippers.

"Seriously," Madam Rowena said, her tone much softer. "Tell me."

Without sitting up, Minjung said, "I'm tired, Madam. Tired of moving from Domme to Domme. I want to belong somewhere. I want to belong to *someone*. I want to be—" *In love.* She couldn't say the last two words out loud. Instead, she blew out an emotional sigh and took a moment to catch her breath. She sat up but remained on her knees as she looked at Madam Rowena. "Each is a hopeful new start. But then I'm shown the door time and time again. With every new Domme, I hope to serve well and find personal satisfaction in my service. I truly do like to serve, Madam. It brings me joy to know that my Domme is happy, thriving, and living a good life because I helped in some way. That gives me joy. I am truly submissive, Madam, which gets me in trouble sometimes."

Minjung reached up and touched her healing cheek without realizing she had done it until Madam Rowena pointed and said, "Tell me about that."

Minjung wiped the tears from her face, grateful that she'd been able to get her emotions somewhat under control. She sniffed back a few tears that tried to escape. She told Madam Rowena about her time with Mistress Kelly and the circumstances with Master Kevin. She told about sleeping on a cot in Master Kevin's pantry and being ignored, never praised, not even by Basil.

"My instincts told me not to move in with Jenna," Minjung said. "It was going to be temporary, I told myself. But, Madam, it was February in Chicago. I had nowhere to go."

Madam Rowena nodded. "Go on."

"These injuries—the black eye, bruised ribs, and concussion were all courtesy of Jenna's Dom boyfriend. They were my reward for refusing to submit to him. He told me to get on my knees. I refused. I said, 'I don't submit to men.' He said, 'You do now.' And when I refused again, he hit me. I continued to refuse even though Jenna pleaded with me to do it 'just this once.' He used me as a punching bag and, apparently, knocked me unconscious. I came to when paramedics were lifting me onto a stretcher to take me to the hospital." Minjung looked Madam Rowena dead in the eye and said, "You may dismiss me at any time, Madam. I will figure something out."

"Come here," Madam Rowena said and patted the spot next to her on the couch.

Minjung didn't move because she didn't understand.

"It's okay," Madam Rowena said with a soft tone. "You need some aftercare, I think."

Minjung got up slowly, needing to use the arm of the couch to help her get up. She moved to the spot next to her Domme and stiffened when she was pulled into a hug. Strong arms went around her, and the show of kindness undid her. She couldn't stop the sob or the tears that followed.

"You're okay," Madam Rowena said. "You're safe now. That's over. I'm not releasing you. That's not what this conversation was about."

"I'm sorry that I'm so weak right now, Madam," Minjung said with a hitch in her voice. Why was she so stupidly emotional right now?

"You're okay," Madam Rowena said so softly that Minjung almost didn't hear it. After a beat, Madam said, "New relationships are hard. We're getting to know each other, and I have my guard up. I'm sure you do, too."

Minjung started to deny it, but Madam Rowena cut her off. "It's understandable." They sat in silence for a while until Minjung felt brave enough to pull out of the embrace and sit up. Madam Rowena cleared her throat and said, "Stool," as she pointed to the low stool in front of her.

Minjung moved swiftly and waited.

"Let's agree to communicate," Madam Rowena said. She stood up, went to her desk, and rooted around in one of the drawers. When she came back to the couch, she was holding a leather-bound notebook of some kind. She opened the cover to lined pages. "The kitchen island is a perfect place for us to put our thoughts, questions, and ideas down for each other. In addition to texts, I can leave notes for you there. I also envision that this will be a place for you to write down your questions and concerns for me." She waved the notebook around. "I'll do my best every morning and evening to have a look at it." Madam Rowena looked at Minjung and asked, "What do you think?"

"That would be a relief, Madam. To have a place for questions."

"And your concerns," Madam Rowena added. "I want you to feel comfortable here. You're going to be working hard for my household and satisfying my personal needs. That's a lot to ask. And, yes, I know that I am compensating you monetarily, which reminds me that we need to discuss what form of payment you wish, but not now. Here, let me—" She wrote in the journal and then showed Minjung.

Saturday, 3:00 pm
Madam:
1. Minjung to provide payment information.
2. Minjung will not be shy about writing in our correspondence journal.

"What do you think?"

A small grin crept up Minjung's face. She looked up and her heart swelled as her Domme visibly relaxed and smiled. It was a genuine smile.

"I love this, Madam," Minjung said. "This will work."

"Excellent." Madam Rowena handed the journal to Minjung and said, "I have some research to look over this afternoon, but I'd like my meal at 6:00. I would like you to join me shortly after in the family room."

"Yes, Madam," Minjung said.

"You're free to do whatever you wish until then. Unpack, maybe." She waved her hand without looking up. "You're dismissed."

Minjung waited until Madam Rowena had moved to her desk, then stood up and backed out of the room, journal in hand. She knew exactly what her first entry in the journal would be.

Hours later, after Madam Rowena had gone up to bed, Minjung sat on her own bed, personal journal in hand. An acquaintance in Seattle had suggested Minjung write her thoughts, fears, hopes, and whatever in a journal for safekeeping. That way, she didn't have to hold on to the thoughts for dear life, and they would be kept safe until she was ready to look at them.

Minjung looked over at one of the unopened boxes containing her various journals over the last decade. She'd somehow managed to keep every single one. Writing small helped. She chuckled out loud, opened to a fresh page, and clicked open her new gel pen.

Saturday, April 21, 10:23 pm

Madam didn't use me today. I thought she would when she summoned me to her office. Maybe she will after the doctor's visit and our impact session tomorrow (hopefully). I need to feel needed, wanted, and loved (I said it). I've never been to Cincinnati. The Company toured there the year after I left, so, anyway, I hope she'll point things out to me.

We watched a baseball game in the family room this evening after dinner. She seems really into baseball, judging by the framed photographs on her office walls. There's a photograph of a younger version of herself smiling next to a baseball player in uniform. And then another of an entire team. I didn't see what team, but it's most likely the Cardinals because that's who she was rooting for earlier while we sorted blue and green pieces on her puzzle.

She definitely got into the game. A lot of expletives flew out of her mouth when a player messed up or the other team did well. I have to learn more about this sport. Maybe I'll start with Wikipedia and go from there. The Cardinals won, beating a team called the Brewers from Milwaukee. That put Madam in a good mood.

Madam started a correspondence journal with me. I put this in it.

Minjung: 1. Menu for the tea party:

Then, I listed popular tea sandwiches like cucumber, crab salad, ham, brie, etc. Next was a vegetable platter and then homemade cookies. I asked what other things she'd like on the menu. Oh, and I asked her what type of tea she wanted and how the service would be done. Those were items two and three. I stopped there, even though I still had a lot of other questions for her.

She may not like all my questions, though, and might rethink the correspondence journal thing. Oh, well. She started it.

I shouldn't be flippant like that. I'm grateful that she has taken me in and is giving me a chance to prove myself despite her reservations about a new person in this role. I can't help thinking about the women that came before me. Were they amazing? Do I have extraordinary shoes to fill? And on the flip side, why did they leave?

My recon walk was good. Might have found a place. We'll see tomorrow if I have time for a walk before we head to Cincinnati for my physical exam. She wants to make sure I am physically fit to serve her personal needs. It makes sense.

Almost forgot! She has the best playroom/dungeon/fitness room in her basement. It's cleverly disguised as an exercise room, but I noticed the hooks in the ceiling and walls. Maybe I'll get acquainted with them tomorrow. Fingers crossed. On rainy days, I can use the treadmill, elliptical machine, or the fancy bike from the commercials on TV. There is even a section of floor near the mirrored wall that I could maybe...

Minjung chewed on the end of her pen. Did she dare think that she could ever move that way again? It had been years, over a decade. With a sigh, she went back to her journal.

> Best not to tempt that ghost, right? Stick to the usual, Minjung. Tired now. Bedtime for me. More tomorrow.
>
> Day rating: 5/10 (First full day in Denton Heights, OH)

~~~

The city went by in a flash as Madam Rowena drove them back toward her home in Denton Heights. Cincinnati was a small city in Chicago, San Francisco, and Seattle terms, but it was definitely a busy one. Minjung drank in the sights as they went by. Not only was she soaking in her new surroundings on that rainy Sunday, but she was also trying to get her bearings after leaving Chicago.

She hadn't been able to walk the property that morning because of the rain, so stashing cash and a small go-bag near the fence would have to wait. Instead, she asked for and got permission to use the treadmill and elliptical machines in the basement playroom. She'd gotten an exhilarating cardio workout that morning and even took time to do a few yoga stretches on the open mat next to the mirrored wall. The mirrors brought back memories. Memories that had begun to leak back into her mind. It had been over fifteen years since the incident, or accident, depending on who you asked, and maybe it was time to let the memories in. If the mental memories insisted on coming back, then maybe she'd try the physical ones, too. Not having an official barre, she used the treadmill's handrail and launched into a routine she'd learned as a child to warm up toes, arches, and calves. She stood sideways to the makeshift barre with her arms on bravo. Music would help, but she knew she'd chicken out if she stopped to open the music app. She grabbed the barre and opened to the second position. Relevé into Demi-plié. Stretch. She had desperately tried to focus on her body and not the memories that morning, but the memories had come on too strong. How fast one's life could change. It had taken mere seconds for hers to.

A truck passing by knocked Minjung out of her thoughts. She snuck a peek at her Domme driving the Mercedes two-door. She was regal, even when driving. She had a demeanor about her that spoke of confidence and power. The doctor they had just left had a similar demeanor, but there was no posturing between the two alpha women. They seemed to respect one another, which made Minjung's physical exam go smoothly. She was given a clean bill of health all around and the green light for an impact session when they got home. The anticipation almost made Minjung squirm in her seat. Would Madam wear that bustier top she'd worn in Chicago?

"Are you okay?" Madam Rowena asked as she glanced at Minjung in the passenger seat.

"Yes, Madam."

"What were you thinking about?" Madam signaled and pulled into the Denton Heights exit lane.

Minjung knew better than to lie, so the truth it was. "I was thinking about our impact session later. Specifically, what you might be wearing, Madam."

Madam Rowena chuckled. "Is that so? I'd better make it good then." She chuckled again and said, "You did well with Dr. Moreau. You did as she asked and acted like a proper submissive."

"Thank you, Madam."

"Did she give you her phone number like I asked her to?"

"Yes, she did, Madam. She also told me I could call her anytime I needed to."

"Perfect," Madam Rowena said. "The communities here in Denton Heights and Cincinnati seem to be unique in the ways we look out for each other. We have certain tastes and many people, most people, don't get us, or they think we're mentally unstable or something. We try to protect each other from folks that don't understand the subtleties of our BDSM relationships."

Madam Rowena seemed lost in thought, so Minjung didn't dare interrupt.

"I'm hungry," Madam Rowena said abruptly. "Let's get to-go orders from Indigo."

"Yes, Madam," Minjung said, not knowing what an 'Indigo' was.

Madam Rowena turned down what looked like the main street of Denton Heights. She pointed out a few of the stores, including a pharmacy, a furniture store, and a trendy clothes boutique that she said had nothing in her size, 'of course.' She'd said this matter-of-factly as if resigned to the fact that boutiques like that didn't carry plus-size fashions. Many buxom women that were Madam Rowena's size were self-conscious about their weight, but she seemed unaffected. Minjung absorbed this information because it helped understand her benefactor's state of mind and view of the world.

"See this coffee shop?"

"Yes, Madam."

"Matilda's grandniece Rikki owns it. She just had her two-year anniversary. It's nice inside, but too busy for my liking. Good for her business, I suppose," she added with a laugh.

Minjung admired the big picture window in the front that read "Rikki's Coffee Shop" in gold lettering. It looked kind of cozy inside, with hanging lights and plants in the window. Minjung wasn't a coffee drinker, but those places typically had a nice selection of teas, as well. But by the sound of it, they'd never go there.

Madam Rowena pulled into an open spot on the street. "Back there is the Indigo Café. Go on in and get me a hot Reuben sandwich with everything that comes with it. I also want Tyttle potato chips. Get the plain, not barbecue or anything else. No drink. We have stuff at the house. Get yourself whatever you want. It's my treat because you made me look good today in front of Dr. Moreau."

"Thank you, Madam. For the compliment and the lunch."

Madam Rowena handed her a fifty-dollar bill and then waved her out of the car. Minjung hurried to the café and placed their order. She was pleased they had a nice selection of salads and went with the salade niçoise. The café was just as quaint as she imagined the coffee shop would be, and a certain level of comfort settled in her chest. Denton Heights, a bedroom community of Cincinnati, seemed to be a lovely little town. She'd been lucky to find Madam Rowena.

She double-checked the bagged order and headed back to Madam Rowena's car.

"Oh, that smells so good," Madam Rowena said. "We're going to need our strength for this afternoon's session, aren't we?" She gave Minjung a predatory glance that almost curled Minjung's toes.

Yes, yes, yes. This is what Minjung wanted—that dominance. Time would tell if it was real and if it would last.

Once back at the house, Madam Rowena took on the full Domme role. She stepped into the foyer and said, "Give me that lunch bag."

Minjung did as requested.

"Strip."

The command startled Minjung, but she complied, making sure to fold her clothes semi-neatly. She didn't want to be reprimanded for sloppiness.

"For the rest of this afternoon and evening, you will be nude in my presence."

Minjung nodded.

"Put those away in your room," Madam Rowena said, referring to the clothes. "Freshen up and come back down. You'll plate our food and serve me at the dinette. After I have been served, you may eat with me at the table."

"Yes, Madam. Thank you, Madam." Minjung wasn't sure if she was dismissed, so she didn't move.

"Go." Madam Rowena pointed toward the stairs.

Minjung took three steps back and then headed toward her room. She tossed her pile of clothes on one of the dressers and then did a quick washcloth bath to "freshen up." Once back downstairs, Madam Rowena was nowhere in sight. Minjung settled the food on plates and covered them with bowls. She looked around for food covers but came up empty. She put that question in the correspondence journal and noticed that Madam had answered all the questions Minjung had asked about the tea party the following Sunday.

She closed the notebook when she heard the elevator whir. She stood in relaxed mode with her hands clasped in front of her. She would keep her gaze down until told otherwise. She wasn't self-conscious about being nude. She'd had many assignments where that was a requirement and had quickly gotten over any embarrassment associated with it. Now, she simply took it as a compliment that her Domme wanted to see her body. Especially because that meant there was a good chance her body would be used to please her Domme at some point soon.

"Serve me," Madam Rowena said as she headed toward the dinette table.

She wore a flowing silk nightgown tied at the waist.

"Yes, Madam." Minjung sprang into action. She didn't head for the food. Instead, she pulled out the chair for her Domme and then asked what she would like to drink with her meal. She found the requested bottle of cola in the refrigerator and, instead of popping off the cap, brought it and an opener to the table.

"Would Madam like me to open the bottle for her?"

"Yes."

Minjung did so and then went to retrieve Madam's sandwich and chips. She brought an empty bowl in case Madam would like to pour the bag of chips into it.

"Go get your food and join me here," Madam Rowena commanded.

Minjung nodded and retrieved her salad and a glass of iced tap water.

"Salad?" Madam Rowena rolled her eyes. "You're not anorexic, are you?"

"No, Madam," Minjung said, although she'd come close back then. Most of the girls were bulimic, anorexic, or serious food deniers like Minjung.

"Whatever," Madam waved her hand dismissively and added, "You do you." They ate in silence for a while until Madam began outlining the tea party for the following Sunday. Minjung made mental notes. She'd write it all down when she got a chance.

"You represented me well today," Madam said and pushed her half-eaten lunch away. "You will do the same next Sunday as well."

"I hope to, Madam."

"If all goes well, then I will plan another tea with very special guests. I've mentioned Domme Matilda to you before. She is the most honored guest I will have in my home. She is La Grande Dame of Denton Heights, or should I say, 'Grand Domme'?" She scoffed at her own joke and then said, "Everything must be perfect."

Madam's expression took on a faraway gaze for a moment, and then she stood and gave instructions on how to save her food for tomorrow's lunch. Apparently, it was to be reheated, but not in the microwave.

"I'm going to rest for forty-five minutes and then head down to the playroom. I would like you there waiting for me." She grabbed Minjung's chin. "Do not disappoint me."

A thrill ran through Minjung at the words. "I won't, Madam." Madam's slight push against Minjung's chin sent another chill.

Minjung waited until the elevator took her Domme away and then sprang into action, clearing the remains of lunch. Would there be a connection down in the playroom? Would she feel Madam Rowena's dominance? Would it be real? She had two weeks to decide if she wanted to stay. So far, she wasn't leaning in either direction.

Chapter 7

Rowena

Rowena stood outside the closed door to the playroom, taking a moment. The submissive waiting for her was seasoned and knew what she wanted and needed. It was up to Rowena to fulfill that for her and, in turn, be fulfilled herself. That was sometimes the tricky part.

She looked down at her regalia. She'd chosen the black leather with black lace for this first official session with her new sub, but she favored the deep plum leather with biscuit lace or even the red with black. The plus-sized corset with skirt fit her well and accentuated her many curves nicely. The leather corset zipped up the back and laced closed in the front, which completely accentuated her breasts. Was Minjung a breast girl? She'd find out soon enough. The lacing trim and decorative sleeves completed the look, and she felt sexy in it. And powerful.

She took a cleansing breath, put her game face on, and opened the door. An involuntary noise, something akin to a moan, escaped her throat when she saw her nude submissive kneeling on the mat. She was facing the now open door but looking down. Her palms turned up at Rowena's entrance.

"Very nice," Rowena said.

Her submissive exhaled noticeably as if letting out nerves.

"Get off those knees," Rowena commanded. She knew her sub was trying to please her, but the scars and stiffness she'd witnessed made it abundantly clear that this was not a sub who should be kneeling. Accommodations were needed.

Minjung leaned to the side and put most of her weight on her buttocks.

"Good girl," Rowena said and watched as a small frown curved Minjung's lips. It was fleeting, but it put question marks in the air. "Do you not like being called a 'good girl?'"

"No, Madam. I do not." Minjung did not look up. "Unless it pleases you, Madam."

"Why don't you like it? Most subs do." Rowena took that opportunity to cradle Minjung's chin and lift it. "Look at me."

"I am submissive, Madam, but I'm not a *little* or a girl."

"Ahh," Rowena said knowingly. "I see. You are a grown woman."

"Yes, Madam." Minjung blinked several times in succession. It was nerves, that was obvious, but Rowena was impressed that Minjung had asserted herself on her second full day in Rowena's house.

"And you want to be respected as such, correct?"

"Yes, Madam."

"Done." Rowena let the chin go and said, "Keep your eyes on me." Minjung complied as Rowena headed to the locked storage cabinet and unlocked it from the key she had squirreled away in the cleavage of her corset. She had a spare key hidden in the room, but it was best not to let a new sub know that. "Am I also correct in assuming that you would like me to be in command, in charge, and making the decisions?"

When Minjung didn't answer right away, Rowena turned back to face her. She had two wrist- and two ankle-cuffs in hand. She raised her head and one eyebrow. That usually got results. And it did.

"Yes, to the first two, Madam, but as far as decisions go, if it pleases Madam, I would like to be able to make a few decisions about running the household independently. With Madam's approval, of course."

"'Independently,' hmm?" Rowena echoed. "We'll see, but I like your initiative. I do. I truly do. It's refreshing." She closed but didn't lock the storage closet. She moved to stand in front of Minjung. "But in this room?" She gestured around her. "In here, I am the queen, the boss, the matriarch of your existence. Is that understood?"

"Yes, Madam. Yes, yes." Minjung leaned forward and kissed one of Rowena's high-heeled feet, then rested her forehead on the shoe. "Yes, Madam. That is a given."

"Sit up," Rowena commanded, and Minjung complied. Rowena said, "I play hard. I want you to know that." Minjung nodded. "But I'm also cognizant that you are a living, breathing human being who is in my care. So, we have the stoplight system for safewords, of course, but if at any time you say, 'stop' or 'no more' or anything like that, I'll stop." She searched Minjung's face for understanding. When she got it, she said, "Tell me you understand that."

"I understand, Madam." Minjung looked like she wanted to add something so Rowena urged her on. Best to get this out early. "Thank you for looking out for me, Madam. It's…"

"Refreshing?" Rowena offered with a grin.

Minjung chuckled. "Yes, Madam. Perfect word."

"Wrists," Rowena commanded and then attached leather wrist cuffs. None of those new-age soft Velcro crap would ever make an appearance in her playroom. "Come." She directed Minjung to sit on what might look like a simple weight bench to the vanillas but wasn't. "Assume the position."

Minjung bowed her head in a deep nod and climbed aboard the spanking bench face down. She was obviously no stranger to the apparatus. Her forearms rested on the padded armrests with her torso draped over the long bench. Her knees were hopefully well-cushioned against the padded nylon knee and shin rests below.

"Knees?"

"Fine, Madam." Minjung added, "Truly." Funny how Rowena had been about to ask if that was the truth. No need to now.

Rowena attached the ankle cuffs to Minjung's ankles one after the other but didn't attach the cuffs to anything just yet. That would come later. She reached down between Minjung's ankles, grabbed hold of the shin rests, and yanked them apart. Minjung made a small noise of surprise. She was now exposed and vulnerable. Just the way every submissive liked it at some point.

Rowena chuckled deeply. She placed her hands on each of Minjung's calves and rubbed gently. She worked her way up the back of Minjung's thighs and made sure to stroke the inner thighs. Minjung pushed back, obviously aroused. Rowena ignored the movement and stroked tight buttocks. Minjung was clearly a woman who took care of her body. She had an athlete's physique, and Rowena was going to enjoy every inch of it. Touching the small of Minjung's back elicited a small squirm. A slight ticklish spot, Rowena surmised. Rowena's hands then caressed Minjung's back and shoulders. She gave a slight squeeze on one shoulder before moving away. The squeeze was a signal that the soft touching was over, and things were about to change.

Back at the supply closet, Rowena pulled out her sturdy yet comfortable playroom shoes. Wielding implements of ass-destruction simply could not be done well in high heels. Shoes changed, she then pulled out several of her favorite implements. She placed them on the adjustable hospital tray table and wheeled the table over to show each one to Minjung in turn. Rowena then lifted her hand to show Minjung her palm. Minjung nodded that she understood.

"Just a bit of a warm-up," Rowena said as she smacked the meatiest part of one of Minjung's buttocks and let her hand rest there. It hadn't been a hard hit; she truly was just warming up her submissive's body. Rowena liked the strike-and-hold technique to ease a submissive into the flow of things. The thwack of her hand on skin was like an old friend. It had been so long. Too long.

After a dozen or so strike-and-holds, she changed her technique. She smacked the skin but let her hand flow off the body. This feathering was quick and repetitive, and it had Rowena's blood pumping. She changed the feathering direction, making sure to evenly distribute the attention to both sides. And then she stopped.

"Breathe," she commanded.

Minjung inhaled and sighed out audibly.

"Again."

Once Minjung complied, Rowena said, "Don't tense up. You're seasoned enough to know that's when you'll get injured. Understood?"

"Yes, Madam. I understand." Minjung let out another nerve-relieving exhale.

Rowena grabbed a handful of pink butt cheek and squeezed gently. This was another signal to indicate that things were going to change again.

Rowena picked up the ping pong paddle and tapped it gently on Minjung's nicely pink and warm butt cheek. Several taps later, she moved to the other side. And then the fun really began. Rowena used her other hand as a backstop when she brought the paddle up. This resulted in fast tapping. She didn't stop tapping when Minjung squirmed. Minjung was simply trying to get relief from the impacts. That was a signal from her submissive to change things up. Best to check in, though.

Rowena put the paddle down on the tray table. "Color?"

"Green, Madam." A contented sigh followed the response.

"Green for me, as well," Rowena murmured into Minjung's ear from behind. She added a deep conspiratorial chuckle, hoping Minjung would understand that they were in this together.

Rowena picked up the final implement and snapped it between both hands. Minjung flinched slightly, but hopefully, it was the sound that startled her and not the fact that the leather belt was next in the lineup.

"Most subs can only take about five of these," Rowena said to Minjung. I'm betting you can take more."

She wrapped the leather around her hand and wrist and whipped the business end on Minjung's upper thigh. Minjung yelped. Two more whacks were delivered on that side, but no safeword was called.

"That was three," Rowena said and changed positions. She whirled the belt around so that it made a whistling sound and then struck. Another yelp. "Four," Rowena said evenly. Another swing. "Five."

"Color?"

There was no answer, just a forceful exhale.

"Color?" Rowena asked again.

"Green," came the quick answer this time.

The last snap of the belt against skin sent a jolt of arousal through Rowena. She grunted at the surprise surge. She folded the belt in half and snapped it once before putting it back on the tray. She squeezed Minjung's shoulder and then ran her hands lightly over Minjung's very red buttocks and upper thighs.

So far, Minjung seemed like she could take what Rowena was dishing out. Now, on to step two, which would quickly morph into the third and final step.

Rowena grabbed a bottle of water from the stocked mini fridge. Impact sessions were workouts for her and pretty much the only time she drank water. Minjung opened her mouth when Rowena tilted the tip of the bottle toward her. Rowena poured a small amount in. Minjung opened her mouth again, and Rowena poured another small amount into it. One more, and then Minjung thanked her by bowing her head and turning her palms upward.

A warm glow flowed through Rowena. All of that had been done without words. She grunted. Best not to get sentimental. New subs were eager to please. That was all it was.

"Up."

Minjung moved slowly off the spanking bench and stood with her hands folded in front of her body. Rowena put the water bottle down and circled her new sub, touching a breast here or tweaking a nipple there. A squeeze of an earlobe elicited an aroused sigh from her sub. Interesting. Clothespins would make perfect earrings at some point.

She's beautiful, Rowena thought. She grabbed Minjung by the other earlobe and pulled her toward what looked like a pull-up bar swinging on chains. A small smile graced Minjung's face when she realized what was next. Minjung gracefully allowed Rowena to clip the leather wrist cuffs to the bar overhead. There was plenty of play in the chains, so Minjung wouldn't have to be on her tiptoes, not today, anyway. Rowena similarly connected the ankle cuffs to the chains she pulled out from behind a side table. Again, there was plenty of play, and Minjung could move easily. Wordlessly, Rowena positioned a padded stool with a wide square seat behind Minjung. The seat tilted slightly so Minjung could move back and lean against it, which she did at Rowena's urging.

One quick trip back to the supply closet brought an eye cover. It was actually a plum-colored sleeping mask called an eye bra. The eyepieces were cupped slightly so the fabric didn't touch the eyelid or the lashes. Rowena put it on her sub.

"Can you see?"

"No, Madam."

Rowena checked for gaps around the eye bra and, once satisfied, said, "I'm not going to gag you today. We're developing and earning trust." Rowena took a few steps back. "I'll be back in a few minutes for our next adventure." She liked to give subs time alone during a session to think or recover or anticipate whatever was coming next. Feeling their limbs chained with no way of releasing themselves was heady stuff, indeed. It fed into their feeling of acquiescence and reliance on their Dominant. Many subs had told her that was the time when they started to let go and feel free. That was the start of sub-space for many. Would it be the same for Minjung? She'd find out soon enough.

Rowena first headed to her supply cabinet to get out her favorite flogger. There would be no cane or whips today. Soon, though, but only if this next session went well. She then headed toward the door, opened it loudly, and then closed it as if she had left the playroom. She hadn't. She stood still and looked down at the floor. People, especially blindfolded submissives, could feel you staring at them. Rowena kept Minjung in sight out of the corner of her eye, though. She smiled when Minjung leaned forward so she could scratch her nose. To her credit, though, she made no move to undo the eye cover.

Rowena waited three more agonizing minutes, then opened the door again and acted as if she were coming back in.

"Color?" she barked as she marched over to her sub in chains.

"Green, Madam," Minjung said, stiffening slightly. Rowena understood that her new sub was trying to impress her and didn't want to do anything to displease her.

Rowena also understood that although she was an experienced Domme, she was trying to impress her new sub as well.

"Your back, Minjung," Rowena said, running one hand over her sub's back. "It's so unpink. So boring. Let's change that."

Rowena moved the padded seat out of the way and draped the flogger over Minjung's shoulder so she would know what was coming. She stepped back and began. It was almost like playing tennis. A backhand swing sent the tails to the left shoulder blade, and the reverse forearm swing hit the right. Back and forth, Rowena swung her hips, but the blows were easy. Now that she was warmed up, Rowena put more force into her strokes. She knew enough not to rely on arm strength alone, though. She swung her hips and followed through. She was careful not to hit the kidney area or wrap the tails around Minjung's shoulders.

Minjung's groans increased in volume as Rowena's hits increased in force. She ran the ladder up Minjung's back and down again. On the next round, she ran up the back and continued down over the buttocks to the back of the thighs. That had Minjung dancing. Back and forth, Rowena swung, then up the ladder and back down. Abruptly, she stopped out of breath. Minjung exhaled in relief.

But Rowena wasn't done. She threw down the flogger and picked up her surprise implement. She didn't warn Minjung or tell her what was next. She thwacked her new sub with her tried and true lollipop paddle. The small half-dollar-sized wooden head left incredible marks on a sub's ass.

Minjung yelped in surprise, or maybe it was pain. Rowena didn't know which. Maybe both. She didn't care. Another yelp followed another thwack as Minjung tried to handle the extremely stingy impacts. The paddle made small rings that lasted for several hours. One day Rowena would try to make the

Olympic rings on Minjung's ass, but her sub was moving around too much for that kind of accuracy. Instead, Rowena attempted to make a face. Two circles for eyes, a circle nose, and a mouth made of five more lollipop paddle circles. Satisfied with her creation, she stopped and stepped back. She moved the chair behind Minjung and then walked to her supply closet without a word.

She took a moment to breathe and then donned her new toy. It was a vibrating strap-on that Victoria recommended to her. It vibrated in the phallus and had a vibrating portion for the wearer. Rowena tightened up the straps and tucked the remote control in her cleavage.

Minjung was still breathing loudly.

"Color?"

"Mmm," Minjung groaned. "Greenish yellow, Madam."

"Understood," Rowena moved behind her blindfolded sub. She leaned back against the tilted seat of the chair and rolled a condom over the phallus. She waited until Minjung's breathing evened out, and she released a calming sigh. That's when Rowena stood up, put one hand on Minjung's back, and pushed her forward. The chains stopped her from falling, but now Minjung was open and available for Rowena's use. One hand grabbed Minjung's hip, and then the other grabbed the end of the phallus to guide it. She slid the phallus between Minjung's legs but didn't insert it. Not yet. Instead, she slowly slid the silicone phallus through Minjung's wet labia, hoping to make contact with her clit.

Minjung jumped, but the aroused moan that accompanied the contact told Rowena all was well with her sub. Enough foreplay, Rowena thought. She pulled back and slid the phallus into Minjung's body. Minjung's legs opened wider. That and Minjung's encouraging moan were all the invitations she needed, not that she needed one.

Rowena slid all the way in until she hit bottom. She grabbed Minjung's hips with both hands and thrust in and out at a slow but steady pace. Rowena's power centers filled at this dominating stance. Her body swelled with energy, and she increased the pace. The back end of the phallus hit her own pearl deliciously.

Minjung's aroused cries became more frequent. Rowena moaned at the sound but then stopped all motion. There were two reasons for this. She was out of breath and needed to regroup for a moment. That and she wanted to mess with Minjung. She needed to remind her who held the power here. Maybe she'd withhold the orgasm. But no, she herself was close to orgasming.

Breath not quite caught, Rowena hit the remote on the phallus vibrator. Minjung inhaled in surprise and bucked her hips. "Madam, please," Minjung begged. "I need release. Please, Madam."

Rowena hit the button that turned on the vibrator in the harness. "Mother of pearl," she said out loud as the vibrations hit her clit just right. She grabbed Minjung's hips and thrust again. In and out, faster and faster, harder and harder.

Minjung's moaning wail as she came sparked Rowena's own orgasm. She kept thrusting as her entire body filled with wave after wave of igniting nerve endings. Her movements slowed as she milked out a few more pulses. When she finally recovered, she sat back against the tilted seat of the chair and pulled Minjung back against her. The phallus was still inside. The chains were stretched to the maximum, but Minjung managed to loll her head back and rest it on Rowena's shoulder. It was an intimate move, but one Rowena would allow for now. Her sub was clearly flying high in sub-space. She reached for the remote and turned off the vibrators.

Rowena planned to hold her sub for as long as Minjung wanted, but Rowena's phone shattered the silence.

"Fuck," she muttered and pushed Minjung off her. She yanked the phallus out and headed to her phone by the storage closet. There was only one person who had that ringtone. Mallory. She had been avoiding her sister for too long and couldn't ignore it.

She reached for the phone and said, "Hey, Mallory. Hang on one second." She didn't wait for her sister to reply, put the phone on mute, and tucked it into her cleavage. She took off the strap-on and placed it in the basket near the bathroom. Minjung would clean it later.

She then stomped her way back to a woozy-looking submissive hanging like an offering on chains, but she couldn't take the time to admire it. Subs were too pampered these days, anyway. And who knew if this one would last? Rowena took off Minjung's blindfold and then undid the chains from the ankle cuffs. When the wrist cuffs came off, Minjung stumbled, and Rowena steadied her.

"I have to take this call," Rowena said. She gestured toward the couch.

"Go lay down over there. There's a blanket draped over the back. Water's in that fridge, and there's chocolate if you want that." She turned her back and, without looking over her shoulder, said, "And clean up our mess before you leave."

Not waiting for an answer from her submissive, Rowena headed toward the door. "Hey, Mal." At her sister's question, she answered, "No, no. Not doing anything important right now." And even though she knew exactly why her sister was calling, she casually asked, "What's up, big sis?" as she let the door slam shut behind her.

Chapter 8

Minjung

One week after their first impact session, Minjung rolled on her side to ease the new set of pains. Her ass, back, and thighs were sore from that afternoon's caning and bullwhip session. Madam had even allowed her to orgasm afterward, but Minjung knew the fresh marks on her body had been put there for Madam's company to see tomorrow. Minjung adjusted the pillow under her side and opened her journal. She put pen to paper.

> *Saturday, April 28, 10:32 pm*
> Last Sunday, Madam said, "Not doing anything important." I haven't had the courage to write that down until now, six days later. It stung then and still stings now. She doesn't think I'm important.
>
> So, I must remember that I am not Minjung Lee in this house. I am just a hired servant and plaything. I'm paid to look after a household and have contracted sex. That's all. Not more. And I can't go looking for more. That only gets me in trouble.
>
> But...Honestly, I thought she would take more care with me. I clearly read her signs wrong. She's mercurial. I must remember that because I naively thought she would give me aftercare. I even fantasized that she would hold me after our first impact session because I thought she was the type of Domme who needed to provide aftercare to ease out of her Domme space.
>
> But she didn't hold me. And I didn't lay down on

that couch or wrap that blanket around my quickly cooling body like she told me to. I did drink some bottled water, though. Two bottles, actually. Was that my tiny act of defiance? At the time, yes. I cleaned the implements she used like she asked me to. I cleaned the equipment as well. I even showered in the bathroom down there and snuck up to my room to put on clothes.

But that was last Sunday. During the week as I was cleaning her office, she told me what she did all day at her computer. Apparently, she invests in stocks and bonds and mutual funds and all that. I know nothing about it, so I said so, and then I got a confusing tutorial about how to pick online brokers, set up brokerage accounts, and diversify holdings. Not that I'm going to do any of that anytime soon, but it was cute how enthusiastic she was about it, which is good because that's how she makes her money. I guess it is, anyway. I don't really know.

Yesterday, she paid me cash for one week of service. I took half of it and stashed it in the go-bag I buried near the fence out of sight of the house. The other half got tucked in a hidden pocket in my to-go backpack here in my room. If this situation turns weird, I'm out of here. And I'll probably head south where it's warm. That way, if I'm homeless, I'll be semi-okay.

Minjung closed her eyes and sighed. She desperately didn't want to be on the streets again, but there was no way she was going to end up in another Jenna roommate situation. She wanted to stay in Madam Rowena's oversized house. She liked her new Domme well enough, but they didn't know each other that well. They were one week into that two-week trial period, and Madam Rowena had every right to dismiss her at the end of the two weeks if she wanted to, with no reason given.

Minjung sighed audibly. To be fair, though, Madam Rowena had given her aftercare every day after that first impact session. And even though Minjung had started her period on Monday, Madam Rowena took it in stride and stuck to sessions where Minjung serviced her, sometimes twice a day, even using the queening chair in the playroom.

That very morning, in fact, with Minjung's period over, Madam Rowena treated Minjung to another impact session. Chained tighter this time, Madam used the cane and a six-foot bullwhip on her. She praised Minjung for lasting so long and rewarded her with an orgasm. Madam had one, too, of course. After the session, Minjung let herself relax when Madam Rowena held her on the couch. Oh, she knew better than to read anything more than obligation into the aftercare, but it felt nice.

Still, as Minjung lay on her bed, she opened her eyes and repeated this mantra, "You are nothing. You are nobody. Don't insert yourself into her life." With this mantra, she vowed not to get too comfortable with her current setup. She hadn't fully unpacked her boxes in case she got the boot. They were tucked away in the closet in case Madam came in to inspect or something.

Tomorrow was the big day. The tea party. Minjung wrote a few more thoughts in her journal, tucked the pen inside, and then closed it. She was too tired to roll over and turn off the bedside lamp, so she simply closed her eyes. She hoped sleep would come quickly. She tried to convince herself that there was no need to obsess over the party. She had the menu down, she'd cleaned the house, and she understood the expectations for her behavior. Madam had drilled her on protocol the entire week. Never speak to anyone unless it was a Domme and she had been spoken to first. And if she did speak, it was to be brief and to the point.

Minjung got the distinct feeling that Madam was more nervous about tomorrow's tea party than she was. Minjung had served at many other Dominants' parties before. She knew the drill. She was more anxious about the cleaning staff coming on Monday. It would be Minjung's first time supervising them. She didn't want to ruffle feathers, but she'd found a few places in the home that needed more care from the cleaning staff. She was, however, going to take the learning approach on Monday. She was new to Madam Rowena's household, after all, so she'd play the ingenue and get a feel for how this particular crew did their job. But in actuality, she did have experience cleaning houses. She'd run Mistress Kelly's household, after all. And she'd learned quite a lot working under Basil at Master Kevin's. If anything, she would hopefully lead with grace and poise.

Minjung laughed out loud. "'Grace and poise, ladies,'" she mimicked the company's artistic director. That was the last company she'd ever been in.

Yes, whatever happened tomorrow and the rest of the week, Minjung would do it with grace and poise.

~~~

The next day, the front gate motion sensor sounded in the house. Madam Rowena looked up from her puzzle and said, "We're on." She got up and headed toward the great room where she would visit with her guests that afternoon.

Minjung followed but then veered off to the intercom camera near the front door. She saw a grinning Ash in the grainy feed. Before hitting the gate open button, she said, "Welcome." It was short and succinct, like Madam seemed to want. And that was just fine with Minjung. There had once been a time when she wanted to be the center of attention, but that had come with a heavy price. Being unimportant and in the background was good enough for her now.

Minjung watched out the side window flanking the heavy front door, and waited until Ash and her Domme and the Domme's male sub were walking up the steps. Madam Rowena assured her that they would think nothing of a servant opening the door in the nude, so she did just that and said, "Welcome" again. And Madam Rowena was right. None of them seemed phased by her nudity. "Please come in." She swept her hand into the house.

"Aren't you a hot little thing," Mistress Hayley said, cupping Minjung's face with one hand.

According to Madam Rowena, Mistress Hayley was in her early forties and a successful local realtor. She had been the one to show Madam this house, and their friendship was quickly born. Mistress Hayley was a short woman with long, flowing dark hair well past her shoulders. She wore a tight white button-up sweater top that showed some generous cleavage. Her tight tan pants hugged her trim figure, showing off her curves. And although she was small, she was also very clearly in charge.

"Come, Terrence." Mistress Hayley tugged on the leash attached to a heavy leather collar around the man's neck. He had to be at least six inches taller than she was, but he obeyed and stepped into the house. "You know Ashley," Mistress Hayley said to Minjung.

"Yes, Ma'am." Minjung nodded at Ashley, who bugged her eyes out at Minjung behind her Domme's back. She was probably trying to get Minjung to laugh. It was either that or she was trying to get Minjung to relax. Probably a mixture of both.

"If you'll come with me into the great room," Minjung said and gestured for Mistress Hayley to go first. "Madam Rowena is waiting for you."

"It's '*Madam*' Rowena now, heh?" Mistress Hayley said with a note of surprise in her voice. "I love that."

Mistress Hayley's pace increased when she saw Madam. "She's lovely," she gushed to her friend. "You never said she was a looker, too." She tapped Madam lightly on the arm in reprimand.

"Good to see you, too, Hayley." After giving Mistress Hayley two cheek kisses, she said, "Please, sit." She gestured to one of the cushioned chairs. Two pillows on the floor flanked it on either side.

"Does your girl need help?" Mistress Hayley asked this as she gave hand gestures for the man to sit on one of the pillows. "Ashley is ready and willing."

"Yes, actually," Madam Rowena said. "I'd like Minjung to serve while Ashley waits by the front door to let our next guests in when they arrive."

"Done." Mistress Hayley turned to her female submissive and said, "You heard the woman."

"Yes, Ma'am." Ashley headed toward the door. She waggled her eyebrows as she passed by Minjung. The smirk on Ashley's face as she went by almost made Minjung grin, but she squelched it.

"She's so exotic," Mistress Hayley said to Madam Rowena as she sat down.

Madam simply chuckled and gestured to Minjung to get the tea service going.

"Shall I pour, Ma'am?" Minjung asked Mistress Hayley.

"Yes, thank you."

Minjung picked up a cup and saucer and poured hot Earl Grey tea from the ceramic teapot into it. She handed the cup to Mistress Hayley and then offered a tray of various sugars and creamers.

"Shall I fix your tea for you, Ma'am?" Minjung gestured to Mistress Hayley's tea.

"No, thank you, Minjung. You may leave the tray." Mistress Hayley turned to Madam and whispered conspiratorially. "She's gorgeous,"

Minjung set the tray down on the table in front of Mistress Hayley and asked, "Will the gentleman be wanting tea?"

Mistress Hayley didn't answer right away but threw Madam Rowena another surprised look as if she was impressed. On second thought, Minjung wasn't sure if that's what the look was about. Maybe she had breached protocol by mentioning the submissive at Mistress Hayley's side.

"You're sweet to ask, Minjung," Mistress Hayley said at last. "And, yes, I think he's been a good boy today and can have some tea."

"Very good, Ma'am."

As Minjung poured the second cup, the front gate motion sensor sounded. She heard Ash buzz in the last guests as she set the teacup down on the table at Mistress Hayley's gesture.

"Madam?" Minjung asked. "Tea?"

Upon her Domme's nod, Minjung fixed the tea and then stood beside her at the unspoken gestured command.

"We'll wait for Victoria and her latest sub to get their tea before serving the treats," Madam said. "Minjung has put together quite an array today."

"I see that," Hayley gushed. "Deviled eggs, finger sandwiches, sweets. Ash will love the pizza rolls, that's for sure." She took a sip of tea and then said, "And speaking of treats, tell me more about the auction where you picked up this morsel." She gestured toward Minjung.

"I interviewed five candidates on Friday, as you know. And then I signed the contract with Minjung on Sunday. The rest is history, I guess."

Mistress Hayley cleared her throat loudly. "You've completely skipped Saturday. What happened on Saturday? That's the best day, I hear. Tell me." She took a sip of tea and leaned closer.

"Not much to tell, actually." Madam Rowena leaned closer, mimicking her friend's posture. "I only had one appointment on Saturday." She stared at Mistress Hayley, whose mouth opened comically into a disbelieving O.

Madam Rowena's words hit Minjung's ears, and she was confused. She had imagined that her new Domme had sampled several prospective submissives that Saturday. But she'd only had one appointment—the one with Minjung. She swallowed hard at the realization. And Mistress Hayley saw it.

"She didn't know that," Mistress Hayley said knowingly.

"I know," Madam Rowena said. "But now she does and will not let that swell her head."

Pride was trying to bloom in Minjung's chest. Madam had chosen her above all the others. But…no. She willed her elation away. It didn't mean anything. *You are nothing. You are nobody.* She repeated this in her head as the new guests greeted Ash and then made their way to the great room.

"Shit," an androgynous woman with stylishly short hair said as they came into the great room. "She's fucking stunning, Rowena. Didn't know you had it in you."

The woman looked Minjung up and down, making her uncomfortable. She didn't like being devoured by this new guest.

"Shut the fuck up, Victoria," Madam Rowena said with a smirk. Minjung's eyebrows raised in surprise, but she quickly regained her neutral expression.

Ahh, this was Miss Victoria, the other Domme attending the tea. She seemed to be in her early thirties and wore black chinos, kick-ass black boots, and a tight white short-sleeve shirt that showed off her physique. This was a woman who worked out, was proud of her body, and liked to show it off. That much was clear to Minjung.

Mistress Victoria's companion, a bleached blonde, wrapped both arms around one of Mistress Victoria's. It was a gesture of possession, but the blonde needn't worry. Players like Mistress Victoria were absolutely *not* on Minjung's radar. But apparently, Minjung was now on Mistress Victoria's. She hoped Madam wasn't going to break their contract and offer Minjung to her friend.

Minjung let her quick-exit strategy run through her head. A head nod from Madam put Minjung in motion. She served the new guests tea and then gestured to the self-help table, which was laden with treats, informing everyone to please help themselves. Minjung wasn't surprised when only the subs got up and served their Dommes first. Minjung waited for Ashley and the blonde woman to serve their Dommes before serving Madam. Only then did Ash, Mistress Hayley's male sub, and the blonde serve themselves. Minjung had nothing. She wasn't hungry and needed to stay available to help.

With a silent hand signal from Madam, Minjung sat on her stool at Madam Rowena's side. The Dommes chatted amicably about their respective lives. Madam Rowena had apparently been doing well with her investments, but her sister had called and reminded her to attend to "the family business." Minjung had no idea what that meant, but it wasn't her concern. Mistress Hayley had also done well recently with a big sale, earning her "buku bucks." Mistress Victoria seemed to enjoy complaining about her roommate Mac and all the guys he brought home. Minjung secretly wondered what this guy Mac thought about all the women Mistress Victoria brought home. Minjung had been in Madam Rowena's house for a little over a week but had already heard about Mistress Victoria's many conquests.

Unfortunately, thinking those thoughts had caused Minjung to unconsciously look over at Mistress Victoria, who was now attempting to give her some kind of smoldering glare right back. Minjung's gaze shot down to the hands folded in her lap. She'd had no business looking up, anyway. She'd get punished for sure.

A strong clearing of Madam's throat made Minjung look up. "Please mind the guests while I go have a reminder chat with my friend." Minjung was certain the last part was directed at Mistress Victoria. And, sure enough, Madam asked Mistress Victoria to accompany her to the office.

When the two of them had departed, Minjung asked, "Mistress, would you or your subs like anything else?"

Mistress Hayley silently questioned both Ash and the man on a leash, and neither of them wanted anything. "No, thank you, Minjung."

Minjung asked the blonde submissive if she wanted anything. The young woman said, "No," but made no move to help Minjung as she started to clean up.

Ash leaned over and whispered into her mistress's ear loud enough for everyone to hear, "Can I please you when we get home, Mistress?"

"Oh?" Mistress Hayley's raised eyebrows were almost comical. "I was planning on it." She tousled Ash's hair, and it was clear that Ash loved the attention. "On the daybed in the playroom. Maybe Terrence can join us." She turned to him and asked, "Would you like that?"

He nodded vigorously but kept his eyes down.

Ash whispered something in her Mistress's ear, but it was so low that Minjung couldn't hear. And it wasn't like she was trying to eavesdrop. She wasn't.

"You want to make him watch for a while?" Mistress Hayley asked.

Ash nodded and whispered something else.

"Work him up to a frenzy, heh?" Mistress Hayley laughed. "So, when he mounts you, he'll be like a wild animal, is that it?"

This time, it was Ash's turn to nod vigorously.

"I like it. And if you please me, I might let you cum this time."

Ash's eyes grew big. Apparently, orgasm denial was big business in Miss Hayley's home.

"Do you need help?" The blonde blurted and stood up. The red tinge of her cheeks told Minjung she'd had enough of the side conversation.

Minjung asked her to cover the remaining food with lids. She did as requested and was returning to her seat when Mistress Victoria came back to the great room. Madam Rowena was not with her.

"Who said you could get up?" Mistress Victoria asked in a mock scolding.

"Sorry," the blonde said and hurried to sit down on her pillow.

"I should take you OTK," Mistress Victoria teased, grabbed her sub's chin, and kissed her deeply. After the kiss, she laid her hand on the woman's cheek and then patted her face affectionately.

"Yes, please, the blonde said. "Please take me over your knee later."

"We'll see," Mistress Victoria said. "But only if you behave." She sat in her chair and said to Mistress Hayley, "You're on."

"Oh, already?" Mistress Hayley asked Minjung to return to her stool. "Rowena asked us to chat with you. We know you're in your two-week trial period, and that can be scary. So many unknowns. Will you make a good sub? Will your new Domme treat you well? We all understand that. But as I'm sure she's told you, here in Denton Heights, we look out for each other. We keep communication lines open. You have Ash's number, correct?"

Minjung nodded.

"Speak, please. I need verbal confirmation."

"Yes, Ma'am. I have Ash's number."

"Good," Mistress Hayley said. "I'm giving you my number, and Mistress Victoria will give you hers."

Mistress Victoria made a show of pulling out her cell phone and tapping it dramatically.

"Rowena already gave us your number," Mistress Hayley continued. "Should you need anything, or should Madam Rowena do something that doesn't sit well with you, please call one of us. It won't be a bother. It won't be out of protocol. Do you understand?"

"Yes, Ma'am. I understand."

"Good. If you feel you need to leave the house suddenly, don't go it alone. We take care of each other."

"You're freakin' her out, Hayley," Mistress Victoria said. "Look at her face."

"Sorry," Mistress Hayley said with an embarrassed chuckle. "Our relationships can be intense. But please know that Rowena is a good person; she takes care of her people."

"Sometimes to a fault," Mistress Victoria added with a roll of her eyes.

"Yes, yes," Mistress Hayley agreed. "She can be overly generous at times."

"Having said that…" Mistress Victoria led.

"Yes," Mistress Hayley picked up the thread. "Having said that, we will not stand for anyone trying to take advantage of her. She is a treasured friend. The kind you don't find that often in life. So, nothing, and no one will mess with her on my watch." Mistress Hayley's demeanor had turned serious. "Do you understand that?"

"Yes, Ma'ams," Minjung said to both of them.

"You will not steal from her," Mistress Victoria continued. She leaned forward and glared at Minjung. "You will not gossip about her." She poked her finger in Minjung's direction. "You will not make false promises." Anger came off Mistress Victoria in waves.

Minjung's heart was pounding at the anger and distrust focused on her.

When Minjung didn't respond, Mistress Victoria poked another finger and boomed, "Is that understood?"

"Yes, Sir," Minjung blurted.

"Sir?" Madam Rowena's voice rang out from the hallway. "Did you just call my good friend 'Sir'?"

Minjung wasn't sure what was happening. Had she called Mistress Victoria 'Sir'? She couldn't remember.

"Speak," Madam Rowena bellowed as she came to stand in front of Minjung.

"I don't remember, Madam," Minjung said. She couldn't look up. All she could do was turn her palms up as a sign of respect and wait for the inevitable slap to her face.

No slap came. Instead, Madam Rowena pulled Minjung's chin up to make eye contact. In the calmest voice Minjung had ever heard, Madam said, "You will be punished for this."

Chapter 9

Rowena

Silence filled the great room until Hayley broke it. "We were coming at her hard and fast, Rowena," Hayley said. "I think we made her nervous."

"Nerves are no excuse for insulting one of my friends." Rowena took a breath and sat down. She wasn't faulting Hayley for coming to Minjung's defense; she just wanted everything to be perfect at Minjung's first tea party. It was kind of her unveiling to the community. It was a dry run for the tea party she hoped to have with Matilda as the guest of honor. Rowena knew Matilda would want to meet and evaluate Rowena's "new slave." However, Rowena knew full well that she was going to be the one evaluated, not Minjung.

"Rowena," Victoria said quietly, "I know you need to follow up on your punishment, but if you don't mind, I'd like to know why she called me 'Sir.' I've been called that by submissives before and haven't been offended."

Rowena flicked her hand in a 'have at it' gesture. "Look at Mistress Victoria when she speaks to you," she said sternly.

Minjung looked up at Rowena first, her eyes filled with remorse, and it took all of Rowena's Domme strength to overlook it. Minjung nodded once and turned her attention to Victoria.

Victoria took a moment to gather her thoughts and finally asked, "You know that I'm female, right?"

"Oh, yes, Ma'am," Minjung said quickly. "Yes."

"And yet, in the heat of the moment, you called me Sir."

"I honestly can't remember now, Ma'am."

"Have you ever called a female Domme 'Sir' before now?"

"Yes, Ma'am," Minjung said but didn't elaborate.

"Tell me about that."

Minjung took a deep breath and said, "One of my appointments at the auction was with a woman who wanted to be called Daddy Shiela."

Hayley made a noise of surprise but didn't interfere.

Minjung continued. "She said I could call her Sir or Ma'am, whichever felt right at the time."

"Genderfluid, perhaps?" Rowena asked the group with a shrug.

"Or non-binary," Hayley suggested.

"Maybe just a masc lesbian?" Rowena countered. She shrugged and looked over at Victoria.

Victoria didn't comment on the suggestions but merely nodded. She turned her attention back to Minjung and asked, "Hypothetically, since I've been informed to keep my hands off other Domme's submissives—" She threw a playful glare at Rowena, who sent it right back. "Anyway, hypothetically, if you were my submissive, would you call me Sir or Ma'am?"

Minjung cleared her throat as if she knew whatever answer she gave could get her into deeper trouble. She hesitated for so long that it forced Rowena to say, "No repercussions on your answer, Minjung. Just be honest."

"Yes, Madam." Minjung looked up at Rowena as if she was a life raft. "Miss Victoria, I would probably start out calling you Ma'am, but you do give off a masculine vibe. Not male, Ma'am. Please don't misconstrue. I mean that the way you walk, carry yourself, and speak is quite masculine." Minjung's nervous exhale signaled how hard that had been for her.

Victoria nodded as she took in Minjung's words. For the most part, Rowena agreed with Minjung's assessment. Victoria was pretty butch and a good-looking one at that. That thought made Rowena chuckle, so she said, "Vic, you're a pretty butch."

Victoria burst out laughing, and the others followed suit. Rowena even caught Minjung suppressing a smile.

"Can I call you Daddy?" Victoria's submissive Sarah asked. And she sounded sincere.

Victoria turned to her and blinked comically. "You want to call me Daddy Victoria?" She scoffed at the sound of it.

When Sarah nodded her head vigorously, Rowena interrupted her retort by saying, "Daddy Vic. How about that?"

"Hmm." Victoria rubbed her fingers along her chin, clearly thinking hard about the suggestion.

"Please, please, please," Sarah begged. She whispered loud enough for everyone to hear, "I want to call you Daddy Vic. It fits you so much."

"Hmm," Victoria said for the third time. She sat up tall, took a deep breath, and let it out slowly. "Rowena, how are your Cardinals doing? Do they play the Reds anytime soon?"

Hayley, Rowena, and the rest of the guests broke out in polite laughter.

"Thank you for your honesty, Minjung," Victoria said. "I have some things to think about, I suppose."

"Sounds like you do," Rowena said. She wasn't sure if her friend had ever thought seriously about gender fluidity, but she'd be available if Victoria wanted a sounding board. "And, to answer your question, the Cardinals are coming to town for three games at the end of May."

"Before or after the spring masquerade ball?" Hayley asked.

"Right after," Rowena said. "I reserved a box for anyone that wants to join."

"Count the three of us in," Hayley said, leaning forward.

"I'm in," Victoria said. Rowena noticed that Victoria didn't say, 'We.' That probably meant that Sarah would be replaced in the month between now and then. Rowena tried not to sigh at her friend's voracious appetite for conquests. It was going to get her in trouble one day, but it wasn't Rowena's place to point that out. "And, hey," Victoria added, "now that you have a sub, you absolutely have to go to the ball and show your face."

Rowena frowned. She hated those things. All the posers and weekend kinksters nauseated her.

"Matilda will expect it," Hayley said softly.

Rowena nodded. "Yeah." That was all she could think of. The unofficial queen of the Denton Heights BDSM community was most certainly going to expect Rowena at the ball with her new submissive. That is if she and Minjung made it past the two-week opt-out mark next Friday, only five short days away.

The Dommes chatted and gossiped for another hour until Rowena grew weary. She had a sub to punish, and then they had to talk about the incident. It was weighing kind of heavy on her mind, especially because she hadn't seen the events leading up to the incident. Perhaps she shouldn't have been so impulsive to announce the punishment. But now she had to follow through.

Rowena stood up from her high wingback chair. She turned to Hayley and said, "Have a fun afternoon."

"Oh, we will," Hayley said, her voice lowering to a low growl.

Rowena chuckled and gestured for Minjung to stay where she was, sitting on her low stool, arms resting comfortably on her thighs. Her gaze was still down, and if that made her feel more comfortable, then that was okay.

"Let me walk you to the door," Rowena said, letting Hayley link arms with her.

"Come, Terrence," Hayley said and tugged lightly on his leash. "Come, Ashley." They both stood and followed their Mistress.

Rowena secretly smiled at the way Ashley followed, her chauffeur's cap in hand. Rowena had suggested the chauffeur's designation to Hayley as a way to give Ashley a sense of purpose and accomplishment. It seemed to be working.

Once she'd hugged her friend and said goodbye, Rowena headed back to the great room where Victoria was whispering low into Sarah's ear. Judging by Sarah's beet-red face, those two were heading somewhere to do wonderful naughty things.

"Get out of my house, Victoria," Rowena said to her friend with a chuckle.

"It's Daddy Vic now," Victoria said as she stood up, grabbed Sarah's elbow, and pulled her to a standing position.

"Really?" Sarah gushed. "I can call you that?" Her eyes sparkled like it was the best gift she'd ever been given. "Can I call you 'Sir', too?"

"We'll see." Victoria rolled her eyes for Rowena's benefit. Clearly, the whole business of being called Sir wasn't resolved in her mind. It certainly wasn't resolved in Rowena's. Victoria told Sarah to go wait for her by the front door and said to Rowena, "You really should come to the ball."

Rowena groaned.

"Just…" Victoria hesitated. "C'mon, make a brief appearance. Make sure Matilda sees you, and then you can leave." She raked a lock of hair off her forehead.

With that gesture, Rowena couldn't help seeing the masculinity of it. She'd never paid much attention to things like that when it came to her friend. Rowena sighed and said, "We'll see."

"Yay," Victoria said with a tiny sarcastic clap. "It wasn't a 'no.'"

Rowena groaned, grabbed onto Victoria's shoulders, and turned her toward the door. "Get the fuck out of my house, *Daddy Vic*."

"Ha!" Victoria said. "I kind of like that."

"Go." Rowena gave her a little shove. "Don't you have a sub to torture?"

"Oh, yeah. Mac won't be home until late, so I have the apartment to myself."

"Have at it." Rowena headed toward the front door, and Victoria followed. When they were out of earshot of both Minjung and Sarah, she said, "Call me this week. I want to talk more about the incident."

"Yeah," Victoria said, sounding pensive. "It was awkward, but she may be seeing something I'm not. And I know this is out of character for me, but please don't be too harsh on her."

Rowena chuckled. "I won't, but she doesn't know that."

Victoria laughed an evil laugh. "Laters." And with that, she increased her pace, grabbed Sarah by the arm, and let herself out.

Rowena watched out the window until the gate closed behind Victoria's pickup truck. She turned toward the great room and bellowed. "Here! Now!"

In less than five seconds, Minjung was in the foyer, attempting to fall to her knees.

"In my office," Rowena barked and led the way. She gestured to Minjung's stool. "Sit."

Minjung kept her eyes downcast as any good submissive who was about to be punished should.

"It was unfortunate that you insulted one of my closest friends," Rowena started. "Victoria seemed to take it in stride, but it may have gone sideways quickly. Do you understand what could have happened?"

"Yes, Madam," Minjung said in a shaky voice. She sounded like she wanted to elaborate, but Rowena wasn't interested in hearing it at the moment.

She walked over to the wet bar and pulled out two stemless wine glasses and a bottle of red wine. She walked over to Minjung and said, "Hold your arms in front of you. Hands face down." She showed Minjung the two glasses and the wine. "Ten minutes. For ten minutes, you'll have to hold these up without spilling a drop. It's not my favorite red but I could do without a sub ruining my Karastan carpeting." She gestured to the luxury carpet she'd had installed after she ended Kaylynn's contract well over a year ago. The carpeting had been a consoling gift to herself. It didn't work, but she liked the look of it anyway.

"Do you understand?"

"Yes, Madam," Minjung said. She sighed as if getting ready for a difficult task. And it would be.

"The punishment needs to fit the crime, though." Rowena went to her desk and pulled out two items. She then went to the bar sink and rinsed off the ball gag. It had never been used, but she was a stickler for cleaning implements before and after.

"You're going to wear this because your mouth got you in trouble." Rowena placed the ball gag in Minjung's mouth and fastened it behind her head. "And this," Rowena pulled out a brand new eye bra that would cover Minjung's eyes, "is just for my enjoyment." She'd toyed with the idea of putting noise-canceling headphones on her sub as well, but she had another idea in mind. Besides, full sensory deprivation needed immense trust, and Rowena knew she hadn't earned that yet, especially not with a punishment about to happen.

Once the blindfold was in place, Rowena said, "Grunt for me."

"Ungh," Minjung grunted behind the ball gag.

"Good. That's what you'll do if you're in trouble and need help. Understood?"

Minjung grunted again.

"Excellent. Arms tired yet?"

Minjung shook her head.

Rowena chuckled. She double-checked to make sure Minjung couldn't see and then went back to the wet bar. She pulled out a room-temperature bottle of water and put about two inches in each glass. She then poured the wine into a third glass. This one, she would drink.

She brought all three glasses over to Minjung, who still sat dutifully holding both arms out in front of her. Rowena placed a glass of water on each of Minjung's downturned hands. Of course, Minjung would think she was holding up two glasses of red wine. It was a bit of Domme trickery, but Rowena really didn't want her carpets stained. She made sure the two glasses were balanced on the back of Minjung's hands and then walked back to the wet bar.

"Nine minutes left." Rowena pulled out her phone and found the two selections she wanted. Connecting to her Bluetooth speaker, she let the first piece play. Minjung didn't seem startled by the sudden music, which was a good sign.

"This is a duet with Renee Fleming and Pretty Yende. The mezzo soprano's name is *Pretty*," Rowena said as if she was having a conversation with Minjung. "Isn't it funny? The piece is called *Sull'aria* from Mozart's opera *The Marriage of Figaro*." Rowena let the voices fill the room but kept a watchful eye on her stoic submissive. She took a sip of wine, allowing the duettino to remind her of long ago when she'd sung that very piece in a recital.

The Mozart ended, and then a longer piece came on. "Ahh, this is a favorite," Rowena said. "How ironic that both duets feature women and their female servants." She chuckled, thinking the music would grate on Minjung's nerves like it did Kaylynn's. Not everyone liked opera. "When this one finishes, that will be ten minutes, and your punishment will be over."

Renee Fleming's flawless soprano filled the room, followed quickly by Susan Graham's mezzo-soprano.

With about one minute or so into the piece, Rowena almost forgot about her submissive when the sweet tones of the blended voices kept her attention.

A soft moan came from Minjung. Although blindfolded, her head had turned toward Rowena. There was a slight shake to the glasses balanced on Minjung's outstretched hands. Minjung's slightly audible exhale seemed to right the ship, and the tremors stopped.

Rowena went back to mouthing the Susan Graham harmonies silently to herself, wishing she could go back in time and sing for real. But those were the days of her youth—good and gone and gone for good. She hadn't been to or watched an opera on television in quite a while. Maybe it was time to change that.

She sighed quietly and then announced, "Two minutes left." Minjung moved little, which impressed Rowena immensely. Kaylynn had never lasted more than five minutes.

"One minute," Rowena said, took another sip of wine, and moved quietly toward her submissive. Most people didn't like punishment, but she'd found over the years that submissives understood the need for it and almost welcomed it. They appreciated that their Dominant not only set the rules but made sure the submissive adhered to them as well. A misstep on the sub's part got an immediate follow-through from the Domme.

When the duet ended, she hit pause on her phone, stashed it in her skirt pocket, and snatched both glasses from Minjung's now shaking hands. "You may lower your arms."

Rowena set the glasses down on the coffee table and then undid the ball gag. The blindfold came off next. "You did well," she praised. She probably shouldn't have praised her sub after a deserved punishment, but she truly had been impressed.

"Thank you, Madam," Minjung said.

Rowena showed Minjung the two glasses of harmless water, and Minjung sighed audibly in relief. A small smile graced her face. "Thank you, Madam," Minjung said again.

Rowena emptied the water glasses into the sink and left them there for Minjung to wash later. She took one last sip of wine and poured out the remains.

Rowena was about to tell Minjung what was going to happen next, but Minjung spoke first.

"Madam?"

"Yes?"

Minjung let out a small breath. "May we listen to the second piece again, Madam? The Flower Duet? I haven't heard it in such a long time."

Rowena let out an unintentional noise of surprise. Some kind of emotion squeezed her chest, but she nipped the feeling before it could blossom. "Yes, of course." She found the piece on her music app and played it again.

The two women sat quietly listening, and Rowena was astounded when Minjung wiped tears from her eyes. "This moves you," Rowena said. It wasn't a question.

"Yes, Madam," Minjung said and then chuckled. "They're only singing about beautiful flowers, but there's something in the music, their voices, the structure, that hits me."

Rowena nodded. "I feel it, too. Do you like opera?"

"Yes, Madam. Very much."

"Do you have a favorite?"

Minjung glanced down as if embarrassed. "Madame Butterfly."

"Puccini," Rowena said with a nod. "*Un bel di, vedremo.*"

"Yes, Madam. A very moving piece."

"Love and betrayal," Rowena said with a laugh.

"Most operas have that theme, Madam. Don't they?"

"Mm hmm."

Rowena found the Madame Butterfly piece. Her favorite was the Ying Huang version, and she played it.

Minjung put a hand to her chest, clearly moved by the meaning of the piece. While it was playing, Rowena found herself in a dilemma. Here they were, Domme and submissive, having a real bonding moment. But it was happening right after a punishment. She could not let the indiscretion and subsequent punishment go unresolved with this tender exchange.

When the music ended, Rowena said coldly, "Go to your room and rest. In one hour, I want you in the family room fully clothed. We shall discuss your indiscretion and this punishment. And then it will be done and over with, and we will move on from it."

"Yes, Madam," Minjung said and stood up. "Thank you for the punishment, Madam." She took three steps backward, turned, and headed out the office door.

Rowena gazed at the back of the closed door for a moment, shook her head, and headed to the elevator at the back of the office. She, too, needed a brief rest in her rooms.

An hour later, Rowena was in the other elevator heading to the family room. She felt refreshed after a much-needed twenty-minute nap and then a shower. As the elevator door opened, she noticed Minjung kneeling in the family room, eyes down.

"Get off those knees."

Minjung complied, and she was still sort of kneeling, but her weight was now on her ass on the carpeted floor. She looked freshly showered and wore a lovely sleeveless linen tank dress. The warm tone of the green complemented her skin tone well. As Rowena sat down in her recliner in the family room, she thought how polished and sure Minjung seemed to be. She carried herself upright and tall, and even though she was clearly submissive, she displayed strength in that role. Rowena was leaning hard toward keeping her on for the full six-month contract, but the decision wasn't hers alone. Next Friday, Minjung could opt out and leave. So that's why Rowena was going to make the most of every moment she could for the next five days.

"Eyes up."

Minjung looked up.

"What were they saying to you when you blurted out the word 'Sir' to Victoria?"

Minjung took a moment to gather her thoughts. It was becoming an endearing quirk that Rowena found refreshing.

"Mistress Hayley and Mistress Victoria were reminding me that I could contact them if I needed help or felt I wasn't feeling right about something here."

"Did they give you their phone numbers?" Rowena asked, knowing that they did. "Those aren't to be treated lightly or given to anyone else."

"They did, Madam, and I understand that." Minjung nodded and said, "I know what a privilege it is for them to share their personal numbers with me like that."

"Then what happened?"

"Then they gave me the flip side. They told me to treat you well, not abuse you, not cheat you." She waved her hand around as if searching for more words. "That sort of thing, Madam. Mistress Victoria was especially forceful and seemed quite angry. I was trying to think what I had done wrong, and then I must have said, 'Yes, Sir' when she asked me if I understood what she was telling me. It was a slip, Madam. It wasn't on purpose or a dig or aggressive or even passive-aggressive. I truly don't remember saying it. And maybe that was my mistake."

"Go on," Rowena encouraged, her tone softening.

"Maybe I put my foot in my mouth because I wasn't fully listening to what I was saying. Not being fully present was rude and arrogant and just plain selfish of me." Minjung leaned down and put her forehead on Rowena's house slippers.

"No, no," Rowena said. "Sit up. I don't think you were intentionally being rude. And I don't get an arrogant vibe from you. Nothing you have done for me in our first week has shown you to be selfish, either." What was she doing? Defending her submissive? Preposterous. She'd insulted a friend.

They sat in silence for a moment while Rowena wrestled with her thoughts.

"You're lucky that Victoria wasn't upset by it. Surprised, maybe, but I think intrigued is the better word. And Sarah, her sub, was dying to call her Daddy. Can you imagine that?"

Minjung simply shrugged.

"Is there anything else you wish to say about the matter?"

"Yes, Madam," Minjung said. At Rowena's encouraging hand gesture, Minjung continued, "I'm sorry if I embarrassed or upset you, Madam. I..." She paused for a moment and swallowed hard a few times. Ahh, she was getting emotional. Her voice was high and tight when she spoke again. "I want to please you, Madam. You and your home have made me think that this might be a place where I can feel safe. A place where serving you and your household will fulfill something inside of me that needs nurturing or attention or something. I'm not sure I'm explaining myself well, but please know and understand that I was in no way acting out."

Rowena had heard pleas before, but Minjung's seemed sincere. Rowena leaned forward and put her hand on Minjung's head. She petted her head lightly and relaxed when Minjung leaned her face into Rowena's hand at one point. Rowena stopped petting and grabbed the chin instead.

She looked directly into Minjung's troubled brown eyes and said, "You have pleased me. Greatly. And as far as I'm concerned, the incident is over and done with. You were reprimanded publicly and punished privately. I won't bring it up again. Is that satisfactory to you?"

Minjung's brow furrowed as if she were troubled, but then she relaxed and said, "Yes, Madam. I...Thank you."

"Good." Rowena let go of Minjung's chin and said, "I heard you say you wanted to please me." Without waiting for a response, she unbuttoned her wrap skirt and maneuvered her body so Minjung could pleasure her.

"No mouth or tongue yet," Rowena said. "I want you to get to know my body. Hands and fingers only."

"No elbows, Madam?" Minjung asked with a grin.

Rowena burst out laughing. "If you can make that work then have at it."

Minjung began her exploration of Rowena's body by massaging her calves. She moved up from there to massage Rowena's thighs. Rowena felt herself relaxing into the touch as she gazed at the downturned head of the sub working to please her. Despite the wrong-gendered honorific, Minjung had done well, very well, at that afternoon tea party. Rowena's instincts had been right when she decided to interview the thirty-six-year-old submissive in Chicago. She usually favored much younger submissive women, probably because they didn't have much experience, and Rowena could mold them any way she wanted to. But when she looked over the candidates at the auction, something impatient inside told her to at least give Minjung an interview.

Minjung looked up as if sensing Rowena watching her. That small smile Rowena had seen over the last week appeared and made Rowena smile back.

"Get to the goal," Rowena said, wanting attention where her body needed it most.

Warm fingers explored Rowena's center from the outer labia to her inner G-spot. The fingers clearly avoided the sensitive nub that sorely wanted to be touched, but Rowena decided to stay out of the mix for a while. This was Minjung's exploration, after all.

Rowena picked up the remote and turned on the television. The game had already started, and she was relieved to see that neither the Cards nor the hometown Mets had scored yet. The Cardinals left fielder got up to bat to start the top of the third inning.

"Come on," Rowena called to the television. "Do something good."

Minjung looked up, and Rowena said softly, "You, too. Use your mouth, your tongue. Make me cum."

That small smile was back but then disappeared as she dove in and went to work.

That was one skillful tongue, and it wasn't even touching Rowena's clit yet. Minjung's nose would bump it occasionally, probably by design. Was she milking this out? Or maybe she was just reading Rowena's body language.

"Ground out to the pitcher?" Rowena groaned at the television. "How much do these guys get paid?" She inhaled sharply when a pointed tongue flicked her clit. The next batter got up to the plate. Minjung wrapped her lips around the sensitive nub and sucked short pulls as if sucking through a straw. Rowena opened her legs wider to let Minjung work unhindered.

"Bums," Rowena growled as the Cardinals designated hitter flew out to right field. She undulated her hips to Minjung's swirling tongue and probing fingers. "Yes." This she said to Minjung as she grabbed her sub's head with one hand. "Fucking right there. Holy fuck." Rowena bucked rhythmically. "Sharp tongue. Don't move it." She pressed herself against it to stimulate her clit. "Move those fingers." Two swipes of Minjung's fingers across her G-spot almost sent Rowena over. "Stop. Full stop." All movement, including Rowena's, ceased. She was breathing heavily as she rode the edge between cumming and losing the orgasm altogether.

"Use your tongue. Move your fing—" She never got the full word 'fingers' out as her climax reached its peak. She bucked her hips into Minjung's face as the orgasm ripped through her. Minjung didn't stop her motions, and soon enough, a second, less powerful orgasm coursed through her body. She pushed Minjung's head away and lay back, breathing hard. She moaned as an aftershock hit her unexpectedly. "Fuck." That one expletive was all she had strength for. After a few moments, she lifted her head and reached down to tousle Minjung's hair. "You did good."

Rowena took a deep breath and let it out in a sigh. "Get off your knees," she reprimanded.

"Sorry, Madam." Minjung changed her position on the carpet. "I had to adjust to, uh, service your needs."

"Mm hmm," Rowena said as a wave of calm overcame her. She waved Minjung out from between her legs and then closed them. She closed her wrap skirt and sat up in the recliner. She tuned back into the game only to find that the Mets were now up to bat. She checked the score. Still scoreless. Good, she hadn't missed anything.

"We need to find suitable accommodations for situations like this." Rowena gestured to Minjung on the floor and then to her crotch. "Do you have any ideas?"

Minjung took her usual pause before answering. "Yes, Madam. They're called 'wheeled kneelers.'" She went on to describe a device that contractors use to work on floors. It was a wheeled seat low to the ground. It had knee supports so the worker could lean forward. Apparently, it also had a chest support that helped take the weight off the knees. Rowena handed her tablet to Minjung, who found one online.

"Knee Saver Creeper," Rowena read out loud. "Is this the one you want?"

Minjung looked down. "I can give you cash, but I have no credit card, Madam."

Rowena was confused until it dawned on her. "I'm buying it. It will be an essential worker's tool." She took back the tablet and did a few minutes of silent research. "Ahh, check this one out." She showed Minjung the picture. "It has sturdier wheels and a stop tab, so you can't accidentally topple over."

"Thank you, Madam," Minjung said, her cheeks pinking.

Maybe Minjung wasn't used to people doing nice things for her. Rowena's brow furrowed at the thought. "I'll order this tonight, and if it sucks, I'll return it, and we'll find other accommodations for your needs. Okay?"

"Yes, Madam. Thank you."

"Good." Rowena clicked on the shopping cart icon and said to Minjung, "Go get our dinners. We can watch the game while we eat and then work on the puzzle."

"It's really coming along, Madam," Minjung said, surprising Rowena, who had expected Minjung's seemingly perfunctory 'Yes, Madam' response.

"It sure is. And I appreciate your help with it. Now, shoo. I'm hungry." Rowena waved her away and ordered the knee-saving device she hoped would work out for her submissive because she planned on using her for activities like the one they'd just had for the entire six-month contract.

Rowena's phone dinged three incoming texts. Her heart sank. They were all from her sister.

> MALLORY: You have to get your ass down to the Cincinnati plant within the next two weeks!!!! Daddy is waiting for your report. There's been too much turnover there, and he thinks a visit from you would help.

> MALLORY: In the least, little sis, show your face. In the most, find out what the frig is going on down there. You're good at that kind of thing, unlike me.

> MALLORY: You always say to 'play to our strengths.' You're strong and take no prisoners. So DO THAT!!!!

Rowena's sister tended to be dramatic in texts, using capital letters and exclamation points. With a sigh, Rowena put a note on her digital calendar to call the plant and set up a visit. An evil grin crept up her face as a plan emerged. Minjung would need a suit. She would be Rowena's administrative assistant during the visit, and later back home, she would probably get draped over Rowena's desk, tight skirt inching up by Rowena's hand. She sighed at the luscious possibilities. She closed the phone app and found her favorite clothes shopping site.

Chapter 10

Minjung

Minjung sat at the new desk Madam ordered for her room and opened her journal. She needed to unload the bulk of things weighing on her mind. Tomorrow was going to be a day like no other, and she needed to be able to focus.

Thursday, May 10, 9:23 pm
It's been one week and four days since my punishment. Madam went rather easy on me during the punishment. Of course, I thought the glasses had wine in them, but when she showed me afterward that they contained water, I realized something. She is a good person. She is fair. Honestly, I think each of us is acting out of caution. Clearly, we've both been burned, cheated, wronged, and whatever other words I can't think of right now to explain the rottenness that people can stoop to. At the two-week mark, we both agreed to continue together and although I am still cautious, I'm hopeful, too. We are both generous and thoughtful people, and we get taken advantage of. I still have both go-bags filled and ready. She still has not let me see her retreat on the third floor. Even the cleaning staff doesn't go up there. It's off-limits.

In the short three and a half weeks that I've been here, though, I think I've helped her. The cleaning staff accepted me immediately and stepped up their game. I'm pleased with the job they do now, but I will be ever watchful. I have no idea if Madam even noticed the now-clean baseboards that had been sorely neglected before. And the landscapers are a jovial bunch, that's for sure. They are a family-owned business and have (so far) had no problem coming to me for guidance.

I haven't had a maintenance issue, so I haven't interacted with Madam's favored handyman yet. She was impressed when I fixed the flickering light under a cabinet in the kitchen. It was a loose wire, which I reattached easily (yes, I turned off the circuit breaker for that part of the kitchen beforehand).

Minjung sat back in the new desk chair and looked at her newly pressed suit hanging on the closet door. Madam bought it for her and brought in a seamstress to tailor fit it to Minjung's body. It was a gorgeous suit from the Victoria Beckham collection. The light gray single-breasted jacket had front flap pockets and four cuff buttons, along with a single pocket on the chest. Madam had picked out a black collarless shirt to go underneath. The new black flats would be worn but probably swallowed up by the flared-leg pants. Madam seemed pleased with the result when Minjung tried on the newly fitted suit.

The suit and tailoring probably cost a fortune, so Minjung was going to do her best to do it justice at the stockholder's meeting the next day, where she would be wearing it as Madam's assistant. Apparently, the stockholders' meeting was at the Tyttle Foods Processing Plant in Cincinnati. Minjung understood that she had a huge role to play as Madam's assistant, and it showed how much trust Madam had in her. Minjung hoped she was up to the task. She only had this evening to get her head wrapped around the idea.

But before she could focus on the big day, she had to dump the thoughts in her head into her journal and be free of them for now.

I write in these journals to attempt to make sense of my thoughts and my life. I'm trying to set these things down so that my future self will see how we felt at this particular moment in time. The opera Madam played during my punishment almost two weeks ago made me think of you, Mistress Isabel. You gave me opera. I hadn't known much about it or had much interest in it until you took me in after my first surgery and nursed me. And how quickly our relationship turned physical and then more structured after that. You were my very first Domme. I was not, however, your first submissive, nor did I turn out to be your last. But while I was yours, you taught me everything about D/s relationships. You taught me to embrace my submissive nature and how not to be a doormat. Especially when it came to … him.

While I convalesced, you helped me understand who I was inside. When I could finally walk on my own, you encouraged me to dance again. But it was too soon. When I tore some of those just-healed ligaments again and needed that second surgery, you had had enough, hadn't you? When I didn't materialize into that prima ballerina, we both thought I was going to be, what happened next, Mistress Isabel?

You tossed me to the curb for an ingenue, didn't you? She was beautiful. And then there was no place for me and my brokenness anymore, was there, Mistress?

Minjung closed her eyes and took a deep breath, letting it out in a long sigh. Why had Mistress Isabel come back into her thoughts again? It happened over fifteen years ago. Minjung had been twenty-one years old, and it was one day after she graduated from Stanford. She'd had a promising dancing career ahead, but he didn't like that. And in one instant, in one fit of ever-present anger, he took it away. Mistress Isabel tried to get it back for her. But it didn't work. What also didn't work was going back to her father's household. He was still him and since she had nowhere else to go, she had to convalesce in his house. Her mother tried to intervene, but it wasn't enough. It had never been enough. Minjung had barely been able to walk when she fled his house. For good, that time.

So, to answer my own question about why you're in my thoughts again, it is because I think I've found someone (a Domme) who respects me for me and not only for what I can give her. I think she genuinely likes my presence and the attention I give her. I like being with her, too. Yes, I'm getting paid, but I've discovered that I would be here without that.

I have feelings, but I'm not going to put them on paper. I can't get ahead of myself. Yes, I caught feels. But maybe that's only because I feel safe (okay, safe-ish). She is dominant, but she is fair and lovely.

There is something about Madam that seems to make people feel protected and able to be themselves. Lower their guard—maybe that's what I'm trying to say. Maybe it's something in the way she speaks. It's direct but measured. She has a way of making you understand that she is, indeed, listening to your words, but she is also hearing everything you're not saying. She seems to read people fairly easily and fairly quickly. Some don't understand that they should not make an enemy of her.

I've decided that despite her sometimes brusque demeanor, Madam Rowena is a beautiful soul. She has truly treated me well and more than fairly. My new wheeled kneeler—that's what we're calling it—

came a couple of days after she ordered it. It is a lifesaver for my knees. She loves it, too, because now I can stay between her legs for a long time, and she isn't worried about my knees. See how thoughtful she is?

And look at this new desk and chair she got me. I mentioned that I wrote in a journal every night and then she got me a desk. Look at this room...no, it's more than a room. It's a suite. Do I require this much? No, of course not. I've done with much less. But Madam seems to like pleasing the people in her life. Apparently, this shareholder meeting tomorrow is a family obligation or something. I can tell she's dreading it. Hopefully, I can be a calming presence for her.

She got me a small tablet for taking notes tomorrow. It's all set up and running smoothly. It's a good thing I'm a fast keyboarder. I wouldn't want them to catch on to our ruse.

Today was a good day. I'm feeling more comfortable in my house manager role and as Madam's companion. She seems more comfortable with me as well. She held off on impact sessions leading up to tomorrow's visit to Tyttle Foods. I guess she didn't want me limping or showing bruises or something.

See? She's thoughtful. But hopefully, we can have a session tomorrow when we return. I have a feeling she'll either need a nap or an impact session, and I'm hoping for the latter.

More after tomorrow's visit to the factory. Or plant.

Or whatever it is.

BTW – Sunday will be one month since signing the contract to work for Madam.

It was a good day. Day Rating: 8/10.

~~~

It took a few minutes for the guard at the front gate to find their appointment on the master schedule, but he finally let them through, and Ash pulled up the long driveway. The flowered signage at the front of the factory seemed a bit untended, and although the grass had yet to be groomed for the season, it, too, looked a little worse for wear, like the company had no pride in its image. But that wasn't Minjung's concern. Her concern was to keep Madam happy and make her look good.

Ash helped Madam out of the car for which Madam thanked her. These were the first words spoken to either of them since they'd left the house thirty minutes earlier. To say that Madam was anxious was an understatement. As Minjung got out of the car, she made firm her resolve to help Madam reduce her anxiety. Minjung had no way of knowing what went on at shareholder meetings, but she was about to find out.

Once Ash drove off with instructions to wait in the visitors' lot for a text to pick them up, Minjung walked at Madam's side. This was their arrangement. Walk side by side unless Madam was walking with someone else, then Minjung was to walk a step or two behind. Madam did love her protocols, didn't she?

As they walked up the long, covered entryway toward the front doors, Minjung clutched her tablet tightly, hoping not to fumble with it during the meeting and make Madam look bad.

They were still quite far from the doors when Madam veered right and sat on one of the weathered benches flanking the walkway.

"Sit," Madam commanded.

Minjung sat and faced her benefactor.

"I have to let you in on something that only Hayley and Victoria know."

Madam held her head high and took a breath as if to calm her nerves. "Even Ash thinks we're here for a shareholders' meeting. We're not."

Minjung remained silent but raised her eyebrows, knowing Madam could see the questions in her eyes.

"I need you to keep this confidence," Madam said. "I feel I can trust you. I know you've only been with me for a short while, but I'm gambling on you. Do you understand?"

"Oh, yes, Madam," Minjung said, still full of questions. "I understand."

"Good." Madam sat back against the bench and paused to gather her thoughts.

Minjung made a mental note to check the state of Madam's blue power suit jacket and skirt before they entered the building. They were sitting on a less-than-stellar bench, after all. It's what a personal assistant would do, right?

Madam searched Minjung's face for the truth in her declaration and must have been satisfied with what she saw because she blurted, "My name is not Rowena Tate. I only use that name to keep my private life private. My name is Rowena Tyttle, and my family owns Tyttle Foods. I unofficially check in on this processing plant from time to time. We own dozens of plants like this one."

Minjung's heart pounded in her chest as adrenaline rushed through her. Madam was a member of the billionaire Tyttle family? She couldn't wrap her mind around that. Madam was an heiress?

Minjung must have had a look of incredulity on her face because Madam placed a hand on Minjung's forearm and said, "I know it's a lot to take in. I don't usually tell people."

"It's okay," Minjung said, her voice sounding strong and steady despite her quaking nerves. "It's a shock, but I intend to represent you in the best way possible, and no matter who you are, I will continue to do that, Madam."

"Thank you for understanding," Madam said. "Sorry to throw you in without a life jacket, but I'm here to be a Tyttle family presence. I need you to have your ears and eyes open. Take notes. This processing plant has been taking a downward turn lately, and my father would like to know why. I'm supposed to fix it." Anxiety had crept into her voice.

"Madam, how do you eat an elephant?"

"What?" She was clearly confused.

"One bite at a time, Madam." Minjung grinned, hoping it would calm down the heiress. "One bite at a time."

"Yes," Madam said and then grinned back. "See? I knew my instincts were right in asking you to come with me." She stood up abruptly and said, "You know what? Let's go in there and find out what these fuckers are doing to ruin my family's business."

"Yes, Madam," Minjung said with equal enthusiasm. She brushed what looked like dust off her Domme's skirt and jacket and then deemed her ready.

Minjung was surprised when Madam ordered her to turn around and then brushed the dirt off her clothes as well.

"Let's do this, Madam," Minjung said. It was her version of a pep talk.

With a reminder to follow her lead, Minjung walked side-by-side with her Domme into the lobby of the Tyttle Foods Processing Center, Cincinnati.

"May I help you?" the young twenty-something receptionist asked, barely looking up.

Madam made a small noise of frustration but didn't say anything, so Minjung stepped up to the desk. "We're here to see Mr. McMahon this morning."

"Good luck with that," the young woman muttered loud enough to be heard. "Let's try Mrs. Ruiz, the vice president in charge of production. She's usually around on Fridays."

Minjung heard a strangled groan behind her.

"That will have to do, I suppose," Minjung said, standing tall. "However, I'm curious about our confirmed appointment. A..." she looked down at the notes on her tablet, "Miss Sinclair called yesterday to confirm today's appointment."

The receptionist just chuckled. "That's Mrs. Ruiz's admin assistant." She clicked on her keyboard and said, "Ah, here. I see your appointment. What was the name again?"

"Tyttle," Minjung said, saying the name with hard t's so the woman would hear it. "Rowena Tyttle. Daughter of the chairman of the board." Minjung turned and pointed to the large portrait of Madam's father hanging on the far wall of the lobby. "That chairman."

The young receptionist's eyes grew wide. "Oh, okay. Yes, that's good. Umm, let me walk you up there myself." She turned toward an open door behind the reception desk and screeched, "Miriam, get out here and watch the desk." Without waiting for an answer from Miriam, she stepped out from behind the desk and led them to an elevator. On the way up to the third and highest floor, she did her best to suck up to Madam by saying how much she enjoyed working for the Tyttle Foods company.

Madam Rowena did not say a word, nor did she bother to look at the now-fawning receptionist. In her younger days, Minjung might have cringed at the awkwardness of the situation, but this young woman had not shown her Domme respect, and respect was everything.

When they reached Mrs. Ruiz's office, Minjung nodded to the receptionist, effectively dismissing her, and said, "Thank you." She then knocked once and opened the door to let Madam enter first. "We have an appointment with Mrs. Ruiz," Minjung said to the middle-aged woman who stood as they entered.

"We're honored to have you visit us today, Ms. Tyttle," the admin assistant said. "I'm Jody Sinclair, Mrs. Ruiz's assistant. She's ready for you." The older woman knocked twice on the office door, opened it, and said to the person inside, "Ms. Tyttle and her associate are here."

"Oh, great," came the enthusiastic voice. "Bring them in."

Minjung followed behind the women. She was surprised to see that Mrs. Ruiz's office windows didn't look out over the landscaped lawns below but instead looked over the work floor and the workers three floors down. The glass must have been thick because you could barely hear the machinery down below. Minjung hoped to get a glance out the window at some point. Madam didn't mention getting a tour of the factory, but Minjung hoped they would.

Mrs. Ruiz stuck her hand out toward Madam and said, "It's a pleasure to finally get to meet you, Ms. Tyttle. Please call me Esther." Mrs. Ruiz was a middle-aged woman, probably in her late forties or early fifties. She wore a suit much like Madam Rowena's. It was power blue in color, and it fit her trim frame well. The woman spoke authoritatively as she greeted them. Her slight Spanish accent added to her charm, and Minjung felt at ease quickly. She sat next to Madam and opened her tablet, ready to be the best personal assistant ever.

"My assistant will take notes so we can focus on our chat," Madam Rowena said to Mrs. Ruiz. Minjung liked her Domme's no-nonsense approach. She didn't ask permission; she just told it like it was going to be.

"Of course. That's fine." Mrs. Ruiz looked at her assistant. "Jody, would you please fetch us three bottled waters." She looked at Madam and said, "Or perhaps you would like something else. Coffee? Tea? Our specialty is Tyttle Pop, of course." Both women laughed, but Minjung wasn't sure what the joke was.

"Water is fine." Madam waited until Mrs. Ruiz nodded to her assistant, who left on her mission, and then said, "Why am I not sitting in McMahon's office right now?"

Mrs. Ruiz nodded her head. "I expected you to get right to the point." She chuckled knowingly and sighed. "To be honest, Ms. Tyttle, I'm a bit frustrated with it. I don't want to throw him under the bus, you know?" She leaned forward. "I'm supposed to keep the company looking good. Keep smiling through it all."

Madam stayed silent. The only thing she did was raise her chin slightly, obviously waiting for the answer to her question.

Mrs. Ruiz must have felt the power because she blurted, "Golf. He plays golf every Friday. And in the winter, he goes to the indoor driving range. We haven't seen the man here on a Friday in…years."

Madam looked stunned. "Thank you for letting me know." She visibly softened and added, "Anything you say here today will be kept in confidence. I should have opened with that." She smiled and then said, "This is a tricky one. McMahon was one of my father's placements."

"So, what brings you here today?" Mrs. Ruiz said, probably trying to shift topics quickly. She waved in her assistant, who brought three bottles of water and handed one to each of them.

"I'm checking in," Madam said. "I want to find out why there's such high turnover here."

"That's a million-dollar question," Mrs. Ruiz said and scoffed. "Mr. McMahon says it's because young people are lazy and just don't want to put in the work. I'm not sure I believe that, but, indeed, we can't seem to retain our new hires. Even some seasoned employees have jumped ship. I started down on the floor in my twenties. I moved up to lead, then supervisor, and then systems manager. I've worked in just about every department here at Tyttle Foods Cincinnati, except maintenance. I rose quickly in the ranks, and when I threw my hat in the ring for this vice president position, I got it. So, it's confusing to me why we can't retain people when there is so much career growth available here. I do have an idea, though."

Madam took a sip of water and wordlessly gestured for Mrs. Ruiz to go on.

"When I first got here years ago, I heard about the Tyttle Family. Not your biological family; I mean the family of Tyttle employees. When I had surgery and had to be out, my coworkers got together and made meals for me and my family, picked up prescriptions, picked up my kids from school." Mrs. Ruiz sighed. "The world is changing, I guess. When Mr. McMahon got here ten or so years ago, he abolished many of the employee gatherings. 'To save money,' he'd always say. I liked those parties. They were informal, except for the Christmas parties at the Hyatt. Now those were big and so much fun. Everyone went home with some kind of present. One year, I got a microwave oven."

"I agree. Those Christmas parties were fun," Madam said. "Do you still give out pins for longevity? Five, ten, fifteen years, and so on?"

Mrs. Ruiz held her lips together tightly and shook her head. "No. Mr. McMahon wanted to save money. He said they cost too much. I used to love it when everyone went out to the courtyard between buildings, and we'd have that picnic ceremony for the milestones. Now *that* felt like family."

Madam visibly deflated. "Hmm," was all she said.

"I don't feel like I've been very loyal to Mr. McMahon, Ms. Tyttle." Mrs. Ruiz's tone held obvious regret.

"On the contrary," Madam said. "Honesty is important. There's something that needs fixing here. Golf on Fridays may have nothing to do with it." She stood up, so Minjung did as well. Madam walked over to the large window.

Mrs. Ruiz followed. "You're lucky. We've got a big run of Tyttle Pop going on today. Ginger ale."

"Nice," Madam said.

Minjung nodded silently to herself. So that's why the other two women had laughed when Mrs. Ruiz mentioned Tyttle Pop. This was a bottling plant. Or part of it was.

"I wasn't sure if you had time," Mrs. Ruiz said, "but I've arranged for the floor supervisor of bottling to take you on a tour and answer your questions. We can meet back here if you wish, or I can find someone to take you on a tour of the tortilla manufacturing building a short walk from here."

"Thank you, Mrs. Ruiz," Madam said, putting out her hand. "You've been very forthcoming. That has been duly noted and much appreciated." She turned toward Minjung. "My assistant will communicate what we'll be doing once we figure that out." She looked toward Minjung, who knew exactly what to say.

"Shall I call your assistant on this number?" Minjung held the phone out with the number and extension of Mrs. Ruiz's assistant.

"Perfect," Mrs. Ruiz said. "Let me walk you down to Manny." She headed toward her office door.

"No," Madam said, sounding surprised. She stopped walking. Mrs. Ruiz turned. Madam asked, "Do you mean Manny Schmidt?"

"Yes," Mrs. Ruiz said.

"I remember him. He was here when I came over twenty years ago to tour the plant with my dad. Maybe more. I wonder…"

"He will," Mrs. Ruiz said knowingly.

"He will? He'll remember me? I was, like, eighteen or something." Something in Madam Rowena's tone made Minjung want to pull her into a hug.

Mrs. Ruiz nodded and led them past her assistant, down the elevator, and onto the floor of the noisy bottling plant.

"Do my eyes deceive me?" A grandfatherly-looking man with a slight limp walked over to them with open arms. "*Mi bella ragazza.*" He enfolded Madam Rowena in his arms and said, "We don't see you enough." He let her go and stepped back, grinning conspiratorially.

Madam turned to Mrs. Ruiz and said, "You were right." Both women laughed and Minjung smiled at the whole exchange. "We'll let you know our plans."

Mrs. Ruiz took her leave, and Madam introduced Minjung to Mr. Schmidt. Madam then linked her arm to his offered one. Minjung trailed behind, straining to hear their conversation. The first thing Mr. Schmidt did was offer them lab coats, protective eyewear, and hard hats. "Company policy," he said with a grin. As they walked the floor, Madam and Mr. Schmidt caught up with each other's families and spent a lot of time discussing each one of his five grandchildren. Madam didn't seem upset by the chit-chat. In fact, she seemed invigorated.

For Minjung's part, she was fascinated when he pointed out the bottling process, clearly showing off his beloved livelihood to his favorite '*Bella ragazza.*' The automation of the glass-filling machines was incredible as they filled each individual glass bottle, capped it, and then sprayed it down with clean water to remove any stickiness. The labeling part was incredibly fast, and Minjung watched in wonder. It was clear that employees were needed for quality control to fix any weirdness. 'Weirdness' was the word Mr. Schmidt used, which made Madam Rowena laugh.

And apparently, the next warehouse filled cans with Tyttle Pop. Beyond that was the tortilla chip baking and packaging building, which was why the air smelled like 'nutty toast.' At least, that was how Mr. Schmidt had phrased it. To Minjung, the air just smelled sour.

As they continued to walk the floor, Madam seemed to be oblivious to the employees' comments as they walked by. Minjung was glad her Domme didn't hear what they were saying. "Who is that?" one young woman asked, nodding her head toward Madam Rowena. "Hopefully, it's a corporate takeover," a second woman said, adding, "Working here sucks." Minjung couldn't hear the response because they were out of earshot at that point.

Another group of middle-aged women spoke Spanish, but Minjung had enough of an ear for the language that she got the gist of the conversation. Apparently, someone named Patrice had gone out on maternity leave and couldn't return right away due to complications with the pregnancy. Since the maternity leave was up, but she wasn't physically ready to come back, she had been fired. Minjung wasn't one hundred percent sure that's what she'd heard, but she did understand that the women were angry at the company.

After watching bottles get placed into cartons for shipping, Madam Rowena and Minjung squeezed into Mr. Schmidt's small office and sat down on two metal fold-up chairs. Madam and he danced around the true nature of her visit for several minutes until Madam blurted, "What's going on around here, Manny? I need to fix it. What can I do?"

Mr. Schmidt's cheery demeanor disappeared as his face fell. "I don't know if there's anything you can do, Rowena. Time goes on. The good old days are gone. There's no loyalty anymore." He smiled sympathetically and said, "Personally, I'm disgusted that no one out there seemed to know who you were."

"I felt that," Madam said. "Not that I was looking for recognition, but it certainly does feel different here."

"There's been a gradual eroding of camaraderie. Of course, we have that ongoing friendly rivalry with the tortilla chip dips next door," he said with a laugh. "But that's all in fun. Or it used to be, anyway." He turned to a cabinet behind his overladen desk and pulled out two uncrimped red bottle caps. He handed one to each of them. It read "Tyttle Pop" on the cap. Apparently, their visit was over, and they had just been handed souvenirs.

They each thanked him, and Minjung could tell by the way Madam shifted in her chair that she was about to stand up to leave. As if sensing that, Mr. Schmidt said, "We ran the gingers today as a show for you, Rowena."

"What do you mean?"

"There isn't as much call for Tyttle Pop these days, so the line is often unplugged. I've pleaded with whoever will listen that we need to use half the floor out there for something else. Maybe plastic-filled beverages? Or we could expand the tortilla chips over here and make other snack foods. I don't know, but this place just isn't what it was. I've only just turned sixty, and in September, I will have been here an even thirty years. Maybe that's enough. I may retire early. At least at home, my wife pretends to listen to me." He chuckled, but Minjung could hear the sadness in it.

Madam Rowena simply nodded, and then she stood up abruptly. She was clearly agitated. They said their goodbyes amicably, and after hanging up their borrowed safety gear, Madam hugged Mr. Schmidt again, and they headed off the processing floor into the blessedly quieter hallway.

"We're going home," Madam said succinctly and took off down the hallway, through the lobby, ignoring the supplicating receptionist, and out the front door.

Meanwhile, Minjung hastily texted Ash to bring the car around and then called Mrs. Ruiz's assistant to let them know that Ms. Tyttle wouldn't be going back upstairs.

Minjung was grateful when she saw Ash's car pulling out of the visitors' lot. The car ride home was quiet, too quiet. Once back at the house, Madam thanked and dismissed Ash. She headed into the house and directly into her office. Minjung tried to follow, but Madam said, "Leave me."

"Shall I prepare lunch?"

Madam Rowena's only response was the closing of the office door. Minjung stood outside the closed door, not sure what to do. When she heard angry muttering and then glass breaking, she tried to open the office door, but it was locked.

Panicked, she shouted, "Madam, are you all right?"

"I told you to leave me," Madam Rowena said quietly.

"Yes, Madam." Minjung moved across the foyer, sat on the bottom step, and called Mistress Hayley.

Chapter 11

Rowena

The sunny May morning was in direct contrast to Rowena's mood when she woke. The cheery sunlight that muscled its way through the closed blinds was not a welcomed accompaniment to her hangover. She had been in bed since seven pm the night before. With almost eleven hours in, she did not feel refreshed at all. No miraculous answers presented themselves overnight. Hayley told her to "sleep on it." She did, although her sleep had been fitful, and there had been at least one nightmare. But last night's nightmare would not compare to the phone call to her father she had to make later. He would want her to explain what was going on at the plant. She didn't really know. And he would want potential solutions. Impossible. It was not going to be a good day.

She stretched her arms overhead, threw the comforter off, and sat up. No sense staying in bed. Nothing was getting accomplished there. She swung her legs over the side and grabbed her phone from the nightstand. A text from Hayley was waiting for her. It had been sent about fifteen minutes earlier.

HAYLEY: How are you feeling this morning, dear? Check in when you get up so I don't spend my day worrying. I can come by if you want to talk more about…stuff.

ROWENA: I'm okay. No need to come by.

Her return text was short, concise, and not very sweet. She should have thanked Hayley for driving over yesterday afternoon but was too embarrassed. She wanted to forget the memory of her friend rushing in like the cavalry. And as for Minjung's role in that, well, Rowena was more than a little miffed. It was clearly grounds for dismissal, wasn't it? But she held back yesterday because Minjung had done an excellent job stepping up when Rowena had been shocked into silence in the lobby when that twinkie of a child didn't know who she was. And with her father's portrait hanging right there watching the whole thing, Rowena had frozen on the spot.

Back at the house, Hayley burst in while Rowena was in the middle of downing her second shot of whiskey while trying to make sense of her visit to the plant. To say that Rowena was shocked at her friend's sudden appearance would have been an understatement. After a half hour of reassuring Hayley that although the trip to the plant had been worrisome, she was okay and would be fine. She just needed time to get her thoughts together before reporting to her father the next day.

After Hayley left, Rowena downed a third shot of the sweet, burning whiskey. Her father had given it to her years ago as a housewarming present. She thought the alcohol would calm her mind and let her muse about the visit to the plant that morning. Her heart ached when she realized that even Manny seemed to be giving up on Tyttle Foods. Working there had always seemed like one of his life's greatest joys—that and his grandkids. She should have gone to the plant more often over the years. She should have visited him.

But the whiskey didn't provide clarity, and she fell asleep on the couch in her office. She woke with a headache and a queasy stomach. After taking something for the headache that she hoped wouldn't upset her stomach, she checked her phone. That's when she saw Minjung's texts about food.

> MINJUNG: As Mistress Hayley was leaving just now, she suggested I leave a lunch tray for you. I'll put it outside your office door. I'll pick it up when you wish.

Minjung's next text had come in several hours later.

> MINJUNG: I picked up your uneaten lunch tray and left your dinner outside your office door. Would you like me to bring your dinner elsewhere? Perhaps you retreated upstairs? Would you like something different?

Rowena realized then that she needed to eat something. That might make her feel better. She grabbed the tray from the hallway, hoping Minjung wasn't lingering near the door. She hadn't been. The food made her feel somewhat better physically but not emotionally. After eating what her stomach would allow, she put the tray outside the office door and then put a thumbs-up emoji on Minjung's text. She hated it when people did that to her because it seemed like a dismissal. And in this particular case, it was. It was a warning for Minjung to butt out and stay out of her personal life.

Barely three minutes after she put her tray outside the door, a third text came in.

> MINJUNG: I picked up your spent dinner tray. I'm glad you ate something. I'll be in the family room if you want to watch the Cardinals game. If it's okay, I'll work on the puzzle.

Rowena didn't respond. A fourth text came in a little while after that. Rowena had already taken her private elevator up to her rooms on the third floor. It was barely seven o'clock, but she was already in bed when she read the text.

> MINJUNG: Good night, Madam. I'll be in my room with my phone on and the volume up if you need anything.

As Rowena reread the texts from the day before, she almost felt guilty for ignoring her submissive. But Minjung was that same submissive who had called Hayley as if the world were on fire. C'mon. That was overstepping. And Minjung needed to understand that. Rowena sat on the edge of her bed. She probably needed to punish Minjung. With a sigh, she groaned. She simply didn't have the emotional energy to deal with it.

Rowena got up, took a shower, and brushed her teeth. When she couldn't get rid of that morning-after-drinking taste in her mouth, she rinsed with mouthwash. Truth be told, she really wasn't much of a drinker.

She had just gotten dressed in loose-fitting capris and a comfy oversized tunic when the ding of a text came in.

> HAYLEY: Good to see that you're okay this morning. I have a favor to ask, and this is it: PLEASE do not punish Minjung for calling me. She was concerned for your well-being. Remember how you asked me to give her that "we're all here for each other" speech at the tea party? Remember? You wanted us to make sure she could call someone if she needed help. She thought YOU needed help.

Another text followed the first as if Hayley was getting everything out of her system.

> HAYLEY: Have a talk with her about what she might have done differently if you feel that's appropriate, but I'm glad she called me. (She said she didn't contact Victoria, btw. So, this can be our secret.)

Rowena snorted out an annoyed sigh. She'd moved away from home ten years ago under the guise of managing this one small plant that was part of the family business. That much was true, but it had been her father who had suggested it. He'd seen how she'd been floundering. Self-admittedly, a career singing opera just wasn't panning out. Social media lambasted her, and she agreed with many who said she should stop trying to be something she wasn't. She knew she could sing, though. She'd studied, learned difficult pieces, and performed with some amazing orchestras.

She'd been good. But she hadn't been great. And that was the difference. She sighed in frustration at the memory and headed to the window in her living room overlooking the driveway and front gate. Yes, her father had initially paid for the house and property. And, yes, she still got a generous allowance from him every month. Everything he sent, she invested, and now she had enough to pay him back threefold. He never accepted her offer, though, and he never would, so she simply invested everything he sent and basically lived more than comfortably.

She looked up at the lightening sky. It looked like it was going to be a beautiful day. Funny how the day didn't match her mood at all. It should be cloudy, rainy, and stormy, just like her.

Her stomach growled. She needed breakfast. Although, she probably needed coffee more than that. She glanced at her coffee machine. Minjung made better coffee. She grunted. She didn't want to deal with Minjung right now.

She plopped herself down in front of the security cameras and saw that Minjung was in the family room working on the jigsaw puzzle. She switched to the kitchen camera, and her heart softened. Minjung had a tray on the counter, ready to be filled with her Madam's breakfast order.

"She calls me 'Madam,'" Rowena said out loud. "That's a true sign of respect." She sighed for the umpteenth time that morning. She mused on the word respect and decided to respect her friend Hayley's concern for her and texted back.

> ROWENA: I hate how you can read my mind. I promise that I won't punish Minjung. But she and I will need to discuss how she handled it.

Three dancing dots appeared. Hayley was reading the text.

> HAYLEY: She handled it correctly.

Rowena raised her eyebrows to the sky. "Getting feisty there, Hayley." She was actually impressed that her friend felt able to give Rowena her opinion. Most people didn't. Rowena laughed. She usually paid them not to.

She was about to respond when the three dots danced on her phone again.

> HAYLEY: I need your help and advice when you have time. Not now. You need to talk with Minjung first.

> ROWENA: What's up?

HAYLEY: Terrence. He wants me to face-slap him. I don't know if I can.

ROWENA: Do nothing until I've shown you the proper technique. You can't just haul off and whack someone in the face. Personally, I loathe face slapping, but if you two kids are into it, then let me help make sure you do it right.

HAYLEY: THANK YOU!! Text me later. I have a showing. Bye.

Before Rowena could sink back into dwelling on all that was wrong in her world, she texted Minjung.

ROWENA: I need coffee. And breakfast. My rooms. Right turn out of the elevator. The last door on the left.

She sent it before she could change her mind. She chuckled as she watched through the camera when Minjung leaped up and clapped her hands two times.

MINJUNG: Yes, Madam.

Rowena chuckled again when Minjung then ran to the kitchen and made two soft-boiled eggs and toast. She put the coffee on to brew. It wasn't long before there was a soft knock on the door. Part of her wanted to tell her submissive to simply leave the tray and go away, but she needed to get the conversation with Minjung over with before she could focus on the one with her father later that very day.

"Come," Rowena said and pointed to the coffee table in front of her.

Minjung nodded as she came in and set the tray down. "Would Madam like me to fix her coffee?"

Rowena nodded. While Minjung added the creamer and sugar, Rowena watched. Minjung didn't seem nervous or clumsy.

Minjung handed Rowena the coffee, handle first. After taking her first sip, Rowena sighed audibly. "You do make good coffee, Minjung."

"Thank you, Madam," Minjung said, clasping her hands in front of her. I'm glad you are well this morning." Without waiting for a response, she asked, "Will you be requiring anything else?"

"Yes," Rowena said. "I have no stool, so why don't you sit on the couch with me. I want to talk about yesterday."

"Y-yes, Madam," Minjung stammered but complied. She sat down, her body tall, and her hands face down on her thighs.

Rowena took another sip of coffee. She then picked up the tray and balanced it on her lap. "I want to chat."

"Yes, Madam." Minjung turned slightly to face Rowena.

Darned if Rowena couldn't read Minjung's expression. Except for the stammer, she didn't appear to be anxious or worried or even happy to be in her Domme's presence. Minjung had a damn good poker face, that was for sure.

Rowena reached down for her toast and swooned. "You made toast soldiers for me." She picked up one of the long strips.

"Yes, of course, Madam," Minjung said, her shoulders visibly relaxing. Aha, she had been tense. "One always needs toast soldiers to dip in soft-boiled eggs. You have strawberry jam if you prefer that."

"What, no fruit?" Rowena teased, trying to lighten the room.

Minjung chuckled and looked down. "It's become clear that Madam does not like fruit in the morning." She glanced up and, with a mischievous grin, added, "Or ever."

Rowena burst out laughing. "You got that right."

Minjung looked down again and shyly said, "Madam?"

"Mm hmm?"

"About yesterday."

"Let me," Rowena took another sip of coffee. She needed it to clear her mind. "I was frustrated yesterday after the visit to the plant. Still am, as a matter of fact. When I threw the glass in my office and broke it? That was childish of me. I needed that burst of release."

"I—"

"I'm not done," Rowena said, and Minjung nodded. "I'm sorry that I scared you so much that you needed to call Hayley. You did the right thing. I was being a brat. A quality my sister says I have in spades." She chuckled and felt gratified when Minjung shook her head slightly as if to convey that she didn't think her Madam was a brat.

Rowena reached over and tapped Minjung's knee. "Again, I'm sorry I scared you and retreated. Thank you for trying to reach out for my well-being. I'll try to do better when life throws me my next challenge. Sound good?"

"Yes, Madam. I wasn't sure what to do."

"As Hayley emphatically told me this morning, you did the right thing."

Minjung took a relieved sigh, and then they sat in silence while Rowena ate the breakfast Minjung had made for her.

"Madam?"

"Yes?" Rowena sat back wonderfully full. There wasn't a speck of food left on the tray.

"I've never been to Cabo or to Bora Bora. I've been to the spots in California, though, like Venice and Laguna."

"What are you talking about?"

Minjung grinned. "The puzzle. I finally figured out what the puzzle is. It's a bunch of famous beaches and vacation spots."

"Oh, you didn't know that?"

"No, Madam. I wasn't sure what it was because the lid is face down. We're making great progress on it."

"I'm grateful for the help." But was Minjung making small talk? Interesting. Rowena wasn't sure what to make of it. "I've been to some of those places. The best way to travel is by cruise ship, though. Ever been?"

"No, Madam. It sounds a little scary."

"They can be fun if done right," Rowena said. She changed the topic awkwardly. "Well, it was only a matter of time before you got to see my lair up here on the third floor." She stood up. "Let me give you a tour."

Rowena purposely avoided the security room with the camera monitors but pointed out the obvious living room first, then the balcony overlooking the west side of the property. Next, she showed her the bedroom, and even though Minjung's eyes were wide already, they grew even bigger at the sight. "Nice, isn't it?"

"Yes, Madam," Minjung said, taking one step toward the bed. "Would Madam like me to make her bed?"

Amused, Rowena said, "Yes, please."

Minjung fairly burst with joy as she went about tucking the sheets, fluffing the comforter and then the pillows. "I noticed that the cleaning staff are not allowed up here. Would you like me to take on this area? Cleaning, straightening, organizing?" This Minjung asked while she picked up the suit Rowena had unceremoniously pulled off her drunken body the night before. All of it had missed the chair she'd been aiming for and lay in a heap on the carpet. "Dry cleaning, Madam?" She asked this without waiting for the answers to her original question. She was eager. Eager to help and eager to please.

"Sure. Yes, to all three. Thank you, Minjung."

"Excellent, Madam." Minjung seemed to visibly puff up at suddenly having new responsibilities.

"We'll work out a schedule later. Once a week, maybe."

"Excellent, Madam." Minjung folded the discarded suit carefully and held the bundle in her arms.

After a quick tour of the oversized bathroom with its shower and jacuzzi tub, an idea sprang to Rowena's mind. "Come sit outside with me." She headed toward the outside balcony. "Put that stuff there." She pointed to the sideboard near the door to the hallway.

"Madam," Minjung asked, "do you have any other laundry I can see to?"

"Relax, Minjung. It's Saturday, and it's our day to chill. And to answer your question, yes, I do have laundry, but it can wait until we work out a schedule."

"Yes, Madam."

Rowena almost laughed out loud at the heartbroken sound in Minjung's tone. Here was a woman who truly loved to serve.

"Come, sit." Rowena gestured to one of the rocking chairs on the balcony as she raised the sunscreen. The morning sunlight was gentle, thank goodness, especially when one had a slight hangover. She sat in the other chair and said without preamble, "Tell me your impressions about our visit to the plant yesterday."

Minjung took her usual pause to think and then said, "Well, the first thing that made me both mad and sad was that, with the exception of a few people, no one seemed to know who you were."

"That may be my fault, I'm afraid," Rowena said. "I figured the plant was on autopilot and didn't need me. Maybe I was lazy? Who knows. But I can't wallow in what I could have done, you know?"

Minjung nodded. "The workers seem to have lost that work-together feeling. That teamwork thing. Mrs. Ruiz and then Mr. Schmidt both mentioned the loss of the family feeling."

Rowena nodded. She'd absorbed the same concern. "What does family mean to you, Minjung?" She shook her head, trying to get the stray locks of hair off her face. In frustration, she swiped at them with irritation and gestured for Minjung to continue.

"Would Madam like me to do her hair today? Or sometime?"

Was Minjung avoiding Rowena's question because her response was definitely not what she had expected. "Sure. Absolutely. You can do me after our chat." She grinned mischievously at her salacious choice of words.

Minjung's cheeks pinked momentarily. She took a breath, looked out onto the trees, and said, "Madam, to be honest, I'm not sure what family means, but I can tell you what it doesn't mean."

"Go on."

"It doesn't mean a father who drinks and takes his anger out on his family or a mother who takes it from him just to keep the peace. It doesn't mean his view is necessarily the right one for all, especially when others' opinions aren't entertained. Family doesn't mean rejecting your only child when she finally stands up to him and gets slapped in the face for it, tries to get out of the way, and finds herself falling down the basement stairs, her dancing career effectively over in one moment. Dancing had been the one and only joy in her life, and he took it."

Rowena launched out of her chair and pulled the now sobbing Minjung into her arms. She pulled Minjung's head into her chest and stroked her hair. "You're okay, honey," Rowena soothed. "They're not here. He's not here. Shh shh shh." She rocked Minjung until the crying seemed to stop.

"I'm so sorry, Madam," Minjung said, pulling away and wiping at the tears on her face. "I didn't mean for that to happen. You were asking me about your company."

"My anger yesterday didn't help. It must have brought up some bad stuff for you." Rowena cupped Minjung's cheek. "I'm sorry for my role in that."

Rowena settled down in her rocking chair, and they sat in silence until Rowena said softly, "Thank you for sharing that with me, Minjung. I'm open to talking more about this if you want. I know how intensely personal that was." A sudden realization hit Rowena. Minjung was looking for a family. She was looking for people to see to her well-being, to listen to her opinions, and to consider what she had to offer.

"You're a good person, Minjung," Rowena continued. "And you did not deserve that kind of treatment. Is your mother still with your father?"

"I don't know."

"When was the last time you've seen or spoken with either of them?"

"I left home over fifteen years ago. I send my mother letters every now and then, but I don't give her a return address. I don't want him finding me."

"How do you know she receives the letters?"

"I don't, but I send them to Embee Labs. She's a biochemist there researching diseases. I check their website often to make sure she's still listed as a researcher there. And she still is as of last night."

"I hope this doesn't come out wrong," Rowena said, "but I completely understand how difficult it is to stand up for yourself. Your mother is obviously an incredibly intelligent woman and yet couldn't find a way for the two of you to leave your father." She put her hand up as if to stop Minjung's response. "Please, I'm not faulting her. Not in the least. Bullies have power; they just do. And it's hard to find—"

When Rowena didn't finish her sentence, Minjung said, "Madam?"

"I just had an epiphany," Rowena said. "Frank McMahon, the plant manager of my beloved Tyttle Foods plant, is a selfish, insensitive bully." She glanced over at Minjung and saw light dawning in her eyes as well.

"Yes, I think you're right, Madam," Minjung said and then proceeded to tell Rowena about the conversations and comments she'd overheard during their tour. "It's no longer a family, Madam. It's chaos."

"People aren't feeling heard," Rowena said. "They clearly aren't acknowledged." She thought about the lack of milestones recognitions. That could be fixed quickly. "They simply don't feel appreciated. That's it. That's the key problem. It's hard to stay excited about something when no one seems to give a shit about you." Rowena pointed her finger in the air and wagged it as the puzzle pieces began to fall together on their own. "We're on to something here, Minjung." She clucked her tongue against her teeth. "Poor Manny. He's stoic, just like you and your mother, trying to pretend everything is okay and keeping up appearances. Manny almost had me fooled yesterday, but then we both saw how tired he was of fighting McMahon's methods."

Rowena stood abruptly, her rocking chair swinging back hard and hitting the balcony wall. "Oops. I'm excited." She stilled the chair and said to a now-standing Minjung, "We have work to do. We need to come up with a plan. My father will want clear action points." She looked at her watch and said, "Shit, we only have six hours. Okay, we can do this."

Energized, Rowena headed back inside her rooms and then toward the door to the hallway. "No, no, leave the dishes," she said to Minjung, who had veered toward the tray. "Leave the suit, and my hair will have to wait, too. There's work to be done." She put her arm around Minjung, steered her toward the door, and said, "If my conversation goes well with my father later, then Tyttle Foods Cincinnati will be getting a new plant manager, and you, Minjung Lee, will be getting a well-deserved flogging this afternoon."

"Really, Madam?" Minjung's entire face lit up.

"Oh, yes. Complete with a happy ending for both of us." Rowena laughed maniacally and steered Minjung to the elevator that led straight down to her office.

Chapter 12

Minjung

Minjung washed and put away the lunch dishes in record time. She then headed back to the office. She hadn't felt this exhilarated in years. She and Madam had been brainstorming and problem-solving all morning. Working together felt so natural that Minjung thought maybe she'd write a day rating of 10/10 in her journal that evening. It was early in the day, though, only one o'clock in the afternoon, and they had one more hour to go before Madam would call her father.

Madam's face lit up when Minjung walked back into the office, making her feel squishy inside.

"I've ordered a desk for you in here with an executive chair. None of those ridiculous little secretary's chairs for you." Madam positively gushed at her announcement. "You have been instrumental in this whole thing." She pointed to her computer screen where she'd been typing in proposed solutions to the lethargy problem at the plant.

"Come, sit." Madam patted the chair next to her. "What are those?" She pointed to the two bottles of cold sparkling water Minjung had brought back in. Madam had certainly had enough caffeine at this point, so Minjung was trying to sway her in another direction. Not that it was her place to judge her Madam's caffeine consumption, but she was going to anyway.

Madam picked up each bottle in turn. "Which is mine?"

"Whichever one you want," Minjung said. She glanced over at Madam's bar on the far side of the room. "You could taste each one first."

Madam nodded, so Minjung retrieved two small cocktail glasses from the bar—no ice. She came back and poured a little lime sparkling water into one glass and a little coconut-flavored water into the other.

Madam tried the lime-flavored one. "Weird. I'm so used to Tyttle Pop with all that sugary taste." She took another sip and then reached for the coconut. "Hmm," she said with a favorable expression. "These are kind of good. No sugar or artificial sweeteners?"

Minjung shook her head. "No, Madam. It's just carbonated water with flavors."

Madam waggled her eyebrows and said, "What if I put the lime in the coconut?"

Minjung suppressed a giggle. "And drink them both together?"

Madam burst out laughing. "We are definitely on the same wavelength today, Minjung. I love it." She poured the rest of the lime-flavored drink into the coconut, swirled it slightly, and took a sip. "Wow. This is kind of good. I mean, it's still weird, but it's good." She handed the glass to Minjung and gestured for her to try it.

Minjung was pleasantly surprised. "I never thought to mix the flavors like that."

"We may be on to something with this." Madam picked up one of the bottles and examined it. "We don't have a sparkling water line. And Manny said the bottling side of the plant has been used less and less. What if—" She looked at Minjung, an idea clearly brewing. "What if we gave sparkling waters a try?"

"I think it could work, Madam."

Madam looked off into space, deep in thought for almost an entire minute, and then blurted, "I need your thoughts on my opening lines."

"Go," Minjung said as she sat. It was odd not to say, 'Yes, Madam' or something similar, but they'd become more colloquial as their brainstorming session wore on. She poured each of them a mixture of lime and coconut.

"Okay, ready?" Madam asked. Her obvious excitement was nothing short of cute.

Minjung nodded.

Madam read from her computer screen, "The Tyttle Foods plant in Cincinnati has become merely a place to work. A means to an end. For the employees, it's a job, that's all. Punch in, punch out, go home. The overall feeling at the plant seems to be one of boredom and uncaring. Workers no longer seem proud to work for Tyttle Foods, camaraderie seems to be waning, and, in short, the plant has lost the family feel. How do we fix that?" She looked up at Minjung expectantly.

"You've certainly captured the feeling there, Madam." Minjung looked at the document on the screen. "And it looks like you have examples of employee behavior in the next few paragraphs to support your introductory statements."

"You sound like an English professor," Madam said with a chuckle.

Minjung shook her head. "I was a biology major, biochemistry to be exact.

"And, what, pray tell, does that mean?"

Minjung smiled. "Basically, it's the study of the chemistry of living things."

"Did you graduate?"

"Yes, Madam," Minjung said shyly. "I have a bachelor's degree from Stanford." She hated this part. The next question would be, why in the hell was she a submissive servant or some variation of that.

Madam's eyebrows rocketed upward. "Impressive. I'm honored that you chose to accept my offer to work for me. I consider myself lucky."

"Madam? What was your degree in?" Minjung pointed toward the framed diploma on the wall. She'd been curious about it, but it wasn't her place to snoop.

"I majored in Fine Arts at Chouteau College. It's a small liberal arts college in St. Louis."

"That was my dream," Minjung said wistfully. "To major in Fine Arts, I mean. Dance. My father wouldn't allow it."

"I'm sorry to hear that. But it sounds like you got your dance on anyway."

"I did. I took as many dance classes as I could and joined the classical dance company there. My mother convinced him it was good for my physical health."

"Good thinking. I majored in music and vocal performance, with a concentration in opera."

This time, Minjung's eyebrows shot up. "Madam," she said, clearly impressed, "you're an opera singer?"

"Was." The reverence in Madam Rowena's tone made it clear she had enjoyed the pursuit once upon a time. "Here we are, two artsy people working on a business proposal." She laughed and then said, "Funny how fate brought the two of us together, isn't it?"

"Yes, it is, Madam," Minjung said.

"Okay, Twinkle Toes, back to work." Rowena patted Minjung on the knee.

"Yes, Madam Songbird," Minjung teased, her eyes wide. She was taking a huge risk, giving her Domme a nickname.

Madam Rowena burst out laughing, shook her head, and hesitated. "This next section deals with my proposed solutions to the plant's problems, and I guess I have to lead with relieving Frank McMahon of his job." It was clearly a difficult idea for her to process. "I mean, he has a family."

"Aren't his children all grown and out of the house?" Minjung asked.

"Yes," Madam said succinctly. She scrunched her face as she thought about what to do. "He has a golf habit to pay for." Madam chuckled and then groaned. "I have to recommend this move to my father, Minjung." It sounded like she was pleading with Minjung not to make her do it.

"What if," Minjung started. "Okay, just thinking out loud here."

"Go."

"What if he wasn't exactly fired, per se? What if his role changed?"

"To what?"

Minjung hadn't quite formulated a full solution but said, "I don't know. Advisor to the plant?"

"No," Madam said quickly. "Advisor to the company. This way, he isn't tied down to my plant." She laughed evilly. "I need him out of my hair."

Minjung smiled, and an idea came to her. "Madam, does Tyttle Foods sponsor golf tournaments? I went to a tournament with a former Domme, and there were hole sponsors, clubhouse sponsors, and overall tournament sponsors."

"The LPGA Queen City Championship is played right here in Cincinnati. September, I think. It's only May, so there may be time to get some kind of sponsorship in. What's your angle there?"

"You make Mr. McMahon the Tyttle Foods ambassador or liaison or whatever important-sounding title you can give him. He gets to hang out with professional golfers for several days while he represents your company. This way, he's still employed, and he gets to be around his first love of golf."

"And, and, and," Madam said excitedly, "he doesn't have to stick to the tournament here. He can travel. He can do the PGA and the Senior PGA tournaments as well. Is there a senior LPGA tour?"

Minjung shrugged that she didn't know.

A five-second internet search produced the answer. "Yes, there is,"

Madam Rowena said. "This is fantastic. 'Legends of the LPGA.' Great name." Madam turned to Minjung and said, "My father plays golf. He's going to love this idea." She smacked Minjung on the thigh twice. It was her way of giving Minjung an 'atta-girl.'

Minjung sat back in her chair. A flood of warm feels overtook her. She had no right falling in love with her Domme, but it was happening anyway. She had no expectations that her Domme would ever feel the same way. And that was okay. Minjung would never let her feelings be known, but in the least, she hoped that Madam would be able to feel her devotion.

~~~

Hours later, Minjung found herself tied face up on a padded medical table in Madam Rowena's playroom. Minjung had just been flogged and now lay on her red and pulsing back. Her arms had been pulled overhead, tied together at the wrists, and then fastened to something behind her that she couldn't see. Her heels rested in gynecological stirrups, with leather straps binding her ankles tight to the stirrups.

Apparently, the phone call with Madam's father had gone fairly well, although he'd told her he had to muse on her suggestions. That part didn't matter to Minjung at the moment because her Domme was happy, and Minjung was getting endorphin-ized.

Thirty clothespins were attached to Minjung's body. Her breasts, torso, and upper thighs had been decorated with the pins, a set of fifteen running up each side. Madam wore a sexy doctor's uniform, her breasts pillowing over the tight white medical coat. A stethoscope hung around her neck, and Minjung didn't see pants or a skirt and wondered what her Domme was wearing beneath the thigh-length coat if anything.

The whole outfit surprised Minjung. She hadn't known about her Domme's medical play fetish. Minjung was to call her Doctor Songbird.

"These medical clips," Dr. Songbird said as she flicked the pins attached to Minjung's right thigh, "will tell me how to treat your condition. Now tell me, what brings you to my office today, Ms. Twinkle Toes?"

Minjung wanted to laugh at the nickname, but she couldn't. She was kind of panicked. They hadn't discussed the scenario. She had to make something up, and quickly. Her brain frantically scanned itself for possibilities. "Restless Nerve Syndrome."

"Indeed." Dr. Songbird grabbed one end of the cord attached to the fifteen clothespins on her right side. "After I yank this string of pins off, I will then examine each spot for redness and sensitivity."

Dr. Songbird yanked the string, and the fifteen pins flew off Minjung's skin in a flurry. Minjung cried out as delicious pain hit her body, sending bursts of arousal to her sex moments later. She writhed when the doctor pressed on each of the throbbing sites. She arched her back to relieve the pain, but all that did was arouse her further.

The doctor only murmured, "Mm hmm," and "I see." Then the doctor sighed. "I have a theory but not enough evidence. I must do the other side in order to get a conclusive diagnosis." She ripped off the second fifteen-pin zipper, making Minjung thrash in the heady mixture of pain and arousal.

"Doctor," Minjung said breathily, "I have an issue."

"What's that, Ms. Twinkle Toes?" She pressed her thumb deep into each of the remaining pin spots.

"My lower region seems inflamed, Doctor." Minjung pointed with her head and chin toward the area between her legs. She would have used her hands, but they were tied behind her head.

Doctor Songbird looked down toward the notch between her patient's legs. "Stop squirming, Ms. Twinkle Toes." Minjung melted at the dominance she heard in the tone. She arched her pelvis as much as the restraints allowed.

The doctor chose to ignore her arching and instead said, "I must be certain about this nervous condition of yours." She pulled a handheld controller out from under the padded table, and the previously horizontal table tilted back. Minjung's head was now slightly lower than the rest of her body.

"I like certain colors," the doctor said as she moved behind Minjung's head. "Do you have a color you like at the moment?"

"Green, doctor. Frustratingly green."

The doctor laughed. "I've never heard of that particular shade before." The doctor chuckled again and leaned over Minjung's body. To Minjung's surprise, the doctor's impressive breasts had been freed from the lab coat and were now dangling over Minjung's face.

"Let's test the strength of those lips and tongue now." This, the doctor said as one massive breast was lowered directly over Minjung's mouth. The table was tilted even lower so the doctor's nipple could be placed firmly in her patient's mouth.

This was the moment Minjung had been dreaming of. She'd only seen the pillow tops of her Domme's breasts before now. She desperately wanted to caress and fondle the soft flesh but could only use her mouth. She sucked the erect nipple into her mouth and was delighted to hear the doctor moan in arousal. Far too soon, the breast was taken away. Minjung heard herself moan in frustration, but then the other breast took its place. The doctor, keeping contact with Minjung, reached lower and dipped a latex-covered finger into Minjung's center.

"Hmm," the doctor said. "This slickness. I've never seen this phenomenon with Restless Nerve Syndrome. I must explore further."

She stood up so fast, effectively removing all contact with Minjung's body, that Minjung cried out at the loss.

The doctor moved to the foot of the examining table and said, "I must get a better idea of what's happening down here." She undid the leather restraints on Minjung's ankles, and Minjung was about to be relieved, but then the stirrups were slowly spread, making her lower region wide open to the doctor. "My color is very green at the moment," the doctor said. "How about yours, Ms. Twinkle Toes?"

"Green still, doctor."

"Excellent." The doctor reinserted one gloved finger and added another inside Minjung, causing her to moan and arch her pelvis again. When she began undulating her hips, the doctor slapped Minjung's thigh. No words were spoken, but the undulating stopped. Staying still seemed like one of the hardest things Minjung had ever done.

The doctor moved behind her head. Minjung couldn't see her Domme. Both breasts were lowered over Minjung's face and pressed down. There was a slight air pocket, so she wasn't suffocating, but it would have been heaven to do so. The doctor leaned further down Minjung's body, and the breasts were gone, only to be replaced by the doctor's ample belly. There was no air pocket this time. Minjung squirmed for breath and was forced to move her head slightly for air. And then something happened. Something was inserted into her body between her legs. She arched her pelvis and felt another odd thing. Rope. The doctor stood up slowly, and Minjung saw the rope in the doctor's hands. She'd inserted a hook plug, it had to be, and the rope was attached to one end so she could pull on it to torture her very willing patient.

The exam table moved again. This time, Minjung was bent at the hips as her upper body was raised. The doctor laid the rope on Minjung's torso and then attached it to the table somewhere beyond Minjung's head.

"This is fascinating research," the doctor muttered and then tugged on the rope.

Minjung jumped. The object embedded inside her rubbed against her clit. Her clit was so swollen and sensitive that she could cum any second.

Another tug on the rope. Minjung groaned.

"This may be Restless Nerve Syndrome after all," the doctor said in a detached manner.

She tugged the rope once more and then did a preposterous and evil thing. She lowered the table in small increments so that Minjung's upper body caused the rope to tighten. The object pulled further inside her, and the rope pressed against her clit.

She was going to cum. "Madam," Minjung screeched as a warning.

The table was raised slightly, relieving the pressure, and Minjung's imminent orgasm vanished.

"Curious," the doctor said and proceeded to lower then raise the table in quick succession, causing Minjung to squirm and reach the brink of orgasm again. She didn't warn her Domme this time. Maybe she would—

"Another approach is needed," the doctor said dispassionately as she released the tension on the rope. She moved between Minjung's legs and removed the curved hook with a ball on the end. Minjung's breath came hard and fast as endorphins flooded her body. She was overloaded. Her eyes fluttered closed and then open. She had not orgasmed, but this feeling was glorious. Addicting.

Before Minjung could close her legs to get some much-needed relief, the doctor stepped in between and lifted her lab coat. Underneath was the infamous double-ended vibrating strap-on that Madam seemed to favor.

"I think I've discovered the source of your Restless Nerve Syndrome," the doctor said. She tucked the bulbous head of the phallus just inside Minjung and rested it there, much to Minjung's ever-increasing frustration. "Judging by the extreme slickness in this lower region, I believe I've found the source. Obviously, I must test this area." She moved forward agonizingly slowly, causing Minjung, in her dreamy state, to moan for stimulation, any stimulation.

Once the phallus had bottomed out, the doctor pulled back, left the head inside, and then pushed forward again slowly. Minjung's legs quaked as her entire body reacted to the stimulus.

"Color," the doctor barked as she increased her pace.

"Gr—" Minjung tried to talk, but a pre-orgasmic wave struck her.

"Color," the doctor demanded.

"Greeeeeeeeeeeeen," Minjung screeched. Her primal scream seemed otherworldly, but she didn't care as the orgasm wracked her now-spasming body. She writhed on the table. An aftershock shook her soul, followed by a brief pause. Another wave rolled through her. When Madam pulled out, she had another orgasm, lesser but intense, just the same.

Minjung lay panting on the table, her eyes fighting to stay open but losing the battle. Her hands and arms were crossed over her chest. She'd been untied. She closed her legs. Another wave hit her, and she rolled into a fetal position. A blanket was draped over her, and then Madam did the weirdest thing. She kissed Minjung on the head.

"I'm here, Minjung," Madam soothed. "That was fucking epic." The awe in her Domme's voice made Minjung smile as she fought to catch her breath. She was fighting hard to stay present, but she was one part of this world and one part of a world of Madam's making.

Minjung woke when the back of Madam's fingers stroked her cheek. "You okay, Twinkle Toes?" The voice was soft. The voice was close. Very close. Somehow, Minjung was now lying on the couch with no recollection of how she'd gotten there. Madam was spooning her from behind with her arms wrapped protectively around her. It was all she'd hoped for, and yet she knew it didn't mean what she wanted it to mean. But that was okay. She'd take what she could get.

No sound came out when Minjung tried to form words. She cleared her throat and said, "Thank you, Dr. Songbird."

"Answer the question."

Minjung moaned at the dominant tone; although soft, it had been authoritative and hit her in places that few had been able to reach. "I am more than okay, Madam." She tried to sit up, but her Domme pushed her down. "But, Madam, I need to pleasure you."

Madam Rowena chuckled knowingly. "What do you think my Twinkle Toes will be doing this evening after she's rested, made me dinner, and nestled between my legs as I watch baseball?"

Minjung laughed and then mumbled, "Ten out of ten."

"How's that?" Madam Rowena asked with a puzzled tone.

"Best day ever," Minjung said and closed her eyes again. Strong arms squeezed her tight.

Chapter 13

Rowena

Four months had passed since Rowena visited the food plant with Minjung. It was now mid-September, and they were back at the plant, but this time, Rowena was sitting on a makeshift stage in the courtyard between the two major buildings of the plant. She was waiting to be introduced to the workers, to give one of them a special award, and then to tell them about exciting new developments for the Cincinnati plant. Rowena suspected that rumors had already gotten around about the new bottling line. But that was okay. She was here to get them excited and let them know they hadn't been forgotten.

When Esther Ruiz, the newly appointed plant manager, asked her to give out the milestone awards, Rowena politely declined and suggested that Esther take the helm. Rowena wanted the employees to see Esther as their new leader and as one who cared about them. Which she did. She was the right choice for the job, and her father was easily swayed to make the appointment. And as far as Frank McMahon, he was now the newly appointed Tyttle Foods ambassador for the PGA and LPGA tours. He was happy. Esther was happy, and Rowena's father was happy. It was win-win-win all around.

"Herman Thompson," Esther said into the microphone, "you've been here twelve years, but I am retroactively giving you your ten-year longevity pin."

Rowena smiled genuinely and joined the employees' enthusiastic clapping. A middle-aged man with an impressive mustache walked up the steps, shook Esther's hand, and took the pin and the envelope with the bonus check in it. Rowena wished they could have given more money with the longevity acknowledgments, but at least it was something. It was more than they used to give, anyway.

"And Herman," Esther said as he was leaving the platform, "I'll see you back up here in three years for your fifteen-year pin."

"You got it, Esther," he said and winked at her. The workers chuckled good-naturedly, and Esther went on to the next group of recipients.

Rowena glanced over at Minjung, who was standing off to one side near the employees. She was impeccably dressed in her new Sunny Bowker suit. Noticing Rowena's gaze, Minjung smiled at her. It was a reassuring kind of smile that said, "You've got this, Madam." Rowena smiled back and then semi-focused on Esther at the podium. It was because of Minjung's input and astute observations at the plant that Esther Ruiz was now the new plant manager, and Frank was off playing golf and still getting paid for it.

And it was also because of Minjung that Rowena was about to announce the big changes coming to the plant. None of this would have happened without the new submissive that had somehow fallen into her life. Lately, she'd been waking up every morning with a hopeful feeling in her body. And every morning she realized that the hopeful feeling came from being able to spend time with Minjung.

The tone of Esther's voice changed, and Rowena tuned back in fully. "We're so pleased," Esther said into the microphone, "to have with us a member of the Tyttle Family. She is the one who has been instrumental in a lot of the new changes we've seen these past few months. Please help me welcome Rowena Tyttle to our happy little plant."

The applause was mediocre, but Rowena didn't mind. They didn't really know her. Once she got in front of the microphone, she gazed at the crowd, catching the eye of several employees and giving them genuine smiles. "Thank you for that warm welcome, Mrs. Ruiz. And I have to say that I have always loved these longevity awards. I am so glad they're back." She turned and grinned at Esther, who was now sitting on the stage with the various division managers, including Manny. Esther grinned and threw her two thumbs up.

Rowena turned back to the crowd and said, "I promise I won't take too long up here because doesn't that barbecue smell amazing?"

An enthusiastic cheer went up in the crowd. Rowena had convinced her father that employees were grateful for free lunches. She had been neglectful of the plant, and this was her way of apologizing.

"About twenty years ago," Rowena said, "I toured this plant with my father. I was eighteen or so, and I met a man named Manual Schmidt. At forty, he was already the division head of the bottling side of the plant and remains so today." Rowena turned to see Manny's face scrunched up with emotion. Oh, crap, she hadn't expected that. She cleared her throat to choke back her own emotions and then said, "And I asked Mrs. Ruiz if I could have the honor of giving Manny his thirty-year pin. She graciously gave me the privilege." Rowena turned back and mouthed, "Thank you" to Esther.

Rowena went on to spout Manny's work history at the plant and his tireless push to make the plant safe for all the workers. "It's because of Manny that we've had so few injuries. I bet you didn't know that. But no one works alone. Manny has had all of you at his side, making him look good." The workers chuckled, and Rowena's heart swelled when she heard Manny laugh behind her. "But, of course, there are other people who have been by Manny's side. His wife, Beatrice, and his two grown children, and their children." Rowena knew Manny hadn't seen them yet and had no idea that his entire family was there, so she stayed silent as the workers made a path for them to move to the front of the courtyard.

A strangled cry of emotion from Manny almost undid her, but she persevered. "Beatrice, would you kindly come up to the stage and pin your husband with his thirty-year pin?"

Manny's wife handed one of the grandbabies to her son and headed up the stairs. Rowena handed her the pin and stepped out of the way. Manny stepped forward, hugged his wife, and stood with shaking hands while she attached the thirty-year pin to his white Tyttle Foods shirt. They hugged again, and she left the stage to boisterous cheering and excited calls from the workers.

Rowena handed Manny his envelope and hugged him. She said into his ear, "I hope you'll stay at least five more years. You should see our new retirement sendoff."

He laughed, hugged her again, and headed back to his seat on the stage. He wiped at his eyes, and Rowena found that she needed to dab at her own as well.

"Okay, one more announcement." She gripped the podium and said, "The rumors are true. We're getting a new product here at the Cincinnati plant. The bottling line won't be sitting idle because we're introducing—" Rowena nodded toward the Chief Officer of Beverages, who had come all the way from the headquarters in St. Louis. The woman pulled the tarp off the gorgeous marketing advertisement poster.

"Our new line is called Tyttle Fyzzle," Rowena said. A cheer rose in the crowd, and she was pleased at the enthusiastic reception. "The admins at corporate are going bonkers over this new product, and this plant right here is going to be the one to produce it." Another cheer went up. Rowena leaned forward as if telling a secret, "I have to tell you. I really wanted to have samples ready to give out today, but apparently, that's going to take a while. The labs need to work out the recipes, and the FDA has to approve them. Yada yada, all that."

The workers groaned good-naturedly. Rowena chuckled, thanked the workers, and handed the podium back to Esther, who released them to have their festive lunch.

After another hour of schmoozing with the plant's administrators and those who had come over from corporate, Rowena and Minjung were finally in the backseat of Ash's car and heading home.

"Good stockholder meeting, Ma'am?" Ash asked as she pulled onto the highway.

"Very good," Rowena said. She patted Minjung on the knee and asked, "Don't you think?"

"Absolutely, Madam," Minjung said. "It seemed as if the other stockholders also approved of the new plant manager."

"Breath of fresh air." Rowena winked at Minjung. She was grateful that Minjung hadn't slipped because Ashley still didn't know Rowena's real identity. That was one of the private reasons Rowena requested that no photographs or video be taken during the event that morning. Esther Ruiz thought it was a precaution against their new product line leaking to their competitors. And Rowena let her believe that. Another reason was that she didn't want any photographs of Minjung to accidentally leak out. Minjung had emphatically stated that she did not want her parents to discover where she was. And since this was a win for Minjung as much as it was for Rowena, she insisted on no visual recording of the event.

Once they had reached the house and Ash was driving out the gate, a sudden tiredness overcame Rowena. She needed to lie down for a while. But she'd hinted unabashedly to Minjung that if the event went well, they'd have a session in the playroom afterward. She checked her watch. There was certainly time for a nap.

"Go rest, Minjung," Rowena said and nodded toward the stairs. "You've earned yourself a session in the playroom later."

"Thank you, Madam." Minjung's cheeks turned pink, which always surprised Rowena. Minjung was a seasoned submissive and yet seemed shy about their sessions. It couldn't be embarrassment, could it?

"Let's say an hour and a half. I may have to set my alarm." Rowena chuckled. She was only thirty-eight years old but sometimes felt a lot older. Afternoon naps weren't a regular thing, but she definitely needed one right now. "Be waiting for me down there."

"Yes, Madam. Thank you."

"Go on." Rowena pointed toward the stairs again. It was funny how Minjung never left unless formally dismissed. The woman had certainly been trained right.

Rowena let herself into her office to drop off her notecards. She placed them on her ultra-neat desk. Minjung must have straightened up before they'd left that morning. Ever since the first plant visit over four months prior, they'd done a lot of things together. Minjung finally got to meet the Grande Domme of Denton Heights for the first time at the masquerade ball at the end of May. Rowena had wanted that meeting to be sooner, but apparently, Matilda's social schedule was packed full, and she didn't have time for a tea party at Rowena's. Matilda was polite to Minjung at the ball but, in true Matilda form, suggested to Rowena that Minjung wear some kind of show of possession like a collar or cuffs or something. Rowena hadn't wanted to put a collar on Minjung. At that point, she'd only had Minjung for one month and a week. Placing a collar on a submissive was a huge statement, and Rowena hadn't been ready to make that statement yet. She'd simply nodded to Matilda. One does not argue with the likes of Domme Matilda. You will not win.

Victoria had been over the moon that night in May when Rowena finally showed her face at the ball. Victoria had shown up with one submissive and, at the end of the evening, not only left with that submissive but had a second one on her arm. Rowena had to admit, the party hadn't been all that bad. Hayley was a proud peahen showing off her two submissives, who also seemed proud to be shown off. Rowena had to laugh at Hayley's constant griping about the decorations, and Rowena politely suggested that Hayley get on the masquerade ball committee that oversaw those things. It was as if that thought had never dawned on her friend before.

Later that same month, the box she'd reserved at the end of May for the Cardinals/Reds game went over well with her friends. She'd only invited the usual suspects, Victoria and Hayley, and their subs. Although the Cardinals lost the game, Rowena had enjoyed her friends' company. She finally had a submissive of her own to show off and interact with. Minjung surprised everyone about how much she knew about the Cardinals' players and team history. This caused Victoria to tease Rowena about getting a submissive so she wouldn't be alone rooting for the mediocre team from St. Louis. Minjung hid a smile at that quip and had to turn away when Rowena told her friend to fuck off—good-naturedly, of course.

But it was at that game that Rowena started to feel like she'd been missing out on something. Victoria talked about Rikki's coffee shop and all the goings-on there. In June, when Matilda invited Rowena to a Sunday afternoon tea dance, she decided it was time to reach out to the community and attend. And what a gathering that was. Rowena got to rekindle her friendship with Seamus and get a look at his new submissive. Rowena was flabbergasted that he'd gone *little*. Seamus was only in his early fifties, but his hair was completely white, and he looked grandfatherly. He was also very fit, as evidenced by his barrel chest and strong hands. His new *little* was in his early twenties, so of legal age, but there had to be at least a thirty-year age gap between them. Although Rowena wasn't about to judge someone else's kink or kink shame Seamus, she didn't understand it. And if that wasn't enough, Shasti, the relatively new Domme in town, was meeting a potential *little* for the first time. Judging by the look on Shasti's face that afternoon, it was love at first sight. And apparently, it was because, in July, that *little* had moved in and was collared. The collaring ceremony was nice, and the young woman seemed appreciative, although a bit confused over the new world she'd landed in.

Minjung turned thirty-seven the last week in August. Rowena had a gathering for her growing group of friends in honor of Minjung's birthday. Rowena was pleased that Minjung took the attention graciously and didn't shy away from it, nor did she puff up like Kaylynn had. As the guests were leaving, Rowena would never forget what Shasti's new *little* said, "It's a nice house, and the cupcakes were awesome, but I thought this was a collaring ceremony." Shasti shushed her and grimaced for Rowena's sake. Rowena just shook it off.

The birthday gathering had been over a month ago, and Rowena still held fast to the notion that it was too soon. Collaring was a big deal. Collaring meant real commitments from both sides, and she wanted to at least reach the six-month mark and the end of Minjung's first contract before even entertaining the idea.

Rowena sighed and headed to the elevator and her rooms. Truth be told, Rowena liked having Minjung near her. She liked Minjung's intelligence and her willingness to please. She wasn't overly fawning, and pleasing Rowena genuinely seemed to make her happy. Now, in her bedroom, Rowena took off her suit and hung it up in the new 'to-be-dry-cleaned' section of her closet that Minjung had set aside for her. Rowena stroked the sleeve of her gray suit jacket. She'd had submissives with that genuine desire to please, but there was something different about Minjung. Whatever it was, Rowena wasn't going to question it.

Forty-five minutes later, Rowena woke, showered, and dressed in a Renaissance Queen ensemble. It had a long white chemise underneath, and the burgundy overdress was cinched at the waist, allowing her ample bosom to become the star of the show. Matching slippers adorned her feet, and she was almost ready to head down to the lower level. She sat at her makeup table and put her hair up in a messy bun. Funny how much Minjung liked doing Rowena's hair. She chuckled out loud. It would be nice to have Minjung here to help her dress and get ready, but she wanted Minjung to be surprised by her clothes and styling. She wanted Minjung to gasp a little at the artistry of her presentation. She wanted to turn Minjung's head.

Satisfied with her look, she headed down to the playroom a half hour ahead of schedule. As she padded toward the room, she heard lovely music coming from within. Minjung was early, very early. The door hadn't latched shut. Curious, Rowena nudged it open enough so she could see what her submissive was up to. A lot could be garnered from a person's behavior when they thought no one was watching.

It was Rowena's turn to gasp. The lovely creature wore nothing but Mother Nature's clothes and a pair of shoes. She moved with such grace and elegance that Rowena could barely breathe. Minjung held onto the handle of the treadmill as if it were a ballet barre. Her graceful bending, elegant arm sweeps, and ethereal movements captivated Rowena. The out-turned feet, the standing up on her toes and back down again—she was incredible. Rowena knew these movements and positions had names, but she didn't know them. Standing in the hallway spying on her submissive made her feel clumsy, like a rhino clomping in the wild. To be fair, rhinos were probably more graceful than she was.

Minjung made a sweeping movement with her arms and turned to face the other direction. It was then that she noticed Rowena watching from the cracked door. "Madam," Minjung said, surprise in her voice. She scrambled for her phone and turned off the music. She lowered her body to the ground, thankfully stayed off her knees, and bowed her head low.

Her obeisance usually energizes me, Rowena thought as she opened the door and walked in. But today, it didn't. She felt like she'd intruded on something personal and private. "That was lovely, Minjung. I'm getting you a barre." Minjung looked up. "Right there on that mirrored wall. It'll be perfect. You have the soft mat unless the mat would hinder."

"Madam, please don't go to any trouble on my account," Minjung pleaded. She seemed embarrassed that Rowena was taking an interest.

Typically, Rowena would barge ahead with her plan no matter what anyone thought, but for some reason, she softened and said, "We'll talk about it later. I won't do anything unless you want me to. Okay?"

"Yes, Madam. Thank you." Minjung remained seated on the floor while Rowena towered over her. For some reason, Rowena wasn't feeling the power dynamic just then. Who was she to make this incredible creature bow down to her? Emotion squeezed her chest, and she had to turn away. What was wrong with her today? It must be hormone flooding or something. She took a breath and moved behind her submissive. She reached down, grabbed a handful of ponytail, and tugged Minjung's head up slightly.

"You are mine."

Minjung made a small noise of arousal and took a quick breath before saying, "And you are beautiful, Madam. Like a queen."

Rowena tightened her core and barked, "You have ten seconds to take off your shoes and land face down on the spanking bench ass up, ready to receive whatever it is I feel like giving you." She released the ponytail and began the oral countdown.

Minjung burst into action. She flung off her shoes and draped herself over the bench with ample time to spare. Rowena strapped her submissive down by the wrists and ankles and then went to her storage closet for much-needed supplies. Out came a fresh eye bra, gag, and a flogger. Or should it be a caning today? No, the flogger. Rowena briefly considered a spanking, but she was much too tired to pull that off. Besides, spankings hurt the spanker as well as the spankee.

After suiting Minjung up with cuffs, bindings, and gag, she walked behind and, without saying a word put a hand on one of Minjung's tight round ass cheeks. This woman under her hand was a fine specimen of womanhood. Her body was toned, her skin practically flawless. Rowena's hand stroked the firm flesh lovingly. She moved to the other cheek and gave it equal time.

"Give me a thumbs up," Rowena commanded.

Minjung put both thumbs in the air as much as the wrist bindings allowed.

"This will tell me you are all right. It's the equivalent of green. Now snap your fingers."

Minjung did as told.

"That will be your safeword since you won't be able to speak, and it is the equivalent of red." Rowena made sure the ball gag was tight without binding. "Do you understand?"

Minjung put two thumbs up.

"Good."

The eye bra went on next. Again, she'd thought about full sensory deprivation. They'd certainly built trust after five months together. But something held her back. Maybe she'd go full deprivation after they renewed the contract in another month. And then there was the possibility of collaring. That might be the more appropriate time.

Rowena moved away from Minjung and walked a wide path around her.

Minjung did something odd. She lifted her head as if searching for her Domme. It was an endearing movement, but Rowena tried not to read anything into it.

"Color?"

Minjung gave her a thumbs up.

Rowena picked up her flogger. The loose leather tails were like old friends. It really was her favorite instrument to use on a sub. She reached forward and touched Minjung lightly on the shoulder. Minjung braced herself, knowing she'd just gotten the signal that the party was about to begin.

Rowena ran the tails of the flogger across her submissive's back so she would know what was coming. If they made it to the collaring stage, Rowena might not be so generous with her information.

Rowena took one swing and made bullseye contact with an ass cheek. She waited. Sometimes, anticipation made a sub squirm. Not this one. Minjung was the most stoic submissive she'd ever had.

Another swing made contact with the other ass cheek. She waited. But then she got impatient and swung right, then left, and back again. The hypnotic rhythm of her strokes, as she moved from ass cheeks up to the back, was entrancing. This sub could take a lot. Rowena increased the power of her strokes. Minjung took it. Rowena increased the speed. Minjung squirmed, but there was no snapping of fingers. That was permission to keep going.

Minjung's entire back and ass and upper thighs were fiery red. As Rowena continued her assault, a flash of Minjung dancing shot through her mind. Rowena pulled her arm back to strike again when something rushed through her entire body. She didn't know what it was, but it felt like remorse, regret, or guilt.

What am I doing? came the unbidden thought.

She dropped the flogger, grabbed the faux fur cloth, and rubbed her submissive's body gently.

How can I hit this beautiful person in my care? This obviously hurts. She's doing it to please me because pleasing me seems to be a reward for her. And this is what I want from her? What the fuck?

Rowena unstrapped Minjung, took off the gag and eye bra, and said, "Rest."

She moved behind her submissive and frantically searched for a solution to her sudden paralysis. The Cowgirl Machine was the solution. Rowena rolled the saddle-like machine out of the closet and toward the spanking bench. She plugged it in. "I want to watch you get yourself off."

Minjung nodded but didn't move.

"Have you ever used one of these?"

"No, Madam."

"All right. I'll help you get on."

Minjung shimmied off the spanking bench and stood still for a moment before moving. She seemed to be giving herself time to regain her balance.

"There's this lovely attachment I'd love for you to use." Rowena grinned evilly and produced a lifelike penis attachment and fastened it to the top of the seat. She helped Minjung straddle the machine and then guided the phallus into her submissive. She then handed her the remote.

"There's an app for this machine, so I can control it, but I'd rather give you autonomy." Rowena moved away and sat down on the couch to enjoy the show.

"Now, Madam?"

"Go for it. I want to watch you cum."

Minjung hit the start button and yelped when the machine came to life. It seemed to take her an entire minute to figure out what each of the controls did, but she finally found a rhythm and undulated her hips to the vibrating machine. Rowena hoped her submissive wouldn't put on a show as if she was in a porn movie. Thankfully, she didn't.

Minjung then changed things up by lifting her body off the phallus and then back down. As she increased her speed, Rowena noticed Minjung's breathing quicken. She was getting close.

Minjung's head dropped back, her mouth opened momentarily, and then her head flew forward as she came. The moans coming out of Minjung's mouth were otherworldly. A spike of arousal shot through Rowena's body. She squelched the feeling. She didn't deserve a reward for the things she'd done to the woman in her charge.

After a few moments, the machine stopped vibrating. Minjung took a deep breath and looked over at Rowena.

"Go put that on," Rowena said, pointing to a thin black robe she kept available for submissives. "And then come back here to the couch."

Minjung did as commanded and sat on the couch where Rowena patted. "That was wonderful, Minjung. Thank you for the honor of watching you enjoy your own body."

Minjung's face was already flushed, but Rowena knew she was blushing at the praise. She put her arm around Minjung's shoulder and pulled her close.

"Madam?" Minjung said, her head resting on the shelf of Rowena's breasts made firm by the Renaissance outfit she wore.

"Yes, Twinkle Toes?"

Minjung chuckled and then said, "Your clothes are incredible. I feel your dominance when I look at you. But Madam?"

"Yes?"

"May I suggest something? Something, err, different?"

"Sure."

"Would it be all right if I…"

"Go on. You've earned the right to ask for what you want. You have that whole free will and all that."

Minjung made a noise of approval and then said, "Would it be all right if I held *you* this afternoon?"

"Me?"

"Yes, Madam."

Rowena was confused at first, but as she realized the truth, tears welled up in her eyes. She blinked them back the best she could but was unsuccessful. Minjung knew something was wrong and was trying to give *her* aftercare.

"Sure," Rowena said, grateful that her voice didn't break from emotion.

After an awkward moment of figuring out how to position her body comfortably within Minjung's arms, she finally settled in. This time, it was her head that rested against Minjung's small but comforting chest.

A hand stroked her hair. "We have a beautiful power exchange relationship, Madam," Minjung said. "You take care of my needs, and I hope I adequately take care of yours as well."

Rowena let out a breath and watched the silk of Minjung's robe move. Why was she suddenly having this wave of self-doubt and second-guessing? She had no idea.

Minjung continued, "And, Madam, sometimes it's okay for the power to kind of flow the other way. I'm still learning your moods, but I sensed something shift earlier. At first, I thought I had displeased you in some way because you had stopped so abruptly. Then I thought perhaps you were physically ill, but then your soft cloth was on me. I felt regret and questioning coming off you in waves, Madam."

"You felt that?"

"I did, Madam." Minjung squeezed the Dominant nestled in her arms. "Know that I participate in what we do willingly and with enthusiasm. I like the pain, Madam. I *need* the pain. And, although I could never do what you do, I understand that it fulfills some basic need in you. Like, it fills up your power centers or something. I may be saying this all wrong, Madam, but I'm okay. As far as I'm concerned, *we're* okay."

Rowena wasn't sure if Minjung was telling the truth. She sounded genuine, though. "I don't think I've ever heard you put so many sentences together in a row like that, Minjung." Rowena chuckled and was rewarded with an answering chuckle and soft knuckles stroking her cheek. "You're a beautiful dancer, Minjung. I wish I could have seen you dance before your accident."

Minjung made a small noise of regret. "That would have been nice, Madam."

Rowena took a cleansing breath and let it out in a long sigh. Minjung moved her arms as Rowena sat up.

"Thank you for this," Rowena said. She took one of Minjung's hands in both of her own. "You're very insightful."

Minjung nodded, and Rowena smiled as she watched Minjung's cheeks color.

"And I was going to spring this on you after dinner, but I have a surprise for you."

"You do, Madam?"

"We're going to New York."

Minjung's eyes grew wide. "I've never been to New York, Madam. Are the Cardinals playing the Mets?"

Rowena burst out laughing. She had created a real baseball fan in her submissive. "The Mets, no. The Met? Yes. We're going to the Metropolitan Opera House in Lincoln Center, Manhattan, to see *Aida*."

"*Aida*? Madam." Minjung's mouth had gone slack. "Me? You're taking me?"

"Of course," Rowena said, her body filling with joy that Minjung was pleased. "Oh, but there's more. Besides awesome restaurants and taking in the must-see sights, we're also going to the David H. Koch Theater."

Minjung's smile faded to an expression of disbelief. "Madam." She said low, clearly anticipating what Rowena was going to say next.

"Oh, yes. We're taking in an American Ballet Theater Performance. I looked for *Madam Butterfly*, but it doesn't seem to be on anyone's schedule this season."

"Thank you, Madam." Minjung wrapped the robe tighter around herself. "I don't know what to say."

"I can tell that you're pleased," Rowena said. "And I'm glad. I'm also happy to finally have someone to go with me to these things. I brought Victoria with me to a performance by the Cincinnati Opera once and—" Rowena scoffed. "That's a story for another day, but needless to say, she never asked to go with me again."

Minjung chuckled. "What will the ballet be, Madam?"

"Oh, it's fun. It's their fall gala or something, and they'll basically have a series of *pas de deux* pieces. I can't remember them all, but there was Sleeping Beauty, Romeo and Juliet, Swan Lake, Don Quixote." She looked up. "There were more, but I can't remember."

"That sounds wonderful, Madam. Like snippets of the great ballets. Thank you so much for wanting me to go."

Rowena smiled, took a deep breath, and touched Minjung's shoulder underneath the robe. It was a signal. Minjung looked up expectantly. Message received.

Rowena stood up. "Clean this equipment, drink some water, and then clean yourself up." She waved her hand up and down Minjung's robed body. "I want dinner in two hours. You will eat with me, and then we can work on the new puzzle if you like."

"Excellent, Madam." Minjung stood up. There was a happy glint in her eyes as a small smile crept up her face.

Rowena couldn't help but smile back at her submissive. But then she turned, strode toward the door with heavy steps, and belted, "Don't keep me waiting."

A soft giggle preceded the "Never, Madam."

Rowena chuckled low and let herself out.

Chapter 14

Minjung

Early October arrived crisp and cool in Ohio, and it was similar in New York. Minjung and her Domme sat in the back of an authentic yellow New York City taxicab on the way to the American Ballet Theater venue. You'd never know the sun had already set because the bright lights from shops, apartments, and traffic kept the city alive with light. The yellow cab turned onto 10th Avenue in Hell's Kitchen, a neighborhood on the West Side of Midtown Manhattan. According to their very chatty taxi driver, Hell's Kitchen got its name for being the place where poor and working-class Irish Americans lived once upon a time.

"HK is a very different place now," the driver said.

Madam Rowena didn't answer or even acknowledge him, but Minjung nodded at his reflection in the rearview mirror. He was one of the chattier taxi drivers they'd had since landing at JFK Airport two days prior. Madam wanted them to take taxis everywhere so Minjung could get a "real" New York experience. The day before, they'd eaten in a neighborhood called "Little Italy" at a restaurant named Lombardi's Pizza, which was famous for being the oldest pizzeria in the entire United States, having opened in 1905. The food was good but wasn't anything Minjung was used to. In fact, she'd eaten so much rich food in the last two days, including an apparently required bagel from Brooklyn, that she was feeling sluggish.

Minjung glanced at Madam sitting next to her in the backseat of the taxi. She was engrossed in sending sight-seeing pictures to her sister. Minjung was grateful for the experiences her Domme was giving her—the *Aida* opera last night, the sightseeing yesterday and today, and the ballet they were heading for now. Yes, she was grateful, but it was all a bit overwhelming. The noise alone was enough to send Minjung's nerves aflame. Why the drivers had to honk their horns so often was beyond her comprehension. When they walked through Times Square after the opera last night, the crush of tourists had been overwhelming. There had been so many different languages spoken that it made Minjung's head swim. The one thing that the movies had gotten right was the aggressive and boisterous ways New Yorkers talked to each other. They were loud and kind of rude. Madam shrugged off the inattention they got at the shops and said, "We're going with the flow."

Minjung's Domme was impeccably dressed in a black Jacquard flare skirt with a golden peony print all the way around. The skirt hit just above Madam's ankles and low heels. Her long-sleeved round-neck pullover sweater complemented the skirt but didn't compete with it for attention. Madam had once said that Minjung had impeccable style, but Madam most certainly did. She owned her plus-size body and knew how to dress accordingly.

Minjung understood what an absolute privilege it was to accompany her Domme to these high-fashion events. And, after spending a lot of time nude in Madam's house, it was nice to get dressed up on occasion. Minjung loved the dress Madam had purchased and had tailored for her before they left Ohio. The black boat-neck A-line dress hit just below the knee. The fit was perfect, accentuating her bust and waist before flaring out into the typical A-shape silhouette.

Madam raised an appreciative eyebrow when Minjung had emerged from her bedroom in the two-bedroom suite at the hotel earlier. Minjung had a secret hope that they'd share a bed in one room, but alas, that didn't happen. They each had their own bedroom. Although Minjung thought she should wear heels with the ensemble, Madam would not hear of it. "High heels are the death of every woman," she'd said, adding something about protecting Minjung's knees.

"Enjoy the show," the exuberant taxi driver said as they got out at the curb of the David H. Koch Theater.

Minjung waved. It was a small gesture. She wasn't sure how one was supposed to interact with New York City taxi drivers and Madam wasn't helping. Madam paid the driver, of course, but other than telling him where to drive and handing him the payment, she'd had no other interaction with him.

Minjung's feelings of inadequacy faded as she took in the excited murmurs of the well-dressed people heading to the theater. She looked in wonder at the lighted steps leading up to the stone plaza that surrounded the lit fountain. The fountain here was much grander than the one at Madam's, but that was to be expected.

A chill ran through Minjung as they walked up the low steps. She paused at the top of the stairs to put on her jacket. Madam had finally decided on a tailored cropped jacket for Minjung that hit just above her waistline. It was perfect.

"You look yummy," Madam Rowena said.

"Thank you, Madam," Minjung said, surprise in her voice. "As do you, of course."

Madam smirked and headed for the steps of the building. Once inside, Minjung delighted at the promenade's high gold-leaf ceilings, with its bright lights and large sculptures flanking the gathering crowds. Madam ushered them toward the women's restroom, and after taking care of business and freshening up, they headed to their seats.

Minjung's heart was beating fast as she took in the sights and sounds of the auditorium. The plush red seats and the balconies along the sides made such an elegant scene that she almost had to pinch herself. She'd dreamed of performing in a place like this one day. Who was she kidding? She'd dreamed of performing in this exact venue one day. Her chest squeezed tight at the loss. The senseless loss. Anger that she thought she'd had buried deep inside welled up. She looked down at the program in her hands and tried to tune out the excited audience noises. She tried to take a deep breath but could only manage a shallow one. She conscientiously lowered her tense shoulders and tried again, this time with success.

"Isn't this wonderful?" Madam Rowena asked her. Minjung wished she could muster the same smile on her face that Madam sported. She did smile, knowing that it didn't reach the rest of her face. Madam narrowed her eyes, clearly sensing something. "We don't have to stay for the entire performance, Minjung."

"I'm fine, Madam," Minjung lied.

"If you're sure," Madam said. She had a concerned expression on her face.

Minjung reassured her Domme that she was fine; she was just a little tired, and that was all. And that much was true. This entire trip was an exceptional gift for someone of the likes of Minjung—a nothing, a nobody. And she should be grateful that her Domme had invited her. Minjung must be sure to remember her place. She had momentarily forgotten. Nothing was about her. If she had anxiety over seeing the stage, the one she'd hoped to touch one day, then that was to be kept to herself. Madam had paid a lot of money and put in a lot of time for Minjung to see and experience these things, so she needed to suck it up and deal. She tried to remember how she'd felt at the opera the night before in order to recapture and mimic that persona.

"These aren't the best seats," Madam Rowena said. "But they're certainly adequate enough."

Minjung tried to hide a smile. Although they didn't have seats in the lower orchestra section, they were sitting just right of center in the first ring of seats above the orchestra and only three rows back.

"The opera was exceptional last night, Madam," Minjung said, sensing that Madam Rowena wanted her to make small talk. "I'd never seen *Aida* in person, only on a PBS broadcast."

"What did you make of Aida's aria, *O Patria Mia?*"

"*Oh, My Homeland,*" Minjung translated. "She was wistful about her home and was basically saying goodbye to it. Her sense of home was gone. She couldn't go back." Minjung paused and then added, "And honestly, Madam, that touched me personally. Unlike Aida, I chose to leave my home, the only home I'd ever known, but like her, neither of us can go back."

Compassion overtook her Domme's countenance. "I hadn't thought about it that way. Verdi certainly seemed to understand that kind of loss, didn't he?"

Minjung nodded. "He was one of the world's greatest operatic composers, wasn't he? I mean, that's why that opera is over one hundred and fifty years old and still going strong."

"Exactly," Madam agreed. "Along with so many others that he wrote. *Rigoletto, Otello, il trovatore, la traviata, Macbeth.*" She chuckled and added, "I could go on, but I don't want to bore you."

Minjung smiled and it was a genuine smile. "Once a music major, always a music major. Right, Madam Songbird?"

Madam shot her a playful face with her mouth in a silent "O" as if to say, "Oh, no, you didn't." She didn't have time for a counter response because the lights flickered and then dimmed.

After an introduction by the chief artistic director from the American Ballet Theater, the premiere ABT dancers took the stage. Minjung let herself relax during the various performances. She had danced some of the pieces before, like the Swan Lake *pas de deux*, but not all of them. In her seat, her body flowed with the dancers. She kept her movements to a minimum, but her soul felt each one.

She was proud of herself for keeping it together and not distressing her Madam, but that was until a new group of dancers took their positions on the stage. They were ballet students from the Jacqueline Kennedy Onassis School. They looked young. Minjung checked her program. The students ranged from age twelve to eighteen. She had once been a hopeful dancer like they were. She had worked hard just like them. And, at age twenty-one, her own father had destroyed her chance at furthering that dream. She'd just started to tour with a junior company, but he didn't like that. He didn't like the way the tight leotard showed off her body. He didn't like the way hundreds of people watched her move. It was disgraceful, he'd said. She was a whore, showing her body like that, he'd said.

The laundry basket she'd been carrying in her arms from the apartment building's basement laundry room had her leotards and leggings folded on top. That's apparently what had set him off, that and the ever-present alcohol on his breath. When she had the nerve to disagree with his assessment of her, he did what he did best and used the open palm of his hand against her face. Not once, but twice. The surprise of it had her stepping backward to get away from him. But she'd been on the stairs. She couldn't get her footing and crashed down the stairs in agony before she'd even hit the damp concrete floor. She'd find out later that she'd torn the ligaments in both knees and had months of healing and rehabilitation ahead of her.

"Excuse us," Madam Rowena said. She reached a strong arm under one of Minjung's and pulled her up.

What was she doing? It was bad form and bad etiquette to get up during a performance.

"She's ill," Madam said to the usher who had come to admonish them.

Minjung allowed her Domme to help her down the steps and then to the lobby. She guided Minjung to the women's restroom and had her sit on the couch in the lounge area.

"Put your head down," her Domme said. "Yes, like that. I'm going to get you a cold, wet towel."

Just then, a worker came with a small bottle of water, which Minjung took gratefully. She took a small sip and handed it back. She couldn't guarantee what her stomach would do. And there it was. She bolted off the couch into the nearest stall. It wasn't very ladylike, but she had to empty the contents of her stomach. "I'm sorry, Madam," Minjung cried between gags. "So sorry," she muttered to herself. She wiped her mouth with toilet paper and then flushed. She was shaking when she finally stood upright.

"Are you okay, honey?" That was Madam Rowena's voice. She'd called Minjung "honey"—not as in lover but as in someone she took care of.

"Yes, Madam," Minjung said. She took a breath, then another, stood up tall, and opened the door.

Madam's hands were all over her, touching her cheeks, her arms, and her forehead. "It was too much. Too much. I'm sorry this evening triggered you, honey." Minjung allowed herself to be pulled into a tight embrace. Being crushed into the bosom of her Domme was a-okay with her.

"Can't breathe, Madam," Minjung said. She was only half serious.

Madam released her immediately. "Oh, honey," Madam rubbed Minjung's arms. "Go rinse your mouth, and we'll get a cab back to the hotel."

"Yes, Madam." Minjung complied and it wasn't long before they were waiting on the curb outside Lincoln Center.

Madam held her arm up high toward the street, hailing a cab. "We can talk about what happened when we get back to the hotel," Madam said. "Or we can postpone it until later."

"How did you know something was wrong?"

"You weren't watching the performance. Your breathing was weird. You were kind of snorting out anger or something. And when your fists clenched and you pounded your thigh, I knew something was happening."

"I'm sorry, Madam," Minjung apologized again. "I ruined your evening."

"Inconsequential," Madam said as a taxi pulled up to the curb. "You are more important to me than any performance." She opened the back door and ushered Minjung in. She gave the driver directions, and this driver was blessedly quiet the entire one-mile trip back to the hotel.

Once inside their suite, Madam Rowena insisted that Minjung take a bath. And then Madam did an amazing and unexpected thing. She got on her knees on the bathroom floor and washed Minjung from head to toe. Being pampered by her Domme was amazing, but the only thing that could have made it better was if Madam had gotten in the bath with her. That was a bucket list item for Minjung, but one she would never share. It wasn't her place to want such things.

Madam Rowena added a bit more hot water to the bath and said, "You soak." She took a minute to get up off the floor, needing to use the edge of the tub to pull herself up. "I'm going to order a few bites to eat from room service. You don't have to eat anything if you don't want to, of course, but I'm going to push those two chairs over to the window so we can look out on Times Square for a bit. I want you to have happy memories of our trip."

"That's very sweet of you, Madam," Minjung said. She wanted to apologize again for her completely inappropriate meltdown at the ballet but had already been admonished on the taxi ride back to the hotel not to apologize again.

Now that her Domme had left the room, Minjung let herself relax. She even dozed for a moment. When she woke, she felt refreshed and got out of the tub. She toweled off and then opened the door. The smell of something savory made her stomach growl. She was hungry, and that was a good sign.

Madam Rowena turned from her seat by the window. "Feel better?"

"I do," Minjung said truthfully. "May I put on a robe, Madam?"

"Yes, of course. I want you to be comfortable."

Once in her robe and donning the comfy slippers Madam had purchased for the trip, Minjung was seated in the chair next to her Domme, looking out over the incredibly bright flashing lights, ever-changing digital billboards, and honking traffic more than ten floors below. The view was nothing like she'd ever experienced before. "This is incredible, Madam. Thank you for taking me."

"Remember how I told you to stop apologizing?"

"Yes, Madam."

"Now it's time to stop thanking me." Madam Rowena chuckled and added in a softer tone, "I know you're grateful, Minjung. You've been a wonderful companion this trip."

Minjung looked down, embarrassed. She hadn't been a very good companion that evening, now, had she? She looked at the uneaten bowl of chicken noodle soup on the room service tray, "Madam, may I serve myself?"

"Yes, yes," Madam said. "I got practically one of everything, including dessert, which I know you won't eat, but I will." She laughed good-naturedly, and Minjung laughed with her. The soup and oyster crackers sat well on her stomach, and when she finished that, she cut off a sliver of the turkey and Swiss sandwich.

"Tummy feel better?"

"Yes, Madam."

"Good." Madam looked out the window for a moment and then said, "You can nix this idea, but I was thinking that since we're here in New York, far away from where you actually live, you might want to send a letter to your mother. Maybe a postcard?"

That was the farthest thing from Minjung's mind. She was momentarily speechless.

"Or not," Madam added.

"I…No, that's a good idea, Madam. I should."

"I don't want to force you." Madam stood up and tightened the belt around her robe. When she came back, she handed Minjung a small flat box. "Open it."

Inside the box was a personalized stationery set with Minjung's name embossed in ornate raised ink across the top of each note card. "Madam, this is lovely." She wanted to fly into her Domme's arms and thank her but held back. That wasn't the kind of relationship they had. Instead, she clutched the box to her chest tightly. "I'll start a letter to her tonight."

"Excellent," Madam said. "We're here for two more days, so you could send a couple of letters. If you wanted to."

Minjung nodded. That might be a good idea. Since living with and feeling secure with Madam Rowena, Minjung had begun to think more about her mother. Perhaps she could help her in some way.

"Now," Madam Rowena said, turning slightly in the oversized chair. "I had a whole litany of things for us to do tomorrow. Statue of Liberty, Twin Towers Memorial, Empire State Building observation deck, lunch or dinner in Chinatown, maybe a boat ride to see the skyline at night. Or even a carriage ride in Central Park." Before Minjung could respond, Madam said, "But we don't have to do any of those things if you're not up for it."

"One last time," Minjung said. To Rowena's confused expression,

Minjung said, "Thank you for all you've done for me. I'm okay now. I would love to do any and all of those things, Madam." What she didn't add out loud was, *If I get to do them with you.* What she did say next was, "I'm okay, but I have some processing to do, I think. Apparently, I haven't made peace with what happened with my father."

"We can find someone for you to talk to."

"Yes, maybe that's what I need." Minjung looked down at her hands. "But, Madam, I want you to realize that I'm pretty tough. I don't know if I'm the kind of person that wants to be treated with care. Do you know what I mean?" Ever since Madam had that sudden case of Domme drop in the playroom two weeks ago, she'd been treating Minjung differently, almost softly. "I want to be handled. Not man-handled, of course, but *woman-*handled. No, *Domme*-handled. I want to serve you, Madam. I want you to need me. That brings me joy. I don't want to be coddled or treated delicately. Taken care of? Yes. Absolutely. But I need to feel your dominance, not your pity." Minjung looked up at her Domme. "I know I'm all over the place with this, but does any of it make sense?"

Madam Rowena didn't answer the question. She simply touched Minjung's shoulder underneath the robe and then stood up. She closed the curtains and slowly pulled the belt off her robe. With a finesse Minjung had only begun to realize her Domme had, Minjung's wrists were tied together. A sharp tug had Minjung on her feet, following her Domme.

"Prepare to be handled," Madam Rowena said evenly. "Handled by a Domme."

Minjung knew not to speak as Madam Rowena pulled her into the bedroom.

Chapter 15

Rowena

Simmering with Minjung had become one of Rowena's favorite activities since returning from their New York trip. It was a Friday afternoon, and Rowena sat at her office desk. The sounds of the landscaping crew cleaning up this week's piles of autumn leaves only added to the realism of the simmering scene. Further in the background, Rowena could hear the bobcat excavator working to create a mulch-covered walking path along the fence line around her property.

Rowena wasn't sure how it happened, but ever since they'd gotten back, she had taken to walking partway around the perimeter of the property with Minjung. Part of it was because she wanted to exercise on a more regular basis, but another part was that she discovered she enjoyed her submissive's company. And that included times like now when Minjung was playing the role of sexy administrative assistant, Ms. Twinkle Toes, to Rowena's Ms. Songbird executive boss role.

Rowena's assistant wore a form-fitting skirt and blouse combination that accentuated all of her lovely assets. Ms. Twinkle Toes leaned over the side of the newly installed secretary's desk. And for today's session, Rowena had legitimately assigned her to research a potential company for Rowena to invest in.

Rowena had dressed the part as well. She wore a black suit with a wrap skirt that would be unwrapped soon enough. Her crisp white button-down shirt had been ironed just that morning by Minjung without her knowing it would become part of this afternoon's festivities. She also hadn't known that the tight bun she'd styled on Rowena's head would also help Rowena play the part of the executive boss.

"Ms. Songbird," her assistant said, "I need your assistance interpreting this company's financials. The price-earnings ratio seems off to me."

"Let me help you then." Normally Rowena would have asked Minjung to bring the financials to her desk, but Minjung had caught on to the game that was afoot. Rowena sidled up next to her assistant and glanced down at the laptop screen, a gift to her submissive to aid in the very real research. Rowena pretended to stumble and reached out to steady herself. Of course, the hand ended up stroking Minjung's firm ass.

"Mmm," Rowena moaned as a small dose of arousal feathered through her. She loved simmering. Tiny touches of excitement were layered with future anticipation. They'd been at it for quite some time that afternoon, but it still wasn't quite the right time to seal the deal. She wanted to introduce Minjung to a small dose of Shibari rope and bondage right there in the office.

Rowena's hand continued to stroke its owner's ass as she said, "Ahh yes, I see you divided the company's stock price by their earning per share to get the price-to-sales-ratio, P/S for short. But where did you get that EPS figure from?" Rowena pinched the flesh beneath her hand. The muted squeal of surprise made Rowena smile. It had been a gentle, playful pinch to let her assistant know she was in charge.

Minjung, or Ms. Twinkle Toes as she was currently known, slid the laptop away from them and leaned even further across her desk. Elation fluttered in Rowena's chest. Minjung knew how to keep the simmering going, didn't she? Two were playing this game, and Rowena loved it. She leaned closer and slipped her hand underneath her assistant's skirt from behind. She stroked the inner thighs and was not surprised to find that her submissive was already wet. Oh, but it wasn't time to finish her off yet. Rowena was going to drag it out for at least another half hour. She wanted both the landscaping and the path-making crews gone and off her property. That way no one would be able to hear Minjung scream as she finally got her ultimate reward.

"I see the issue," Rowena said as she inserted the middle and ring fingers of her upturned hand into her submissive. A soft moan from Minjung was the reward. Rowena pumped slightly, making sure she grazed the G-spot with her knuckles as the fingers moved. Minjung opened her legs wider, clearly needing relief.

"I see the issue," Rowena repeated. "The figure you used here isn't the EPS. EPS is calculated without the dividends included. See here?" Rowena pointed to the correct figure.

"My…" Minjung undulated her hips to get more friction.

"Yes, Ms. Twinkle Toes? You were saying?"

A soft moan was the only response. Uh oh, the simmering had intensified to a soft boil. That was not in the plan. To reduce the heat, Rowena slowed her hand and pulled out.

Minjung's head dropped as she struggled to get her rapid breathing under control. "My mistake," she finally managed to get out.

"We all make them." Rowena made her way back to her desk, pulled out the wipes stashed in the bottom drawer for such occasions, and cleaned off her fingers. What she admired about her submissive was that the question had been genuine. Minjung was doing actual research. She was learning how to analyze companies for investing and learning quickly.

Ever since they'd gotten back from their trip to New York, Minjung had spent a lot of time in the office doing research for Rowena's investments. Minjung seemed quite adept at finding companies with growth potential. Rowena checked over Minjung's recommendations, of course, but found that Minjung's "diamonds in the rough" seemed promising. Time would tell, of course, but it pleased Rowena that Minjung seemed to be enthusiastic about the research.

Rowena wanted today's simmering session to be special. Tomorrow marked the end of Minjung's six-month contract, and Rowena was going to offer her another contract for just as long. She'd begun to hope that this particular submissive would last longer than any of the others. But Rowena didn't want to get ahead of herself. In fact, the only gift she'd purchased for Minjung was the gold charm necklace she had in her top desk drawer. She opened it slightly and saw the box. If Minjung said she wanted to renew for another half year, then Rowena would ask her to put the lock charm on the necklace and wear it in Rowena's presence. Rowena planned to do the same with her key charm. She sent Miss Kat's Domestic Servants Agency a silent thank you for its role in sending Minjung to her.

Rowena closed the top drawer and figured that if Minjung decided to move on and not renew the contract, then Rowena would give her the necklace as a parting gift. The woman had done a spectacular job, above and beyond, really. And now the woman was helping her with the financials of potential investments. That was an amazing woman. Minjung herself was a diamond in the rough.

With a mental sigh, Rowena forced herself to refocus on the business at hand. The business that paid the bills. She had been watching one particular stock for a while now. She was waiting for it to reach a certain price before selling a few shares. It was boring stuff, so she treated herself to a glance at Minjung. Minjung noticed, and accidentally-on-purpose, dropped her pen on the floor. Naturally, she needed to retrieve it. She bent at the waist, ass toward Rowena, and lingered in this vulnerable position as she "struggled" to pick the pen off the carpet.

"Here, let me help you," Rowena said. She carried a small bottle of water with her, and as Ms. Twinkle Toes stood up, Rowena accidentally-on-purpose splashed water over her submissive's tight white blouse. "Oh, my goodness," Rowena said. "Look what happened there. I'm so clumsy." Rowena was about to touch the newly made wet spot, but her submissive did something next that sent Rowena's libido into high gear.

Minjung reached up and circled one nipple, now visible under the practically see-through wet spot. She reached a second hand up and circled the other. "It will dry soon," she said and kept circling the nipples with the middle finger on each hand. "Perhaps you can aid the process, Ms. Songbird."

A rush of excitement hit Rowena's sex when Ms. Twinkle Toes lifted one breast with both hands in offering. Rowena lunged at her submissive and sucked at the nipple through the blouse like she was starving. She backed her toward the desk and, with one hand, swept all of Minjung's papers and notes to the floor. If she'd had the strength, she would have lifted her submissive onto the desk but had to motion for Minjung to jump up instead. Rowena put her hand on Minjung's back and gently laid her down on the desk. She maneuvered between Minjung's legs and ripped open the soaked white blouse.

"Offer one to me," Rowena said, her voice husky.

Minjung offered one small breast, and Rowena eagerly latched on to the presented flesh. She sucked and licked and then realized she needed to hold off. The workers were still there. With her teeth, she nipped the sensitive skin. Minjung yelped at the surprise attack but then moaned as the pain turned to pleasure, just as Rowena knew it would.

"Sit up," Rowena commanded. "Take that off." She gestured to the torn shirt hanging off Minjung's body. "And that." The skirt would be next. Rowena moved out from between her submissive's legs and opened the bottom desk drawer. She pulled out the coil of soft cotton rope and commanded her submissive to sit on the desktop again.

The rope session would cool them down enough to wait out the workers who were due to leave in about fifteen minutes.

"I know just how to dry that wet skin of yours, Ms. Twinkle Toes," Rowena said. "Cotton." She held up the coil of rope and grinned. She could see Minjung fighting a smile, and that was just fine. She wanted her submissive to enjoy their sessions together.

Rowena in no way, shape, or form considered herself a rigger, but she had learned a few easy ties that her past submissives seemed to enjoy. But you never knew with submissives. Some were fawning sycophants, biding their time, and putting up with whatever Rowena threw at them. They did this so later they could get what they wanted. Like Kaylynn.

Rowena halted her thoughts of Kaylynn. Happily, she had been getting better at stopping the intrusive thoughts of her former submissive quickly. Instead, she focused on the beautiful woman in front of her. She ran a doubled-over section of rope underneath Minjung's small breasts and around her back. She threaded the loose ends through the lark's head loop and tightened it. She wrapped the strands over one of Minjung's shoulders and then across one breast in front until snaking it around the rope underneath both breasts. The rope went up and over the other side. That was pretty enough, indeed, but Rowena had it in her head to do a Cupcake Tie. She might need to abandon it if Minjung's breasts proved to be too small, but she hoped she could get at least one coil around each breast. Three were preferable, but she'd find out soon enough.

She separated the two sections of rope and focused on the first breast. Two strands wrapped around just fine; the third slipped off. No worries. Rowena simply made sure there was enough tension to keep the two in place and then wrapped up the second breast. She tied down the rope strands, keeping her creation in place. Each one of Minjung's breasts was squeezed at the base and forced to point straight out into the room like two cupcakes with hard cherry nipples on top. Rowena resisted the urge to flick the beautifully erect nipples. That would come later.

"You should be feeling much drier now," Rowena said. She didn't look her submissive in the eye as she checked the bindings.

"Yes, Ms. Songbird," Minjung said, staying in character. "Much drier.

Thank you."

Rowena took that moment to look her submissive in the eye. Her expression changed to one of evil intent, and Minjung made a small noise of anticipation.

"Hop down."

Minjung hopped off the desk with an athleticism that Rowena envied. But not for long, there was mischief to achieve. Rowena took the long ends of the rope that were dangling from the breast harness and pulled them down, snaked them between Minjung's legs, and up again. She'd never been successful creating a happy knot, one that sat directly on the clit, so she didn't bother trying. Instead, she tucked the rope ends through the breast harness and around Minjung's wrists in front of her body.

"Lift your hands."

When Minjung did so, the rope slid between her legs and the slickness there. She lowered her hands and then raised them again.

"No, no, Ms. Twinkle Toes," Rowena admonished. "You must be very still and allow yourself to dry." Rowena stepped closer. "In fact, I noticed a red bump down here." She slid her middle finger through Minjung's slickness and then swirled it around the swollen clit.

"I meant to ask you about that, Ms. Song…"

"Ms. Who?"

"Ssss…"

When Minjung's breathing reached a certain point, Rowena stopped all motion and backed away. "I need to answer this call," Rowena said, even though no phone had rung. With an evil laugh, she headed back to her desk and sat down. She swiveled her executive chair away from her clearly desperate submissive and, after cleaning her fingers, picked up her phone. She turned on the mirror app and positioned it high overhead so she could watch Minjung try to regain her usually stoic demeanor.

Rowena chuckled and then lowered her phone but held on to it. The workers should be packing up at this point. In fact, she didn't hear the blowers, rakes, or even the far-off bobcat. Excellent. She'd glance out the window to be sure before ravaging Minjung, though. There was a certain decorum to these things, you know.

She placed the phone face down on her desk, and just as she did, the front doorbell rang, making her jump. She put a hand over her chest and said, "That scared the crap out of me." She glanced at Minjung and quipped, "I'd tell you to go answer that, but you're a little tied up at the moment, aren't you?" Rowena let her head fall back as she laughed out loud. Before opening the office door, she called back. "Don't go anywhere." She laughed again and headed for the front door. The newly hired walking path worker stood on the porch.

"Afternoon, Ma'am," the middle-aged, clean-cut man whose name Rowena couldn't remember said. "We're heading out for the day, and we'll be back on Monday."

"What kind of progress did you make today?"

"We did great," he said enthusiastically. "We're weaving around and leaving the big trees like you wanted. We dug up a huge boulder on the far north end. It's a beaut. Jacob put it off to the side. It could be a nice resting spot for you."

"How many more days, do you think?"

"Two more. Monday and Tuesday should do it. On Tuesday, we'll lay down and rake out the wooden mulch all the way around."

"Fantastic," Rowena said. She was grateful for the information but wanted him gone now. "I'll see you on Monday morning then."

She started to close the door, but he stopped her by saying, "Oh, and Ma'am, Jacob dug this up on the east side." He held up what looked like a small blue gym bag.

"What is that?"

"Oh, we didn't open it, Ma'am, but I don't think there's anything dead inside or anything like that. Kind of feels like clothes, actually. Jacob thought it was a time capsule or something." He still held the bag high in the air. "Should I have Jacob bury it again?"

"No, no." She opened the glass storm door and reached for the dirt-covered bag. "Thank you." She closed the door against the chilly October air.

He tipped his ball cap and said, "See you on Monday. Oh, we're leaving the bobcat here. Is that okay? It's in the back end of the property."

"That's fine. That's fine," she said. "See you Monday." She closed and locked the front door. She held the heavy bag in her hand and watched as the workers drove out the front gate.

Who had put this relatively new bag on her property? Maybe some neighborhood kids had thrown it over the fence. Or maybe they had sneaked onto her property at some point and buried it there. She had been toying with the idea of putting cameras all along the perimeter fencing but thought it unnecessary until now.

She opened the door to her office and plunked the bag on the coffee table. There was no way she wanted that nasty thing on her desk.

Rowena turned to Minjung and said, "The workers found—" She didn't finish her sentence. The look of surprise mixed with dread on Minjung's face halted Rowena's words.

"You know something about this, don't you?"

Minjung didn't answer. She merely swallowed and continued to look like a deer in the headlights. If the woman hadn't been tied, she might have run out of the room. Hell, she still could. Rowena casually closed and locked her office door.

"Tell me what I'm going to find in here."

Minjung's countenance ran the gamut of emotions. Surprise, dread, and fear were the main ones, but then she finally sighed and lowered her gaze. She clamped her lips shut and slid down the side of her desk until her ass hit the floor. She leaned to the side and moved until she was on her knees. She brought her arms forward as much as the rope would allow and reached toward Rowena. She placed her forehead on the carpet and lay still.

Her submissive's obvious supplication moved Rowena, but she didn't yet know what she was dealing with.

She sat on the couch and pulled the bag toward her. Minjung flinched at the sound of the grimy zipper sliding back. Rowena pulled both sides of the bag open and peered in. She pulled out clothing: sturdy jeans, a long-sleeved shirt, and a hooded sweatshirt. There were also a few bras, underwear, and socks. Well-worn sneakers that had seen better days came out next. Underneath the clothes was a folder containing paperwork of some kind.

Rowena didn't have a chance to look because as she pulled out the folder, she saw that the bottom of the bag had been lined with cash. Fifty-dollar bills had been carefully spread out on the bottom. Rowena grabbed a handful and marched over to the woman cowering on the floor.

"What is this?" With her foot, she nudged Minjung's chin off the floor.

"Look at me," she screeched. "Are you stealing from me?"

"No, I would never steal from you, Madam."

Rowena paced. Blood rushed through her ears. How could this woman betray her? All submissives were the same. Why had she bothered to try? "What is this then?" She threw the bills at the betrayer. "Are you selling drugs? Or buying them?" She stomped her foot on the carpet. It was not satisfying at all. "No, I don't even want to know. Just get out." She pointed toward the door. "Get out of my house. You have thirty minutes to grab your shit and leave."

Minjung sat up so abruptly that Rowena took a step back. "This, Madam. Exactly this." She breathed back a sob. "That bag is my emergency go-bag. If I had to flee from here, which it looks like I have to, that would help me live for a little while."

"It's your *what*?" Rowena couldn't believe she was listening to the malcontent on her floor.

"It's a bag with some money and clothes. It's some of the money you've paid me. The fifties. When you pay me, I put them in the bag and then bury it again."

Rowena let the words enter her ears. She quickly counted the money she'd thrown. It wasn't much. And it did look like the crisp fifty-dollar bills she'd given her. Submissives were cunning, though. And this one was smart. Very smart.

"You've been free to go at any time, Minjung," Rowena said, suddenly feeling tired. She sat down on the couch. "I'm not abusing you or holding you hostage. You're not chained here." She scoffed at her statement when she remembered that Minjung was currently in rope bondage. She took a breath and picked up the folder. She needed more information. Inside were copies of Minjung's personal identification—her Illinois driver's license and passport. There was also a short, signed note inside. Rowena forgot to breathe. Minjung had been telling the truth.

"In case of death, contact Ye-eun Lee," Rowena read softly. "That's your mother, isn't it?"

Minjung nodded. "Living on the streets is hard, Madam, and I wanted my mother to know if…you know."

Rowena sat back. She was still attempting to digest this new information.

"Madam, if you can untie me, I will go get my things and leave you in peace. Our contract is up tomorrow anyway."

Rowena frowned. The thing was, she didn't know what she wanted exactly. She found herself standing up and undoing the Shibari ropes while Minjung sat on the floor. Once freed, Minjung stood and headed toward the door.

Wait. This isn't what I want. Rowena grabbed Minjung's arm and said, "No. No." She moved and blocked Minjung's exit. "I don't want you to leave. I want to talk about this more." She released the arm she was still holding. "Would that be okay?"

Rowena moved away from the door with both hands up as if in surrender. She sat on the couch and put everything meticulously back in the bag. "These are your things. They belong to you." She gestured toward the money on the floor. "That, too. You've earned every penny. Keep it."

Minjung made no move to pick up the bills on the floor. She just stood there frozen.

Neither woman moved. Neither woman spoke. The woman on the couch had no clue what to do next.

Chapter 16

Minjung

Minjung didn't know what to do. She was standing nude in Madam Rowena's office. She'd never intended for the outside go-bag to be found. In fact, things had felt so right in Madam Rowena's home that she'd almost forgotten about it. Almost. And then it blew up in her face.

"Come sit," Rowena said, patting a spot on the couch. Let me get your robe." She headed to the bathroom and returned with the long red kimono wrap.

Minjung still didn't move. She was in flight mode. Flight mode had saved her ass on many occasions. The bag was right there. She could grab it and a few of the bills and bolt if the talk went sideways. She took a step toward the couch.

Madam Rowena let out a small breath of relief and then sat down.

Minjung took the robe, put it on, and then took the helm. She needed to guide this tenuous conversation lest it get away from her. Her body wasn't quite ready to sit, so she stood off to the side. "I've been burned in the past. I've learned to live in survival mode. A few times, I've been lucky enough to find a community of homeless folks who took me in and offered protection, but those situations never last long. The cops get bees in their bonnets and come crashing in to clean the vermin from the streets. And then it's off to find another safe haven." Minjung shook a loose strand of hair off her face. "Sometimes I mistake a Domme's home as a safe haven. But people with power and people with wealth sometimes think those without power don't matter and no one will miss them. Sometimes, they think they can do outrageous things to someone's body despite hard limits. They feel no shame. There are no repercussions for their actions."

Madam Rowena groaned. It was clearly a groan of distress.

Minjung looked up and said, "The police used to use the acronym NHI to describe sex workers, transients, or people they didn't feel worthy of their time or efforts. Do you know what NHI meant to them?"

Madam Rowena shook her head. "No."

"NHI stood for No Human Involved."

Madam Rowena gasped. "What the fuck? Do they still use that?"

"Madam, they may not use the term, but the attitude is prevalent. I'm telling you this so you'll understand that there is little help for people like me. No one thinks I'm important. No one will come to my aid. No one will deem me human enough to help me."

Minjung's hands shook as she spoke. The anger inside was too much. She stumbled toward the couch and sat down hard.

"Oh, honey," Madam Rowena said, leaning toward her.

Minjung put up both hands. "Don't touch me." She heard the fright in her own voice. She softened her tone and said, "I need a minute, Madam. I'm sorry."

Madam Rowena moved back. "You're fine, Minjung. You're fine. I'm appalled that you've had to endure this. It hurts my heart that anyone has to go through this. I want to help you. When you're ready, tell me how to help." She stood up and got a bottle of water from the small fridge. "I promise not to spill this one on you this time." She smiled.

Minjung grinned back, but it was a small grin acknowledging that the first water spill had been something fun they shared. Her expression also conveyed that there were more serious things afoot. She did, however, appreciate Madam Rowena's attempt to ease the tension. She took the water and drank. She took another gulp, capped the bottle, and handed it back. Madam Rowena took it without question.

"I have a question for you," Madam Rowena said.

Minjung raised her head slightly to indicate that she was ready to listen.

"All those walks around the property, were they truly walks, or have you been plotting your escape?"

Minjung scoffed politely if there ever was a thing. "At first, the walks were to help me formulate an exit strategy. I needed to make sure that I would have a chance out there if things in here turned sour."

Madam Rowena nodded her understanding. "Did I do something that made you think things would turn 'sour?'"

"No, Madam," Minjung said. "There was one moment in the first week that I thought, 'maybe.'"

"When was that?" Madam set the bottle of water on the coffee table and then sat back on the couch. She let out a long sigh as if to relieve some tension.

"When I was punished for the Mistress Victoria incident. And you had every right to punish me, Madam. I had overstepped and embarrassed you."

Madam Rowena nodded. "But what made you realize things hadn't turned 'sour.'" She used air quotes around the word *sour*.

Minjung sighed out a smile and found her own body relaxing. "When you took off my blindfold and showed me the glasses I'd been balancing on the backs of my hands held water, not wine. You didn't have to show me that. And then you played the opera pieces again after I asked. It showed your humanity."

"So, this bag of yours is a way for you to have a sort of insurance policy in case something catastrophic happens and you need to leave quickly and be able to take care of yourself. Do I have that right?"

"Yes, Madam," Minjung said. She toyed with the idea of confessing about the other go-bag in her room, but she wasn't quite ready for that much honesty. Especially because they were at a major decision point in their arrangement. Would Madam Rowena still want to renew the contract, or would she give Minjung the boot after this bag incident? "I have relaxed here, Madam, but there have been times in other houses when I thought I was safe but wasn't. At Mistress Kelly's, for instance. Out of the blue, she gave me to Master Kevin. The services I provide can wear off for some mistresses, Madam. I realized then that I couldn't get too comfortable anywhere. But I've always known that I needed to protect myself."

"I think—" Madam Rowena started to say and then had to clear her throat. Minjung looked down. It sounded like Madam was getting emotional. "I think you've been a good fit here, Minjung. Hayley thinks I should renew your contract. Victoria thinks the same. They say I've been more outgoing and vibrant and not so much a hermit since you've come along. They even say I seem happy. Can you imagine that?" Rowena scoffed. She'd never been unhappy. Yeah, that was a lie. "Now, may I ask you another question?"

Minjung looked over at Madam Rowena and nodded.

"Why are you a hired submissive? I mean, you have an impressive college degree from an equally impressive university."

"I never wanted to study Biochemistry. I got the degree to please my father, and there were only so many majors he would approve of. Since he was paying for it, he got to approve the course of study. My mother took me aside and said she'd help me with the biochemistry studies if I needed it."

"Did you?"

"Need help? No." Minjung chuckled. "No, I was a good and dutiful student. I was a good and dutiful daughter until…"

"Until he did that, and you left."

"Yes, basically." Minjung gave Madam Rowena the short version of her convalescent stay at the home of her first-ever Mistress, a matron of the arts for the ballet troupe Minjung was part of. She didn't mince words and impressed herself that she didn't get emotional when she told the part about Mistress Isabel replacing her with a younger submissive. "After discovering my submissive nature and finding fulfillment like none I'd ever known, I had to get back into the lifestyle. There was no way I could go work in an office or a lab in a nine-to-five job. I never wanted that. Since dance was officially out of the picture, I only knew of one other type of fulfillment, and even though I didn't quite know how to get it, I left San Fran in search of it."

"And then, by some long and winding path, you somehow ended up here with me."

Minjung nodded. "And despite what a lot of people think, this lifestyle isn't all about sex."

"No, it is not."

"I'm not just a nameless female body to be used for someone else's enjoyment." Minjung paused for a moment to organize her thoughts and was grateful that Madam Rowena waited patiently. "I always felt fulfilled helping the younger dancers and thought maybe teaching dance or elementary school would be in my future. But apparently, teaching wasn't a career worthy of my father's approval. He refused to pay for a degree in education. So, instead, I got the science degree. I like to think that I would have somehow found myself in this lifestyle anyway, but it was because, in an odd twist of fate, my father causing my fall led me to find fulfillment as a submissive to a dominant woman. I've found fulfillment…" She couldn't stop the tears welling in her eyes. She grabbed her thigh and pinched hard, forcing herself to focus on the pain. The emotions stopped. "I get fulfillment helping you, Madam. I have relaxed knowing that you trust me to help you with Tyttle Foods and with your investments to a certain extent." Damn, those tears were back. "But I'm afraid I've blown that trust with you now. And for that, I'm truly sorry."

Madam Rowena didn't say anything for an overlong moment. When she did speak, she used soft tones to say, "I'd like you to stay." Madam paused, so Minjung looked up, knowing a hopeful expression had taken over her countenance. "I want to offer you another contract. It can be the same, or if you want to renegotiate some things, we can discuss that, but either way, I—" Mistress Rowena pressed her lips together tightly. Tears glimmered in her eyes. She wiped them away with short, jerky strokes. She caught Minjung's gaze and smiled. It was a sad sort of smile. A lonely one. "We can go month to month if you want."

Minjung started to respond, but Madam cut her off. "Wait a moment." She stood up and retrieved two boxes from her desk. "I was going to give this to you after we concluded our scene this afternoon, but we got interrupted." She handed the box to Minjung. "Go on, open it."

Minjung opened the small white box and pulled out a lovely gold chain. It was thin and had an adjustable clasp. "Thank you, Madam." She didn't know what else to say.

"Even if you decide to leave me tomorrow or next week or whenever the chain is yours. It's fourteen-carat gold. If you ever needed to, you could sell it for quick cash, I guess."

Before Minjung could say she would never sell it, Madam blurted, "I have one, too." She opened the second box and pulled out the same type of chain, but hers had the key charm from the auction attached to it. "I thought you could put your lock charm on yours, and we could..." She paused for a moment, clearly trying to figure out how to phrase what she wanted to say next. "I mean, it's corny, but it would show—" She sighed and threw her hands up in frustration. Clearly, this hadn't been the way she wanted to give Minjung the necklace.

"Madam," Minjung said and sat up tall. "I apologize for the misunderstanding with my go-bag. I didn't mean to upset you in any way."

"No, no," Madam Rowena said. "I understand now."

"I was hoping you would want to extend my contract. And I hope you still do."

"Yes, I do."

"I accept," Minjung blurted before Madam could change her mind. "And I will wear this every day as a symbol of my commitment to you. As soon as I put the lock charm on it, that is. But there's one condition."

"Oh?" Madam Rowena's expression was one of bemusement, which was good because Minjung was about to make a demand.

"The condition is that you put the necklace on me."

"This won't mean I'm collaring you, Minjung."

"I know," Minjung said. And she had known. "I understand you take collaring very seriously, but I was hoping these necklaces could maybe symbolize our commitment to each other. You know, in terms of trust and looking out for each other."

"Of course," Madam Rowena said, melting right in front of Minjung's eyes.

"Thank you, Madam. Thank you for having faith in me."

Madam Rowena opened her arms, and Minjung leaned in for a warm hug. Madam stroked her robed back, and it felt good.

When they broke apart, Madam said, "I want you to feel comfortable here. If you feel you still need your go-bag, which is totally fine, I'd like you to find a different place for it. You don't have to tell me where, but somewhere cleaner, maybe?" She chuckled and made a show of wiping off her hands.

Something clicked inside Minjung. She wasn't sure if the necklaces had pushed her over the edge or the hug or just the whole way Madam was willing to listen without judgment. Whatever it was, Minjung made a split-second decision.

"I don't need that go-bag anymore, Madam." A certain calmness filled her chest as she realized it was true. "In the six months that I've been here, I've seen many of your moods, and I feel safe here with you."

Madam Rowena nodded once and said, "I'm glad. I feel safe with you, as well." She let out a sigh and added, "I don't know about you, but I could use a rest."

Minjung nodded her agreement.

"Okay, then," Madam said as she stood up. "How about we each go clean up, rest, and then have dinner in an hour and a half? There's a puzzle that needs finishing, I believe. And there may just be a certain themed scene that needs to be finished. Someone's administrative assistant has made her executive boss quite happy, and the boss wants to reward her."

"This assistant loves all of those ideas, Madam."

"Shall we?" Madam Rowena put out her hand to help Minjung off the couch.

Minjung took the hand, even though she didn't need it physically. But apparently, she needed it emotionally. It was a small gesture from her Domme, but it was one of kindness and acceptance.

The fact that something huge had just happened between them wasn't lost on Minjung. Neither one had made any kind of declaration of love or anything remotely related to that, but what had been conveyed was respect and a certain amount of affection between an upper-class person and a beloved servant. And Minjung knew that would have to be enough.

~~~

Two months after the go-bag incident, Minjung sat at the desk in her suite. The gold lock charm felt smooth as she rubbed it between her thumb and fingers. Wearing the necklace these past two months had been comforting. Although Madam said the necklace wasn't an official collar equivalent, Minjung couldn't help thinking of it in those terms.

She was supposed to be up here in her room resting, but she was too antsy for that, what with the pre-party set to begin in an hour downstairs. She was already dressed for her Domme's pre-party to the Holiday Masquerade Ball. But beforehand, she needed this quiet moment to jot down some thoughts. She picked up the pen and opened her journal.

> *Saturday,* December 18, *2:30 pm*
> I wanted to update this journal since a few major things have happened since I renewed a six-month contract with Madam Rowena. She understood my need for a go-bag, but now I only have the one right here in my room. I don't feel I need the one outside anymore. If I'm wrong, then it will be a harsh lesson for me.

Anyway, Madam suggested I take the money I'd stashed in that go-bag and set up an online investment account of my own. Since I'm learning how to research companies to invest in anyway, this would make it all the more real for me, she'd said. I now read prospective companies' annual reports and letters to shareholders on a regular basis. Madam says this will give me a sense of the tone and futures of those companies. That stuff supplements the number crunching I do and helps me get a gut feel for what might make a good investment. Of course, the moment I bought ten shares of VisorTech, the stock prices dropped and dropped. Madam Rowena laughed and said that I had to be patient and let it ride. She said there was a reason I was drawn to that particular company, so I had to chill. I have a couple of safer investments, though, but I didn't start out with much investment capital, after all.

I never, in a million years, thought I'd be learning words like investment capital, price-to-earnings ratio, or earnings per share. Not only am I learning those terms, but I'm also getting a better understanding of how to make decisions based on them. It's fascinating.

Madam seems to trust me more, too. I guess trust is a two-way street, isn't it? She's been going out two to three times a week lately. She never tells me where, and it's not my business, anyway, but I'm curious. She's probably just going to the food plant to check up on things. I hope she's not ill or something because I need to take care of her.

Minjung heard a sound in the house through her open door. It was only the far elevator. Madam must be heading downstairs. Minjung knew better than to leave her room. When Madam gave explicit instructions to rest, then you rest. The pre-party and then the masquerade ball were going to wear them both out, that was for sure. She checked her phone and didn't see any new text messages from her Domme, so she went back to her journal.

Madam Rowena's birthday was on Halloween. Can you imagine that? She turned thirty-nine this year, and Mistresses Hayley and Victoria took us to a place called Dominique's Dungeon in downtown Cincinnati. Ashley and Terrence were there, too. And Mistress Victoria had a young sub with her. "Too young," Madam Rowena said to Hayley under her breath. Mistress Rikki Carmichael, the owner of the coffee shop, was also there that night. She is a beautiful, tall, redheaded Domme with a stoic demeanor, yet there is a kind of permanent twinkle in her eye. I shouldn't say it, but her submissive Eileen is not a nice person. She barely spoke to me or Ashley. She barely acknowledged us, but that's okay. I don't want much to do with her. Why Mistress Rikki is with her is a mystery. Even Madam Rowena said so to Hayley. Those two can gossip, that's for sure. But maybe that's what I'm doing here in my journals, so I'll move on.

That night at the dungeon, Madam Rowena had one of the hired Dommes there flog me while she watched. Afterward, Madam wouldn't let the hired Domme soothe my sore body. Nope. Madam Rowena did it. It was a really tender time. She held me and even kissed me on the back of my head. She's never kissed me on the lips, though. And she has never come up to see my room. I'm not sure why. To give me privacy, maybe? I have to stop wishing for these things. They aren't going to happen. To her, I'm like a puppy, I guess.

Anyway, back to the downtown dungeon. Apparently, Terrence had been jonesing for his Mistress to slap him in the face, but Mistress Hayley seemed tentative about doing it. Madam Rowena said point blank, "He's trying to top you from the bottom, Hayley. You are the one in charge. If you don't want to do it, then it doesn't happen." Ashley's eyes got really wide at Madam's bluntness. And Terrence was right there. He heard it. Wow. That's my Domme. I felt myself puff up at her dominance just then.

Anyway, it turns out that Mistress Hayley actually did want to do it. She just didn't quite know how. Madam said she would show her right then but told me to go get some of the free water. She leaned in close to me and said she didn't want me to watch because it might trigger some bad memories or something. See how thoughtful she is?

Minjung fondled the charm around her neck thinking how lucky she had been ending up at the same auction with Madam and then getting chosen out of the hundreds of submissives Madam could have picked. She vowed not to take their arrangement for granted. She checked the time on her phone. She had a few more minutes before needing to head downstairs. She put her pen back on the paper. Wow, she'd already used up two whole pages so far. She guessed she had a lot to get out.

I hadn't even turned to leave when she said, "Gentle pats at first. Put your left hand on the other side of his face to absorb the blow from your right. Have him loosely clench his teeth. Your blow must stay on his cheek. No eyes, nose, ears, chin. Never backhand; use the pads of the fingers only. And no jewelry or gags of any kind." She said more, but I was out of earshot at that point. I don't think she hit Terrence herself; she only instructed Mistress Hayley how to do it. When I got back with the waters, Terrence's right cheek was bright red, and his Mistress was stroking his head lovingly. I guess it had been a success all around.

Oh, for Madam's birthday, I got her a 1000-piece puzzle of the NYC nighttime skyline, just like the one we'd seen on our boat trip in Manhattan Harbor in early October. It was a good, solid brand, she told me. I just ordered from the company she usually used, but I checked her puzzle closet (there are over one hundred in there) and she didn't have this one yet. I knew we'd be busy on her actual birthday, so I gave it to her the day before. She seemed very happy with my present. She said that it was very thoughtful. We even had an incredible impact session afterward.

I need to go; I'll write more soon to get down my thoughts about the Holiday Masquerade Ball. But I wanted to say that we had Thanksgiving at Mistress Hayley's, and it was a nice day. Terrence got fed from Mistress Hayley's plate, and although I know he's her husband, it makes me wonder if they are D/s 24/7 or only at certain times, like when other D/s folks are around. I don't know, and I won't ask.

More Later.

Day Rating (so far): 9/10 (only b/c I'm anxious about this pre-party)

Minjung tucked her pen inside her journal and stashed it in her bedside table. The sound of the front gate bell put her feet in motion, and she sprinted for the front door. Someone was early. When she checked out the front gate camera, she saw it was Mistress Deidre Roberts, the hired pianist. The woman had been one of Mistress Hayley's Thanksgiving guests and Madam hired her for this pre-party. She was an older woman in her mid-fifties with so many tattoos that Minjung had a hard time finding any virgin skin. She was fascinating to look at. Minjung buzzed her car in the gate.

Minjung let Mistress Deidre and another musician into the house. Minjung hadn't known about the hired vocalist.

"Nice to meet you, Minjung," the vocalist named Becky said. "Might there be a private place where I can do some vocal warmups?"

"Yes, yes, of course," Minjung said. She hung up their coats on the coat rack in the foyer and then led both of them to the great room to show Deidre the piano. "Madam had the piano tuned this week, Ma'am. She even played it a few times to make sure it was still in."

"Excellent," Deidre said. She held up a tablet and a charger. "Outlet?"

Minjung showed her an outlet on the wall near the grand piano, well within reach of the charging cord.

"Cool," Mistress Deidre said. "Oh, and Becky here is a member of our kinky church, btw, so no worries there." She winked at Minjung and gestured to Minjung's form-fitting, very kinky ensemble.

"Good to know, Ma'am," Minjung said. She took three steps back and guided the kinky Becky to the butler's pantry behind the kitchen. Becky loved the space and, before Minjung was even out of the room, began a series of odd noises. Those were presumably her vocal warmups.

Minjung checked in on Mistress Deidre, who said she was fine and then headed to the kitchen to get the light refreshments ready. She heard the east-side elevator whir and knew Madam was about to appear. Minjung's heart sped up. She would finally get to see what Madam was wearing to the masquerade ball. It had been some kind of closely guarded secret, so much so that Minjung was not allowed to help her Domme get dressed or do her hair.

When the elevator doors opened, Minjung forgot to breathe because standing right in front of her was the most majestic woman she had ever seen.

"Madam," Minjung gushed. "You look incredible." The deep red floor-length A-line dress had a wrap-around mid-section that suited Madam's buxom figure nicely. The long pleats of the bottom half nearly hit the floor but were the perfect height over Madam's low heels.

Madam Rowena simply smiled, crooked her finger, and bent it in a come-hither motion. "Zip me." She turned around, and with shaky hands, Minjung slowly zipped the back of the deep red dress that was an exact match to her own ensemble. Minjung admired the construction of the garment. Madam always said that her ample bosom was difficult to manage in formal clothing, but the thick straps held Madam up elegantly.

Once zipped, Madam waved her fingers and said, "Carry on." She walked toward the great room where Mistress Deidre was tinkering on the piano. Minjung watched the dress move exquisitely away from her.

"Wow," Minjung said to the magnificence that had just left. "No wonder she kept that a secret."

Chapter 17

Rowena

Surrounded by her closest friends, Rowena should not have been this nervous. The drinks and light refreshments Minjung had prepared were going over very well. Ashley was especially over the moon because Minjung had baked some pizza rolls for her. Rowena stood off to one side of the great room, taking in the happy chattering of her guests, all while trying to keep her heart from racing.

Earlier that week, Rowena had taken charge of the Christmas decorations, although she'd done more directing than actual decorating. Minjung and Ashley were willing participants and seemed to enjoy wrapping the lighted garland around the stair rails and setting up the two-story-high Christmas tree. The white tree now stood tall in the corner, basically anchoring the great room. Minjung reassured Rowena that she and Ashley could handle the overlarge tree and that calling in the maintenance crew for help was simply not necessary. And she'd been right. Although the tree looked the same as any other year with its white garland, white lights, and white ornaments, it felt different this year. Maybe because the women putting up the tree treated it like a privilege, not a chore, and they seemed to infuse love, devotion, and dedication into the task. Rowena wasn't sure if that was the reason, but all the decorations in the house seemed that way. Of course, when Minjung suggested hanging gauche red stockings off her precious walnut fireplace mantle, Rowena put her foot down. None of those bourgeois trinkets would ever grace her house, thank you.

The holiday decorations definitely set the stage, and Deidre, playing soft background music on the piano, completed the scene. Her friends were dressed for the holiday masquerade ball they would all attend later. Hayley was quite the sexy Mrs. Claus with her two submissive elves at her feet. Victoria wore gray but managed to pull it off like she pulled off anything she wore. Today, she was decked out in suspendered slacks with a charcoal button-down shirt. There wasn't a holiday theme in sight for Victoria, but Rowena knew her friend did things her own way. The odd thing was that Victoria had no submissive with her. Not that Rowena was worried; she'd bet cash money that Victoria would not be going home alone to her fancy new apartment on the hill overlooking downtown Denton Heights.

Seamus and his boys were there, four in all. How he had the stamina for that many was beyond her. Her gaze finally settled on her own submissive—the beautiful woman in the dress that was designed to match her own. Minjung's spaghetti strap lace romper had been modified to look less lingerie and more like her own dress with pleats and a wrap-around waist. Even the long waterfall earrings Minjung wore matched Rowena's. There would be no mistaking who Minjung belonged to at that masquerade ball. Minjung's dress, if it could be called that, was designed to turn heads. More than once, Rowena caught Deidre looking Minjung over from head to toe.

Minjung must have sensed Rowena looking at her, because she turned around searching. Her face relaxed when she settled on Rowena. Minjung raised her eyebrows. At this point, eight months into their arrangement, they could communicate fairly well without words, and Rowena knew Minjung was asking if Rowena needed anything. Rowena shook her head. No, she didn't need anything at that moment. She simply smiled at her submissive and decided to do something about her nerves. She looked over at Becky who had been clearly waiting for the signal, because she stood up and headed toward the piano. Rowena moved so she was in Deidre's line of sight and nodded at her. Deidre artfully ended the piece she was playing and waited.

"If I can get your attention, please," Rowena said, standing in front of the piano. Victoria put two fingers in her mouth and whistled so loudly that most people covered their ears. "Umm," Rowena said to Victoria, "thank you?"

"You're very welcome," Victoria said with a cheeky smile.

If there hadn't been a room filled with guests, Rowena most certainly would have called Victoria a dumb-ass or some similar construct. Instead, she just shook her head as she laughed.

"We are in for a real treat," Rowena said to her guests. "Please find a comfortable seat. We're so fortunate to have Becky Whitehurst here this evening. She has graciously agreed to sing for us." Excited applause erupted, and it was just the response Rowena had hoped for.

Rowena looked over at two of Seamus's submissives and nodded. The young men hustled over to the piano and closed the lid gently. Rowena didn't want Becky's voice to get lost in the piano. She then put her hand out and moved off to the side, giving Becky the makeshift stage.

Becky's face was cherubic pink. She was in her early thirties, and according to her Domme was just a doll of a submissive. Becky giggled, most likely a nervous tic, and said, "A medley of Christmas songs to get us in the mood." She gestured to the tall white Christmas tree in the corner of the great room.

Becky nodded to Deidre, who began a well-known peppy Christmas song. Becky's voice was heavenly, but Rowena knew the soprano could belt much bigger than that. The song morphed into another, and then, with the third, Becky gestured for people to sing along with her. Rowena was positively delighted when most of her guests joined in. Even Seamus sang in his gruff way, which greatly delighted his new *little*, whose name Rowena simply could not remember at the moment. Right. That was her own nerves taking over. She took a calming breath and focused on relaxing her shoulders on the exhale.

Enthusiastic applause accompanied Becky's last note. Deidre beamed from her seat at the piano as Becky bowed her thanks to the guests.

"Oh, but there's more," Becky said. "If we cheer her on, perhaps our wonderful hostess will join me up here."

Out of the corner of her eye, Rowena saw Minjung's head swivel in surprise. The happy encouragement from her guests helped settle Rowena's core. Of course, Becky's request had not been a surprise because she and Rowena had been practicing with Deidre since Thanksgiving. And to her knowledge, no one knew. Not even Minjung.

"Fine, fine," Rowena said as if giving in. Truth be told, right before the party, she'd snuck down to the soundproof playroom to do her vocal warmups. "If I must."

"Yes!" Hayley pumped a fist in the air. Even she hadn't known about this surprise.

Rowena stood at the piano next to Becky, took another breath, and nodded to Deidre. The opening bars of *O Holy Night* filled the house. Rowena blocked out her guests to calm her nerves and sang the harmonies against Becky's melody. By the time the song was finished, Rowena had relaxed enough to enjoy the music they were making. Enthusiastic applause filled the great room, but Deidre didn't stop playing. Soon enough, Rowena's friends cheered when the *Carol of the Bells* began. This was a wonderful song to sing. Becky and Rowena took turns singing the main melody and the backup vocals.

When the song finally finished, Rowena grinned at Becky and then Deidre. They were pulling off this surprise like nobody's business.

"One more duet," Becky said to the crowd. It always blew Rowena's mind when submissives like Becky took the helm and led convincingly and with confidence. She'd seen Minjung do it, too, with the cleaning and maintenance staffs and, to a lesser extent, with Ashley.

"Yes, yes, yes, yes, yes," Seamus's *little* chanted.

"I guess we have to now, don't we?" Becky said to Rowena as she gestured to Seamus's *little*.

"I suppose we do."

Becky's beautiful soprano began the duet. Rowena's mezzo-soprano accompanied her soon after. Rowena chanced a glance at Minjung but had to look away quickly. Minjung's hand was splayed across her chest. She was obviously moved by the song selection. Rowena thought she'd even caught a glimmer of tears.

Rowena let herself get lost in the *Duo de Fleurs* piece, admiring the smooth blending of their voices. She had to concentrate because she was so very rusty on the French words, but she managed well enough. When the song finally slowed, and then they finished, the room was silent until Seamus stood up and started a slow clap. Rowena put a hand to her chest as the other guests joined in. She looked over at Minjung and was surprised to see Hayley's arms wrapped around her submissive as if holding her up.

Rowena must have had a questioning look on her face because Hayley simply nodded in a manner that conveyed that all was well with Minjung. Rowena nodded her thanks to Hayley and then turned her attention to her guests.

Becky took the helm again. "Folks, I think if we're clever, we might be able to get our hostess to grace us with one more."

"Yeah," Seamus's *little* shouted.

"What he said," Seamus quipped, making everyone, including Rowena, laugh.

"Okay," Rowena said. "But just one because we'll have to wrap things up and head over to the venue for the ball." She turned her body to face Becky and said, "Isn't she wonderful? We've been so lucky to have you, Becky." Rowena clapped, and her guests followed suit.

Rowena took a cleansing breath, relaxed both shoulders, and nodded at Deidre who played the opening notes to *Ave Maria*.

"Jesus, Rowena," Victoria said, sitting down hard on her chair. She wiped at her eyes. "You're killing me," she murmured to no one in particular.

Rowena would have smiled, but she had a moving song to sing. Regardless, her chest filled with love and thanks for her encouraging friends. Once the song was finished, Rowena said, "Thank you for your generous applause. This has been such a fun evening for me." She called Becky back up to stand next to her and thanked her and Deidre publicly to much applause.

"And now I'm thinking we'd better wrap up and head out." Rowena looked at Seamus and said, "We can't let the master of ceremonies be late to his own ball."

Seamus laughed and said, "We all know this is Matilda's grand affair, and I'm mere window dressing."

Everyone laughed, but they also stood up to give their thanks to Rowena for hosting. Once the last guest had left, Rowena sat down in the high wingback chair she normally sat in and let herself come down off her high. She heard the shuffle of Minjung's slippered feet and looked up.

"Madam, you look like a queen sitting on your throne." Minjung gathered up the last of the refreshments and started heading back to the kitchen.

"Did you like it?"

"Oh, yes, Madam," Minjung said, spinning around so fast it startled Rowena. "You have a wonderful voice. So soothing and pleasant. That was such an incredible surprise."

"That's where I've been going all these weeks. To Becky's classroom at Blackwell College in Cincinnati."

"How nice," Minjung said. "You've gotten back into singing. I'm so happy for you, Madam."

"It's been...wonderful," Rowena said and sighed. "Give me about five more minutes on my throne here," she chuckled at the thought, "and then I'll freshen up so we can go. Sound good?"

"I'll be ready, Madam."

Minjung turned on her heels and headed back toward the kitchen. After five minutes or so, she let out a happy sigh and headed for the first-floor restroom. When she stepped out, she noticed Minjung in the kitchen writing in their shared communication journal. It was probably something mundane about next week's menus or something similar. Either way, Rowena made a mental note to read it when they got home.

~~~

Minjung sat on the low stool they'd brought to the ball for her to sit on. Rowena knew Matilda would approve because, like Rowena, Matilda was old school when it came to D/s relationships. The dinner had been palatable, and Rowena now sat stirring her coffee at the table she shared with Hayley, her two subs, and Victoria. Victoria, however, barely graced them with her presence, obviously on the prowl. She was now, however, currently dancing to that silly YMCA song with Shasti's new *little*, Madison. As far as Rowena was concerned, the jury was still out on the existence of *littles*, but she was softening a bit toward them, having witnessed Madison's endearing antics when she'd pulled Victoria away from a particularly flirty prospective submissive.

Once the too-loud song was finished, another one came on and Madison turned her sights on Billy, Seamus's *little*, and was teaching him some weird dance. His name had come to her once they got to the ballroom of the old hotel on the outskirts of town.

"What in the world are they doing?" Rowena asked no one in particular.

Minjung answered, "It's called *The Floss*, Madam."

Rowena wasn't sure what to make of it. She looked over at Madison's Domme, Shasti, who had turned her chair all the way around so she could watch her submissive's antics. She seemed pleased by the silliness, but Rowena had to sigh. Submissives weren't what they used to be. Her own was sitting dutifully at her feet. If Minjung didn't have knee issues, she would be sitting on the floor.

A loud voice pulled Rowena's attention in the other direction.

"She's using you," Matilda said to her grandniece Rikki Carmichael, the owner of the local coffee shop. "Be a strong Domme and forbid her from doing that." Matilda was much shorter than her niece but was still imposing. Her beehive hairdo stood tall, a Josef creation, no doubt, and her posture exuded confidence and power, even with the cane. She was in her late seventies, maybe early eighties, but she could still command a room like she had done as Mistress of Ceremonies that evening. And currently she was trying to command her niece.

"She's just volunteering for Dominique's flogging demonstration, Aunt Tilda," Rikki said quietly, but anyone who was watching could see how stiffly Rikki held herself.

"Eileen's looking for her next best fix, Rikki," Matilda warned. "She's using you. And I won't stand for it any longer." Neither woman said a word until Matilda added, "Did she even ask you for permission?"

"No," Rikki said. "But I would have given it. She's helping out, and I don't want to hear any more about it." And with that declaration, Rikki stood to her full height and walked away toward the St. Andrew's cross in the demonstration area.

Matilda made a beeline for Rowena's table. Not many people had heard their tiff because they had been off to the side of the ballroom, but Rowena's table had heard every angry word.

"All of you," Matilda said, "leave us." She waved her hand at Hayley and her subs and at Minjung. Clearly, she wanted Rowena to stay.

Minjung looked up and Rowena nodded that she should do as Matilda asked. Minjung stood, took three steps back, and then turned to join Hayley's group as they headed toward the demonstrations.

Matilda sat down hard in Victoria's unused seat. "I need you to promise me something," Matilda said. "You must make her understand that she is the heir-apparent to our little community." Her gaze shifted toward Rikki, who was watching her submissive Eileen getting primed for a flogging by Dominique, the local dungeon mistress.

"What do you mean?" Rowena wanted to help but wasn't quite sure how.

"People already look up to her," Matilda said and then joked, "And not because she's tall. She doesn't see how much of a role model she is. She doesn't know that the members of our unique community already see her as their de facto leader. Oh, they still give me that honor, but let's get real for a moment." She cleared her throat, but that turned into a coughing fit. Her alpha submissive, Josef, was there in an instant with a bottle of water. She drank some, and that seemed to help.

"Are you okay, Matilda?" Rowena asked softly.

"Yes, yes," she said and gave the sit signal to her submissive. He sank to the floor and sat cross-legged. She patted his head for a moment. "He's so good to me."

Rowena smiled at the tenderness.

"I need you to support her, Rowena," Matilda continued. "She won't want to lead, but someone must. Our way of life might be in jeopardy if some of these new-age folks grab the reins. Rikki must lead. She has it in her. She already shows her leadership at that coffee shop of hers. She just needs to understand the crossover."

"I'll do what I can, Matilda," Rowena said. A small part of her was hurt that Matilda hadn't recognized Rowena's own leadership potential and asked her to participate in running the community. But then again, Rowena wasn't sure she wanted all that responsibility. But if she could support a qualified leader, she could certainly get on board with that. "You know I'll do whatever it takes to keep our community safe and protected."

"I know you will, darlin'," Matilda said and patted Rowena's hand twice. "Now, about this submissive of yours. We have a problem. Actually, *you* have the problem."

"What do you mean?"

"She's succumbed to one of the many pitfalls of submissives. It's quite common these days, I'm afraid."

Rowena frantically scanned Minjung's behaviors and couldn't find a single fault. Her submission was exemplary. Leave it to Matilda to find something.

"She's in love with you, Rowena. And once they fall in love like that, it ruins the entire dynamic."

Rowena was at a loss for words. When they'd first arrived at the ball, Hayley told her how nice it was to see Minjung's strong devotion. Rowena had agreed with her friend because Minjung was appreciative of and grateful for

Rowena's care and attention. That was all. But love? That couldn't be accurate.

"I see you didn't know," Matilda said with a laugh. She then patted Josef on the head and said, "Take me home." And with that, Matilda left the ball without saying goodbye to anyone.

Perplexed, Rowena murmured to herself once she was alone, "In love? With *me*?"

Chapter 18

Minjung

It was an unseasonably warm day in mid-April as Ohio tried to shake off the last dregs of winter and slide into spring. Ashley pulled the town car into a parking spot at the Korean grocery store on the outskirts of Cincinnati. "Can I come in with you?" she asked Minjung.

"Of course," Minjung said as she waited for Ashley to open the passenger door and help her out. She had no idea why she was being given the princess treatment, but apparently, Madam wanted this for her, so Minjung had no choice but to go along with it. Madam also insisted that she wear the wool-blend Ralph Lauren wrap coat for her errands. She'd given Minjung the coat the night before, but it really was overkill in the warm afternoon. She kept in on, though. Her Madam wanted her to.

"I just need to get a few things," Minjung said. "We've been gone so long already; I need to get back to Madam." Minjung was still perplexed as to why Madam had asked Ashley to drive her as she ran errands that Friday afternoon. She scoffed quietly. Maybe Madam believed the old stereotype that Asians were bad drivers. But Madam Rowena knew that wasn't true. She'd given over the driving detail to Minjung for about four months now, ever since the masquerade ball.

"You're making Mistress Rowena a Korean meal?" Ashley held the door open for Minjung. It was funny how Ashley had dressed to the nines in a black suit, white shirt, and black chauffeur's hat.

"Yes," Minjung said. "I suggested a menu change last week and offered to make *Beef Bulgogi* and *Kimchi Fried Rice*." Minjung laughed. "It took some convincing, but she finally agreed. And," Minjung poked Ashley in the arm, "she said that if the meal passes her inspection, maybe we'll have Mistress Hayley and her subs over next time."

"Ooh, goody," Ashley gushed and clapped her hands several times. "Wow. This place is so cool. I'm going to look around. I'll let you do your thing and find you at some point. Okay?"

"Sounds fine." Minjung headed for the produce section to look for onions, garlic, Korean cabbage, and a host of other things. After the produce section, which would fill most of her basket, she'd move on to meats.

"Holy crap," Minjung heard Ashley gush. "Look at all this Korean candy. Gettin' some."

Minjung smiled at her young friend's antics. Because Madam Rowena and Ashley's mistress were besties, that threw Minjung and Ashley together often. That was okay. Ashley was youthful and full of fun.

Again, Minjung wondered why her Madam sent Ashley to drive her. Although she'd never driven Madam's two-door Mercedes sports car, she'd driven the Lexus many times to run errands. She'd even driven them to Mistress Matilda's funeral in February. Mistress Matilda had apparently had a stroke. The church service had been on Valentine's Day, of all days. But everyone thought that was fitting for Queen Mistress Matilda. Madam Rowena had gone through a rough mourning period and didn't leave her rooms on the third floor for several days. Minjung did what she could to simply be available for whatever Madam needed, like bringing her meals, which she ate half-heartedly.

It had been a sad time for the entire Denton Heights BDSM community. The church had been packed for her funeral. Mistress Rikki had a stunned look about her that day, but Mistress Shasti stayed by her side. That was a good thing because after a short while, maybe a couple of weeks later, Mistress Rikki's submissive Eileen up and left. Took all her things "and then some," according to Madam Rowena. Maybe the woman realized the money chain was gone or something. At least, that's what Madam Rowena surmised to Mistress Hayley. Minjung knew nothing about their financial arrangements. The only thing she knew was that it wasn't any of her business.

Eileen's betrayal seemed to help their group wake up and get beyond the sadness and into remembering Mistress Matilda with fond stories. Apparently, Daddy Vic, which a lot of people were calling her now, had trained under Mistress Matilda and told story after funny story about learning how to flog, cane, and whip Mistress Matilda's very willing contract submissives.

Madam had Minjung drive her to the coffee shop several times in the days following the funeral. She even spent time with Mistress Rikki alone in the coffee shop's office. Minjung knew her Madam was there to console her bereaved friend, and it made Madam that much more endearing. In fact, today was the third anniversary of Rikki's Coffee Shop. Minjung had asked if there would be a celebration, but Madam said she hadn't heard of one. Minjung thought there should be, but here again, it was none of her business.

Minjung was so deep in thought that she barely registered that Ashley had asked her a question.

"Sorry?" Minjung said.

Ashley looked at her phone and said, "I asked if you were almost done."

"Oh, yes. Yes. Let me check my list." A quick perusal of her handheld basket against her digital list told her she needed to get one more crucial item. "Ssamjang paste," Minjung said and led the way to the aisle that held condiments. She opted for the mild since she didn't want to upset Madam's senses right off the bat.

Once she paid, Ashley held the door open for her again.

"You're treating me like a princess today," Minjung said.

Ashley just laughed, led the way to the car, and, after putting the groceries in the trunk, opened Minjung's passenger door for her.

Minjung got in, and once Ashley sat in the driver's seat, Minjung said, "Look at them in there." She gestured secretly to several of the employees gawking out the store's windows at them.

Ashley just laughed. "Apparently, you're some kind of big deal today." She put the car in reverse and said, "Let's get you home."

They chatted amicably on the way home, and when they reached the Denton Heights exit off the highway, Ashley said, "My mistress says you're a dancer. Ballet. Is that true?"

"I was. When I was a few years younger than you."

"Didn't Madam Rowena put a bar-thingy in her playroom for you? That's what Mistress said."

Minjung wasn't sure if Ashley had been eavesdropping on conversations she shouldn't have, but she wasn't Ashley's Domme, and as always, it wasn't her business to know.

"Yes, Madam Rowena had a ballet barre put in for me down in the playroom. Do you remember her Christmas party? The pre-ball party in December?"

"Yeah."

"Well, she'd already offered to put a barre in for me, but I originally said no. And then her singing inspired me so much that I thought maybe I'd take her up on her offer. I saw how fulfilled she seemed to be after reconnecting with her passion, and I thought maybe I could recapture that same feeling for myself."

"Aww," Ashley said. "That's so sweet."

"I was too shy to ask her outright, so right before we left for the ball, I got up the nerve to ask her in our communications notebook."

"And then she just had it installed." Ashley seemed impressed by that. "Will we ever see you dance?"

Minjung's eyes grew wide. Dance? In front of people? Those days were over. Her body couldn't take the difficult movements anymore. "I don't think so," Minjung said shyly.

"Maybe you could teach kids to dance or something."

"I have a job. I serve Madam Rowena. You know that."

"Yeah, I get it." Ashley put her signal on at Madam Rowena's driveway and said, "We're here."

"I can give you the gate code," Minjung said.

"Nope, I'm not supposed to have the new one. I get buzzed in like every other guest at Tate Manor."

"Tate *Manor*?" Minjung had never heard her Domme's home called that and started to laugh. The laugh died in her chest. Panic seized her as the front gates opened.

The entire front yard was filled with cars.

"Ashley, hurry." Minjung reached for the door handle. "I must have forgotten something."

Ashley grabbed her arm. "Wait until I get to the door."

Minjung whipped out her phone. There were no texts or phone calls from Madam. She checked the joint calendar. No events were scheduled for that day.

"Am I toast, Ashley?" Minjung said quietly. Her stomach was in knots.

"There's only one way to find out." Ashley pulled up to the front of the house and said, "Listen, I'll take care of the groceries and packages. You go in and find out what's going on. Okay?"

Minjung blew out a strangled sigh. She found herself nodding and then opened the car door. She saw the curtains next to the front door fall back as if someone had been watching.

Minjung walked up the steps to the front porch and, with her heart pounding, used her key to unlock the heavy door. She didn't hear any noise inside. Perhaps the guests were in the playroom downstairs. Minjung started to relax. Madam was probably having a demonstration day down there.

She was about to be relieved by this fantasy until she opened the door and saw dozens of people lining the hallway leading to the great room.

"What's going on?" Minjung's heart was pounding in her ears.

She didn't see her Domme anywhere, and no one spoke. No one answered her question. She tried to bide time by taking off her new coat and hanging it by the front door with the dozens of guest coats already hanging there. She took one step backward toward the door, ready to flee, when a hand slid into one of hers. She turned. It was young Madison. Madison was smiling. Another hand slid into her free one. She turned. It was Billy. The two *littles* tugged on her arms and were now leading her through the rows of people she recognized from the community. Seamus and his subs smiled at her as she went by, but no one spoke. She heard shuffling behind her and realized that the people were now following her.

She stopped walking, closed her eyes, took a cleansing breath, and then let the *littles* lead her on. There she was, right there on her throne—Madam Rowena.

"What's happening, Madam? I'm frightened."

Madam Rowena stood up and gestured to her wingback throne. The *littles* led Minjung toward the chair, but she resisted. "Madam?"

Madam Rowena gestured to the chair again as the *littles* tugged hard on Minjung's arms. Minjung complied and sat. Her flight mode was dialed way up, and she looked around at all the faces. Mistress Rikki was smiling, and so was Mistress Shasti, who made a calming gesture with her hands and mouthed, "It's okay. You're okay."

Mistress Victoria walked over with Mistress Hayley by her side. They helped Madam Rowena sit down on Minjung's low stool.

"No, Madam, please," Minjung said, standing up. She heard the confused desperation in her voice. "I should be there."

Madam Rowena gestured once more to the wingback chair.

Minjung hesitated and then did as her Domme commanded.

"Minjung," Madam Rowena said in a clear, strong voice. "It's been one entire year since we signed that first contract with each other."

Minjung nodded. Was she being released? In front of all these people? She held her breath.

"I sit below you now as a symbol of my commitment to you. You have taken care of me, my household, and our community in ways that are both easy and difficult to express. I want to honor your obvious dedication to me by making a formal commitment to you in front of our friends."

Madam turned, and that's when Minjung saw the collar sitting on a pillow held by Madison. Madam took the collar and turned back toward Minjung. "If you accept this collar from me today, it will mean that I will do my utmost to see that you thrive and grow and explore your every desire. I will keep you safe and protect you. We've spent an entire year gaining and earning each other's trust and respect, and I want you to know that I completely understand the great responsibility I will be taking on as your Domme, the leash holder to your collar."

Minjung's heart was racing, but not out of fright anymore. Madam was collaring her. Here. Today. Now. She splayed a hand over her chest. She never felt so overdressed in her life.

"Minjung, here in front of all these friends and chosen family, do you accept my collar and acknowledge that you are mine? My sole submissive. And that I am yours? Your sole Dominant."

Madam Rowena stopped talking and held the collar up toward Minjung.

"Yes, Madam," Minjung said and slid out of the chair and onto her knees. Madam's gently raised eyebrows caused Minjung to slide lower to get the weight off her knees. Madam was always looking out for her. "Yes, Madam, I'm yours." Emotion closed her throat, so she mouthed the words, "Thank you, Madam."

Madam smiled, showed Minjung the date stamped on the underside of the thin leather collar, and then slid it around Minjung's neck and buckled it closed. Madam Rowena leaned forward and kissed Minjung on the crown of her head. Cheers and applause rang out around them.

Minjung practically melted and slid lower to rest her forehead on one of

Madam's shoes. She remained in her pose of prostration while Madam's guests continued to clap. Madam leaned down and pulled Minjung up.

"Thank you, Minjung. You've made me very happy." Madam's smile was so genuine that Minjung couldn't help returning it.

"I wasn't expecting this, Madam," Minjung said. "I'm floored."

"Quite literally," Madam said with a chuckle. "Now, a lot of people would like to congratulate you, so be a good hostess, not a servant, and let it happen. Let me repeat. You are *not* to serve anyone today. You are *not* to fetch anyone anything. Seamus's subs and Ashley are in that role today."

"That will be difficult, Madam."

"I know, but after you graciously receive gifts and then have something to eat, you're going to sit by my side and be an object."

Those words were a balm to Minjung's soul. "Nude, Madam?"

"Oh, yes."

"Thank you, Madam. I'm so very lucky to have you."

Madam Rowena stroked Minjung's blushing cheek and said, "I'm the one who got lucky. We'll talk more about your contract later. I'm renewing it if you haven't figured that out. Renewing it with an open ending."

Madam Rowena looked up. "Uh oh, looks like the line has begun. DeShawn," she called to Seamus's tall sub with amazingly sculpted facial hair, "please help me up."

He nodded and boosted her up from the low stool like it was nothing. His muscular frame clearly had something to do with it.

"Thank you," Rowena said. "Please go help Ashley. She's running the show this afternoon."

"Yes, Ma'am," he said and took his leave.

"You," Madam said to Minjung, who still sat on the floor, "are here." She pointed to the wingback chair, or the throne, as Minjung liked to think of it.

Minjung reached up and touched the new leather collar. "Might I be on my wheeled kneeler, Madam?" Minjung asked meekly, knowing full well she would be denied.

"No. And do not make me ask you to get in that chair again."

Minjung smiled. Madam's clear dominance had hit her in the core again. Once seated, Mistress Shasti and her *little* approached.

Mistress Shasti said to Madison, "Go on. You can ask her."

Madison leaned closer to Madam Rowena and asked, "May I speak to your slave, Ma'am? And give her this gift?" She held up a medium-sized box wrapped in solid green paper.

Madam Rowena's eyes grew big, but she fought back whatever thoughts she was having, and her face returned to neutral.

"Of course you can, sweetie," Madam said. "But she's not a slave. She's a contracted submissive. Like the ones Mistress Matilda had. She has free will and can leave or call red at any time."

"Oh," Madison said and took a deep breath. "I call red sometimes. Like when Mistress has me tied up too long or something."

Mistress Shasti took a deep breath as if her *little* tried her patience at every turn. It wasn't true, though. The two of them were an amazing match, and both seemed fulfilled.

Madison turned toward Minjung, who wasn't sure what to expect from the twenty-three-year-old. Madison handed Minjung the box and said, "I asked Mistress to get green paper because green means go, and you got collared today, and that means you and your Mistress can be super happy and go go go into the future together."

Minjung suppressed a chuckle. The young woman had said all of that with one breath. How can one not be endeared by this young one, Minjung wondered. Even Madam Rowena was smiling with her whole face, even her eyes.

"It's a set of—" Madison started to say but stopped when Mistress Shasti's hand went over her mouth.

"Let her open it first," Mistress Shasti scolded and removed her hand.

"Oh, sorry," she said behind her Mistress's hand.

Minjung wanted to take the paper off carefully, but a long line had formed behind Madison and her Mistress, so Minjung tore off the paper in short, quick spurts, making Madison laugh. When she opened the box, she pulled out a set of expensive-looking knee pads.

"Mistress told me you have some knee problems and can't kneel that well, so I told her we needed to get you knee pads for when your Mistress wants you between her legs to make her cum."

Minjung almost choked at the young woman's bluntness.

Madison continued. "They're made with this cool space-age foam, and there's cooling gel inside, too, which is good, especially if you have to be down there forever like I do sometimes with my own Mistress."

Minjung pressed her lips together and desperately tried not to burst out laughing. Madison was being sincere. It was clear that she felt comfortable in their community and didn't feel the need to hide behind social expectations.

"And look," Madison said, pointing to the knee pads. "They have neoprene thigh straps, so they won't fall off in the heat of the moment when she grabs your head and rides you like a bucking bronco."

"This is a very thoughtful gift, young Madison," Minjung said. "You took a lot of care to find something useful that I would like."

"You like them?" Madison puffed up so comically that Minjung reached out for a hug.

Madison glanced over nervously at Madam Rowena, who nodded her okay.

Madison flew into Minjung's arms and said, "I'm glad you're in our community now. It's nice having someone else who looks like me."

Mistress Shasti made a small noise of concern behind Madison.

"Same," Minjung said. And as she said the word, she realized it was true. It had been comforting to meet another Korean member of the Denton Heights BDSM community. She wasn't sure why, but it made her feel less of a novelty.

Madison stood back up and said, "Welcome to the community." She swiveled so quickly on her feet it was as if she was doing a *fouetté* in sneakers. She glanced back over her shoulder and asked, "Why aren't you naked?"

The entire great room, filled with people, chuckled at her antics, but Mistress Shasti ushered her away with a scolding.

Minjung knew some of the guests who came up to greet her and give her gifts and well wishes, but not all. Somewhere toward the end of that first hour, the gift giving finally ended, and Madam allowed her a short break to use the restroom and get something to eat. As Minjung filled her plate with the obviously catered food, Ashley sidled up to her with a bottle of water and a grin.

"You knew, didn't you?" Minjung accused playfully. She put a forkful of rice and beans in her mouth. She was ravenous. She hadn't realized.

"I did," Ashley said with a grimace. "My mistress said I was key to them pulling this off. Don't be mad."

Minjung laughed. "I'm not mad. Not at all. This whole event is amazing." She leaned closer. "I'm still in shock, actually." She balanced her plate, fork, and water bottle in one hand and reached up to touch her new collar with the other.

"Getting collared is the best," Ashley agreed. She touched her own silk collar and melted. "I love her so much. And Terrence, too. They treat me so well and let me have my own job."

"The driving."

"Yeah."

Minjung took a bite of the spicy *carne asada* on her plate. Apparently, Madam had a hankering for Mexican food. Not that Minjung was complaining. "Does being collared make you feel more settled?" she asked Ashley.

"Yes. It makes me feel like I'm home." Ashley's cheeks turned red. "They're just what I'd been searching for."

Minjung looked up to try and spot her Domme. She was talking with Mistress Rikki. It seemed like a serious conversation, so Minjung felt like she had a few more minutes to eat before going back to her Madam's side.

"Why are people giving me gifts? I've heard of a Dominant giving a collar or jewelry, but not other people."

Ashely laughed. "That's what makes this community so neat. Us subs all remember getting collared and how special we felt. And the Dominants remember the feeling of offering the collar. I think it makes them feel protective or something. I'm not sure, but it's a lot of fun."

Minjung ate a few more bites.

"You went to Madison's collaring, right?" Ashley asked.

Minjung nodded. "She was so cute. She had no idea what was going on."

"That's part of the fun. And you got a lot of cool gifts. Electric nipple clips, anal plugs, of course. Mistress loves putting those light-up ones in me. And, I mean, Daddy Vic always gives huge dildoes named Rocky or The Terminator or something."

"That thing was huge." Minjung's eyes were wide. "I hope Madam doesn't ever want to use that thing on me."

Ashley laughed, but then her face grew serious, and her eyes widened. "I think you're being summoned," she said.

Minjung looked where Ashley had pointed with her chin. Minjung handed Ashley her mostly eaten plate of food and the water bottle and excused herself.

"Yes, Madam?"

"It's time."

"Oh, thank you, Madam." Minjung heard the relief in her voice and knew that Madam did as well because she chuckled quietly.

"I'll help you prepare."

Madam walked toward her office, followed dutifully by Minjung. Less than a minute later, they walked back into the party, but this time, Minjung was nude, and Madam Rowena's leash was attached to Minjung's new collar.

Madam led her to the low stool while she moved to sit on her usual throne. Things were back to normal, which made Minjung relax.

Mistress Rikki walked up and petted Minjung on the head. She said to Madam Rowena, "She's a good solid submissive." She then looked over Minjung as if prizing a show cow. "She'll bring you happiness."

Another line seemed to be forming. This was heaven. To be treated like an object and know that her Domme saw her as a *valuable* one hit Minjung hard. Arousal hit her lower region.

Deidre, the pianist, stepped up next, grabbed Minjung by the chin, and lifted gently. Her hand then moved lower to fondle one breast and then the other. "Rowena," Deidre said, "you are a lucky woman, but you're making me a sad one. Everyone knows you don't keep subs very long. There were a lot of us waiting for this one to be released." She tweaked one of Minjung's nipples and added, "I was going to snap her up so fast all our heads would spin." She reached over and tweaked the other nipple.

"Thank you for your candidness, Deidre," Madam said evenly. Minjung detected a hint of protectiveness in her Domme's tone.

Mistress Deidre simply nodded and moved on.

On and on the line went. No one touched her too close to her actual center, which was dripping wet and aching with need. It was funny that Mistress Shasti simply touched Minjung's shoulder and nowhere else. Daddy Vic patted her twice on the head as if she were a pet. And that was definitely okay. Seamus didn't touch her at all, and for that, Minjung was grateful. She relaxed visibly after he gave Madam Rowena his congratulations.

"You're okay," Madam said low to her as Mistress Hayley approached.

"I'm so happy you finally put a collar on this gem, Rowena." Mistress Hayley leaned down and looked Minjung in the eye. "You're a gorgeous creature, Minjung. Such a boon for your Domme. And I know you two will not only give each other amazing pleasure, but you'll support each other's growth and be each other's champions." She stroked Minjung's cheek and smiled.

Minjung couldn't help the grateful smile creeping up her face.

"There she is," Mistress Hayley said softly. "You're a treasure." She stood up and hugged Madam Rowena, then moved away, leaving Minjung alone with her Domme.

Madam Rowena leaned toward Minjung and whispered. "I think we'll try out some of your new gifts this evening. What do you think?"

Arousal sparked Minjung's core. "Yes, please." She remembered herself and said more clearly, "Yes, Madam."

Madam wasn't offended by the slip in protocol. In fact, she seemed amused.

It seemed an interminably long time before guests started leaving. The sounds of Ashley, DeShawn, and Vikram cleaning up and putting food away in her kitchen were excruciating. The kitchen was her domain, and they were in there. She took a deep breath and let it out slowly. She'd fix it in the morning. She reminded herself that they were helping out of love for her and Madam.

Minjung looked up at her Domme, knowing that the love she felt could be seen by any and all who looked at her. Well, not all. The one person she desperately needed to notice didn't.

Chapter 19

Rowena

Rowena took a moment to look around before lifting the box. It was mid-August, and Rikki had put out the call for help moving her things from the house she'd inherited from her Aunt Matilda. She had to get her personal items out so the estate sale company could come in and organize the rest. Rowena had no idea there was an apartment over the coffee shop, but apparently, that's where Rikki was moving to. There had been so many memories made in this house, Rowena thought nostalgically. She'd learned so much watching Matilda interact not only with her subs but with the other members of their unique community. Matilda's stoic strength and forthright manner were unparalleled.

"Always ask, then listen," Matilda told Rowena once. "Never assume." And that's exactly what she'd been doing in the year and four months since Minjung had been with her.

Matilda had been very giving, especially to new Dominants coming up the pipeline. Rowena had been one of those Dominants all those years ago. Rowena vowed to continue Matilda's example and help new Dommes like the one currently taking the box from Rikki. "Go do your final walk-through," the tall woman named Jaleesa said to Rikki. "The rest of us will be in the driveway getting your stuff organized in the vehicles. Take your time in here."

"Thanks," Rikki said, her voice high and tight. She was obviously emotional. She patted Jaleesa's arm once. "I think I will." She headed up the stairs to the bedrooms. One of them had been hers ever since she'd moved in with her aunt over ten years ago. Her now-ex Eileen had apparently been the only one of Rikki's submissives to have lived with her, but she was gone, too. Poor Rikki. She'd not only lost her beloved aunt, but she'd lost a submissive, too. She'd even lost Josef, Matilda's loving companion. Although Rikki had asked him to stay, he said he couldn't remain in that house with so many memories and reminders. According to Rikki, he was happily living in a retirement community in Florida somewhere. Rowena knew some financial issues had crept up for Rikki, and that was one reason for her move, but maybe, like Josef, she was also trying to escape the memories and get a fresh start.

"You okay?"

Rowena came back to the present. Jaleesa's smile was one of concern. She seemed to be quite attuned to those around her and understood that Rikki wasn't the only one grieving the loss of the matriarch who had once lived there.

Rowena sighed. "Matilda was an amazing woman. I'm sorry you and your family didn't get to meet her."

Jaleesa said nothing. She only smiled and nodded knowingly.

The woman's compassion moved Rowena. She'd only relocated to Denton Heights in June, two months prior, but she and her three female submissives seemed a natural part of their group already. Jaleesa often referred to her submissives as her family. It was endearing. Jaleesa was in her late thirties. Two of her subs were younger, but one was older. They all seemed very giving, and Rowena had been surprised when she received an invitation to their housewarming party. The party had been a great way to get to know Jaleesa and her subs.

"We'll give Rikki some space," Rowena said, picked up the small box, and headed out the front door that DeShawn held open for them. Once outside, DeShawn relieved Rowena of the box and headed to the rented truck.

Minjung was busy helping one of the other new Dommes, a woman named Marta, who was in her mid-thirties or so and had grown up in Denton Heights. She'd been in the life for years but had only recently found their community. She and her new sub, uncollared at this point, were helping out. This boggled Rowena's mind because they had known Rikki for less than two months.

"These are good people," Rowena murmured to herself.

Minjung looked up and smiled at her as if hearing her words. It was a smile of greeting but also a smile of concern. Clearly, collaring Minjung last April had been one of her better ideas. She smiled back to reassure her submissive that she was okay. Jaleesa meanwhile handed the box to Mark, one of Seamus's subs who was also an assistant manager at the coffee shop. Jaleesa then went over and kissed two of her submissives affectionately. Her third submissive walked over, but there was no kiss, just a quick squeeze of a forearm, which contained the message of affection. That was Jaleesa's family. Rowena looked back at her own submissive handing boxes up to Marta to pack in the bed of the woman's pickup truck.

Was Rowena Minjung's family now? Rowena thought this as she watched Minjung's graceful movements. Her submissive might be sore later from lifting all those boxes. Maybe a required bubble bath was in order. Hell, she would be sore, too. Maybe they could take a bath together in her spa tub. The Cardinals were on, so they could have dinner and watch the game after that. Minjung had become a true fan. Although it was August and there was plenty of season left, Minjung was holding out that the third-place Cards could rally and come back to win the division. And she just might be right. They had a good team, having made it to the playoffs last year as the wild-card pick in the National League, so hopefully, Minjung was right, and they could turn that ship around. The solidly in last-place local Cincinnati team had a lot of the people at Rikki's moving event grumbling when someone suggested they all go to a game sometime. Rowena tried not to let it be known in this group that she was a Cardinals fan because her team had just swept theirs in a three-game homestand in St. Louis. Minjung hadn't brought it up, either, not that Minjung spoke much at gatherings. Rowena preferred her not to, but it wasn't a hard rule.

The trucks and cars were all packed and ready to go, but Rikki still hadn't come back out of the house. It was clear that everyone was giving her space during this emotional time. The group gathered around Jaleesa's pickup truck and drank the bottled water that Shasti had so thoughtfully brought for everyone.

"You all missed a great masquerade ball in May," Shasti said to Jaleesa, Marta, and their subs. "Rikki took over as Matron of Ceremonies with Seamus as Patron."

"I'm sorry we missed it," Jaleesa said. Her subs seemed to understand that Jaleesa did the talking for them. That was interesting. Rowena still hadn't quite figured out what kind of Domme Jaleesa was, but she was getting the impression that she definitely ruled their roost.

"Was there dancing?" Marta's submissive Shanice asked. The two had recently found each other and had worked out a cute and loving Mommy

Domme/little girl relationship. The poor twenty-something Shanice had been in a bad car accident a few months before and was now in a wheelchair.

"There was a lot of dancing," Madison said and did a medley of funky dance moves ending in a pirouette. "Miss Minjung is a dancer, too, but she doesn't dance at the balls." Madison reached her hand out to Minjung, who, for some reason, took it. Madison pulled her away from the group and raised their linked hands, nudging Minjung to twirl, which she did, much to everyone's delight. Madison let go, and right there on the concrete driveway before everyone's eyes, Minjung kept moving and danced for them. She turned into the beautifully elegant ballet dancer that Rowena had only seen glimpses of.

Their group burst into applause just as Rikki was coming out the front door. "Did you miss me that much?" she quipped, making the group laugh.

"Miss Minjung was dancing," Shanice said. "Come watch, Miss Riri."

Minjung waved a hand, indicating that she didn't want to dance anymore. Her cheeks had turned crimson.

"Sorry I missed it," Rikki said as she came down the steps leading to the driveway.

"I wish I could dance like that," Shanice said.

A mortified hush fell over the group. Shanice would never be able to dance "like that." Rowena was astonished at what her submissive did next. Minjung moved to stand directly in front of Shanice. She elongated her spine and lifted her head. She motioned for Shanice to do the same. Minjung mimicked a string or rope coming from her head and pulled up on it. Shanice did the same, understanding that she must have good erect posture.

Minjung put her arms out in front of her like she was holding a beach ball. She waited patiently until Shanice copied her.

"First position," one of Jaleesa's subs said. Tina was her name, Rowena thought, but she wasn't a hundred percent sure.

Minjung could have spoken at any time but chose not to. She simply nodded at Tina and then opened up her arms out to both sides. She reached over and corrected Shanice's drooping elbows.

"Second position," Tina said quietly.

By this time, Madison had moved next to Shanice and was also doing the moves. Miraculously, the young woman was quiet.

"Third position," Tina said as Minjung moved one arm back in front but kept the other arm out to the side.

"That's a combo of the first and second positions," Madison said, breaking her silence.

Minjung nodded and Madison seemed so pleased that she ran around chanting, "Happy dance. Happy dance," until her Domme put a finger over her lips to hush her.

Madison stage-whispered to Shasti, "I bet fourth position is next."

Minjung nodded again and moved one arm up over her head as if she were about to pat herself on the head. The other arm stayed out to the side. Minjung reached over and adjusted Shanice and then Madison. She nodded, satisfied with her two pupils' progress. She mimicked the string coming out of her head, and both young women sat and stood taller, respectively.

Next, both arms went overhead in the classic ballet pose everyone knew, and Madison said, "Fifth position," at the same time Tina did.

Minjung then went through all the positions quickly. She had an exquisite way of moving. Rowena had teared up, but Shanice's Domme, Marta, was now out and out balling.

"Mama," Shanice said, "why are you crying?"

Marta took the tissue Shasti offered and then shrugged her shoulders.

"She's very sensitive," Shanice said to the group. "I'm okay, Mama."

"I'm okay, too," Marta said. She looked at Minjung and said, "Thank you."

Minjung nodded, her cheeks flaring bright red. Rowena's chest filled with pride at what her submissive had just done. She would be rewarded. That bubble bath was now officially on the schedule for that evening, but Rowena was also thinking about another reward, one that would take a while to set up. Her father had offered a cruise as a thank-you for turning the Cincinnati plant around. Tyttle Fyzzle was out now, available everywhere, and doing remarkably well. Minjung had been an integral part of that endeavor and would need to benefit from the reward. Rowena had a destination in mind but not the port from which they'd need to sail. That was going to take some research and planning before she mentioned anything to Minjung.

~~~

Three months had passed since the day they'd packed up Rikki and moved her into the second-floor apartment above the coffee shop. It was November. Where had the time gone? In the months that followed, Rowena found herself looking forward to meeting up with the women in their community for social events like the one scheduled for later that day. In a few hours, they were going to head over to Marta and Shanice's home to celebrate Shanice's twenty-sixth birthday.

She glanced over at Minjung, happily wrapping yet another present for Shanice. They didn't know what to get her, so they got her a variety of things. Rowena quickly discovered how much fun it was to shop for a young-at-heart person.

And, seriously, time really did seem to be flying. Guess she was having fun, as the saying went. She'd had Minjung for over a year and a half at that point. And the other mind-blowing thing? Six days ago, she turned forty years old. How did that happen? She tried not to get lost in her musings and refocused her attention on the computer screen in front of her. She was researching a company she was seriously considering investing in, but she couldn't focus.

Her birthday dinner a week ago had been wonderful. Although she had entered a new decade, she felt oddly at peace about it. Hayley and her crew were there along with Victoria. Minjung taught Ashley how to make her fabulous Korean *Bulgogi*, this time with pork and the *Kimchi* side dish. Apparently, Hayley decided to expand Ashley's jobs, which now required her to learn how to cook for their family. Minjung had genuinely and graciously offered to show her how to make the Korean meal. Rowena briefly considered inviting the new friends she'd made to her birthday dinner but realized that since her birthday fell on Halloween, the group was probably busy, especially the families with *littles*.

Rowena chuckled as she mumbled, "The ever-growing *little* population."

"Madam?" Minjung said peering over her shoulder without turning around.

The two of them had been simmering all morning, and Minjung certainly knew how to make Rowena's body respond. Like now. Minjung's form-fitting boy-shorts hugged her ass deliciously, and Rowena's predatory instincts threatened to take over. She scoffed. "Just muttering to myself. How's the wrapping going?"

"Great," Minjung said. "I hope she likes the tickets. Thank you for allowing this to happen. I think she'll find it uplifting."

"I wouldn't miss it," Rowena said and looked her submissive up and down lecherously. Lately, Rowena had taken to having Minjung dress provocatively instead of nude. The black lace bra pushed Minjung's breasts together and upward, creating an enticing pillow top. Rowena wasn't quite ready to ravish her submissive just yet but was delighted to see Minjung's cheeks turn pink as she took in Rowena's new bustier. Minjung had gotten it for her as a birthday present. It was clearly the gift that kept on giving. Rowena felt sexy in it, and Minjung apparently liked looking at her Domme in it. It was a win-win situation.

Without a word or gesture, Rowena turned back to her research, much to Minjung's obvious dismay. The soft moan of disappointment made Rowena smile, but she bit it back. The rewards would come soon enough.

Focusing on company assets and earnings was simply not keeping her focus. With a sigh, she allowed her mind to wander where it would, and it went to some deeply buried places. She'd never really had a friend group before. Hayley and Victoria were sort of her first foray into that kind of thing. Growing up in St. Louis as the daughter and heiress of Joseph and Carrie Tyttle of the Tyttle Foods dynasty was a lonely venture. True friends were difficult to come by. The ones she thought were friends only wanted what her wealthy family could give them. Others either left her alone or tried to knock her down off her high horse. Admittedly, she had grown up with servants and anything she wanted, but she wasn't arrogant or entitled. She didn't think so, anyway. So, having this growing group of friends was nothing short of amazing.

There was that one day in early September when they'd met for a Saturday brunch at Rocco's Diner, of all places, and they'd formed the Denton Heights Women's BDSM Collective. Rikki came up with the suggestion, and Rowena surreptitiously looked skyward, hoping Matilda saw how much Rikki had grown and eased into the natural leadership role. The collective was open to anyone who identified as a woman. Someone, it might have been Shanice or

Madison, helped the group understand that when they used the term 'woman,', it should mean 'woman-identified' and not 'biological female.' No, it was Dana, one of Jaleesa's younger submissives, who had suggested it. She was a cute young woman and very smart.

The other wonderful thing that came out of that gathering was the plan to meet informally on the first Saturday of every month. Unfortunately, someone also suggested they always meet at Rocco's, and the rest agreed, so Rowena went along with it. It would be a "join if you can, okay if you can't" venture. They'd have more formal meetings, of course, and had already had one at Jaleesa's home. It felt good to be included.

"Madam?" a cool voice said from across the room.

"Hmm?"

"Would you care to inspect?" Minjung gestured toward the wrapped presents stacked one on top of another on Minjung's desk.

"I'd be delighted." Rowena stood up, ignored the colorfully wrapped presents, and ran her hands over Minjung's tight lace bra. "Very nice." Then, in one swift maneuver, she pushed the presents aside and held Minjung face down on the desk. Minjung subtly opened her legs and received a swat on her behind.

"So eager. So readily available," Rowena murmured out loud. She sucked air through her teeth and let out a genuine moan of arousal.

Rowena slowly eased the boy-shorts off Minjung's body. "Always ready for me. Always available." Minjung was very wet, probably as aroused as Rowena was.

"Thirty total," Rowena said just before administering the first-hand swat on Minjung's now-bare ass. She divvied up the swats equally and was satisfied as the cheeks reddened up nicely. That and the fact that Minjung was squirming slightly told Rowena it was time. She tapped Minjung's inner thighs. This was the clear signal to open her legs.

Rowena ran her hands near her submissive's sex but didn't actually touch. Minjung grunted her disapproval of this oversight, making Rowena laugh at her sub's predicament. From her skirt pocket, she pulled out one of the anal plugs Minjung had gotten at her collaring seven months prior. She pulled out the small tube of lube she'd stashed in her pocket and lubed up the insertion spot.

Judging by Minjung's movements, it was clear that she was more than aroused. That's why Rowena carefully avoided any sensitive areas other than the one she was currently priming for the vibrating plug.

She slid the narrow tip past the strong ring of muscles and then pulled it out again. Minjung's head drooped.

"Madam, please," Minjung murmured softly.

Rowena said nothing. She inserted the head again but went a little deeper. She continued in this fashion until the plug was neatly seated inside her submissive.

"Stay," Rowena commanded her sub. She backed up a few steps and drank in the arousal coursing through her core. Seeing her submissive so obviously open and available to her was intoxicating. What was also intoxicating was knowing that Minjung felt safe and protected in Rowena's care. And that was what a D/s relationship was all about.

Rowena moved away to wash her hands in the small bar sink. Without turning around, she said, "Two things. One. You're way overdressed. Two. You'll need to be in the family room servicing me within the next five minutes." And with that, Rowena headed out the office door.

A nude Minjung arrived promptly three minutes later and settled into her wheeled kneeler at Rowena's command. Rowena opened up her wrap-around skirt and motioned for Minjung to service her needs. Rowena's head rolled back when Minjung's tongue hit her clit. Sometimes, she wanted her orgasm to build slowly, but not today. Today, she was ravenous. Simmering all morning had her at the boiling point. But first, she was going to make Minjung's job a little more interesting.

She reached for the remote on the arm of her recliner and pressed the vibrate button.

Minjung jumped when the plug sparked to life. She clearly hadn't expected that. Rowena grabbed her sub's head and smashed it back down to her center. One more press of the vibrator's button increased the intensity and caused an interesting side effect. Minjung's tongue, mouth, and fingers also increased in speed and intensity.

It was there. Right there. She pressed Minjung's head tighter and waited for the spark to ignite. That impossible moment of stillness as she rode the incredible wave before exploding into orgasm engulfed her, and then, when she couldn't hold onto it any longer, her entire body spasmed as she came. She flooded Minjung's chin and lips. She pushed away the head between her legs and flopped back, absolutely spent. She used her one working brain cell to find the remote and stop the vibrations. Everything was blessedly still. Her submissive knew not to speak or even move when Rowena was floating like this.

Rowena's soft moaning sighs accompanied every small aftershock. After a few more moments, she took a deep, wakening breath and sat up. She grabbed her submissive's wet chin and yanked her face up slightly. "I look good on you." She laughed and released the face. She twirled her finger, and Minjung knew what to do. She spun the wheeled kneeler around and leaned forward on the chest plate, her ass up.

Rowena reached into the toy box on the floor near her chair and pulled out a medium-sized dildo. This one was not one Minjung had gotten at the collaring but a rather run-of-the-mill dildo. It didn't vibrate or heat up or even have a clit attachment, but it would absolutely do the trick. Sometimes, the old-fashioned way was best.

"No need to check for readiness," Rowena quipped. Her submissive's arousal was clear and evident, slicking up her inner thighs.

Minjung's moan was shaky. It was shaky from anticipation, no doubt.

Rowena slid to the edge of her recliner and set both feet firmly on the floor on either side of Minjung's kneeler. With one hand, she eased the dildo into her submissive in slow increments until it bottomed out. "I bet you feel so full right now," Rowena said. "Ass filled? Check. Vagi filled? Check." She pulled the dildo out and then pumped it with a steady rhythm. Sometimes, it was easier this way since strap-ons could be a pain to get in and out of. She did like the power of pumping her hips, however. There was something dominating in that motion.

"Pain, Madam," Minjung burst out.

Rowena smiled. Minjung did like that pain-to-pleasure connection. Rowena made doubly sure both of her feet were firmly planted and then reached forward with her free hand. The other continued to pump the dildo in and out. She found the nipple her hand had been searching for, latched on, and twisted.

"Ahh," Minjung yelped in pain. "More, Madam. Please, please, please."

"Begging women are so sexy," Rowena said and tweaked the nipple again, holding it tightly for a long moment.

"Yes, yes, yes," Minjung screeched. She was about to cum.

Rowena sat back and swatted her submissive on the ass cheek. And again. It only took one more before her sub screeched out in ecstasy, her body writhing in orgasm. Rowena swatted the now-red ass one more time and waited.

Once Minjung's breathing became more even, Rowena said, "I enjoy using your body like this." She rubbed the ass cheek she'd reddened. It pleases me to give you pleasure."

"Same, Madam." Minjung took a few deep breaths, waited for the two objects to be removed from her body, and turned the wheeled kneeler around. She looked Rowena right in the eyes and repeated, "Same."

Rowena drank in her submissive's vulnerable but very clear message. Matilda had been right. Minjung did have deep feelings for her. Why hadn't Rowena seen it before now?

Chapter 20
Minjung

Minjung pulled the Lexus up to the curb in front of Mistress Marta and Shanice's home and turned off the engine.

"Do you have your coat closed, Madam? It's chilly out there."

"You fuss over me too much," Rowena said and opened the passenger door to get out.

Can't help it, Minjung thought. *It's my job*. She got out of the car and headed for the trunk. In the time between the sex they'd shared that afternoon and now, Minjung scolded herself over and over about showing her affections so openly. She knew Madam had seen the love in her face. Her Domme didn't see her the same way, and intellectually, Minjung knew she needed to stop having those kinds of feelings, but…

When her brain finally registered that Madam was lifting the case of Tyttle Fyzzle out of the trunk, she was knocked back into reality.

"Madam," Minjung scolded. "I'll come back for that."

"Nonsense," Madam Rowena said. "Ever since you've shown me the joys of going on daily walks, I feel better, have more energy, and just feel stronger, too."

"Could also be all those fruits and veggies you eat now, Madam," Minjung teased. Her grin made Madam smile even more.

"Could be, but don't get cocky about that. I get enough grief from Victoria now whenever she sees me eating something green that's not a gummy bear or pistachio ice cream."

Minjung chuckled and picked up the bundle of presents. The most important one was tucked in the front pocket of her dress slacks. Madam said it was a vanilla party, so they were both dressed modestly. Minjung wore no collar. Madam wore a soft cardigan sweater over a mock turtleneck. She said she wanted to wear layers in case the house was cold.

The door opened before they even got to it. Although they had already met, the woman reintroduced herself as Harriet and relieved Madam of the case of sparkling waters. Harriet directed Madam to one end of a new-looking couch and then showed Minjung where to put the presents.

"Wow," Minjung said at the stack of presents.

"We do love our *littles* around here," Harriet said. "Come into the kitchen and help me unload these waters?"

After receiving Madam's permission, Minjung followed the older woman.

Once in the kitchen, Harriet introduced herself as one of Jaleesa's three submissives. She was a service submissive and happy to see to Minjung and Madam Rowena's needs. "Miss Marta would like you to be a guest, Minjung. Not a servant." She cleared her throat and added, "Or a slave."

There was an awkward silence for a moment while Minjung weighed the options of explaining that she wasn't a slave. But she might have to mention that she was paid to work in Madam Rowena's home, but that would make her look like the sex worker she was trying not to be. The only thing she said was, "Thank you, Miss Harriet. I appreciate that. I'd best get—" She gestured over her shoulder awkwardly toward the living room.

Miss Harriet patted Minjung on the arm and nodded. She then turned to attend to something on the stove.

"Would you like something to drink, Madam?" Minjung asked.

"No, no," Madam Rowena said, patting a hassock pushed against the wall near her Domme. Apparently, her hosts thought that would be a fitting alternative to sitting on her low stool at the vanilla party. It was a thoughtful compromise.

Minjung sighed and looked down. Was that how they all saw her? As a slave? As a nothing and a nobody? At one point Minjung had even used that as a mantra. Maybe it was true. *You are nothing. You are nobody.* This she thought to herself twice in succession. Sadness washed over her. So many things felt right with Madam Rowena and their situation, but all this socializing only proved Minjung right. She *was* nothing. She *was* nobody. And they all knew it.

She closed her eyes and tried to find a good breathing rhythm that would keep her tears at bay. It wasn't working. She shifted her focus and listened to the party sounds to distract herself. Madison and Billy were in another room playing video games. Ahh, there was Shanice's voice. She was cheering them on. Mistress Jaleesa was having some kind of serious chat with DeShawn in low tones. It seemed private, so she shifted her focus to Mistress Shasti, who was talking excitedly about Madison's excellent SAT scores to Mistress Rikki. She was a proud Mommy Domme.

Minjung wondered if her father had ever been proud of her. She'd tried to meet his expectations but never seemed to be able to. And her mother? Had her mother ever stuck up for her? Had she been proud of Minjung's accomplishments as a dancer? Like when she got into that elite dance troupe right before the 'accident'? Did her mother even wonder where Minjung was after all these years?

Something reached in and twisted her heart to bits. She leaped up and said, "Excuse me," to her Domme and bolted for the bathroom. It was blessedly empty. Once inside, she turned on the fan to hide her sobs. It was a fantastically noisy fan, and she thanked the universe for that.

She knew she was living on borrowed time, and sure enough, someone knocked on the door. Minjung took a clear breath, hoping she would sound normal. "Almost done," she called to whomever had knocked.

"Are you okay?"

Minjung's heart sank. It was Madam Rowena.

"Yes, Madam. I'll be right out."

She flushed the toilet, even though she hadn't used it, washed her hands, and then splashed water on her face to flush out the evidence of her crying. When she opened the door, Madam Rowena blocked the way.

"Are you okay?" Madam looked her over from head to toe, inspecting. "Have you been crying?"

"Yes, I teared up, Madam," Minjung said, frantically scanning her brain for a reason. She found one which wasn't too far from the truth. "Dust, Madam."

Madam rolled her eyes, looking relieved. "Tell me about it," she said in commiseration and led the way back to the party. "Tyttle Fyzzle time." She veered toward the kitchen.

Minjung asked for Harriet's help setting up the fun, and then Madam called the *littles* into the kitchen.

"Have you ever had Tyttle Pop?" Madam asked Madison directly.

"Of course," Madison blurted. "Ohhhh," she sang and looked over at Billy and Shanice to join in. Once they did, the others also joined in for a rounding chorus of the Tyttle Pop Song, which any and every person growing up in America knew.

"Give me some Tyttle Pop, Tyttle Pop, tit, tit, Tyttle Pop," the group sang. They burst out laughing. It was every child's joy to sing the song at the top of their lungs so they could say the naughty word under the cover of a children's rhyme.

"Ohhhh," Mistress Jaleesa boomed as she entered the kitchen. Everyone in the house joined in again, including Madam Rowena this time. "Give me some Tyttle Pop, Tyttle Pop, tit, tit, Tyttle Pop." The gathering of people, which now included Mistress Marta and her vanilla sister, brother-in-law, nephew, and a couple of other vanillas, burst out laughing.

"We're trying to limit sugar, though," Mistress Shasti said to Madam once the song was over. "But thank you for being so generous."

"I'm limiting sugar, too." Madam shot Minjung a smile. "Ah, but this isn't actually Tyttle Pop," Madam said, laying out small, colorful plastic cups on the kitchen counter.

"Ohhhh," Shanice sang, and another round of the Tyttle Pop song burst from the group.

Madam Rowena chuckled at their antics and said, "There's no sugar in these and no calories. It's called Tyttle Fyzzle, and they're simply flavored sparkling waters."

"Tyttle Fyzzle," Madison repeated, her eyes narrowing. She then broke into a rap beat complete with the word 'tit' repeated several times in succession.

"Catchy," Mistress Rikki said afterward.

"Let's make a TikTok," Billy suggested, and Shanice agreed, gushing her approval.

"I will approve of this TikTok before it's posted," Mistress Marta said and winked at Madam.

"Cool," Madison said, now bopping around in true Madison fashion.

"It *is* cool," Madam said. "I wanted to show you guys some interesting flavor combinations." She poured a bit of orange into each glass. Minjung jumped in and opened a second bottle because everyone seemed to want in on the fun. They handed out the sparkling waters to all, and Madam said, "Just a sip now. Tastes like orange, right? Just orange."

Madison drained her glass and made a satisfied smacking sound that made everybody laugh.

"You were supposed to take a sip, dufus," Billy said.

"Oh."

Madam simply smiled and poured more into Madison's cup.

"This actually tasted great," Mistress Marta's sister said. "I've been looking for some flavored waters."

Madam smiled at Mistress Marta's sister and said, "Yeah, these are pretty good."

Minjung bit down a smile. No one here knew that Madam Rowena Tate, as they knew her, was actually Rowena Tyttle. It was kind of funny.

"So next, we take pineapple flavor and pour a little into the orange."

"Ooh, tropical," Mistress Shasti said after taking a taste. "This is really good."

"Can we buy some?" Madison asked her Domme, swaying from side to side.

"I think we're going to have to." Mistress Shasti held up her glass. "Where did you find these, Rowena?"

"They're everywhere. It's a new Tyttle Foods product. Minjung was actually the one that got me into sparkling waters."

All heads turned toward Minjung. She acknowledged Madam Rowena's statement with a nod and willed the gazes of the others to go away.

"Let's try a few more," Madam said. The pineapple and coconut combination seemed to be a party favorite, with Marta's brother-in-law commenting that it almost tasted like a piña colada. Mistress Victoria said she liked the orange and vanilla combo best because it reminded her of the creamsicles she'd get at the ice cream truck growing up in Indiana. Jaleesa got playful grief from her family for declaring that the black cherry and lime combination was her favorite. She took their teasing in stride because that seemed to be part of her family's love language.

All in all, Madam's flavor mixtures were a big hit, and she was positively beaming. Minjung and Harriet cleaned up after the taste testing, and then Minjung was ordered to "go be a guest" by Mistress Marta. It was a role she wasn't used to, but she sat down next to Madam, who was deep in conversation with Mistress Victoria on the couch.

After eating Shanice's favorite meal of smoked turkey and collard greens, it was finally time for cake and presents. The happy birthday song was sung, and Shanice seemed quite humbled and emotional at the mountain of presents she'd received. The poor young woman had had a rough start in life without a stable home or a family of her own. And now, like Minjung, she had found a place among caring and nurturing people.

And even though they still thought of her as a slave, they had brought her a smaller mountain of gifts at her collaring ceremony, hadn't they? Did these people truly care for her? How could they? They didn't even know who she was. It was not that she was begrudging their generous gifts, but none of the gifts were specific to Minjung. No, they were specific to a submissive or a slave. Not the actual person inside the label.

Minjung lowered her head. She was happy for all the attention Shanice was getting and allowed herself to enjoy it. Minjung had always said she wanted to help a Domme find success and happiness. She wanted her Domme to thrive because of *her*, because of what Minjung and not some generic submissive brought to the relationship. Madam was still glowing from her Tyttle Fyzzle demonstration earlier, and Minjung knew she'd been a huge part of the company's creation of the product. She reached up, pinched the lock charm between two fingers, and ran it up and down the chain. The slight sound of metal on metal soothed her for some reason.

Minjung had to knock herself out of her funk because Shanice was opening the presents Minjung had wrapped for her. "Love her," Shanice said and put on the Beatrice Prior T-shirt over her own T-shirt.

"She is one bad-ass chick," Mistress Victoria said from her seat next to Madam. This caused the *littles* to gasp at the use of the bad word. "What? She is. Going from Abnegation to Dauntless?"

People's faces lit up with understanding when they realized the woman on the T-shirt was a character from the Divergent book and movie series.

"C'mon," Mistress Victoria continued. "We're all a little divergent, aren't we?" Knowing chuckles politely filled the space. They all, except for the vanillas, knew that Mistress Victoria was referring to their chosen lifestyles.

Shanice kept opening the gifts from Madam Rowena and Minjung and thanked them after each one. When she finally got to the big box, Madam said, "You might want some help with that."

DeShawn moved instantly and helped the young woman in the wheelchair tear the paper off the box. Together, they opened the box flats, and then Deshawn pulled out an identical version of the wheeled kneeler that Minjung used.

"This might help save those knees, kid," Madam Rowena said. She looked over at Mistress Marta and added, "Supposedly, it's safe for floors like these." She pointed to the vinyl planking.

Mistress Marta nodded, approached the device, and inspected it. "Wow, this is cool. Do you want to try it out?"

Shanice nodded enthusiastically, and it took them a minute to get her situated on the device. She figured out how to maneuver and was scooting around the room in a matter of moments.

"Halt," Mistress Marta said to her charge. "Put these on." She handed Shanice a new set of wheelchair gloves that Mistress Marta's nephew had gotten Shanice. Since the young double amputee had no feet to propel herself, she had to lean on the chest plate and use her hands instead. Once the gloves were on, Shanice zipped around the room, prompting Madison to whine that she wanted one, too. Mistress Shasti spoke to her in low tones, but Minjung didn't hear what she said.

Shanice zipped across the room, pulled up short in front of Minjung, and sat up taller. She put her arms out in the first ballet arm position and then went through the rest. She was beautiful. Both Mistress Marta and her sister cried at the sight. Minjung was wispy-eyed as well.

"That was beautiful, little miss," Minjung said quietly to Shanice. "We have one more present for you if that's okay."

"Thank you," Shanice said and looked back at her Domme, who came over.

Minjung leaned back on the hassock and pulled the envelope out of her front pocket. It was a little crinkled but none the worse for wear.

Shanice opened the envelope and pulled out two tickets.

"Read it, baby," Mistress Marta said to Shanice.

"Dancing Wheels." Shanice pointed to one of the tickets, "Look, Mama, there are two girls in wheelchairs doing ballet."

"It's a dance group made up of people of all abilities. The performance is in Cleveland," Madam Rowena said. "We'd love for you and your Mama to be our guests. We'll take care of everything."

Mistress Marta's waterworks began again.

"Can we, Mama?" Shanice said, looking up.

"How can I say no when you hit me with those baby brown eyes?"

"Yay," Shanice said and bounced up and down on the wheeled kneeler. She thanked Minjung and Madam Rowena profusely and said, "The Benjies' concert is in March. And now this will be in June. That's such a long time to wait." She groaned.

"I have an idea," Madam Rowena said. "What if you, Madison, Billy, and any other *littles* in our community put on a dance performance at the Holiday Masquerade Ball? Minjung is doing a ropes demonstration with Miss Shasti."

"A suspension," Mistress Shasti added, beaming.

Minjung had worked with Mistress Shasti a few times and discovered they had a good rapport with each other.

"Cool," Shanice said. "Will you choreograph us, Miss Minjung?"

Minjung's eyes grew wide. She swallowed hard as anxiety bubbled up inside. She looked over at Madam Rowena for help.

"It's up to you, Minjung," Madam Rowena said. "But I think you'd enjoy it. Yes, I think you should do it."

"Okay," she said to Madam, hearing the weakness in her voice. She cleared her throat as she turned back toward Shanice and said, "If it's okay with all your—" She caught herself before saying the word Dominants and instead said, "People."

"It's fine with me," Mistress Marta said.

"Me, too," Mistress Shasti chimed in which sent Madison jumping in place.

"Ma'ams," DeShawn said, "I'm sure Mr. Seamus will be fine with him participating."

"Excellent," Madam Rowena said. "Then it's all settled. I'll contact you all on when and where the first rehearsal will be."

Minjung swallowed. Hard. What had just happened? She wasn't sure she wanted to do this. But maybe this would be a good way for them to get to know her. Maybe they would see that she was more than a slave, more than a mindless robot. She let that sink in for a moment and then said, "Thank you," to Shanice. "It will be my honor to teach you."

"Yay," Shanice said quietly. "Oops. I have to go." She looked up at Mistress Marta and said, "Mama, I have to go."

Marta scooped her up out of the wheeled kneeler and whisked her toward the bathroom. When they came back out, Marta's sister, her family, and the other vanilla guests all took their leave. Once they left, the party was no longer vanilla. Mistress Marta announced that "the vanillas have left the building," making everyone laugh.

Upon Mistress Marta's request, DeShawn stepped over to move the kneeler out of everyone's way.

"Where's Seamus this evening?" Madam Rowena asked him.

"He's spending 'quality time' with Mark and Vikram, Ma'am."

"Ahh," Madam said, "and how are you holding up?" She lowered her voice and asked, "Isn't your contract up soon?"

DeShawn moved the kneeler out of the way and sat on the floor in front of Madam. He, too, was submissive and, like Minjung, always felt uncomfortable standing over Dominants. He spoke in low tones. "I'm going to be okay, Ma'am. Thank you for asking. Master Seamus has been talking to someone for a while now. Someone who, I think, has agreed to take over my contract."

"That's fantastic, DeShawn," Madam Rowena said. "You've always been a gentle soul. I'm glad good things will be happening for you. Will you be staying in Denton Heights?"

"Yes, Ma'am," DeShawn said.

Just then, someone tapped a metal object against a glass. It was Mistress Jaleesa. Once the room was relatively quiet, she said, "I want to get ahead of this since rumors are going to fly, and I want you all to understand the truth."

Minjung's mind went to a million different places, wondering what drama Mistress Jaleesa was trying to squelch.

Mistress Jaleesa gestured for DeShawn to come to her. She pointed to the floor, and he knelt in front of her. "Master Seamus and I have reached an agreement, and I'll be taking over DeShawn's contract starting December 1st."

A cheer went up around the room.

"I don't know how she's going to handle one more submissive," Madam

Rowena muttered low to Mistress Victoria.

"She's got a big heart, I guess," Mistress Victoria said back.

"And a big house," Madam said.

"My family approves," Jaleesa continued. "And, like me, they're ecstatic that he'll be moving in with us."

A streak ran through the people and landed on top of DeShawn. It was Billy. "I'm going to miss you."

DeShawn picked the young man off of him and said, "I'm still around, kid. Just a few miles away."

"She's a good lady," Billy said, obviously talking about Mistress Jaleesa. "She'll take good care of you."

"That I will, young one," Mistress Jaleesa said. Billy leaped to his feet and hugged her. She took a few minutes to reassure him that DeShawn would indeed have his own room and that he could make whatever he wanted in the kitchen as long as Miss Harriet said it was okay first.

"Her family is growing," Madam Rowena said. It took Minjung a moment to realize that her Madam was talking to her.

Before she could answer, Mistress Victoria said somberly, "Sometimes the best families aren't biological. Chosen ones are pretty damn good, too."

Madam Rowena patted Victoria on the thigh. "Speaking of family," Madam Rowena said, turning back to Minjung, "I have a surprise for you."

"Me, Madam?"

Madam nodded. "Have you ever been on a ship before? A cruise?"

Dread filled Minjung's chest. "No, Madam. Why?"

"We're going on a cruise to Cabo San Lucas and the Mexican Riviera. You said you've never been there, remember?"

"I do remember, Madam."

"We'll fly out to the port city, do some sightseeing, and set sail for a week-long cruise and tour of Mexico." Mistress Rowena was beaming. "What do you think?"

"Can I wear a life vest at all times, Madam?" Minjung asked this half-seriously.

Mistress Victoria leaned over and whispered, "I doubt she's going to let you wear much of anything at all."

Minjung smiled for Mistress Victoria's benefit, but she was apprehensive.

"What port will we be leaving from, Madam?"

"San Francisco."

Minjung's smile fell. San Francisco was where she had grown up. San Francisco was where the accident had happened. San Francisco was where *he* was.

~~~

"Maybe this was a bad idea," Minjung said, looking away from the plain concrete building.

"We've come this far, Minjung," Madam Rowena said softly. "You should at least give her a chance."

It was the first of December. They'd flown into the San Francisco area the day before, had a nice dinner, and a quiet evening in the hotel room. That morning, though, Minjung went through the motions of sightseeing with her Domme. She never thought she'd be back in the Bay area ever again. She had vowed never to go back. Yet here she was.

Minjung stopped picking at the wrap-around tie of her new full-length raincoat. It had been one of the many gifts Madam had given her for their upcoming cruise. She looked up into Madam's eyes. Madam's expression softened. She clearly understood how difficult this was going to be for Minjung.

"If he's here. I'm out," Minjung said.

"You were very clear about that in the letter to your mother," Madam said matter-of-factly. "If your father shows his face, to me, that is a clear violation of your wishes and destroys the tentative trust you sought."

Minjung's breaths were shallow. She was in a bit of a panic mode, but a hand reached over and snaked its way into hers as they sat in the back of the hired car in the visitor's lot of Embee Labs, where Minjung's mother worked.

"I'll be right here in the car, in your line of sight. If you give the signal, then Miguel and I will scoop you right up, and we'll leave." She gestured toward the back of their driver's head.

Minjung had the oddest thought just then. Ashley looked so much better in her chauffeur's uniform than Miguel looked in his. She smiled.

"That's my—" Madam laughed and then said, "I was going to say, 'That's my *girl*,' but I know you don't like that."

"I don't mind, Madam."

"Really?"

Minjung sighed. "It's a pet name, and you weren't using it to degrade, so it's okay."

"We'll talk more about this later, okay?" Madam obviously understood that Minjung had a lot more on her mind at the moment.

Minjung looked toward the concrete tables that Embee employees used if they wanted to go outside for lunch or breaks. The overcast afternoon was a fitting accompaniment to her dampened mood. Would she even recognize her mother? It had been over seventeen years since she'd last seen her.

The side door to the courtyard opened, and Minjung's heart leaped into her throat. The hand that still held hers tightened. The woman who walked out stood tall and strong, and Minjung would have recognized her anywhere.

Minjung flew out of the car. "*Eom-ma*," she called, her chest heaving with emotion as she ran.

Her mother was also crying. She opened her arms and let Minjung fly into them.

"I've missed you so much," Minjung cried in her mother's arms. "I'm sorry I stayed away so long."

Minjung's mother stroked Minjung's back and said, "Have you eaten?"

Minjung laughed as she said, "I'm fine." Her mother wasn't actually concerned about her food intake; it was a thing Korean moms did to check in on a person's well-being. Minjung stepped back and said, "It's been seventeen years. I shouldn't have stayed away that long."

"Come, sit," Minjung's mother said, pulling her by the hand to one of the concrete tables.

"Are you okay, *Eom-ma*?" She wanted desperately to ask if he was there lurking. She also wanted to ask if she had stayed with him.

"I'm okay," Minjung's mother said. "Still at Embee, obviously. I'm a supervisor now."

"Fantastic," Minjung reached across the table, grabbed one of her mother's hands, and held it.

"Thank you for your letters. When I got the first one and knew you were okay, I finally relaxed a little. I was always searching for you, *Jagiya*. I kept tabs on every ballet company in the US and in Canada. Sometimes I'd search other countries, too." She wiped at the tears on her face.

"You kept looking?"

Minjung's mother nodded.

"I'm glad my letters and postcards found you," Minjung said. There were so many mixed feelings battling in her chest, but the one leading the pack was regret. "I wanted to reach out more, but…"

"I understand." Minjung's mother brushed a lock of graying hair from her face. "What have you been doing in your life? Job? Husband? Wife? Children?" She sobbed once and added in a tight voice, "You've grown into a beautiful woman, *Gongjunim*."

"I'm far from a princess, *Oem-ma*." Minjung laughed and then said, "I've traveled a lot over the years."

"I could tell by the postmarks on your letters."

"I mainly work as a personal assistant to important people." Certain that her mother was disappointed with that career choice, Minjung quickly added, "It's very satisfying and important work. I like it, and I'm good at it."

"It seems to suit you, *Jagiya*. You look healthy and strong."

Minjung was melting inside at her mother's endearment. Her mother used to call her *Jagiya* and *Gongjunim* throughout her childhood and into her early twenties. "I've tried to take care of myself. I'm not married and have no children, either."

Her mother nodded and sighed. "I left him."

Relief seeped from Minjung's pores.

"The moment I got that first letter from you in Seattle, and you told me you were fine and exploring life, I knew you'd be okay." She looked up at Minjung with tear-filled eyes. "And that's when I realized that if you had the strength to leave, I did, too."

Minjung inhaled sharply. She hadn't expected that.

"What happened, *Oem-ma*?" She squeezed her mother's hand but didn't let go.

"I gave him his walking papers. I divorced him. I moved out, closer to the Labs, and got a restraining order when he showed up here drunk, yelling at me for not being a proper wife or even a proper woman. It was a mess, but I had the support of really good people." She gestured toward the building. "My colleagues rallied around me and got me the help I needed, including that restraining order."

"Where is he now?"

"Do you remember Mr. Park?"

"Our neighbor in the apartment below ours?"

Minjung's mother nodded. "He maintains contact with your father. He says it's so he can make sure I feel safe."

"He's not my father," Minjung said evenly. "He lost that right a long time ago, and I just can't think of him that way. Drinking was more important to him than us. He has mental issues, and I wish I could forgive him, but I just can't. Not now and not for the last seventeen years. I just can't." Foreign yet familiar arms went around her and rocked her back and forth. A soft Korean lullaby wrapped itself around her heart. "I've missed you so much, *Oem-ma*."

The rocking continued. "I should have been there more for you back then," Minjung's mother said. "My therapist has helped me understand that I was fighting for my own safety and just wasn't able to protect both of us." The arms around Minjung squeezed harder.

"We shouldn't have had to fight for our own safety." Minjung took a deep breath and let it out in a gush. She sat up, wiped the tears from her mother's face, and said, "Neither of us should be apologizing. We were the victims, *Oem-ma*. We should be mad, not apologetic."

"Yes, I agree," Minjung's mother said. "He moved to a Korean community somewhere in the Los Angeles area and hasn't bothered me since."

Minjung sighed in relief. Her mother was safe and had been for years. "Thank you for raising me, *Oem-ma*. Thank you for giving me an education and trying to make it a loving home. I know you tried."

"Thank you. I needed to hear those words." Minjung's mother looked toward the town car in the parking lot. "Is that your love interest?"

Minjung followed her mother's gaze. Madam Rowena was watching intently from the backseat.

"She's—That's—" Minjung huffed. She hadn't thought about how to explain who Madam Rowena was. "She's my employer. I manage her household, and I'm her personal assistant. She's rewarding me with a cruise to Cabo. We're leaving from the port tomorrow for a weeklong cruise. That's part of the reason we're here. You're the other part."

Her mother smiled, and it went straight to Minjung's heart.

"She sounds like a very generous employer." Her mother glanced at the car again.

"Would you like to meet her?"

"Yes," came the quick answer. "I want to meet the woman who takes care of my baby."

Minjung digested her mother's words. "Yes, she does take care of me."

"Good."

Minjung stood up and waved for Madam Rowena to walk over and meet her mother.

Five or so hours later, it was time for them to part. And in that time, Minjung kept reaching for her mother as if the physical contact would erase the seventeen-year absence. Madam treated them to a nice dinner near Minjung's mother's apartment, and then they went up to the apartment for tea and Minjung's favorite childhood cookies. Minjung's mother made them with the hope that Minjung would come back to the apartment.

They stood at the door, still saying their goodbyes, when Minjung's mother said, "I'm ecstatic to have my *gongjunim* back." She held Minjung tightly as if reluctant to let go. "I'm counting the days until your cruise ship returns."

"As will I," Minjung said. "We'll spend the whole weekend together when I get back."

Just then, the doorbell to Minjung's mother's apartment rang. When she opened the door, a delivery girl handed her mother a package. "What could this be?"

Madam Rowena was grinning like a Cheshire cat when she said, "Open it."

Inside the package was a framed photo that Madam had taken of Minjung and her mother in front of the greenery outside the Italian restaurant they'd gone to that evening.

Minjung's mother hugged Madam Rowena and thanked her profusely. "You're very generous. Thank you for taking care of her for me. And thank you for—" Emotion closed her throat before she could finish her thought. When she recovered enough to continue, she said, "And thank you for making this happen." She gestured to Minjung and herself.

"I'm glad it turned out so well."

They said their goodbyes, and Minjung decided the rating for that day was 20/10.

Chapter 21

Rowena

Rowena had been on many cruises in her forty years, but she never fully got used to the gentle rolling of a ship. Rowena let herself relax into the swaying motion as much as she could. They'd left the San Francisco port that afternoon, unpacked in their suite located in the stern of the ship, had a buffet dinner on the pool deck during the sailaway party, and were now relaxing in the forward starboard lounge.

Minjung was saving their choice lounge seats near the large picture windows. The open seats had been a lucky boon. The infinite horizon of the Pacific was mesmerizing, and the early evening sun was low in the sky, promising a gorgeous sunset. Minjung had looked so peaceful dozing in her chair that Rowena offered to get her own coffee at the self-serve beverage station, much to Minjung's surprise.

Rowena fixed her coffee just the way she liked it and then pulled the hot water handle to fill a second cup for tea. She snagged a variety of tea bags to give Minjung some choices. Oh, the look on Minjung's face when Rowena said she would get her own coffee had been priceless. Hopefully, Minjung would again be surprised at how thoughtful Rowena was in bringing the tea. The poor dear had such an emotionally draining day reconnecting with her mother and cried all the way back to the hotel. At one point, she'd heard Minjung mumble, "So much time lost."

It had broken Rowena's heart, so she vowed to relieve some of her submissive's burden, like getting hot after-dinner beverages.

Rowena weaved her way through the first-night crush of cruisers. If she got back to the lounge chairs without wearing one form of liquid or another, it would be a miracle. Something protective and even a tad possessive settled in her chest as she thought of the many trials Minjung had endured and dealt with in her life. And despite that, Minjung never complained, never took advantage, and never asked for handouts.

When Rowena finally turned the corner to their spot near the windows, her ire piqued instantly. "Oh, hell, no," she muttered under her breath. She put the drinks down on the low table and was about to tell the two interlopers to move along like little doggies when Minjung put a hand on her arm to stop the tirade.

"Hello there," the overly friendly middle-aged man in a tropical shirt said to Rowena. "Kimchi here has been telling us you're going down to Cabo for a ballpoint pen convention. It sounds very interesting."

"And what an exotic place to hold a convention," an equally overly friendly woman in a gaudy tropical dress added.

Rowena blinked several times. "Uh, yes. It should be ink-credible." She waited until the joke landed and then laughed with the couple, who were obviously just getting started on their cruising campaign and not the nautical kind.

"Can we get you a drink?" the man asked.

"We're not available," Rowena said quickly. She'd had enough. Who knows what poor Minjung had to endure before Rowena walked up.

"Just one drink," the clearly thirsty man said.

"Honey, they said no." The woman placed the back of her hand on his shirt, which was covered with upside-down pineapple prints, a clear sign that they were swingers and looking for fun.

"Look for us if you change your mind," he said to Rowena. He shook Minjung's hand and said, "You, too, Kimchi." This he purred.

Rowena took a step closer. She would have growled next if he hadn't stepped back and moved on, his companion in tow.

"Madam," Minjung said after Rowena sat down. She leaned closer. "You didn't book us on a swingers' cruise, did you?"

"No," Rowena said. "I mean, I hope not." She thought about it for a moment. "No, there are a lot of kids on board and families." She realized something. "Wait, you knew they were swingers?"

Minjung laughed. "Yes, Madam. Even without the way overdone pineapple motif shouting their intentions to the world, they were quite aggressive. He was, anyway."

"You handled them well," Rowena said and then added, "Kimchi."

Minjung grinned. "They didn't seem to catch on."

"Can I call you that from now on? Oh, *Korean-sour-cabbage-dish*, I require something."

Minjung laughed and thanked her for the tea, which she seemed quite appreciative of.

"Ballpoint pen convention?" Rowena asked, finally taking a sip of coffee.

"They were on me so fast; it was the first thing I could come up with." Minjung's smile waned. It was clear that something had made Minjung slightly uncomfortable, so Rowena asked her what it was.

"Getting tea for me was a nice surprise, Madam, but I'm the one that's supposed to get *you* things."

"I wanted to surprise you."

"You did, Madam," Minjung said. "This is a lovely treat. Thank you." She picked up the vanilla chai tea bag. "This one looks interesting."

"I got a variety for you."

"Thank you," Minjung said again. "This is perfect."

It was clear to Rowena that Minjung wasn't used to being served or having people do things for her. Maybe that should change. Just a little, though. Submissives could get spoiled so easily, couldn't they? Maybe that's what Matilda was warning her about, getting soft and blurring the lines between Dominant and submissive.

Minjung took a sip and, without turning toward Rowena, said softly, "As Aida sang in the opera, you can't go back again." She looked up and made eye contact with Rowena. "He not only took ballet from me, but he took my mother, too. Maybe now I can have a relationship with her again." Tears filled her eyes, and she looked down at the cup in her hands. "I don't know how I'm going to make up for lost time. I should have tried sooner. And I have you to thank for pushing me to do this." She looked back up, her posture softening, her eyes grateful.

"I'm glad it worked out so well for you," Rowena said. "You can send your mother a postcard from Cabo."

"No, Madam," Minjung said, a slight grin creeping up her face. "I will **bring** her postcards not only from Cabo but Mazatlán and Puerto Vallarta too."

"Perfect," Rowena said, but she needed to change the subject so Minjung wouldn't dwell on the time she'd lost with her mother. As subtly as she could, she turned the conversation to the satisfying progress Minjung had been making getting the *littles* ready for the masquerade ball.

"That has been so much fun," Minjung said. "I don't think Mistress Marta likes her role as the nutcracker prince, though."

"She'll get over it," Rowena said with a chuckle. "She'll do anything for Shanice. We all know that."

"That's true, Madam. They adore each other."

They settled into a pleasant conversation and then watched the sun set over the water in the distance. Clouds marred the overall effect, but it was still a sight they'd never see in Ohio. After the sunset, they found two seats closer to the dance floor. The energy of the vacationers was high, and the drinks were flowing. Rowena had a white wine, and Minjung had sparkling water with lime. She wasn't much of a drinker, and that was okay. Rowena wasn't really a drinker, either.

The music was definitely suited for couples, and many were making their way around the floor. When the song "Pink Sunsets" came on, Rowena felt the urge to dance. Whether it was the wine or the fun all around them, she wasn't sure, but when she looked over at Minjung, she just couldn't ask her. It wasn't right. Rowena didn't feel it was right to dance intimately with a submissive. Sex? Yes, all day, all night, but holding a submissive close, cheek to cheek, that was too close to being intimate, and that's not what their relationship was about.

Rowena cleared her throat and announced that she was tired. Once back in their suite, she got ready for bed and listened to Minjung moving around in her smaller room on the other side of the small suite. When the sounds finally settled down, Rowena silently wished Minjung a good night's sleep. The last few days had been quite emotional for her submissive, and she needed the rest.

The bed was comfortable enough, but sleep wouldn't come. Too many thoughts swirled around her mind. She threw on her robe and, as quietly as she could, made her way from her bedroom through the shared living room and out onto the balcony. Their suite sat at the back of the ship, overlooking the walking track a few decks below and the glorious Pacific Ocean beyond. She settled into one of the sturdy lounge chairs and let the sounds and swaying of the ship calm her racing mind.

The song in the lounge had awakened something in her. She'd wanted to reach her hand out, have Minjung beam as she took it, and then lead her to the dance floor. She wanted to feel Minjung's clothed body pressed against hers as she led her around the floor. She wanted everyone to know the amazing woman in her arms was hers.

"Oh, shit," she said to the ocean and bolted upright. "Shit," she said again. "What the hell do I do now?"

Rowena clutched the lapels of her robe tighter. She finally realized what had been knocking on her heart for quite some time now.

"I'm in love with Minjung." The words, although spoken out loud, got lost in the ocean.

~~~

Over the next six days of the cruise, Rowena kept a close guard on her feelings. The night they left Puerto Vallarta, the last port of their trip, Rowena made sure to reward Minjung with a nice D/s session in their stateroom. She had to gag Minjung, of course. She didn't want Minjung's cries to alert anyone official. Minjung looked rather yummy, tied to the bed face down. Rowena had only brought a small paddle that doubled as a charcuterie board, but it reddened Minjung's ass and legs nicely. It only took a few strokes of Minjung's very aroused sex, and she came. Her moans of release were beautiful music to Rowena's ears.

Rowena untied her submissive from the bed and had her turn face up. Rowena shimmied her way up Minjung's body, surprised at how nimble she was as she positioned herself over Minjung's now ungagged mouth. The new walking path back home and Minjung's guidance about nutrition and healthy eating had helped Rowena build more strength and stamina. She made quick work of her own needs using Minjung's very talented tongue and lips. When her orgasm hit, she made sure not to collapse on her submissive. They were both very satisfied as Rowena held Minjung close for a short aftercare session. After that, they took showers, had dinner, and then headed to the forward starboard lounge for a cocktail on their last night.

"This has been a memorable trip, Madam," Minjung said as she sipped her sparkling water with a wedge of lime.

"It has," Rowena said. "Those dancers on the pier at Mazatlán were incredible."

"Thank you for delaying so we could enjoy them."

"Of course," Rowena said. What she wanted to add was, 'Anything for you.' But she didn't. Long ago, she'd resigned herself to a loveless life. Sexual companionship that she paid for was all life was going to give her. As each day of the cruise progressed, Rowena realized that Minjung might leave her once the trip was over. She'd rekindled a relationship with her mother, and there was not much Rowena could do to compete with that. Minjung was not a slave like some wanted to think. She could leave whenever she wanted. They had a contract, but contracts could be broken. Minjung was collared, sure, but that unwritten contract could also be broken at any time.

"Another wine, Madam?" Minjung stood up, knowing the answer would be "Yes."

"Sure, why not."

Minjung grinned and walked across the fairly empty dance floor. She stopped and then did several ballet pirouettes. She grinned back at Rowena, her shoulders hunched in a coquettish giggle, and then headed to the bar.

Rowena's heart pounded as the love she'd just come to realize for her submissive filled her chest. Unfortunately, other feelings were tagging along, making themselves known. Sadness, loneliness, emptiness.

She pictured being all alone in that big house again. She was going to miss not only Minjung's service but also the way she smiled when she placed a piece in the puzzle or whenever Rowena invited her to eat at the table with her. There were those afterglow, sub-space smiles, too.

A numbing misery bubbled in her chest and threatened to undo her. She opened her mouth and let out a frustrated sigh. She watched Minjung at the bar, knowing this was probably the last vacation they would spend together. How long would Minjung stay now that she'd found her mother again? Would she even fly back to Ohio with Rowena?

Rowena jumped when someone spoke to her. "She's a beautiful woman," the pineapple-wearing woman from their first night on the cruise said.

Rowena coughed and then cleared her throat to remove all emotions. As a Dominant, she knew how to remain in control of herself. The familiar veil of stoicism settled over her like a mask.

"She is," Rowena said to the woman who was holding a tropical-looking drink.

The woman stood off to Rowena's side, her male companion nowhere in sight. "How long have you two been together?" the woman asked.

"Almost two years now," Rowena said. That was a bit of a stretch, but saying one year and nine months would have been awkward.

The woman took a sip of her drink. "Being in love looks good on you both." Her hand briefly touched Rowena's shoulder. Without waiting for a response, she said, "Enjoy the rest of your cruise," turned, and walked away.

Rowena was too stunned to respond. Her face flushed with heat. Was it that obvious? Minjung made her way back over the dance floor, no pirouettes this time, holding two glasses of wine.

"Madam," she said and handed Rowena her usual white wine. "I thought I'd try one if that is okay," Minjung said, holding up a second glass.

"Fine, fine," Rowena said in her best imitation of cool, calm, and collected. She had to keep her walls up. She was going to get her heart broken after the cruise ended. Minjung would have to tell Rowena she wanted to break the contract, though. Rowena was not simply going to hand that to her, even though it was probably inevitable.

~~~

Rowena sat in the first-class plane seat heading back to Cincinnati from San Francisco. Asking Daddy to use the company plane hadn't seemed appropriate, so here she sat surrounded by strangers. She surreptitiously looked at the woman in the seat next to her. Minjung was casually playing a game on her phone to pass the time, but she was the most beautiful woman on the entire plane. Rowena looked away. Did the woman sitting next to her know how amazing she truly was? How beautiful and graceful? Did she know how Rowena's heart lit up every time she walked into the room?

Even after Minjung spent most of the weekend with her mother while Rowena did some sightseeing on her own, Minjung still didn't mention breaking their contract and leaving her. Maybe she was going to wait until April, four short months from now. That would be their two-year mark. That must be it. She was going to move out in April.

"Madam?" Minjung said. "Are you all right?"

"Yes, of course," Rowena said sternly.

Minjung nodded and went back to her game.

How could Rowena tell her submissive that she was aching inside? That the fear of losing her was taking over her every thought. She couldn't. And she wouldn't. Matilda had been absolutely right. Dommes should not fall in love with their submissives or vice versa. It just ruins the entire dynamic.

Rowena closed her eyes and willed sleep to come.

~~~

Once back home, Rowena poured herself into her trading. The Dow Jones and the S&P 500 had done some interesting things while they'd been away, and she had to make sense of it. Minjung, meanwhile, was downstairs in the playroom, pouring her energy into rehearsing with Marta and the *littles* for their Nutcracker dance. The masquerade ball was in a few days, and this was their very last rehearsal.

Rowena heard the sound of the main house elevator whirring and headed out of her office to greet Minjung's guests and show them out.

The elevator door opened, and an out-of-breath Madison emerged. "Hi, Miss Rowena. Miss Minjung says we're in 'prime shape' for Saturday." She used air quotes around the words prime and shape.

Before Rowena could respond, Billy and the other *littles* loudly voiced their agreement with Madison.

All that loud, youthful energy jarred Rowena's frayed nerves, but she managed to remain a gracious host. "That's fantastic," Rowena said, a natural smile creeping up her face. "I'm looking forward to seeing it on Saturday."

Shanice squealed. "That's only two days from now."

Shanice's Domme, Marta, grimaced at Rowena as she pushed Shanice's wheelchair out of the elevator. "They're ready. Your Minjung is a miracle worker."

"Mama!" Shanice protested the perceived insult.

"No, no," Marta said quickly, "I mean, she got us looking so good in such a short time."

"Okay," Shanice said, but she still pouted in disbelief.

Rowena chuckled. Marta was in the doghouse, that was for sure. One thing she'd noticed about the relationship between *littles* and their Dommes was that the *littles* seemed to be the ones in charge. As she walked with them toward the front door and they said their goodbyes, she realized that wasn't exactly true. It was more of an exchange between them. She'd witnessed Shasti taking charge of Madison, and on the flip side, she'd seen Madison making sure Shasti knew what she needed. Seamus and Billy were similar as well as Marta and Shanice. There were clearly defined roles and mutual respect, of course, but they also let their needs be known.

She closed the door behind them just as Minjung bounded up the stairs.

"My office," Rowena said. "Now." It sounded gruffer than she had intended. Her nerves were practically shot, and she couldn't help it.

Minjung didn't say a word but followed Rowena. She made a beeline for her stool, but Rowena guided her to the couch. She looked lovely in her leotard, a slight sheen of sweat on her face.

"Water?" Rowena asked.

"Yes, Madam," Minjung asked with surprise in her voice.

Rowena got the bottle of water and sat on the couch next to her sub. "I'm going to cut to the chase." Her throat got tight with emotion. Her head chimed in, though, telling her she was going about it all wrong. Rowena made a course correction and softened her tone. "Well, first, you're doing such a great job with the group that just left. And I'm proud of the work you're doing."

"Thank you, Madam," Minjung said tentatively. She knew something was up.

Rowena decided to rip off the band-aid. "Are you leaving me?"

The look of surprise on Minjung's face was genuine. "No, Madam. I…Are you releasing me?"

"No, no," Rowena said. "You just rekindled your relationship with your mother. I thought you'd want to go back and make up for all the time you've lost."

Understanding flooded Minjung's face. She flung herself to the floor and put her forehead on one of Rowena's shoes. "No, Madam. I don't want to leave you."

Rowena leaned down and squeezed Minjung's shoulder. Minjung sat up.

"You want to stay? With me?"

Minjung nodded. "Of course, Madam." She reached up and ran her fingers along her silk collar, the one Rowena had put on her right before the group rehearsal.

"You won't leave in April when your contract is up?"

"No, Madam." Minjung looked like she wanted to say something but couldn't find the words. She searched Rowena's face.

"I don't want you to leave, Minjung," Rowena blurted before Minjung could find her words. "I'm…" Now, it was Rowena's turn to search Minjung's face. She couldn't just blurt it out, so she said, "I love the way your face lights up when we finally finish a puzzle, the way you adopted the Cardinals as your favorite team, the way you subtly helped me understand the value of veggies." She chuckled but wasn't finished. "Minjung, I love the way you accept my dominance and seem so strong and confident in your submission." She was probably revealing too much, but she couldn't stop now. "I love the way you take care of me. You put your heart and soul into it." She reached down and stroked Minjung's cheek. "Minjung—" She had to pause to gather her emotions. "Minjung, in case you haven't figured it out yet—I'm utterly in love with you."

Minjung made a strangled sound and then said in a rush, "You don't know how long I've wanted to hear those words from you, Madam. I've been secretly in love with you for a long, long time."

"You have?" Rowena pulled Minjung back up on the couch. They turned to face each other. She reached for and held both of Minjung's hands. "Are you sure?" Her voice broke on the last word.

This time, Minjung did not take her usual pause and said, "Madam, I think I've been in love with you since our first interview. You set up those tests—the stale coffee, the dirty cup, and the papers on the floor. And just so you know, even though I knew they were tests, I would have taken care of those things anyway."

"You knew?" Rowena found herself leaning closer.

Minjung nodded. "You're not like other Dommes, Madam. You care for and take care of your subs. After a time, I'm not sure when, I felt something shift between us, and I could tell that you also cared for me as a person and not just a hired submissive. The New York trip that I tried to ruin, for example."

"No, no, you didn't ruin it," Rowena said.

"Suggesting I reconnect with my mother. The ballet barre. The whole go-bag in the ground incident. Through all of it, you put me and my feelings front and center. How could I *not* fall in love with you, Madam?"

"What do we do now?" Rowena asked. It wasn't like her to be unsure about anything, but this was entirely new territory. She understood Domme Matilda's concerns, but she had to try to make this work.

"I don't know, Madam," Minjung said. "But I do know one thing we can do right now." She leaned closer.

Their lips met shyly; they'd never kissed like this before. Tentative exploration turned into something else altogether, and it wasn't long before Rowena laid back on the couch and pulled Minjung on top of her. Hands roamed over each other's bodies. Clothing was removed frantically but systematically. They were making love. It wasn't just sex. Rowena could feel the difference. This was a pure exploration of each other's bodies fueled by love, and to Rowena's total surprise, Minjung turned into the aggressor.

Minjung pushed Rowena's arms over her head and held them there. She wasn't bound, of course, but it felt like Minjung was giving Rowena a chance to feel free and let someone else be in charge for a moment. The pure love she saw in Minjung's eyes allowed Rowena to let go and let herself be loved. They kept eye contact as Minjung slipped her fingers inside, moving them slowly in and out. Minjung's expression encouraged Rowena to let go and that it was okay to be vulnerable.

At first, Rowena's stoic Domme barriers stayed up, but she let herself trust the woman giving her pleasure and allowed them to dissolve. The moment Minjung's tongue made contact with Rowena's aroused clit, her arms flew back down, and she stroked Minjung's head lovingly. Rowena's orgasm sparked and built quickly. It took effort to let go so freely; she wasn't used to seeming so vulnerable, but she let her head loll back over the armrest of the couch. She held her breath as the orgasm hit and then wailed in unguarded cries she hadn't heard from her own throat in decades. She ground her sex against Minjung until her body collapsed in release.

Minjung shimmied back up Rowena's body and kissed her deeply. Tasting her own essence on Minjung's lips sent another shot of arousal through her, and after the kiss waned, she flipped Minjung onto her back and did something she never did with submissives. She gave Minjung a taste of her own medicine and kissed her way down Minjung's body toward her dripping wet center.

"You taste so lovely," Rowena sighed, her face finally buried between Minjung's legs. Minjung grabbed Rowena's head and pulled her back to her extremely hard clit. The Domme in her almost balked at this bold move but let herself soften and pleasure the woman she had come to love over the last year and nine months.

Minjung's screeching release was not the last that evening. After making love on the couch again and then eating dinner, the puzzle remained untouched as Rowena took Minjung's hand and led her to the suite on the third floor.

"Start a bath," Rowena commanded. "Make it hot and add the rose-cypress body soak." She'd purchased the body soak during their New York trip, and it reminded her of the bonding she and Minjung had done there.

"Yes, Madam." Minjung was in complete submissive mode. The woman couldn't help it, and Rowena loved her for it.

Once the water was running, Rowena said, "Undress me."

Her submissive didn't respond verbally. She simply moved closer, made eye contact, and then silently removed Rowena's robe, the one she kept in her office for moments like these. Minjung folded the robe and laid it on a chair. Rowena stood fully nude in front of her submissive, who still wore her robe fully fastened closed. This was something she had never done with submissives and had never done with Minjung. Until now. Until today, when she wanted the woman standing before her to understand that Rowena was leveling the playing field.

A quick glance at the spa tub filling with water told her she had time. She stepped toward Minjung who looked up, a slightly confused expression on her face. The expression turned to one of understanding as Rowena untied Minjung's robe and pushed it off her shoulders. It fell to the floor, and Rowena made no move to pick it up. She simply kicked it off to the side. Someone would pick it up later; it might even be her.

Rowena guided the beautiful woman into the tub and got in afterward. Once the tub was full and the creamy foam from the body soak reached a nice peak, she turned off the water. "Let's soak for a few minutes." She rested her head on the side of the formed seat and then reached underneath the water to hold Minjung's hand.

She wouldn't say that she'd dozed off, but she couldn't be certain. Once thing *was* certain, she was never going to let go of the hand she was holding. She sighed, completely relaxed and content. Her eyes opened when Minjung moved with purpose in front of her.

"You're beautiful, Madam."

"Call me Row—"

Minjung's finger over Rowena's lips stopped the word. "I can't. Not yet. One day, perhaps."

Rowena nodded and pulled Minjung into her arms. Lips met willing lips. Her passion for this woman was never far away. Minjung broke off the kiss and turned in the oversized spa tub. She backed up against Rowena, the back of her head coming to rest on Rowena's shoulder. With initiative unlike any Rowena had ever experienced from her submissive, Minjung pulled Rowena's arms around her. She then guided one of Rowena's hands to her small breasts and forced the hand to massage them one after the other. Rowena let out a soft sigh, watching a wisp of Minjung's hair move with the exhale. Rowena's hand was then guided down Minjung's stomach and straight to business.

Minjung forced Rowena's fingers inside, making them pump in and then out repeatedly.

Rowena whispered, "You're so ready for me."

"Mmm," Minjung moaned as she helped the fingers move within her body. The fingers were pulled out, and one was promoted to a special task. "Make love to me, Madam." She directed Rowena's middle finger around her engorged clit, now slick with desire. The guiding hand left as Minjung twisted slightly to kiss the woman she had pinned against the side of the tub. "I want to cum for you, Madam," Minjung whispered in between kisses.

A jolt of desire hit Rowena as a whimper escaped her lips into Minjung's. She did as commanded, and it wasn't long before Minjung's hips undulated to the rhythm Rowena set. Minjung broke off the kiss, fell back against Rowena's shoulder, and sucked air in through her nostrils. She held her breath. Rowena kept up the frantic pace until Minjung's body stiffened, and she exhaled in repeated moans as she came. She turned and kissed Rowena with a fierce hardness that Rowena understood completely. She returned the kiss with matched fervor.

Rowena held a drowsy Minjung to her chest and said, "I've dreamt about you sleeping in my bed with me."

"Mmm," Minjung moaned her approval.

"Will you? Tonight?"

"Yes, Madam," Minjung said breathlessly. "I've dreamt of it, too."

Rowena pulled her arms tighter around her submissive. Things had definitely changed between them. Rowena would still be the dominant one because a leopard can't change her spots. Minjung would remain the submissive, of course.

Fifteen minutes later, Rowena mumbled, "A fresh start," as she fell asleep in her bed with her arms wrapped around the woman she loved.

Chapter 22
Minjung

The *littles* huddled around Minjung in a side room just off the main banquet hall at the masquerade party. The dinner had already been served and eaten, and the *littles'* abridged version of the Nutcracker ballet was about to begin. Demonstrations, including Minjung's rope bottom suspension with Mistress Shasti, would commence after that.

"Always tall," Minjung said to the young people gathered around her. She pulled the imaginary string from her head, and they followed suit. They were understandably nervous. Even Marta, the lone Dominant in the dance troupe, seemed anxious. Minjung remembered that feeling as a dancer long ago, but now it was *her* job to calm the performers.

"Breathe," Minjung counseled. "Let it out slowly. Madison, please relax those shoulders."

Uncharacteristically, Madison didn't speak and simply nodded. Minjung knew the performers would loosen up once their short interpretation of one scene from Tchaikovsky's Nutcracker got started. "You are well rehearsed," Minjung told them. She made eye contact with young Shanice, who was playing the main character, Clara. Minjung smiled and winked at her. Shanice visibly relaxed, which filled Minjung's heart. They were listening and accepting her guidance.

"Now remember, if anything goes wrong—"

"'Which it inevitably will,'" Madison interrupted, quoting Minjung's pep talk from their last rehearsal.

"Right," Minjung said with a grin. "If anything goes wrong, no worries, just go with it and keep on." She paused to look each one of the *littles* in the eye and then said, "Hands in." Mistress Marta and the five *littles* put their hands in the center of the circle. "You know what to say. On three. One, two, three!"

"*Merde*," the *littles* shouted with glee and then giggled. *Merde* was the French word for 'shit.' Telling a dancer to 'break a leg' before a performance was not an accepted tradition but saying 'shit' was the equivalent. Plus, the *littles* got a kick out of saying a curse word in another language.

Minjung ushered them out of the side room and had them line up in order of appearance. Mistress Marta was last. The stage was actually the dance floor, a fitting place for a ballet. She winked at Shanice, who was the first to go on. Minjung looked up toward Mistress Rikki, who had been waiting expectantly for her signal. Minjung nodded and gave her the thumbs-up that her troupe was ready. She then stole a glance toward Madam Rowena. Her heart melted. The look of pride Madam shot her was an instant balm to her nerves. She smiled back and then returned to her charges.

"What a treat we have this evening," Mistress Rikki said into the microphone. She and Master Seamus were the hosts of the December ball. She paused while the partygoers found their seats. "Just a reminder that there will be no recording of this event. None. Zilch. Nada. Our only recording will be in our memories." A disappointed murmur ran through the crowd, prompting Mistress Rikki to lean into the microphone and say, "Is that understood?"

Murmurs of agreement answered her authoritative question. Cell phones and recording devices were strictly prohibited at events like these.

"Good," Mistress Rikki said. "And now, may I present *A Nutcracker Sampler: The Mouse Battle*." She began clapping, and the audience enthusiastically joined in.

The lights dimmed, and using her hands, Shanice propelled her wheeled kneeler into the center of the dance floor, a nutcracker doll in her lap. She then closed her eyes and pretended to be asleep. The other dancers stood at the ready along the sidelines, mouse masks in place. Minjung moved off to the side in clear sight of her dancers. She nodded at the DJ.

The music started. Shanice/Clara woke, looked around frightened, and clutched her doll. Madison, wearing her mouse mask, did two *saut de chat* leaps across the stage, ending in an impressive third position. The crowd burst into applause, obviously enraptured. Madison bowed, and then Billy ran in from the other direction, paused to do a *pirouette,* and then moved on, also to much applause. One at a time, the other *littles* moved across the floor in leaps, turns, and *plies*. Minjung beamed with pride as her charges moved. They were clearly nervous, but it didn't seem to affect their performances.

Madison, as a mouse, crept up behind Shanice and spun the kneeler around. Shanice faked being startled and then allowed herself to relax. She then went into various ballet arm movements as Madison pushed the kneeler to Billy, who was also on his belly. He spun her to the next *little* and then to the next and all around the large circle. Shanice was beautiful with her perfect arms and soft ballet hands.

Minjung's tears marred her view, and she wiped them away with agitation.

The *littles* lying on the floor shimmied in closer, making the circle smaller and smaller until Shanice spun in place to the swelling music. When the music slowed, the spinning of her kneeler also slowed, and she looked around, scared, clutching her nutcracker doll. The mice backed out of the way. Shanice reached down to the floor with her hands and moved slowly in circles, her eyes darting back and forth as if hoping the mice would not return.

She laid the nutcracker doll on the edge of the floor and then turned in fright as the mice *littles* began running, leaping, and pirouetting around the stage, feinting jabs at her.

She wheeled back to get her doll for protection, but then her eyes grew wide when her doll had grown to full height. Mistress Marta stood tall in her Nutcracker costume, a mask over her face. Shanice reached up, grabbed Marta's arm, and pointed to the taunting mice. Marta the Nutcracker leaped into action, sword brandished, and made short work of the mice.

Each one of the *littles* had their dramatic dying scene and then lay still. Minjung's heart soared as the audience clapped and cheered for the Nutcracker's victory. Mistress Marta then turned, reached down for Shanice's hand, bowed, and then ripped off her mask, revealing herself to be the gallant princess. She reached for Shanice's hand and kissed it. She then bent at the waist to allow Shanice's character to kiss her handsome, brave princess.

Mistress Marta completely broke character and kissed her little one on the head, beaming. The audience leaped to their feet, Madam Rowena included. They applauded so loudly that it startled a few of the performers.

"Weren't they great?" Mistress Rikki said from the podium. The applause only increased in intensity.

Minjung motioned for them to take their bows, which they did, but then, to her ultimate surprise, Madison ran to Mistress Shasti and came back with a big bouquet of flowers for Minjung. Billy pulled Minjung onto the dance floor, and they all stage-pointed to her. Minjung, crying, bowed in reverence to the audience and then to her charges, who, to her surprise, bowed in reverence back to her. She hadn't taught them that.

To the sound of waning clapping, Minjung opened her arms wide, and all the *littles* pushed in close. The group hug filled her heart so much that she couldn't help but continue crying.

"Thank you, Miss Minjung," Madison said. "You're an awesome teacher." Madison's sentiments were echoed by the others, including Mistress Marta, who added, "Thank you for everything you've done for her." She nodded her head toward Shanice, who was now deep in hugs with her new fans. "She has found so much passion for this. And confidence. I've been trying to find ways to—" And with that, Mistress Marta started sobbing. Mistress Shasti pulled her into a quick side hug and gave her a tissue.

"Thank you for this," Mistress Shasti said to Minjung. "You made them all feel special. You are a real asset to your Domme."

"Thank you, Ma'am."

Mistress Shasti grunted and hastily excused herself to put an end to Madison and Billy's impromptu pirouette competition.

Minjung's inner core began to shake. She wasn't used to so much direct attention from people. She tried to keep her breathing under control but felt it slipping away into fast, shallow breaths.

Standing in front of her now was her own Domme. She was like the savior angel Minjung needed at that moment. She lowered herself to the floor and put her head on her Domme's dress shoes. She hoped Madam understood that Minjung needed her dominance right now. She needed to feel her Domme's strength, her possessiveness.

Madam reached down and applied slight pressure to Minjung's head. It was just enough to let Minjung know she was there and would remain there.

"You did well, Minjung," Madam said. "Very well."

Minjung heard the authority in her Domme's voice. It washed over her like a soothing balm. She pulled it inside her soul and assimilated the possession. When the applause was directed at her, it had been overwhelming, but now, under her Domme's control, she was recovering. Knowing that

Madam was right there and in charge, her breathing became more regular.

"Sit up," Madam said. "Eyes on me." Minjung did as commanded. Madam studied her face for a moment and must have determined she was ready for the next instruction. "Stand up."

A shudder ran through Minjung as she stood. The people in the hall faded. She only had eyes for Madam Rowena. Madam pulled her into a tight hug and whispered, "I love you, *yoebo*."

Minjung inhaled sharply. "Where did you learn that, Madam?"

"An online translator," Madam Rowena said with a chuckle. "I hope it means 'sweetheart.'"

"It does, Madam. It does." Minjung snuggled against her Domme. It was then she realized they were dancing. It was the first time they'd ever danced together. And they were doing it in public. Madam loved her, really loved her, and wasn't afraid to show the world.

"I want to dance with you all night," Madam said softly. "But Shasti needs you."

"I want to stay in your arms, too, Madam," Minjung said, breathing in her Domme's slight rose scent. They had agreed to let their relationship go where it would go naturally, and dancing in public was apparently part of it.

"Shasti's getting a little antsy, my dear," Madam Rowena said. "I guess I have to share you again, don't I?"

"Yes, Madam," Minjung said. "But then you have me all to yourself once we get home."

"Oh, the possibilities," Madam teased and released her. "Go on. Go do me proud."

"Always," Minjung said. She wasn't exactly expecting a kiss, so when she didn't get one, it was okay.

~~~

Minjung sat nude on the floor in the playroom the morning after the Holiday Masquerade Ball. After getting home late the night before, they showered together in Madam's suite and then fell into Madam's bed, exhausted. Minjung loved the pillow talk she and Madam had been sharing recently and last night's was no exception. She fell asleep in her new favorite spot—in the crook of Madam Rowena's arm, her head resting on Madam's chest.

And now Minjung was apparently getting rewarded for representing her Domme so well at the ball.

"Eyes on me," Madam Rowena said. Her breasts were enticing, spilling out of the top of her black and purple bustier. The short wrap-around skirt would most likely be removed at some point that morning; Minjung was certain of it. "I want you to start talking. You are only allowed to pause to gather your thoughts, but I want you to spill everything."

"Madam?" Minjung wasn't sure what her Domme was asking her to do.

"Finding balance through impact play is glorious," Madam said. "I know how much relief you find with it, but I need you to clear your head a bit first. So, let loose. Nothing you say will be off-limits. I won't punish you for anything. I may ask questions, though."

"Yes, Madam," Minjung said. It was true. She did have a lot of random thoughts swirling around her brain. "One moment, please. I'm not used to being asked for my thoughts or my feelings."

"And that," Madam said softly, "is going to change as our relationship evolves."

Minjung's posture relaxed. Clearing her head sounded like a good idea, and with the promise of no punishments, that was positively freeing.

"Thank you, Madam." Minjung didn't need to pause and launched into a stream of thoughts. "I'm grateful that you volunteered me to be a rope bottom for Miss Shasti's suspension last night. I enjoyed getting to know her and her *little*, Madison. The suspension itself was freeing. Knowing you were right there, where I could see you, helped me stay calm during the tie. And I am also grateful that you said you would handle those requests for me to be a rope bottom for all those Dommes. I don't want to bottom for any males, though, Madam. I hope that doesn't make you mad."

"It doesn't."

Minjung paused but then remembered she was supposed to keep talking. "I liked dancing with you to that song 'Pink Sunsets.' I think maybe people could see how much I loved you when you held me in your arms around the dance floor last night."

"And that's okay."

"But, Madam," Minjung grinned, "when you, Mistress Hayley, and Mistress Victoria—"

"Daddy Vic," Madam Rowena corrected.

"Oh, that's official now. Sorry, I didn't realize," Minjung apologized. At Madam's urging, Minjung amended, "When you, Mistress Hayley, and Daddy Vic were joking around about how you wanted to see all the submissives serving naked at the balls, Mistress Rikki overheard you. I think she thought you were serious."

Madam burst out laughing. "As if that would ever fly in this modern BDSM community." She laughed again. "Well, that's what she gets for eavesdropping. I'm going to let her think that." She shook her head as she rolled her eyes in disbelief.

"And I wanted you to know that that woman made me jealous."

"What woman?"

"Pineapple woman on the cruise," Minjung said. "When she touched your shoulder, I wanted to growl at her and tell her that you were mine and she wasn't allowed to touch."

"You were just being territorial," Madam said. "I kind of like that in you."

"That fits," Minjung said and then continued. "I liked working with the *littles* and Mistress Marta on the ballet."

"Would you like to explore dance, *yoebo*?" Madam asked softly. "Teach young people or take classes?"

"Not right now," Minjung answered quickly. "I mean, I already have ideas for next year's holiday ball, though."

"Tell me."

"Something with the Nutcracker toy soldier army, I think. I'm not sure yet." She adjusted her seat on the floor and looked up at her Domme with admiration. Madam had shown time and time again that she was respectful of Minjung's thoughts and emotions. The mere fact that they were having this casual 'porch talk' only made Minjung love her Domme more. "But I think I want to continue to explore us and our *evolving* relationship, as you call it. And I've just gotten my mother back in my life. I want to keep room for her." Minjung bowed her head and added, "If that's acceptable to you, Madam."

"Of course, it's okay." Madam paused and then said, "Perhaps we can fly your mother in for Christmas. Would you like that?"

"Yes, yes," Minjung said, leaning down to kiss her Domme's shoes repeatedly. A hand squeezed her shoulder, signaling a transition. She froze and waited.

"Maybe we'll even have snow," Madam said with a happy lilt in her voice.

Was Madam Rowena real? Was Minjung dreaming? Madam Rowena was everything she'd hoped for but never thought she'd get.

"Sit up," Madam commanded. She held a sturdy leather collar in her hands. "Lean forward." Madam placed the inch-wide leather collar with four evenly spaced D-rings around Minjung's neck. "This collar indicates your role this morning. It indicates that I will play with your body in any way I see fit. It also indicates that you trust my judgment to protect you by honoring your safewords, boundaries, and hard limits. Do you understand?"

Minjung was too busy melting at the dominance to respond.

A rough hand grabbed her chin and pulled her head up. "Do. You. Understand?"

"Yes, Madam," Minjung blurted, arousal streaking through her.

Madam slapped a leash onto the collar and tugged gently. Minjung stood. She wondered what adventure Madam had in store for her that morning. A medical roleplay? Office roleplay was upstairs in the office, so that couldn't be it. Spanking bench? Chained to the overhead bar with an ankle spreader? The mere conjecture of what could happen sent another rush of arousal through her body, and she moaned.

"Music to my ears," Madam said. She pulled Minjung over to the mat near the mirrored wall. There was an unopened box on the floor. "Open it."

Minjung did as instructed and was delighted to see another wheeled kneeler.

"This one will stay down here in the playroom," Madam said. "I will not have those knees of yours ruined by my insensitivity."

Minjung moaned again. She was so aroused that if Madam touched her at that moment, she would combust.

"Get on. Unlock the wheels. Lean forward."

Minjung did as asked and leaned, knowing exactly why Madam wanted her to.

"Do you see that beautiful woman in the mirror there?" Madam pointed to Minjung's reflection. Without waiting for a response, she whispered, "She's about to get spread and used. She's going to take everything I give her, not only because *I* want it, but because *she* wants it. She deserves this reward for representing herself with grace, determination, and, most of all, humility. I'm proud to be her Domme."

Minjung's breathing became labored as she took in the praise. It was arousing. And her reflection was intense. She was leaning forward on the chest plate, ass in the air, ready to receive. She started undulating her hips and received a swat on her ass for her trouble.

One swat became twenty, and there was no soothing interval in between any. Madam threw a thick pillow on the floor, tossed off her skirt, and lifted the tip of the strap-on toward Minjung's center.

"You will not cum until I command it."

This time, Minjung's moans were moans of frustration. She didn't have time to dwell on her problem when two fingers speared her from behind and opened her wide. The tip of the strap-on entered. Just the tip.

"Look at her," Madam commanded, pointing to the mirror. "Look how she takes it." Madam's hands gripped Minjung's hips and pulled. The kneeler rolled back, impaling Minjung on the phallus. Madam's grip on her hips tightened. The pain was amazing and went right to Minjung's already over-aroused nerves. An orgasm sparked. No, no, no. She had to hold off. Cumming was forbidden.

"Such a beautiful woman," Madam taunted. "Opening her legs for me. Getting her reward." Her thrusts increased in pace.

"Madam," Minjung blurted, "I can't hold off."

"Oh, but you will," Madam said calmly. "You'll cum by my command."

By her command, Minjung screeched silently to her body. *By her command*! Her mind tried its best to overrule her body, but it wasn't working. She started panting. Her entire body tensed, and she held her breath. The orgasm speared her core as she screeched her release. She bucked her hips while Madam kept thrusting. Minjung's orgasm spasmed around the phallus, making her feel full. As the orgasm waned, her body turned to rubber, and she drooped forward over the chest rest.

The thrusting stopped, and her Domme pulled out. She commanded

Minjung to stay right where she was and got up to remove the strap-on. Minjung basked in the afterglow of her release. Through half-lidded eyes, she watched Madam clean and sanitize the strap-on and hang it up to dry in the storage cupboard. That was usually Minjung's job. She wasn't sure what to think about that; she was too floaty to care.

Madam moved with purpose toward Minjung, grabbed the leash, and tugged lightly. Minjung rose.

"You've been a bad girl, Minjung," Madam said and clicked her tongue two times. "Cumming without permission. There are consequences to every action, aren't there?"

"Yes, Madam," Minjung said. She was a little wobbly on her feet, but she was able to follow behind her Domme well enough. Within minutes, Minjung was chained to the upright bar, legs spread at the ankles by a spreader bar. In the past, Madam had allowed her to be flat-footed on the mat, but not this time. She was chained higher, so she could only rest on the balls of her feet.

"What color are your knees?" Madam asked as she pulled up a chair in front of Minjung.

"They're okay, Madam. Green."

Madam nodded and sat on the chair. "Do you know what happens to a submissive who cums before commanded?"

"No, Madam."

"She gets to watch her Domme pleasure herself." Madam spread her legs and stroked herself with the middle finger of one hand. She scooched forward in the chair, which allowed room to thrust two fingers inside and move them slowly back and forth. "The submissive has no way to participate in her Domme's pleasure. She won't feel the slick nectar on her tongue or experience her Domme's sweet taste. Her head won't get squeezed between her Domme's thighs as she cums." Madam alternated thrusting in and out with two fingers and swirling her nub with one. Madam's breathing was becoming labored. She tried to speak, but no words came out. She moaned instead.

Watching Madam so aroused and moaning, clearly about to cum, made Minjung gush with her own arousal. The wetness trailed down her leg.

"Mmm," Madam moaned, finally finding words. "Bad subs have to watch and suffer the consequences of their actions." She moaned once more and undulated her hips. She caught and held Minjung's gaze as her obvious arousal reached its peak. She rolled her head back and let out a strangled cry as she came. "Fuck," she groaned.

Minjung moaned in sync with her Domme. She wasn't cumming, but one or two strokes and she would. They kept eye contact with each other as Madam caught her breath. Madam finally stood up wordlessly, turned, and headed to the bathroom. She came back out wearing her skirt and apparently had freshened up. There was one addition to her ensemble, though. A crop.

Madam's eyes were dark with intent. She marched directly to Minjung and ran the business end of the crop over Minjung's body—her breasts, ass, back, inner thighs. She moved behind Minjung and tapped her ass lightly. It was so gentle that Minjung was almost lulled into complacency. But then the taps increased in intensity until Minjung cried out at the stings.

"Color?"

Minjung couldn't answer. She cried out as another stroke hit her already blazing ass. The strain of standing on her tiptoes was starting to wear her out, but there was no way she was going to say *yellow*. "Gr—"

"Gr? Your color is gray?" Madam asked with a laugh. Another stroke, this one on a burning hot spot.

"Green!" Minjung blurted.

"Green? Oh, why didn't you say?" Madam teased. The strokes became stronger and more rhythmic and seemed to cover every square inch of her ass and thighs. "Oh, my," Madam said, stopping suddenly. "I've forgotten something." She walked in front of Minjung.

As Minjung's body pulsed, the delicious chemicals in her body made her trippy. Sub-space was always such a rush.

Madam Rowena pulled a small chain out of her pocket. At first, Minjung thought it was a set of nipple clamps, but then she realized it was something else entirely. Madam held up a gold necklace with gems. Were those diamonds?

"I love you, Minjung," Madam Rowena said. "I saw this and thought of you. I thought of *us*." She lowered the overhead bar that was holding Minjung's arms up high. This allowed her to settle on both feet. Madam then put the necklace around Minjung's neck. She splayed her hand over Minjung's chest and leaned in for a kiss.

Minjung wanted to wrap her arms around her Domme, but she was still frustratingly chained and spread. She leaned in and kissed her Domme hungrily. Too soon, Madam pulled back.

"This looks good on you," Madam said. "Imagine how it will look when you actually have clothes on."

Minjung smiled. Her Domme was adorable when she was playful.

Madam looked up to the ceiling. "Domme Matilda, with the utmost respect, I think you were wrong. Falling in love with my submissive is the most beautiful thing that could have happened." Madam seemed to be voicing some worry she'd had for a while, and it sounded like she had made peace with it. "Relationships change," Madam mused out loud. "They have to." She looked at Minjung directly. "I had given up on love, Minjung." She swallowed hard, obviously emotional. "You've helped me see that it's still possible." She kissed Minjung quickly and undid the chains on Minjung's wrists. "My sister says she wants to visit after the holidays."

"I'd love to meet her, Madam."

"She knows something's up with me." Madam rolled her eyes. "She can always tell."

Madam helped the now unchained Minjung to the couch. One entire bottle of water chugged later, and she was lying in her Domme's arms. She sighed her contentment, and Madam pulled her closer.

"I love you, Madam," Minjung murmured. "Can we stay like this forever?"

Madam chuckled and said, "How are you feeling, *naekkeo*?"

Minjung snuggled against Madam's body. "You're full of surprises, Madam. You even pronounced it correctly."

"You inspired me." Madam kissed the top of Minjung's head. "I heard you and your mother use some Korean words and I'm interested in learning."

"You aren't real," Minjung said, deciding semi-firmly that Madam Rowena was her AI reward for something.

A swat on her hip dragged her out of her fantasy.

"Call your mother later this afternoon," Madam said. "Ask her if she'd like us to fly her out here for the holidays. But we do have to remember Marta and Shanice's domestic partnership party at the coffee shop after Christmas. Of course, you'll remind me what day, but I know it's before New Year's."

"We have a busy social calendar, Madam. Don't we?"

"We certainly do."

"Perhaps my mother won't mind if we excuse ourselves for one evening, Madam," Minjung said. "But we must remember that Mistress Rikki will have a birthday after Christmas, too. We should find out if anyone is throwing a party or having a dinner or something."

"You're so thoughtful," Madam said and gave her a light squeeze. "I never realized what an amazing group of people we have here in Denton Heights. It took you coming into my life to allow me to see it."

Minjung sat up and looked her Domme in the eye. "And through you, I've learned that family isn't always made of blood and genetics. Maybe families can also be made up of people who accept you for who you are and support you no matter what." She grinned at her Domme and added, "Unconditionally."

"Well said, *naekkeo.*"

"*Naekkeo,*" Minjung repeated. "It's true." A mischievous smile crept up her face.

"What's true?"

"That I'm yours."

"You'd better believe it," Madam said.

Minjung let herself melt against her Madam as she was pulled into the most tender, soul-affirming kiss that spoke of promises and a future worth living for.

~~~ The End ~~~

Additional Resources

Dancing Wheels
Founded in Cleveland, OH in 1980
dancingwheels.org

From the Dancing Wheels Website:
"If dance is an expression of the human spirit, then it is best expressed by people of all abilities. That is the fundamental belief behind the Dancing Wheels Company. Considered one of the premier arts and disabilities organizations in the U.S., Dancing Wheels is a professional, physically integrated dance company uniting the talents of dancers both with and without disabilities."

Newsletter Signup

Sign up for Danielle Grainger's newsletter to keep up with new releases. She also likes to recommend books to read (other than her own, of course)

Find the sign-up on Danielle's website:
www.daniellegrainger.com

Reviews

Reviews help get books like this one to readers who enjoy books like them. It's often difficult for readers of certain, err, tastes to find books they enjoy. Would you consider writing a review? Get the word out?

Thank you for the help.

About the Author
Danielle Grainger

Dani is an instructor who currently resides in the southeastern USA and has several pampered fur babies. She has always been an avid reader and ventured into writing after reading several novels she felt didn't accurately represent the BDSM lifestyle. With so many rampant misconceptions, she took a chance and crafted admittedly idealized versions of possible experiences. Dani hopes not only to entertain her readers but to enlighten and educate them as well.

Dani's Amazon Author Page:
www.amazon.com/stores/Danielle-Grainger

Dani's Facebook:
facebook.com/danielle.grainger.7777

Dani's Instagram:
DaniGrainger84

Dani's Pinterest:
danigrainger84

Dani's Goodreads Page:
www.goodreads.com/author/show/19699760.Danielle_Grainger

Books by Danielle Grainger

THE DENTON HEIGHTS SERIES

The Denton Heights Series comes BEFORE the Bernadette Series. This group of books tells the stories of the beloved characters who populate the Bernadette Series world and live the BDSM lifestyle. We find out more of the origin stories of Madison and Shasti; Jaleesa, Tina, Harriet, Dana, Deshawn, and Kari; Marta and Shanice; Rowena and Minjung; Lisa and Rachel. The Denton Heights series is basically the "Prequel" to the Bernadette Series.

Under Her Wing (Denton Heights Book 1)
(The Shasti and Madison Story)
A lesbian age-gap erotic romance with light BDSM aspects.

2023 GOLDIE FINALIST

Madison Kim finds herself on a bus headed to Denton Heights, Ohio, a suburb of Cincinnati. Her mother sent her there without notice to care for an elderly Korean woman Madison had never met. Madison is twenty-two-and-three-quarters years old, has a high school diploma, but isn't smart enough to go to college...so they tell her. Now she spends her time caring for Mrs. Park, going to the beloved Cincinnati Zoo, and watching movies on her outdated phone. She's not really sure why she's there, but she's taking it day by day. And then she meets strong nurturing Miss Shasti at a tea dance.

Shasti Balakrishnan has been looking for someone to call hers for more years than she cares to count. She wants a woman to love and care for in a nurturing Mommy Domme/little girl scenario. She's thirty-two and already a partner in a thriving medical clinic in Denton Heights, but truth be told – she's lonely. She thought she'd found a companion in Amber back in D.C., but that fizzled out once they realized they weren't what each other wanted—or needed. And then she meets adorably precocious Madison at a tea dance.

ISBN: 978-1-953734-10-5 (e-Book)
ISBN: 978-1-953734-13-6 (Paperback)

In Her Cage (Denton Heights Book 2)

(The Jaleesa and Tina Story)

A lesbian/asexual interracial polyamorous erotic romance with BDSM aspects including Dominance and submission.

Jaleesa Whitmore is a lesbian Domme in and out of fast relationships fueled by sex. She didn't understand addiction. Not yet, anyway. Although she had almost one full year sober, she was done with it. She was moments from heading down the familiar road of drinking that always made her feel good and filled that void. She was about to get her life back on its old track when a fateful encounter with a stranger, who would become a trusted friend, halted her downslide. She didn't know it then, but this encounter would not only lead her to a series of events and people that would change how she looked at life but how she approached it.

Tina Jenkins likes women but is asexual and afraid to try for another relationship. She does understand addiction. Just shy of eleven years clean of her opioid addiction following a dental procedure right out of high school, her parents carefully constructed and monitored everything in her world. It didn't matter that she was thirty-one years old and still living in the pink bedroom in her childhood home. It didn't matter that her mother now had to work from home, and her parents had to track her location and do routine searches of her bag, car, computer, phone, and room. None of it mattered because she was clean.

And then asexual Tina meets promiscuous Jaleesa. And everything changed. For both of them.

ISBN: 978-1-953734-28-0 (e-Book)
ISBN: 978-1-953734-29-7 (Paperback)

Within Her Grasp (Denton Heights Book 3)
(The Marta and Shanice Story)
A lesbian age gap interracial erotic romance with light BDSM aspects.

"Within Her Grasp" is an age-gap interracial lesbian romance that tells the tale of two women who had settled for unhappy lives. And then they meet.

White, thirty-something Marta Ingersoll was done with people. She just wanted to be left alone at work and at home, thank you. Her inside cat and the outside stray were all she needed. And her sister, Nora, too, of course. But that was it. And then, one fateful afternoon, her instincts to save a woman in obvious distress kicked in, and her life was shoved onto a strange new course.

Black, twenty-something Shanice Ward never got a break. Life had thrown challenge after challenge at the young woman, and this latest thing was too much, but it wouldn't stop. Woken up from a sound sleep by someone trying to remove her clothing, she shrieked for him to leave her alone. He didn't, but then, the most amazing thing happened. She discovered that superheroes were real, and one had just flown into her room to save her, and her life was shoved onto a strange new course.

ISBN: 978-1-953734-30-3 (e-Book)
ISBN: 978-1-953734-31-0 (Paperback)

By Her Command (Denton Heights Book 4)

(The Rowena and Minjung Story)

A lesbian interracial erotic romance with consensual BDSM aspects.

"By Her Command" is an erotic interracial lesbian romance containing consensual aspects of BDSM. It finds Rowena Tate in need of a submissive who can also manage her household. It's also the tale of Minjung Lee, who is desperate to find a Domme so she won't find herself homeless again. Trust does not come easily for either of them.

Rowena is a white Domme in her late thirties. Through experience, she has come to believe that most, if not all, submissives are selfish creatures who only want what she can provide without considering the person behind the flogger and the paycheck.

Minjung is an East Asian submissive in her mid-thirties. Through experience, she has come to believe that most, if not all, Dominants are selfish creatures who go well beyond contracted limits because there is no one to tell them not to.

Despite their reservations, both are told by members of the Denton Heights BDSM community that they are a good match and lucky to have found each other. Rowena isn't so sure. Neither is Minjung. Time will tell, won't it?

ISBN: 978-1-953734-32-7 (e-Book)
ISBN: 978-1-953734-33-4 (Paperback)

THE BERNADETTE SERIES

Dr. Bernadette Garneau holds a Ph.D. in Mathematics and has just gotten out of a four-year relationship. Shortly after the breakup, she began an exploration of her repressed sexual desires. One message from a beautiful and powerful online Mistress and Bernadette leaps into the world of BDSM. The Mistress takes charge, and Bernadette reels in the heady power this stranger has over her. She has gotten a taste of the life, and she wants more. She needs more. Several online and in-person experiences with BDSM and Power Exchange have led to cravings she doesn't quite understand. A brief sexual exchange with an online Goddess unleashes an incredible pain-to-pleasure connection that she hadn't understood before. As she sifts through the posers and one-night stands, she homes in on what her submissive nature needs from a Domme.

The Bernadette Series follows Bernadette's journey into the world of BDSM and her search for love and sexual satisfaction. As she said, "I want a monogamous partner who wants to not only love and nurture me but who also wants to drape me over her lovely couch and have her way with me."

Wrecking Bernadette

(Book One in the Bernadette Series)
A lesbian erotic novel with heavy BDSM aspects featuring Dominance and submission.

Dr. Bernadette Garneau holds a Ph.D. in Mathematics and is four months out of a four-year relationship. One good thing about breaking up is that Bernadette is free to explore her repressed sexual desires. One message from a beautiful and powerful online Mistress, and Bernadette leaps into the world of BDSM. Mistress Ciara takes charge, and Bernadette reels in the heady power this stranger has over her. She has gotten a taste of the *life*, and she wants more. She *needs* more.

ISBN: 978-1-953734-00-6 (e-Book)
ISBN: 978-1-953734-14-3 (Paperback)

(S)mothering Bernadette

(Book Two in the Bernadette Series)
A lesbian erotic novel with heavy BDSM aspects featuring Mommy Domme,
little girl.

Dr. Bernadette Garneau's universe is pushing her toward change. Her initial experiences with BDSM and Power Exchange have led to cravings she doesn't quite understand. A brief sexual exchange with an online Goddess unleashes an incredible pain-to-pleasure connection she hadn't understood until that encounter. But after sleeping on it, she clearly understands that this Goddess would never be the long-term relationship she seems to be seeking.

Disappointed, she wonders if she should just give up and move back to California to be closer to her family. That is until she meets Mama_Luvs, an online Mommy Domme. The woman is nurturing yet stern from the start and is just … perfect. And then Mama_Luvs wants to meet. Starry-eyed Bernadette packs for a New Year's Eve weekend, hoping that this time she's found *the one* – the one who wants to love and nurture her but who also wants to drape her over a couch and have her way with her.

ISBN: 978-1-953734-01-3 (e-Book)
ISBN: 978-1-953734-15-0 (Paperback)

Becoming Bernadette
(Book Three in the Bernadette Series)

A lesbian erotic novel with heavy BDSM aspects featuring Dominance and submission.

University professor Dr. Bernadette Garneau has fallen in love with the world of BDSM. She has a nascent interest in the pain-to-pleasure connection, but she has yet to find partners interested in nurturing the soul within her body that they play with. Admittedly, she's had incredible sexual encounters with experienced Dommes, but all of them left her feeling cold for whatever reason. Most of them simply wanted a sadistic roll in the hay. Bernadette wants a strong Domme who will love and nurture her *before* flogging her on a St. Andrew's cross and *afterward* when her body is spent.

One afternoon, she finally musters up the courage to venture out and meet some new friends in the local BDSM community. In walks a tall, handsome butch woman with fantastic hair and a confident stride. When this woman asks Bernadette, "Are you collared," Bernadette truthfully answers, "No," and accepts a dinner invitation for that very evening. She is walking on stars when she gets home at 2 a.m. after an ethereal sexual liaison. On the one hand, she wonders who she is becoming – she's never been this promiscuous. And on the other hand, she wonders if this strong butch woman could finally be the Domme of her dreams.

ISBN: 978-1-953734-02-0 (e-Book)
ISBN: 978-1-953734-12-9 (Paperback)

Desiring Bernadette
(Book Four in the Bernadette Series)

A lesbian erotic romance novel with heavy BDSM aspects featuring Dominance and submission.

Rikki Carmichael finally feels that deep Dominant/submissive relationship she has been craving ever since her Aunt Tilda introduced her to *the life*. She embraced her dominant side early on, but finding a suitable submissive woman who wanted more than a quick roll in the dungeon proved elusive. That is until Professor Bernadette Garneau arrived on the scene. Now collared and committed to Rikki, will Bernadette prove to be different, or will she turn out like all the others — fickle and full of lies and deception?

And will this perfect sub stay with her when she realizes Rikki's ship is sinking? She'd almost lost the coffee shop she owns when creditors came knocking down her door en masse seeking payment for debts that weren't hers. Rikki managed to keep most of her staff and friends in the dark about it, but she has not been able to get out from under it. With high stakes all around, Rikki looks for the peace she is seeking within her relationship with Bernadette. If this one fails, it may be time to leave the life entirely and go live in a cabin somewhere isolated in the woods. But buying a cabin takes money – money she just doesn't have.

ISBN: 978-1-953734-03-7 (e-Book)
ISBN: 978-1-953734-09-9 (Paperback)

Loving Bernadette
(Book Five in the Bernadette Series)

A lesbian erotic romance novel with heavy BDSM aspects featuring Dominance and submission.

Bernadette Garneau, a beloved professor of mathematics, is a natural submissive. She likes structure and rules and finally found a way of life and a woman who would provide those things for her. The BDSM community she stumbled upon in Denton Heights, Ohio is where she found Rikki Carmichael, now her dominant partner and fiancée. Rikki is everything she's dreamed of. Yes, Bernadette found the captain of her ship. With Rikki's support and guidance, maybe other parts of her life can finally come together, too – like the respect she deserves but hasn't gotten at the university. Why won't anyone see that she deserves to teach those upper-level courses? And to move out of that closet of an office? What do they know that she does not?

Rikki Carmichael, the respected owner of Rikki's Coffee Shop in town, has finally found the woman of her dreams in super-smart and super-real Bernadette Garneau. Bernadette is a submissive who instinctively knows how to take care of Rikki and accepts Rikki's need to be in charge. Bernadette is the first submissive Rikki's ever had that wasn't solely out for her own gain. Once Rikki can climb out of the deep financial debt she's found herself in, she will finally make their engagement to be married public.

Miscommunication, faulty assumptions, and unmet expectations threaten this union seemingly made in heaven. When life comes at them hard and fast, they must rely on their bond and their loving self-made family of friends.

ISBN: 978-1-953734-08-2 (e-Book)
ISBN: 978-1-953734-11-2 (Paperback)

www.ingramcontent.com/pod-product-compliance
Lightning Source LLC
Chambersburg PA
CBHW051246260626
47162CB00002B/629